NOBLE REVENGE

JACK NOBLE
BOOK 15

L.T. RYAN

LIQUID MIND MEDIA

THE JACK NOBLE SERIES

Get your very own Jack Noble merchandise today! Click the link below to find coffee mugs, t-shirts, and even signed copies of your favorite L.T. Ryan thrillers! https://ltryan.ink/EvG_

Receive a free copy of The Recruit. Visit:
https://ltryan.com/jack-noble-newsletter-signup-1

PART 1

PART 1

CHAPTER 1

THE WEIGHT OF HIS HAND ON THE BACK OF HER NECK prevented her from looking up. Not that she'd see anything. Not with the burlap sack over her head. The last image she could recall was that dirty-brown bag coming from the side. Whether the world went dark or the breath left her lungs first was up for debate. It had happened so fast. Then her shoulder crashed against something metal. The impact reverberated through her chest and back, and for a moment, Clarissa wondered whether her aortic artery had severed. The pain was so intense.

The pinch where her neck met her shoulder had been the last thing she felt. Her shouts turned to slurs. The words turned into strange slow music. Her taut muscles turned to Jell-O.

When she came to, she was freezing. Her wrists were bound behind her. Her ankles were tied to a chair. And the damn sack was still on her head. The man had visited her six times that she knew of. He berated her, alternating between yelling in English and the local language, which she barely understood. Answers were met with a slap. Non-answers received the same treatment. The guy must have figured he'd beaten her enough. He untied her ankles from the chair.

"Powiedz nam, gdzie on jest!"

She'd started picking out the words in the phrase. Polish. *Tell. Where.*

He. She knew that because she'd been in Warsaw, Poland for the past two months and had started figuring out a few words and phrases.

"Powiedz nam, gdzie on jest!" His voice rose higher.

Clarissa didn't answer. When she had told him she didn't understand, he decided that smacking her upside the head with what felt like a roll of coins was the proper punishment.

He shoved her hard enough she fell off the chair and hit her head on the floor. The door slammed shut. Clarissa remained in place for several seconds, cheek pressed to the floor, knees drawn as close to her chest as possible.

The ringing in her ears settled, and she heard the ticking of the radiator as it kicked on. It ran on a forty-five-minute cycle, equal parts on and off. Equatorial heat was followed by an arctic blast.

After a few minutes, Clarissa moved. She had to roll over and get her knees under her, then use all her core strength to straighten up. Pain seared through her chest. Breathing grew increasingly difficult.

Shuffling along on her knees, she collided with the chair. Why hadn't he re-tied her ankles to the legs? It made no sense. Every visit had come at one and a half cycles of the radiator. If they stuck to the same schedule, she'd have plenty of time to shed her bindings. Did the man come alone? He was the only one that spoke, but since she couldn't see, she had no idea. And, if there were two of them, were they the only two there?

Managing to get to her feet, she walked until she met the wall. She paced the layout of the room, estimating it to be ten-by-ten, with a single point of ingress and egress and no windows she could find by touch. An interior room, but too big to be a closet. Perhaps a framed in room in an attic or basement. She'd ruled out the basement. It wasn't dank enough. While the burlap sack had a strong odor, she'd adapted and could smell fumes from the kitchen, a fire burning, and the man's rancid body odor whenever he'd approached her. The closer he'd gotten to her, the more she wanted to throw up, which she dared not do with the sack over her head.

She didn't dwell on the location of the room. It really didn't matter until she managed to exit it. Once she saw what was next, she'd plan accordingly and figure out which direction to go. Whether to take stairs up or down. And when she reached the exit, she'd have to figure out whether to turn left or right. Was she a block from where they abducted her? Or a hundred miles? With no way of knowing, why worry about it now? *Be flexible, not rigid.*

Clarissa settled in and enjoyed the remaining heat piping out of the radiator. She imagined herself somewhere tropical where warmth and humidity soaked her unless she was on the beach. Her breathing slowed. Her thoughts followed, envisioning how the next visit would go. What the man would say. What he'd do. She thought about his patterns and isolated the moment when she would make her move.

The radiator banged and heat ceased to flow. In another minute, the frigid air would billow out, freezing the sweat that soaked her clothes. Though uncomfortable, Clarissa welcomed it. The man would return soon as long as he stuck to the schedule.

She worked the rope around her wrists until enough of a gap had formed to allow her to slip her right hand free of the binding. She lifted the sack. The room was brighter than she had anticipated. Light knifed through her eyes, penetrated her brain. The air slapped her in the face like an arctic blast. She glanced around the space. It was as she had imagined, except there were windows, they were just higher than she could reach and they were on two walls. The room was on the corner of a building.

Setting the chair on its side, she stepped on the bottom legs. Then she pulled the front top leg until it broke free. Then she did the same with the back, only leaving it slightly attached. She set it upright and eased onto it to test it. It held. But the moment she shifted her weight, it would collapse.

Then the fun would begin.

Enjoying a final moment of cool air on her face, she took one last look at the room, internalizing all the bleak details. Clarissa lowered the hood and threaded her free hand through the rope. She waited. Focusing on her breathing. Grounding herself in the moment. However long it took for the man to return, that was OK. She'd be ready. She replayed the scenario on a loop in her mind until she'd achieved complete automation.

The door succumbed to the man's rough touch and creaked a foreboding serenade. The man took his time walking around the room. Hard heel-to-toe footsteps. He was a big man, or perhaps wore big shoes. He dragged something along the wall. Fingernails? A knife? A baseball bat or some other weapon designed to bludgeon her?

Clarissa fought the urge to free her hand, rip the hood off, and launch an attack. If he did have a weapon, he'd have the advantage. He'd strike her down before she could get off the chair. If she could get off the chair. She *had* sabotaged it to collapse. Any attempt to lunge forward or sideways would result in her flat on the ground as the chair fell apart.

"Your name is Clarissa, yes?" the man asked.

"So, you do speak English," she said.

He smacked the back of her head. Her chest screamed as she tensed her core to keep from shifting. This wasn't the right moment. The guy had engaged her in dialog. She wanted to see where it led.

"Don't make me ask twice," he said.

"I am Clarissa."

"Abbot?"

She nodded, then said, "Yes."

"Do you know why you are here?"

"You were feeling lonely?"

He chuckled as she braced for a strike that didn't come. He moved, coming to a stop in front of her.

This was unexpected. He'd always remained behind her. The sack tugged down, side-to-side, then upward. Pain stabbed her brain as artificial light penetrated her eyes from a single source inches in front of her face. Maybe it had been his flashlight she'd heard him dragging along the wall.

"Do you mind?" she said. "I got a bit of a hangover from whatever you injected me with and that light ain't helping."

He clicked the light off. The ghost of a circle of light lingered where his face should be. Almost looked like a happy face emoji. Clarissa blinked rapidly, but the afterimage remained.

"Ketamine," he said.

"What?"

"I injected you with Ketamine."

Clarissa's brain raced to find everything she knew about ketamine. Some of the guys used it to deal with their PTSD, depression, and other ailments. They had told her the high lasted around forty to forty-five minutes. The timeline of her abduction started coming together. He wouldn't have traveled more than thirty minutes with her under the effects of the drug. Maybe even less than that. It would have been better to get her into the room while unconscious, preventing any chance of her figuring out where she was or becoming combative with him.

"You ever tried it?" she asked.

His face began coming into view. Handsome, with a square jaw, fair hair, and blue eyes. Dead eyes, she noted. The smile faded. His eyes narrowed. Crow's feet expanded to his temple. His forehead creased down the middle.

"I'm going to ask one more time, Clarissa. Do you know why you are here?"

She could give him a hundred reasons dating back twenty years. Further, if her father's career was considered. She settled on the truth.

"No clue, man. You doped me up with Ketamine. Why don't you tell me?"

The shift was subtle, but Clarissa noticed it. The way he adjusted the flashlight in his hand, turning it into a club. And when he reared back, she was ready and slipped her hand free from the rope.

She jostled to the left, then shifted her weight hard to the right. That was all it took to collapse the chair.

CHAPTER 2

DIFFUSED LIGHT SPILLED THROUGH THE GAP BETWEEN THE curtains, illuminating Jack Noble's hand as he peeled the fabric back. His phone had notified him of activity in the apartment across the courtyard. The apartment he'd been watching for the past few days as he attempted to get a glimpse into the life of his recently acquired target.

Noble lifted the high-powered lens to his eye and adjusted the focus until the fine lines at the corners of her eyes came into view. Setting her cell on the kitchen island, she reached into a drawer and pulled out a wooden spoon, which she dipped into a pot on the stove. Her light blue yoga pants accentuated every curve, leaving little to the imagination.

Turning away from the stove, she lifted the wooden spoon coated in tomato sauce and wafted the steam into her face. After a taste, her head tipped back. Her chest heaved, settled. When she opened her eyes, it felt as though she peered into Noble's soul.

Could she capture the essence of his life? All he'd been through? The ups, downs, and more often than not, sideways motions of his journey?

Even he couldn't accurately recall the timeline of everything that had happened over the past decade that had led him to this apartment in the middle of Denmark. At one point in his life, he'd been on the right track. He'd done the right thing. Doing what his country needed him to do. His repayment? Death and destruction. Following him like a wake that never stopped growing. It threatened not only him, but everything and everyone he held dear.

He hoped this would be the last job that would reveal the final piece of the puzzle, because once that happened, he'd be free.

Jack held steady in front of the window, cautious that any movement could cause a reflection off the lens's glass, revealing his position. Did it matter, though? It was dark out. Every light in her apartment was on. All she'd see in her window was her own reflection. Still, he couldn't shake the feeling as she leaned against the counter, arms folded across her chest, wooden spoon hovering inches from her lips, that she was watching *him*.

Seventy-eight hours. That's how long he'd been confined to the studio apartment that smelled like marijuana and fish. The first two days were the slowest he'd ever experienced. He really shouldn't have minded. After all, he needed a break as much as anybody. But he never got one. Not from his mind at least. The thought that he'd been found out always lingered in the back of his mind. Every time he moved to a new location, either on his own accord or due to a job, he wondered if somebody would be there waiting with a bullet that had Jack Noble written on it.

And when he hit those really dark moments, he found himself welcoming the thought.

The woman had been in his sights for the past twenty-four hours. Her life was boring. He'd watched her work through a myriad of domestic tasks and activities. Cooking. Cleaning. Watching TV. Reading. Playing on her phone. The same routine again tonight as it had been the night before.

There had been no clues as to what she had done to bring Noble there. He didn't even have a name. Whether she was a witness someone wanted silenced, a government official who had screwed up, or someone a jilted lover could no longer stand the sight of, her days were numbered. To most in this profession, the reason wouldn't matter. But for Jack, who was still piecing together the puzzle of who was behind the mess his life had become, he had to know.

He needed her story. The background, what had happened to put her in this position. Calling it a story was the right way to go about it. It would be skewed. Would paint her in a better light than the person at the other end of the deal. He'd get false information or diluted information at best. But somewhere in what was said would be a clue. And if he could match that clue up with the others he had collected, he might just figure this damn situation out. Might finally get his freedom.

That was the reason he had assumed the identity of Dylan Van de Berg, the last man who had accepted a contract to eliminate Noble. The first job assigned had been to terminate Clarissa. The game changed at that moment; the next day, the contract changed as well. It vanished, replaced with another. He learned the contract on Clarissa hadn't been moved to someone other than Van de Berg. It had been canceled outright. Breathing room, he figured at the time. But Clarissa was on someone's radar. The same person who wanted him dead? The only way to find out was to find that person.

Or find Clarissa.

That had proven difficult since the last time they spoke was some six months ago.

So far, he'd *completed* eight jobs since first logging into the terminal in Amsterdam. At least one of the targets had been a vile individual who deserved the contract put out on their life. One definitely didn't. The rest were debatable.

Did the beautiful woman across the courtyard deserve death? Had she been in the wrong place at the wrong time? Would she part with information in exchange for her life, like all the others?

Her expression changed and her head turned toward her front door. She set the wooden spoon down, peeled off the apron, and untucked her shirt, covering all that the yoga pants revealed. As she walked to the entrance, Jack zoomed in tight just over her shoulder to get a view of her guest—the first he'd seen since he had begun watching her.

She pulled the door open and stepped aside. The man who entered had nothing distinguishable about him. Average height and build, dark hair, trimmed beard, black-rimmed glasses. He shrugged off his coat as she turned away without a hug or a kiss or even a handshake and headed back to the kitchen. The man followed. He stopped and grabbed a bottle of beer out of the refrigerator, then took a seat on the stool at the island.

Jack zoomed and snapped several photos of his face. He could use those to determine the guy's identity later. For now, he wanted to capture as much of this meeting as he could. How could he be sure it was a meeting and not something else? He considered the way she met him at the door. There was nothing cordial about it. In fact, it felt cold. Would she have bothered to untuck her shirt if this guy were something more than an associate? Then again, perhaps she wanted it to be something more and backed out at the last second so as not to seem overly aggressive.

The man reached into his messenger bag and pulled out an item smaller than his index finger. Black. Metal connector on one end. A USB drive. He slid it across the island to the woman, who looked down at it and remained silent for a few moments. Her face tightened, like a catcher's mitt closing on a ninety-five-mile-per-hour fastball. She picked it up and held it in front of her chest. Her face relaxed. Her eyes closed. Her fist enveloped the device, and she shoved it into the lone pocket of her yoga pants.

When she began to speak, Jack cursed at the angle he had. There was no way he could make out the words by reading her lips. Whatever was being said didn't last long, though. The man stood, nodded, and made his way to the door. She remained at the island, only glancing up once when he looked back and said something. She didn't reply.

The door closed.

The woman laid her head down on the island.

Jack zoomed in and saw the tear slipping free from her cheek.

CHAPTER 3

THE STENCH OF THE MAN, A MIX OF RANCID BODY ODOR AND vodka, reached Clarissa before his attack. She twisted to lessen the impact. The movement altered her plan to allow the length of her right side to absorb the impact when she hit the floor.

The man swung hard. The flashlight passed just in front of her face. She collided with the ground. Going for the kill shot threw him off balance and he stumbled forward. Clarissa kicked hard, tripping him and feeling the resulting impact on her lower shin. He hit the ground. Two thuds. Upper body. Lower body.

Clarissa clawed at the wall in an attempt to get to her feet. She spun as he made it to his knees. He stretched out for the flashlight. She took a step, pulled the other leg back, looking like a place kicker attempting a long field goal. Swinging through, she kicked the guy in the solar plexus. The air left his lungs with a hollow scream. She kicked again, and again, hitting him in the stomach and crotch and neck until he collapsed to the side.

Her pulse pounded in her head and chest. The mix of adrenaline, fear, and rage surged, causing her to hyperventilate. She gulped down as much air as she could.

The guy continued to scratch his way toward the flashlight, barely able to lift his chin off the floor.

Clarissa hopped over him. Mid-air, she thought better of it, but the man was in no shape to trip her up. She landed with the grace of a ballerina, snatched the flashlight up, and spun on her heel. Holding the flashlight like a club, she drew it high, smashed it over the back of his head.

Unsatisfied with his loud groan, she brought the light down again. The back of his head split. Blood matted the handle. She struck again. And again. Kept going until he no longer moved. She watched to ensure he didn't draw in another breath.

Tears streamed down her face, no doubt from the pent-up rage she experienced. If the guy was dead, fine. If not, she'd leave him incapacitated for the rest of his worthless, meaningless life.

Seated on her knees, her hands fell to her lap. The flashlight dropped to the floor. She wiped the tears from her face, saw the blood smeared on her hands. Someone pounding up the stairs alerted her that this was not over yet. She scooped up the flashlight.

No time to feel sorry for yourself, girl.

She moved to the wall, inches from the door. Heavy breathing announced his presence outside the room. The gun entered before he did, trained on the man lying in a puddle of his own blood. The guy drew in a sharp breath. Hesitating, he pulled the gun back. Would he retreat? Call for backup?

When the gun reappeared, Clarissa decided not to wait. She dropped her arm back as far as her shoulder would allow and then whipped it forward, creating a massive amount of torque. The metal club collided with his wrist. The bone snapped. The gun dropped. The man howled. She reared back again, stepping diagonally to keep out of his reach while preparing her next attack.

The guy came into view, occupying about half of the open doorway. He wasn't tall or short. Neither fat nor thin. Just average. A pained look on his face. With his good hand covering his broken one. His eyes widened at the sight of the flashlight as it completed its arc through the air and landed square on his forehead. The skin split, blood spattered at first. Poured from the gaping wound right after. He stood there for what felt like ages but was only a few seconds in real time. His eyelids fluttered. His eyes rolled back as he stumbled toward her. She kicked him in the groin. He bowed forward. She kicked him again, hitting him in the face. Blood covered her feet. He stood there, not quite upright, not quite bent over. She swung again with the flashlight, catching him on the side of the face, cracking his jaw, splitting his lip, knocking a few teeth out. The guy fell back, tried to catch himself on the wall next to the stairs, but he couldn't. The echoes of his body rolling down the stairs like a boulder filled the hallway. He hit the landing at the bottom of the steps and didn't move.

Clarissa stood at the top of the stairs, listening for signs of anyone else present. The hall extended to the left and right. The knotted, worn hardwoods led to closed doors with a crystal knob on the right side. After a few seconds of waiting and only hearing her breathing, she checked the doors. Locked. She debated breaking them open, but after further investigation, she could see they had been sealed shut on the other side. Other apartments, she figured.

Clarissa glanced down at her bloody feet and dirty clothes. She looked like she belonged on the street. And that's where she needed to be. Not waiting in the apartment for someone else to show up. Walking back to the stairs, she looked over her shoulder, spotted the pistol. Knowing it would come in handy, she scooped it up and attempted to tuck it in her waistband. It wouldn't stay. So she sprinted down the stairs with the pistol in hand.

At the landing, she stepped over the guy she'd beaten a few minutes before. He posed no threat. Lifeless eyes stared up at her. His right hand rested on his heart. She kicked it to the side and patted him down, and checked his pockets. He had nothing on him. Were they storing their stuff somewhere? Made sense if they were in danger of being raided.

She glanced around the room. There was nothing other than a couple of folding metal chairs and a single plastic folding table. Nothing on it but a notebook. Grabbing it, she rifled through the pages. Everything was written in another language. About twenty pages' worth of gibberish, but twenty pages that someone else could make sense of. Clarissa ripped them from the notebook, folded them, and stuffed them in her waistband.

Sunlight sliced through a parted curtain. She peeled it back to reveal a wide street with wide sidewalks, a few stores, and a few people milling about. Would they call her out when she stepped into the open air, looking as though she'd dragged herself out of a cave? Would they care at all?

Clarissa took one last look around the place and realized a space existed behind the stairs. A cubby of sorts. She pulled the door open. Inside were her things. A pair of flats. Socks. A coat. Her wallet and phone were missing. But they'd missed the hidden pocket along the bottom hem of her jacket. A little cash and a burner phone. She resisted the temptation to rip it open and pull them out. There could be someone waiting outside. She'd lose the phone forever.

There was no option but to leave. The door groaned as she pulled it open. The breeze found its way through the crack, cooling her flushed skin. She opened it a bit farther. Nothing happened. She stuck her leg out. Nothing happened. She emerged from her captors' dwelling and hit the sidewalk and started walking across the street. A car honked. She ignored them. They shouted something as they passed. She didn't understand, and she didn't care.

On the other side of the street, she turned right. Behind her, a car engine roared to life. She didn't look back. The tires screeched against the asphalt. She still didn't look back. The vehicle raced forward. The driver slammed on the brakes. She almost looked back. Doors opened and slammed shut. Men shouted.

Clarissa ran.

CHAPTER 4

AN HOUR LATER, THE WOMAN EMERGED FROM HER BEDROOM dressed in black jeans and a matching sweater. After downing a shot of vodka, she grabbed her clutch off the coat rack and exited the apartment, which faded to black as the door closed. Was this the opportunity Jack had been waiting for?

He threw on his jacket, patting his chest to feel the burner phone concealed in a hidden pocket. He grabbed his regular cell and a pistol off the table. Given how little he knew about the woman, the gun offered a bit of security, though he doubted he'd draw it this evening.

Stepping out into the cool evening air, he scanned the sidewalk in both directions. She wouldn't be there. Her building was on the other side of the block. Noble had a feeling he wasn't the only one in town, so he made sure to take in any and all faces, noting those that looked familiar.

He raced to the corner, kept his speed up as he turned left. A lone orange streetlamp hummed and cast a small pool of diffused light on the alley. A dark green door with a busted doorbell was the only beneficiary. The name on the door had been scratched out and someone had spray-painted something in Danish.

Jack neared the intersection and slowed his pace a good thirty feet from it. He didn't want to draw any attention. Foot traffic was heavier here. The street was wider, busier. Several businesses, storefronts, and restaurants lined the lower level of the buildings. There were dozens of lights, and the chatter of pedestrians drowned out the electrical hum.

At the corner, he paused, reached into his pocket and pulled out a vape. It wasn't a habit he had any intention of keeping, but it allowed him to blend in while he scouted an area. It beat lighting up another cigarette, something he swore off not too long ago.

Noble sectioned off the surrounding area and scanned for the only marker he had for the woman. Black clothing. Everyone here was dressed in black. None of them were her. He wove through the crowd, picking his way between small groups. Most were younger. Made sense, given the hour. People going out for the evening, not returning home after dinner. Was she joining them?

The entrance of her apartment building was twenty feet away. Jack positioned himself on the curb. The foot traffic was heavy enough to obscure him from anyone inside. Movement in the lobby caught his eye. Someone checking their mail, dressed in black jeans and a red coat. She hadn't left with a coat, though. Perhaps she kept one outside of her apartment? Though the building was large, it seemed the apartments took up a small slice of the structure. Separate entrances dotted the block. She might only have one or two neighbors on her floor.

He stepped off the curb into the street and used the vape again to buy some time while waiting for the woman to finish checking her mail. A group of twenty-somethings laughed and spoke in fast, excited tones, as though their brains were already racing from speed. They walked slowly, blocking Jack's view of the lobby for more than five seconds.

And in that time, the woman disappeared. Jack swept the street from left to right and back again. The lights created large orange swaths that merged together like colliding thunderheads. He spotted a flash of red through a throng of tweaked-out clubbers.

Weaving through the crowd, Noble kept one hand close to his gun. The other threaded around anyone in his path. The woman in red stepped off the curb. Jack slowed, taking in the scene on the street and the opposite sidewalk. A man in a black wool overcoat leaned against a light pole. Hands in his pockets. Staring at the woman. No expression on his thin face.

Red lights hindered traffic at either end of the block. A single car turned left, headed in their direction. The woman stopped in the middle of the street. The car slowed. Its window lowered. Jack lifted his shirt, grabbed his pistol. Only he wasn't sure who he would target. If someone else did the woman in, he'd lose the contract, but more importantly, he'd be on the hook for not completing the job. That would invite scrutiny. And the last thing Noble wanted while living as someone else was some shadow organization digging around and discovering his identity.

The car stopped. Some guy with a full beard leaned out of the open window.

The woman took a step back and slipped a hand in her pocket.

The guy watching her straightened up and pulled something from his pocket.

Jack's skin tingled. Every sense was heightened in this moment. He used to live for this feeling. Now the adrenaline left him with a hangover the next day.

The back doors opened. Two guys jumped out. The bald guy rounded the back of the vehicle. The other, a guy with bleached and blue hair, had nothing impeding his path to the woman.

But these weren't trained operatives. Far from it. They were lanky kids wearing ripped jeans and death metal band t-shirts. They had chains attached to their wallets. They had nose rings and huge holes in their earlobes. The passenger door opened, and a third guy emerged with a pipe or bat in his hand. The three men all paused and glanced at each other. Nodded. Presumably that meant the attack was on.

The guy across the street was halfway to the man holding the pipe, who must've noticed the incoming attack because he brought the weapon up, spun, and swung violently. The man in the overcoat jumped back, bowing his body as he did so. The pipe missed his stomach by inches.

The woman didn't wait for the man facing her. She stepped forward and delivered a kick to his groin. He collapsed to his knees. Held out a hand as though he were begging her to stop. She kicked through his hand and landed a blow to his chin. He fell to the side. She whipped her head to the side, but not in time to catch the bald guy before he caught her. He wrapped her up in a bear hug from behind. He wasn't much of a physical specimen, but he was tall and had long arms that gave him leverage.

Noble had already moved off the curb before the woman delivered her first kick. He reached the guy seconds after he had wrapped her up. The woman was scrappy and already had her attacker off his feet and draped over her back. She leaned forward, working herself free from his grip. She broke it quickly. But he regained his footing, and his arm went to her neck, locking her into the V where forearm and upper arm met. He hoisted her off her feet. She clutched his arm with both hands, dug her nails into his skin, but struggled to break the hold he had on her.

On the other side of the car, the man in the overcoat was in a tug-of-war for the pipe. The third thug could see his team had bitten off more than they could handle. He had one hand on his weapon and the other reaching for the car door. Was something else in there?

Jack turned his attention back to the woman. He knew his next move would put her at risk, but failing to do anything would lead to her death at the hands of this tweaked-out thug. He pulled his pistol, ratcheted his arm back, and with all the power and torque he could muster, brought it down on the back of the guy's neck.

The woman fell to the ground. She sprawled like a wrestler and scrambled to her feet, spun, and was ready to fight again. The guy stood there, motionless. A few seconds passed. By this time, onlookers had stopped, and the murmur had risen. Sirens rose in the background.

The guy collapsed, eyes wide with panic as he processed the fact that his body was immobile. Not permanently, probably. Immediate swelling likely pinched his spinal cord. He'd be normal within a few hours, probably. As normal as a guy like that could get.

The third guy abandoned the pipe and lunged into the open door. Seconds later, wheels screeched on the asphalt as the cowards sped off, leaving behind their friends and a cloud of smoke that vaporized into the shimmering night sky.

The woman stared at Jack, mouth open, no words escaping, and her head shaking slightly, as though she wanted to ask, "Who? Why? How?"

The man in the overcoat called to her. She held up her hand either to tell him to hold on or to shut up. She didn't know Noble. She didn't want Noble knowing her name.

The sirens drew nearer. The crowd gathered nearer. The murmurs and gasps became one unified voice. Cell phones, ever-present, were out and recording.

"Come on!" the guy yelled.

She nodded at Jack, jutted her chin toward the other guy, and gestured for Noble to follow.

He hesitated. This wouldn't be his only opportunity to encounter the woman. And in the future, it could be an encounter he controlled and not this chaotic scene. Not this random moment. He'd never have *this* opportunity again, though. Despite not knowing him, she trusted him. If he didn't follow, that confidence would erode, and he'd never find out why he was sent to kill her.

She looked past Jack and winced. The cops were closing in. He knew if he turned around, he'd see their lights flashing in the distance.

"We should go."

She spun and sprinted toward the alley.

Jack followed.

CHAPTER 5

SMOKE TENDRILS ROSE FROM THE PAN, INTERTWINED, dancing toward the vent. The bacon popped and sizzled. The aroma enveloped Brandon Cunningham and, as he inhaled deeply, he forgot about Kimberlee, and enjoyed the moment for once.

He braced himself with his left arm and rose out of his wheelchair to a fully standing position to turn the strips over. Grease exploded from the pan, raining fire over a three-foot radius of the stove. Brandon brought up his left arm to shield his face, feeling the sting from the splatter.

"That's right," he said to himself, glancing down at his thighs, which hovered over the chair at a slight angle. "I'm still standing."

Hard to believe this was the reason he and Kimberlee weren't seeing eye to eye. For the first time in as long as he could remember, he could almost support himself on his feet. Every week, hell, every day, there was improvement. The photos he took did not lie. Muscle was building around his thighs and calves. Sensations he'd never felt wormed through his muscles. Morning, day, and night, his skin tingled as though the cells were multiplying, or rather, going to war against all those who were bent on keeping him down.

And *she* didn't like it.

Well, who the hell was she?

Brandon winced at the sharp pain in his ear. It always came with the anger. He clenched his jaw so tight, he wondered how he hadn't cracked a molar. They were battle-tested, that's why. Years of this being his only viable response. Wasn't like he could ever get up and fight a bully. Lord knows, he'd had plenty of those throughout his life. It wasn't until he was actually useful that there were people like Jack Noble who looked out for him.

But this pain was different.

For good reason.

It wasn't until Kimberlee that a woman had ever truly cared for him.

There'd been a few before. Brandon had amassed a small fortune as a for-hire hacker, and there were occasions he wasn't above flashing that wealth in order to get laid. It worked. At times. Being in a wheelchair, he could lead with pretty much any line and have no fear of getting slapped. Though it happened.

At times.

When Kimberlee came along, everything changed. She saw him for him. Fact was, she didn't even know about his money.

Or his career.

She loved him *despite* both.

So why had she stormed out five days ago, telling him to call her when he respected her opinions?

The medicine.

The Godforsaken pills.

Three guys had shown up at his door following his involvement in a non-sanctioned operation. If all three had been stereotypes dressed in black suits, he probably wouldn't be here today, given everything that had happened. Only two of them were in suits. The other looked like he belonged in an L.L. Bean catalog. That guy introduced himself as Doctor Michaels. The other two flashed badges. They ran through the house with devices in their hands that Brandon figured were bug sniffers. He found that offensive. Like anyone could've managed to pull that off in *his* house. After they had finished, the pair remained by the front door.

The doctor presented an option to Brandon that he could not pass up. As a thank you for his assistance, a benefactor wanted to grant him access to a next-generation treatment for his condition. Something that could allow him to walk in a year or two.

Or possibly kill him.

Brandon had everything already. Plenty of money. All the tech he could ever dream of and the ability to buy more when it debuted. He had access to channels most people had no idea existed. If he needed a favor, he got one. He even had the love of his life. What was missing?

The use of his legs.

The ability to take a damn walk to the mailbox.

Everything able-bodied people took for granted.

Kimberlee put up a fight when he told her about it. The treatment was unproven and potentially harmful or fatal. There could be numerous other side effects. She heard all that. He didn't. All he knew was this could be his only chance to gain the ability to walk on his own.

So he took it.

And she refused to let that go.

With good reason.

Brandon didn't believe her when she said he'd changed after starting the treatment. How? Nothing seemed different other than the strength he was building and the dedication he had toward doing everything in his power to help the meds. Sure, they caused some physical side effects at times, but those had mostly faded. Other than that, he was great.

Except when he wasn't, according to her.

The outbursts.

The crying.

The anger.

The fighting.

The demeaning attitude.

He recalled none of this and would argue any time she brought up an incident. The tension ratcheted up over the months. She put a hidden camera on the fireplace mantle and began keeping a file of his erratic behavior. When she showed him, it was as though he were watching a terribly crafted movie. One starring him, one he could not remember for the life of him.

"They did something to you, baby," she had said. *"I see it is making you*

stronger, but I can't shake this feeling that they want to use you for something else. Look at how it arrives every week. Some guy shows up and hands you a bottle full of pills. You don't know what's in it! You don't even know who this is coming from!"

That led to the final argument. Which led to him saying some things he couldn't quite remember but knew he shouldn't have said. She cried. He yelled. He yelled some more. He threatened her. He took it back. But that didn't matter.

The next day, she told him she was going away for a while. It might be for a long while. She demanded he not use his skills and contacts to find her. If he did that, she'd never come back. Not only that, she'd make an anonymous tip about him. When he said she was bluffing, she recited a string of contacts and how he'd helped them. He'd spent the better part of a day trying to figure out how she knew. He'd been careless somewhere. Had to have been.

He tried calling. She didn't answer. He tried again. She didn't answer. He went for it a third time. The number had been disconnected.

It had to be up to her, he supposed.

Brandon shook the memory free as he ate his bacon. The taste melted all his troubles away for a few moments. Funny how that worked with certain tastes and smells. For a moment, he was six years old in his grandma's kitchen, eating the same meal. She was a short, round lady with a smile that never faded no matter what troubles she faced. She always told him he'd do amazing things one day, and that God didn't take away one ability and not increase others. Her words got him through a lot of rough years.

The meowing of his cat, Titus, broke the spell. He pulled a piece of bacon apart and offered it to him. At first, the cat shunned the offering. When Brandon pulled it away, the cat swiped and stopped him.

"Told ya, it's good stuff," Brandon said.

After cleaning up, he returned to his office, cat in his lap. A half-dozen unread messages were waiting for him. His breath caught as he scanned the list for Kimberlee's number, hoping she'd reactivated it. The chances of her reaching out to him through this channel were slim. It was reserved for people with codenames and access numbers. Those who reached out only when they needed something because someone's life was on the line.

He skimmed the list, recognizing five of the six who had contacted him. While it wasn't unusual for a stranger to contact him, he was typically given a heads up by the referrer. This was unexpected.

"Let's see what my regulars want first." He stroked Titus on the top of the head and the cat's purring intensified. "Background checks. Same old boring stuff, Titus." He copied the details from each request and pasted them in a note app. None were high priority. He could handle them later.

Titus hopped up on the desk and tried to pull Brandon's hand away from the mouse. Brandon petted him on the head for a few seconds then nudged him toward the edge.

"Now, Mr. or Mrs. @pric0tl0v3r..." He chuckled. *Apricotlover*. Not the toughest sounding name for a spy. "What the hell do you want?"

Clicking on the message revealed three pieces of information.

A city.

Warsaw.

A situation.

Captured. Escaped. In trouble.

And a name.

Clarissa.

CHAPTER 6

LIGHTS FLASHED RHYTHMICALLY IN TIME WITH THE thumping bass. The crowd moved as a single organism spilling over the dance floor into the seating. They were half-bathed in red light, half-doused in neon green. Dressed down to the layers soaked with sweat to their skin. They were fueled by alcohol and various drug cocktails, the never-ending beat further entrenching them in the moment.

Noble threaded his way through the crowd, wishing his brain could focus on one thing like these people focused on the music. He stuck close to the woman. She moved with the grace of a gazelle. When anyone took offense at her passing, she neutralized them with her smile. Often, they'd return it and attempt to pull her into their circle. She'd lean into Jack, grab his hand, and continue forward.

Jack had lost sight of the man from the street within moments of entering. He had moved with a purpose into the belly of the beast, and the beast had swallowed him whole.

When Jack asked about him, the woman said, "Don't worry. We'll meet with him soon."

Had this been pre-planned? Was the club the ultimate destination regardless of what had happened in the street? Hell, Jack hadn't had time to process that, and here he was in another uncertain situation.

"What's going on?" he asked, not expecting an answer.

She didn't give him one. Tightening her grip on his hand, she pulled him toward the DJ's stand. The guy on the platform looking down on the mob wore a mirrored jacket and top hat. The lights reflected off him, masking his face in a starburst of colors. The guy stared right at the woman. Lifting his right index finger an inch or two, he pointed over Jack.

The woman glanced back, her gaze dancing around Jack. Her eyes widened. The guys from the car? Was it not as random as it appeared? The thought crossed Jack's mind that someone else had it in for the lady. That he wasn't the only one after her. Perhaps the idiots they had encountered outside were the first wave of attacks from another group.

Jack turned to see what she had noticed, but before he could single out a face, she yanked his arm, pulled him closer to the DJ. They made eye contact. For a moment, Jack thought he knew the guy. Whether he did or not, the recognition meant the DJ was not who he seemed to be. They shared a look that Noble only shared with men like him. Was the DJ involved in whatever was going on? Hard to know. Could've been active when he was younger. Could've been a grunt. A cop. Special Forces.

Jack saw five hundred puzzle pieces in front of him, scattered about as though a child had taken their small hand and knocked them all around a table. A few pieces had finally come together. The club had been the destination regardless of what happened in the street. He knew that now. The encounter with the young thugs only enhanced the anxiety of the situation.

Reaching back, she tapped his chest. "In there."

The woman pointed at a door behind the platform, standing open an inch. Blue light spewed out of the crack. Two men stood on either side. Tall. Built. Wearing glasses with obvious cameras built in and wireless earpieces they didn't try to conceal. Both were printing. Neither cared Jack could see their guns. Why didn't they just keep their guns in their hands? Too many people around. Drunks and addicts and people on a combo of the drugs and alcohol just to have a good time at the club. The stuff that turned normal people into idiots at times. Idiots who might do stupid things around armed men in a club. Idiots who could escalate a simple situation into a bloodbath.

The guy on their left made eye contact with the woman, nodded, opened the door. The guy on the right stepped up, stuck out his arm, put his hand on Jack's chest. Noble bit back the urge to snap the guy's wrist.

The woman snapped her head toward the armed guard. "He's with me."

"Not until we check him," the guy on the left said. He nodded at his partner.

Jack spread his arms. "I can tell you what you're gonna find. If you try to take it, it won't end well."

"For you," the guy said, his accent was thick. Eastern European. Romanian? Czech or Slovak? He worked his hand down Jack's side.

"You really want to find out, don't you?" Noble said.

The woman knifed herself between them, knocking the guard back. "Not now. We don't have time for this." She faced Jack. "If you're armed, hand it over. We'll get it back."

There's a little red light that exists somewhere in the back of Noble's mind. One that goes off when a situation has the potential of turning real ugly real quick. It had been solid for the past ten minutes. It was now flashing, accompanied by a blaring siren. Maybe it was the lights, the music, the never-ending *thump-thump-thump* all disrupting the messaging in his brain. A scenario played out in his mind where this entire situation was a setup. From getting the job. Following the woman. The men in the street. Now here, in this club, pulling out his pistol and handing it over to some two-hundred-fifty-pound ogre. The person handing out the jobs he'd been taking for months had caught up. She worked for them. These guys worked for them. On the other side of that door, maybe that person was waiting for Jack.

Ignoring the warnings, he pulled his pistol and handed it to the guy. Deed done. Not too painful, not entirely painless. Plus, trust had been earned. Now they wouldn't search him and find his backup piece.

The guy on the right went back to his post, eyes on the crowd. He'd forgotten the annoyance already. The guy on the left opened the door and nodded and ushered them through.

The door slammed shut. Hard. Heavy. Clicked loudly. The music died to a muffled whine. The soothing voice of Antônio Carlos Jobim overtook the *thump-thump-thump* of the bass. They'd landed in a private room in Ipanema. He was with a girl who didn't know his name, but it was Jack that didn't care.

His eyes took a few minutes to adjust from the strobes and neon to the soft blue light emanating from LEDs that lined the walls where they met the ceiling. There were five phones mounted around the room, spanning a century's worth of innovation. They rang at intervals. Gaudy Victorian furniture ate up every square inch of wall space. Two women leaned back on opposing couches. Their long hair appeared as blue as the walls and splayed out across the velvet fabric like large blooming fireworks. They stared into each other's glassy eyes, oblivious to the newcomers. Wasn't hard to figure out why. Needles and spoons and lighters and baggies were laid out on the table between them. Every time a phone rang, their eyelids fluttered, rolled back, and all Jack could make out was the whites of their eyes, which also looked blue.

What the hell was this place?

The woman studied him as he took it in. She started to speak, "We'll just—"

"Who are you?" he asked.

She seemed taken aback he'd cut her off, but if she was angry, it dissipated as quickly as steam rising from boiling water. Her open mouth formed a smile that indicated she was more intrigued than anything else.

"You've been watching me for a few days," she said. "Figured you already knew."

Jack tried not to appear shocked that she had spotted him. Had he been that careless? While his mind raced through his actions since entering his temporary dwelling, he tried to place her accent. She spoke perfect English and did so in a way that offered no clue where she was from. Maybe she'd spent some of her formative years in the States, or at some boarding school in Switzerland where they turned kids into perfect global citizens.

"I've been trying to figure out why I was sent here."

What else could he say? He knew he was screwed. This might be his only shot. The guards could be her people. Or maybe her people were waiting on the other side of the door at the other end of the room, past the drugged-up pixies.

"You're either here to help me or kill me," she said. "Which is it?"

"I'm not sure yet."

"That's a bold answer."

"It's the truth."

"Maybe the truth isn't the best option. Ever think of that?"

"Thinking gets me into trouble."

"So does stalking. Or is it spying?" Pausing a beat. she inhaled. Her eyes were wide, but unfocused. She was taking him in, attempting to spot the slightest tell.

Jack didn't give her one.

The woman to his left planted her hand on the couch's arm and tried to stand. She got about halfway up before falling back, rolling to the side. Her legs were in the air. She wasn't wearing panties. A moment later, she was laughing as she tried to pull her skirt back down. She did a poor job of it.

"You frequent this place often?" Jack asked his target.

"No. And don't change the subject. I need to know who sent you."

"Why are we here?"

Pinching the bridge of her nose, she glanced at the woman who had finally righted herself. "Unfinished business."

"You were coming here no matter what, then? Guys who tried to jump you, they don't matter?"

She held his gaze for several seconds. The woman on the other couch made a sound like she was about to throw up. The other laughed again.

"Tell me your name?" she demanded.

"Asked you first."

"You're a pain in the ass, aren't you." She didn't wait for Jack to answer. "Johanna. Satisfied?"

"Satisfied." He waited a moment, then added, "Jack."

"Should have figured." She took a few steps and scooped up a trash can, handed it to the woman in time for her to vomit in it.

"Why?"

"All you guys are named Jack."

"You're my first Johanna."

"I'll be gentle then."

Jack chuckled at the comment, but as his brain processed the exchange, he knew she wasn't what he thought. Not some activist or lawyer or corporate jackwagon who'd pissed off the wrong people.

She was like him.

"Well, Johanna, what the hell are we doing here?"

"You're about to find out."

CHAPTER 7

THE DIM LIGHT EMITTED BY THE EDISON BULBS HANGING ON strings dangling from the ceiling wasn't the only contrast between where they now stood and the overstimulating club and the blue room. There were no tweaked-out women in here. The thump of the bass was missing. An oval wooden table with more scratches on it than the ground in a chicken coop took up more than half of the room. Past the table, another door loomed. Jack glanced over to see if he could spot a lock. It didn't take long for his attention to go back to the two men in Armani suits and a guy in a t-shirt seated at the other end of the table.

Two of them faced each other. They wore dark glasses. They had trimmed beards. One was graying. The other bald. Thick gold chains peeked out from their unbuttoned shirts, snuggled against mounds of chest hair. Each had a hand on a black briefcase. The other hand remained out of view, under the table, presumably holding a weapon of some sort. A gun, Jack figured, because what else would they hide under the table in a soundproof room?

After a second of sizing up the lackeys, he turned his attention to the man seated between them. He was thin and lanky, wearing a white V-neck t-shirt that his arms poked out from. Jack could tell he was strong. It wasn't the kind of muscle that bulged. There was no bloat on the guy. But his forearms rippled as he drummed his fingers on the table in between the briefcases. A guy like that, probably six-four, maybe six-five, with extra-long arms, could whip up some torque, and if you weren't careful, he'd knock you out in one or two shots.

Silence pervaded the space. The low-key ringing that persisted in Jack's ears rose as he became more aware of it. A stress thing, sometimes. A neurotic thing, at other times. Tinnitus, they called it. He figured it had to do with too many loud bangs and blows to the head. But what did he know? Over the years, he'd learned to like it. When everyone else ultimately faded away, he had his personal Siren wailing in his ears.

The man at the head of the table cleared his throat, attempted to smile, and gestured to the chairs in front of Jack and Johanna.

"Please, sit."

Johanna pulled her chair back. The legs scraped against the floor. The bald lackey grimaced as though she'd run her nails down a chalkboard.

"Thanks for seeing us, Oskar," she said.

"Where's Rupert?" Oskar asked.

"Lost sight of him in the club," Johanna said. "Figured you had someone round him up. Has no one seen him?"

Oskar leaned toward the graying lackey, covered his mouth with the backside of his hand, and whispered something. The lackey nodded once. He got up and pushed his chair in and walked behind Jack to the door leading to the blue room.

"Might wanna watch out for those ladies," Jack said. "They were a handful a minute ago."

Johanna kicked him under the table. The bald lackey didn't acknowledge Jack's advice.

Oskar grinned. "They are nobody. Just a couple of VIPs."

"You call all your VIPs 'nobody'?" Jack asked.

"They aren't *my* VIPs."

"Whose then?"

"What's it matter?" Oskar picked up the rocks glass filled with two fingers of whiskey or bourbon and no ice and took a sip. He aimed the glass at Jack. "Apologies. Would you care for some?"

"Does that make me a VIP?"

Oskar laughed. His shoulders slumped a little. His muscles relaxed a lot. "I like him, Johanna. And you, my friend, were born a VIP." He leaned over to the remaining lackey, the bald one, didn't bother to cover his mouth, or whisper, and said, "Go get the bottle."

The bald guy rose.

Oskar placed his hand on the man's arm. He held up a finger. "The good stuff."

"Hope by 'good stuff' you mean good for both of us," Jack said.

"You don't trust me?"

"I don't know you."

"But you know Johanna."

Jack felt her gaze jolt toward him. They hadn't time to discuss what was going on here. She knew he had been watching her. Maybe she knew he was on the street.

"We're recent acquaintances," Jack said. "Plus, she's beautiful."

"What's that got to do with it?" Oskar said.

"I've learned to never trust beautiful women."

Oskar laughed again. A big, wide smile lingered. He was even more relaxed. It made Jack nervous. Only crazy people acted this way in this kind of situation with a potentially dangerous stranger in the room. Either Oskar was nuts, or the guy had an ace hidden somewhere.

"Johanna, I got to hand it to you. This guy is great. I wanna deal with him. Forget Rupert."

The door behind Oskar opened, and the bald lackey appeared with a decanter. Brown liquid sloshed around as he set it on the table. The smell of whiskey worked its way toward Jack and Johanna. Oskar refreshed his glass and filled two more with two fingers of whiskey each. The lackey set them in front of Jack and Johanna. The smell was even stronger up close. It singed his nose a little.

Oskar lifted his glass to his lips and held it there. He didn't sip. No, he was waiting for Jack to do so first. A test, maybe. Poisoned, perhaps. And if that was the case, Jack was dead, whether he drank it or not. He figured he might as well take a sip and feel the burn one last time. So he did. And it burned. In a good way, of course. The whiskey snaked its way down to his throat and coated his stomach, leaving a trail of fire in its wake.

Oskar's eyebrows hiked up a quarter inch. The bald guy continued staring at the briefcases. Johanna held her breath, which told Jack maybe she didn't trust this guy. Her reasons for coming to see him had to be business related, or out of desperation.

"Well?" Oskar asked.

"Astounding," Jack said.

Oskar slapped the table with his free hand and then downed the contents of his glass, slapping it on the table after. Jack did the same. Why not? They both turned toward Johanna.

"Oh, piss off. Do I gotta act like one of the boys, too?" She didn't wait for an answer, opting to down her whiskey in one gulp. If she felt it, she didn't show it. That impressed Jack a little. "Mine's bigger than both of yours put together."

The guys laughed, and everyone breathed a little heavier for the next twenty seconds as the burn subsided.

Oskar was the first to speak.

"I was surprised to receive your call, Johanna. Things didn't go so well between us last time we saw each other."

"I had a job to do," she said. "You know it was nothing personal."

Oskar lifted his shoulders a couple inches, turned his outstretched hands palms up, and set them on the table. "'Nothing personal' still got my partner five to ten in jail."

"And we're working on getting him out."

"Working? It's been nearly a year."

"He's guilty as hell, and you know it, Oskar."

"He aided you with the understanding he'd remain free."

"He *should* be free."

"What good is '*should*'?"

She took a moment to measure her words. "He will be free. The plan is in motion. You already know this." She slid her glass down the table toward him for a refill. "Frankly, I'm a little confused why we're having this conversation now with more pressing issues at hand."

Oskar leaned back, crossed his arms. Those sinewy forearm muscles rippled as he worked his fists. He reached for one of the briefcases, made a production out of undoing the locks, and sighed and rolled his eyes. He set his hands flat on the briefcase instead of opening it.

"I know, Johanna, and I trust you. Just yesterday, I followed up on this with one of my guys, and they said he should be out in the next thirty days."

She shook her head. "Why are you giving me so much grief about it now?"

Oskar ignored her as he retrieved the contents of the briefcase before pushing it away. Some folders. A phone. A couple of USB drives. He placed them on the table in front of him. The bald lackey continued staring at the closed briefcase in front of him. Didn't even attempt to glance at the items in front of Oskar.

Oskar organized the items largest to smallest in two rows. Folders, photos and papers on top. Phone and USB drives on the bottom. He placed them back in the briefcase in that order and had his guy hand it to Johanna.

"I'm really not trying to be difficult," he said. "Giving you a hard time, perhaps, to see what you'll say. But there's no hate coming from me to you. Honestly, if he had been more careful, he wouldn't have wound up in a cell, and you wouldn't feel as though you owe me for him being there."

"So you admit I don't owe you." Johanna arched an eyebrow as a slight smile curled up the left side of her lips.

Oskar looked up. His hardened expression dissipated as he returned the gesture. There was history between them, and it wasn't all bad.

"Oh, you still owe me, Johanna, and it'll be time to pay up soon."

CHAPTER 8

THIRTY MINUTES LATER THEY WERE ESCORTED THROUGH THE back door by Oskar and his men. A car waited just beyond the reach of the porch light halo. It was larger than most Jack had seen on the streets in Europe. It was black with windows tinted as dark as the paint. The moon reflected off the glass sunroof. Jack noticed the wheels were dirty and streaks of mud caked the bottom of the fenders and doors.

"Is there a shovel in the trunk?" he asked.

Oskar laughed and patted him on the back. "No, my friend. That was disposed of after the body was buried."

"Club casualty? Or...?"

Oskar turned to him. The moonlight illuminated half his face. The lines on his forehead and around his eyes and mouth etched deeper in the pale light, while the whites of his eyes stood out. He looked like both a menacing bull about to charge and a heifer locked in a stall.

"Better not to ask these questions. Not after what we just discussed."

What they had just discussed had little to do with Noble. A lot of it was code. Made up names and places. Johanna and Oskar knew the real names. The real places. Jack assumed he'd find out in due time. If he stuck around, which he wasn't sure he wanted to do. He glanced up at that bright moon and stifled a laugh into a single chuckle because he knew he didn't want to stick around and he couldn't get the image of Oskar munching on hay out of his head.

Since assuming the assassin's identity, Jack was eight-for-eight in completing jobs. And he was eight-for-eight in giving the targets he'd been sent to terminate a second chance. Why should Johanna be different? Either there was a legit reason for the contract on her life or there wasn't. That wasn't for him to decide. He'd already made up his mind. He wasn't going to kill her. Just like he hadn't killed the others. Not physically, at least. They all suffered an end to their life. And enjoyed a rebirth as someone new.

A second chance.

Jack accepted the contracts that stood out to him when he could. Sometimes it was slow, and he grabbed what was there. This time, he had been asked to go to Copenhagen to await further instruction.

From the beginning, he swore he wouldn't kill any of the targets. He only wanted the guy sending the jobs. Because that guy either wanted Jack dead or knew the identity of the person who did. Each target had something to offer Noble. Each of them with their own five-hundred-piece puzzle. Some puzzles were completed. Others not so much. Each offered at least a clue to the shadow figure's identity. Once the targets learned the alternative to living was death, they answered all of his questions. Were they always truthful? No. No one is. Not all the time. Especially those people.

Patterns emerged that painted a picture. More of a Picasso than a Homer. But Jack knew that Picasso started his process by creating a realistic image and deconstructing it until he had a masterpiece.

People were often the same. Misinformation came from a place of honesty. How else could it? And if you asked the right questions enough times to enough people, something akin to the truth came out. It wasn't version one of Picasso's bull. Nor was it version nine. It fell somewhere in the middle. From one angle, the image looked real enough. From the other, you could almost see the form of the masterpiece taking shape.

At this point, he felt like he had eight somewhat clear versions of realistic images, and soon he'd find the thing that helped him deconstruct them all to lead him where he needed to go.

What would he learn from Johanna? She was more than a random woman living in an expensive apartment in an upscale section of town who had managed to screw someone over or screw up somewhere. This lady had the kind of chops Noble had only seen in experienced operatives. Of all the people he'd been sent to terminate—a banker, a CEO, two lawyers, a surgeon, a teacher who actually deserved to die, a witness to a murder, and a man who seemingly hadn't done anything—Johanna had the highest chance of holding the key that unlocked the door that would lead to the person dealing the death card.

"Those ladies in that room," she started after close to twenty minutes of silence other than the talk radio the driver listened to in a language Jack didn't understand.

Jack snapped free of his thoughts and angled his face toward her. "Yeah?"

"I know one of them."

"How?"

"She's a bank teller."

"Hope you don't hand your cash over to her."

Johanna shrugged, turned toward the window. "I was surprised to see her in there."

"The bank?"

"The back room in the club."

"We all got vices, right?"

"Heroin is a hell of a vice."

"Isn't it, though?"

"Do you know much about that?" She shifted in her seat so her back was against the door. She tucked her left ankle under her right leg. Her jacket opened up. Her pistol's grip angled toward him. He could reach for it, shoot her, the driver, grab the wheel in an attempt to control the car.

Instead, he remained seated.

"Not really."

She sighed heavily. "I hate when people say that."

"Not really?"

"Yes."

"Why?"

"Why can't you just say no?"

"I do say no."

"Do you?"

"Not really." Jack couldn't help himself. And he couldn't stop from smiling. "What was all that about back there? The made up names and places. What's on those thumb drives he gave you?"

She pulled her jacket closed. She'd shoved the thumb drives in an interior pocket for safe keeping. Perhaps his questioning had left her feeling less than secure about them.

"It's better that you don't know specifics, Jack."

"Is it?"

"Yes, really."

"That's definitive. I like it." He craned his neck and looked out the front window. After driving a few miles out of the city, they were now heading back in. "Why are we going back?"

"Had to make sure no one was following."

"So we're going back to stay?"

She shrugged. "Depends."

"On?"

"How compromised we are."

"Because of the dudes on the street. And the people with the phones with cameras. And the CCTV that likely exists on every corner."

She nodded and said nothing.

"What are the chances we can stop and get some food?"

She laughed and said nothing.

"What are the chances you're gonna fill me in on all this?"

She sighed and asked him, "Were you sent to kill me?"

Competing thoughts jostled for the lead in Jack's mind. Before a winner could be declared, he blurted out his answer.

"Yes, but I had no intention of completing the job."

She seemed unfazed by the acknowledgment. "At any point were you close enough to pull the trigger?"

"I am right now."

"Yeah, but I can retrieve my gun faster than you."

"Wanna find out?"

"Not really."

Jack stifled a laugh. A moment of silence lingered for a second too long and he felt compelled to fill it. "What's your background?"

She shifted in her seat. Her gaze traveled from Jack to the windshield and back. "How do you mean? Where I'm from?"

"More like where you've been?"

"Here, there, anywhere, really."

"Who have you worked for?"

"I've held a few different jobs."

Noble placed his thumb and index finger in between his brow and massaged outward. The tension in his forehead and around his eyes receded for a moment.

"Not the most forthcoming, are you?"

"Should I be?" she said.

"Just trying to get to know you."

"Let's turn it around. Who have you worked for, Jack?"

"I was military."

She rolled her eyes. "Then so was I."

"What country? Branch?"

"I was eighteen."

"So was I."

"What's it matter now? That was what, twenty-five, thirty years ago for you?"

Noble shrugged and shook his head and turned his attention to the encroaching city lights. The woman's background would come out eventually. His would too, he supposed. He had other concerns at the moment. Like, were they going back to the club? To her apartment? To find the young thugs and pay them back for what they attempted?

The driver wove through city blocks, always ending up on the same main road that would travel past her apartment. A few blocks out, he diverted. A new pattern. Jack resisted craning his neck to get a view through the rear window. The guy behind the wheel seemed to know what he was doing. If someone was following, there had to be a protocol he would enact. Backup would come in. The other car would be pinned in. They'd get what they needed out of the driver then dispose of him. If necessary. It would probably be necessary if all that came to fruition.

It didn't, though. Presumably he was being evasive, just in case.

They drove past Noble's building first. Didn't have to get to the entrance to see it was hot. There was no chance he was getting into the apartment for his things, including the camera he'd used to snap pictures of Johanna. There were a couple of guys standing at each corner. One by the front door. Another across the street from the front door. They tried to blend in with skinny jeans, black boots, black jackets. Two of them were smoking. But not a single one was looking at their phone. One had failed to hide the cord to his earpiece.

"You're compromised," Johanna said.

"What gave it away?" Jack said. "How much you wanna bet you are, too?"

She lifted an eyebrow, shrugged with her left shoulder.

The driver turned away from the main road, away from her apartment, and drove as though he were stuck in the middle of a maze. Ten minutes passed before they drove past Johanna's apartment. Half as many men were out front. They looked the same as the others.

"Any of these guys, the one who visited you in your apartment earlier tonight? Rupert, was it?"

She leaned back as though she'd been shoved in the chest by the words. Her mouth opened, but whatever thoughts ran through her head failed to generate corresponding words. Her left hand fell on her upper thigh, presumably the location of the drive Rupert had handed her in her apartment.

"Sorry," Jack said. "I figured that had something to do with the job. If it was personal, forget I mentioned it."

"How should I do that? You just said it." She hesitated, but when Jack began to speak, she cut him off. "It was a personal matter, but one related to this. I..."

"Look you don't have—"

"I'm processing the information is all, and I'd rather not discuss it."

"Fair enough."

The driver cleared his throat.

"Yes?" Johanna said.

"Sorry, Johanna, but as you've seen, the block is teeming with people who would prefer to see you dead."

"I noticed."

"Where should we go? Sweden?"

She gazed up at the moonroof as though a map were printed there. "I don't want to chance it in Copenhagen, nor the bridges to there and then to Sweden. Let's go to Germany. From there, we can regroup and determine our next steps."

"Comfortable with the E45?" he said, referring to the highway. "That'll turn into the A7 in Germany."

"Yes," she said. "Just be ready to pivot if necessary."

"I'm like a ballerina; I can pivot so hard." He winked at them in the rearview.

"And you're damn good at it," she said.

CHAPTER 9

THE COLD SEEPED INTO HER BONES. HER CLOTHING AND hair were soaked. The blanket she sought shelter under smelled like the man she'd taken it from. It had done a decent enough job of keeping her warm through the late hours. Until the rain started.

Clarissa peeked out from under her cover. Through the buildings, she saw the promise of the sun. The storm clouds racing overhead were thin now, their underbellies turning from deep purple to pink.

Shedding the blanket, she rose and took in the alleyway, now with the advantage of the pale morning light. The clatter of silverware rose from not too far away. A breakfast diner, maybe? She sniffed the air, but all she could smell was the lingering stench of the blanket. How long would that take to dissipate? First step: get away from it.

She hugged herself tight, taking several rapid, deep breaths, which not only made her lightheaded, but also warm after a few moments. She steadied herself, cleared her mind, opened her eyes again more in tune with her surroundings.

Every twenty seconds or so, a car passed on either end of the alley. It wouldn't be long before traffic picked up and pedestrians littered the sidewalk. She'd be safer on the street then. If she left the alley now, anyone looking for her would have an easy time spotting her.

They were out there. She knew it. Could feel them close by. That was a given, though. She estimated she was within two miles of the apartment she had escaped from. Maybe a bit further than that, which would be to her benefit. Every tenth of a mile expanded the search radius that much more. Circles within circles. And the more circles she added, the chance they would stumble upon her shrunk exponentially.

In the wake of the damage she had left in her path, not to mention whatever had led them to her, they'd do everything in their power to find her. Three of their men were dead at Clarissa's hand. One prior to her capture. Two during her escape. And she had no issue adding to that tally.

But it was the money they were after. The two-hundred-million-plus the criminals had stolen. That Beck had stolen from *them*. Beck converted much of it to Bitcoin and a few other cryptocurrencies. After locking forty percent of it in a couple of cold storage wallets, he tornadoed the rest through a series of decentralized exchanges and wallets that would never be used again. Now, some one-hundred-and-twenty-five million dollars' worth of crypto was spread out among thirty wallets. Maybe more by now. She never saw the more recent transactions, so she had to take his word for it. At least he had trusted her with a couple of accounts she could cash in if things went really sideways.

How they had tracked her down and not Beck was a mystery. They'd spent more time apart than together in the past year. Safer, she supposed, as they were *technically* on the run. Beck had told her not to worry, this went as high up as it could within the Treasury Department. They had to operate clandestinely, though, and if they were caught by authorities or otherwise, they had no recourse from the United States government.

Why had she agreed to go along with this? There had been nagging feelings all along that Beck was not who he claimed to be. Or rather, there were two distinct sides to the man.

The Patriot who would do anything for his country.

The Shadow who looked out for himself.

She feared she now only dealt with The Shadow.

But after knowing both versions of the guy, she couldn't decide which was worse.

She'd dragged Jack into this, pulling him away from Mia and his retirement in the Keys. She fed him the story Beck had fed her. She now knew that was a lie. She just couldn't figure out the truth.

Now her only chance at survival might be to drag Jack further into it. Risking his life again.

She fought back against the guilt by telling herself that Noble got himself into trouble easily enough on his own. Not only that, he'd risked his life for Clarissa time and again and did so willingly. At least this time there would be a payoff and neither of them would have to worry about money again. Not with that much socked away in various crypto wallets.

Beck hadn't explicitly taught her how to obfuscate the coins, but she'd picked up on the process by taking what he'd told her, watching as he worked, and doing her own research. At the end of the day, there were maybe five people on the planet who could make sense of the spaghetti trail Beck had already left behind. Once she repeated the process with the wallets she controlled, no one would ever find them.

She reached down and pulled the burner phone from her sock, which had protected it from the elements. The flip phone felt as reassuring as her father's hand had when she was a little girl.

Everything is gonna be all right...

Closing her eyes, she felt the warmth of her father's embrace. His image vaporized like a lone cloud in a bright blue sky. Her thoughts transitioned back to Jack, to the feeling of being wrapped in his arms. The two men who had always protected her. Noble stepping in as her protector after her father's murder. The tradition that usually happens when a father walks his daughter down the aisle and hands her over to her husband-to-be was not to be for Clarissa.

Was Jack even that man?

He'd proven year after year that he wasn't.

There was no doubt in her mind that they were still in love.

However, he wasn't the kind of guy who would settle down for love. Not then. Not now. It wasn't that he didn't want to. She knew of his desire to lead a normal life. It simply wasn't in the cards. He was incapable. The allure of the job was too strong. Even in retirement. Even with his daughter by his side, free from the government's reach, he couldn't resist the pull of the mission.

Of helping her again.

And she'd screwed him over.

Would he ever forgive her enough to be friends?

The phone vibrated in her hand, shaking her free from thoughts of her father and her history with Noble. She took a few deep breaths to settle her racing pulse.

The notification on the screen indicated there was a message waiting. She flipped the phone open and pressed the soft key to open her texts. One unread message waited for her. The image of the closed envelope shone brightly on the light blue background, like a lighthouse beacon at dusk. The number that sent the message didn't matter. In much the same way as crypto could be tunneled through multiple exchanges and wallets, a phone call or text could be sent through switches around the world.

Obfuscation. Confusion. Bemusement. Mystification. The sender's reasons didn't matter.

Especially when it was sent from Brandon.

She'd remembered the dial-in correctly.

He'd figured out it was her.

His reply was, "Stand by."

CHAPTER 10

ALL: TARGET MARKED FOR TERMINATION: CLARISSA ABBOT.

All: Job rescinded.

PRIVATE: Assignee possibly compromised.

Six months later.

PRIVATE: Job re-opened. Previous assignee confirmed compromised. Only solicit most trusted associates.

Five days later.

PRIVATE: Van de Berg dead. Identity assumed. Notify most trusted associates.

Two days later.

PRIVATE: Noble alive. On job in Odense, Denmark. Notify all associates with no ties to Noble.

One day ago.

PRIVATE: Noble job re-opened. Any and all associates with no known ties to Noble qualified to take job. To clarify, ALL can take the job. This is winner takes all. $5 million USD to whoever brings me Noble's head.

Brandon stared at the trail of messages originating from an IP address located fifty miles south of Paris, France and twenty miles east of Orléans, France. He doubted the location mattered. Anyone running an organization like this would have their own *Brandon* to make sure their internet and cellular traffic could never be pinpointed.

Did that mean they were located in another country or on another continent? Not necessarily. Sometimes it was the people who hid in their own backyard that never got caught. Of course, the backyards Brandon dug around in when performing this kind of work spanned miles upon miles. The further from the epicenter, the more ground to cover.

This seemed different, however.

He worked through the traffic logs. He traced the messages forward and back. One server to the next to the next to the next. Dozens in all. A complete circle, finishing where it started.

"You have gotta be kidding me," he muttered. The cat thought Brandon was talking to him. He pawed at Brandon's keyboard. Brandon pushed him away. "Not now." The cat tried again and backed off when Brandon blocked his paw.

What the hell was the person running this operation thinking? They were either incredibly brave or incredibly stupid. Maybe both. Probably both. And that could be worse than the individual options on their own. Were they so secure that no threat bothered them? Or were they foolish enough to believe they could survive any threat? A fine line, for sure, existed between these two realities. One that Brandon would need to figure out sooner rather than later.

First, he had someone in apparent immediate danger he had to help.

Tabbing through his open windows, he stopped on the picture of Clarissa. Her last known image. Her hair was darker and longer than normal. She wore big sunglasses and a blue parka. Her cheeks were red from the cold. The photo had been snapped in Poland. That matched the text she'd sent. Was it real? Any of it?

Brandon opened a new terminal and typed in a string of commands. A new application popped open. Green text stood out amid the black background. A few keystrokes led to hundreds of lines of data. A few more keystrokes summarized all that data into coordinates.

Titus climbed over his arm and sat on the middle of his armrest.

"Just can't get rid of you today, can I, Titus?"

Titus purred and rubbed his head against Brandon's wrist.

"Can't you go find a mouse to kill?"

Titus ignored him.

Brandon scooped him off the desk and sat him in his lap. Should keep him quiet for a few, Brandon figured.

The new program occupied half of Brandon's screen. An image of the world occupied half the program's screen. He pasted the coordinates into a text box and waited while the magic happened.

"Better make this quick, Mr. Titus. The Chinese don't take kindly to folks using their systems."

Displayed on his screen was a real-time image of a slice of Warsaw. He panned out at first to get a good look at the general area, taking screenshots at intervals before zooming to the street level. If he had to explain it to someone, he'd say it's like Google maps, just with a little more detail. Well, a lot more detail. And in real time.

Because of those two things, he had confirmation that Clarissa, or someone with enough info on her and him to fake this whole thing, was exactly in the middle of the coordinates he had collected.

"I'm gonna get you help," he whispered. The cat purred in response. Brandon scratched between Titus's ears.

A soft alarm beeped, indicating it was time to close the connection. Last thing he needed were sleeper agents of the Chinese government showing up at his door, dismantling all his gear, then dismantling him.

Brandon killed the connection, changed his location through the VPN so it appeared he was in Buenos Aires, and then took the system offline.

But he wasn't done.

He pressed a switch mounted under the desk. The monitor flickered and connected to a different computer. A simple database was all he needed. One full of contacts. He filtered it for Warsaw, Poland, and someone who could go to Clarissa and deal with any situation. He waited a few seconds until a single record populated.

The guy was a former member of the Polish Special Troops Command. Following his military career, he joined the Agencia Wywiadu, or the Foreign Intelligence Agency in English. There, he protected foreign diplomats his first five years before moving to more clandestine operations. He'd retired five years ago and remained in Warsaw providing private contract work. Security services. Extractions.

Negotiations. He was exactly the guy Brandon needed in exactly the right place.

He created an encrypted note on a secure server and logged the location using the same nomenclature Clarissa had in her message. He'd provide her access once he established a connection with Kasper, which, presumably, wouldn't take long. It was mid-morning there.

Following the instructions in the file, Brandon drafted and sent a message to the man. Then he waited. Some thought waiting for a guy who had to wheel himself around should be second nature. Not for Brandon. Not with his brain. And definitely not since the medicine.

He felt the fire begin to burn with every passing minute. He stifled the questions his mind threw at him. *Who is this guy? Why is he taking so long to answer? What's he got better to do? Where's he at this early? Doesn't he know my friend needs help?*

The questions ebbed and flowed, as did the rage.

His Apple watch buzzed against his wrist. "Time to take your pills," he said mockingly. The phrase took him back to being a child. His mother. His teachers. The school nurse. *Time to take your damn pills, you broken child.* Only now, the medicine made him stronger. Once he had full strength, he could begin more vigorous exercise. That would ease the anger. The doctor had told him that.

The terminal window flashed blue, indicating a new message. He read the one-word response and frowned. The guy couldn't help. Then he fired off a message to Clarissa telling her to keep safe, he was working on getting her help. It wouldn't arrive immediately, but soon enough. All she had to do was stay in place.

"But I'm not gonna do the same, Titus."

Brandon scooted back a couple feet, grabbed the crutch next to his desk and pushed up from his chair, scooting the cat from his lap. Once standing, he attached the brace to his wrist, then did the same with the second crutch.

The cat watched on, unimpressed.

"Yeah, simple for you, right?" He shook his head at him. "Live in my world for a day."

He made his way to the doorway, stopping to rest there for a moment. While his legs were stronger than they'd ever been, even ten feet of movement was taxing on his heart and lungs. But the work had to be done, or he'd never make it to the mailbox. Hell, he'd never make it past the front door.

The cat scampered past him, racing down the hallway and out of sight.

"Show off."

He straightened up and took the first step out of the office. A wheelchair waited for him past the end of the hall. Twenty-five feet. Furthest yet. And he was going to do it solo. No nurse and no Kimberlee to assist.

Brandon's pulse quickened. His breathing became short and shallow. Sweat coated his brow. He grunted with every step. Halfway there, he thought about leaning against the wall to rest. Cursed himself out for it.

"You got this, man."

He reached the end of the hallway. Last chance to rest. He opted not to. The chair was six or seven feet away. Just had to make it, and he could collapse into it.

Another step.

Sweat dripped off his nose.

He felt a pain in his chest. Heart? Lungs? Fear?

"Come…and…get…me…reaper."

Another step. The crutch scraped the floor. He had to swing it out wide and started to lose his balance. The world tilted. He blinked it back to normal. Then he adjusted and stabilized his body. An image of himself looking like one of those wiggly blow-up things outside of car dealerships popped into his head. He would've laughed if he wasn't panting.

Inch by inch, he dragged the crutches closer together and straightened up. His hands, forearms, and upper arms screamed in agony. His chest was tight. His breathing had gone to panic level.

Could it really end like this?

If it did, he wouldn't mind, though he'd like to at least get Clarissa help first. Even still, it would be better than dying in a hospital bed, unable to wiggle his pinky toe.

After a minute of holding himself in place, he resumed the journey and made it to the chair with minimal support from his crutches. Relief washed over him like a smooth wave. The undertow came around and eased him back into the chair. He turned his attention to his watch and stopped the timer. Seven minutes, fifteen seconds. Not bad, he thought. Soon he'd make it down the driveway and back in that amount of time.

Soon.

Several minutes passed before he attempted anything. He sat there, eyes closed, calming his breath, slowing his heart. The operatives he'd known through the years taught him all kinds of techniques for getting in and out of the zone. Brandon never figured they'd come in handy for this.

The cat returned, hopping up on his lap. He knew what that meant.

"Ready for bacon, Titus?"

He hopped back off his lap and dashed to the kitchen. Brandon chuckled and started in the same direction. A knock on the door stopped him in his tracks. He glanced at the monitor and saw the back of a head. Dark hair with some specks of gray combed neatly. Looked like a blue suit. Mormons or Jehovah's Witnesses, he figured, redirecting his chair toward the door to get rid of them.

But the man that greeted him wasn't there to spread the word of any god.

The man peered down at Brandon with the kind of smile that said, "I caught you."

Brandon's heart ticked up, like when he was halfway down the hall. He tried to stifle the increasing panic, but it was useless. How could he not panic with a Glock aimed at his crotch?

"What the hell are you doing out here?"

"Was gonna ask you the same thing, old friend," the guy said.

Brandon shook the panic off and retorted, "We were never friends."

"True."

With that, the man lifted the pistol and aimed it at Brandon's head.

CHAPTER 11

THE YELLOW LIGHT POOLING ON THE STOOP FADED AS THE last of the deep blues and purples retreated. The door looked as though it had been replaced recently. Of course, recently could've meant three decades ago when compared to other doors on four-hundred-year-old buildings.

Clarissa had confirmed it was locked. She also confirmed she could pick the lock. She wiped grime off the windows from the stoop and corner of the building. She confirmed no one was inside the store. A women's boutique, she guessed by the flowers on the front signage and the contents she could see from outside.

She didn't have an aversion to breaking and entering, stealing what she needed. She just didn't want to get caught. Though the thought crossed her mind that she might be better off in a cell than out on the streets. At least until whoever was after her caught wind of it. Then she was as good as dead. No chance she could defend herself while locked up. Someone would be bought. Someone with nothing to lose. Someone serving a life sentence. A shiv to the kidney or liver or neck. Any would do. Just depended on how deranged the assailant was.

Mold covered the steps to the landing, leaving them damp with the night's condensation. Her feet slipped as she made the short trek up again. She waited there for a few seconds, taking in the sounds around her. The clattering continued. A baby cried. A couple argued. A man and woman were having sex. In the end, she determined that Polish people must not feel the cold since they all had their damn windows open, allowing anyone and everyone to hear their business.

The knob felt like an ice cube made for a rocks glass in her sweaty palm as she closed her hand around it and twisted, half-expecting it to be locked again, throwing off her plans. But it wasn't. The door gave with a slight nudge from her shoulder, and she stepped into a warm embrace of lavender, lilacs, and lilies. Tension escaped. Her eyelids felt heavy. Her breathing slowed. Could she just find a way to hide out in the store for the day? Though the idea appealed to Clarissa, it was not grounded in reality. Even if she found the perfect spot to hide, she'd put the owner and patrons at risk.

Whoever was after her had been brazen enough to abduct her in broad daylight. They drugged her with ketamine. They knew how long it lasted. She knew how long it lasted. That meant they had no qualms with pulling an unconscious woman out of a vehicle and dragging her through the front door of an apartment that any of five hundred people could have been watching at that moment.

More than a dozen clothing racks were arranged around the store. If she could see them from above, she was certain they were arranged like flowers. They were loaded with short dresses and tops and bottoms. Along the walls were long dresses, coats, more shirts. One section was floor-to-head-height jewelry. Another section was the same, but with makeup.

A pair of jeans drew her eye. She walked over and stopped herself as she reached for the item, aware of her blood- and grime-caked hands. She glanced toward the back of the store. Curtains hung from rods, covering three openings. To the right of them was a door. She couldn't read the writing on the plaque, but the male and female image on it told her it was the bathroom.

She hurried in and located the light switch. She shut the door first, then switched it on. Three globes hovered over the mirror. Either they were too yellow, or she just looked like trash. While the hope was for the former, she couldn't deny it was probably the latter.

With a turn of a handle, ice-cold water rushed out of the faucet. Clarissa slipped off her shirt and gathered a handful of towels off the shelf. She ran her hands under the faucet. The water had warmed. She placed six towels in the sink until they were soaked, then set them off to the side. Inch by inch, she wiped down her face, neck, chest, arms. Bruises covered her arms and upper chest. A cut ran along her jaw on the left side of her face. She brushed the knot on her forehead and reeled from the pain.

"What a mess," she said. Her gaze settled on her eyes. She stared at them for a minute. "Might be the only pretty thing about you anymore."

She turned away, peeled off her pants and socks. Her feet were still stained with the man's blood. She shuddered to think what diseases he'd carried. Fighting against stiff muscles, she lifted her right leg, let the water rush over her foot. She did the same with the opposite leg and foot.

The entire process took five minutes, give or take, but it felt like a day at the spa. Hot water spewed from the faucet. Steam rose and coated the mirror. She leaned forward and let it wrap around her face. She breathed it in. Felt the heat dissipate into cool vapor.

Clarissa turned the handle again, and the room fell silent. She exited the restroom and peeled the curtain back to the first changing room. A full-sized mirror greeted her. She turned left, then right.

"Good as it's gonna get," she said.

The pictures lining the wall between the changing rooms caught her attention. They were of the same woman, but there had to be thirty years from the first to the last.

Alone, young, and vibrant.

Slightly older, different hair. A toddler and a baby.

Kids growing up. Flecks of gray in her hair.

Short hair. Teenaged daughters.

Three grown women.

Three grown women with two babies.

Babies were now school-aged children.

A record of the stages of the owner's life, she supposed. Each one lacking a husband.

And when she turned around, the store made a lot more sense. Like the pictures, there was everything one needed for every stage of life, all under one roof.

Through the windows, the other side of the street began burning brightly with the emerging sun. Time was running out. She needed to pick out clothes, get dressed, and get out.

She returned to the jeans that had caught her eye and found a pair in her size. Then she grabbed an athletic bra and panties. Knowing it would be freezing most of the day and definitely through the night, and that she had to keep on the move and possibly defend her life, she opted to choose layers for the rest. A pair of yoga pants. A long-sleeve merino undershirt and sweater. A zip up fleece. A down-filled vest. She grabbed gloves and a hat and a scarf, which could come in handy later.

Finally, she picked out some makeup to cover the bruises and scratches on her face.

She estimated the total cost of the items to be over five hundred dollars. Without nearly enough cash to cover what she was taking, the only thing she could think to do would be to write the woman an IOU. When this mess was over, Clarissa would show up and hand her ten-thousand dollars.

The thought made her smile. And when she turned around to head to the dressing room, her lips fell, her eyes widened, and she almost dropped what she was holding as she came face to face with the woman in the last picture hanging on the wall.

And she was holding a handgun aimed at Clarissa.

CHAPTER 12

THE MORNING SUN CRESTED THE TREE LINE AND REFLECTED off the rolling door on the back of a semi-trailer. It knifed through Jack's eyes. It amplified the headache from a lack of sleep. Around three in the morning, he'd moved to the front seat so Johanna could stretch out in the back. She rested her head on his balled-up jacket and hadn't moved in the hours since.

For Jack, every jostle from a dip in the road or lane change startled him awake. He could fall asleep anywhere. He'd learned to do so in his line of work. Remaining in dreamland, well, that was a different story, also a side effect of his line of work. So he struck up a conversation with the guy next to him.

He'd managed to get a little intel out of the driver. The man would only speak of himself, often glancing in the rearview while measuring his words. He'd been in the Swedish Security Service. Counterespionage, counterterrorism, countersubversion. In short, a hell of a lot more than *just* a driver. When his time had come, he bowed out quietly and took up contract work, not with governments, but corporations. Same work, though. Few realized the amount of espionage and subversion that occurred in the upper echelons of the world's most powerful companies.

After five years of that and watching his youngest daughter become a mom, he decided he couldn't miss his grandkids' lives the way he missed his own kids' lives, so he took up this job. Sure, it resulted in sometimes multiple nights away, but the pay was good and he rarely got his hands dirty. The reduction in stress did his heart good, he said. Of course, there were days and nights like this, but he was up for it.

They bullshitted a bit more about the driver's love of American football. Though his choice of teams left a lot to be desired. It'd been over two decades since the last time the Cowboys were even relevant. A little spirited debate gave way to the hum of the tires traveling ninety miles an hour on the faded asphalt skirting Hamburg, Germany. They took a route to the northeast of the city until the driver's head started dipping and he announced they were pulling over for breakfast a little past Lübeck.

Noble had no interest in eating, but a cup of coffee or three sounded like a good idea, so he hopped out of the vehicle before it was in park and stretched his legs and arms and back and made his way through the door. An attractive woman with silver and black hair in a bun greeted him. He nodded, pointed at an open table, and took a seat. Johanna came in after him, looked around, and joined him. The driver leaned against the car with his phone to his head.

Noble looked from the guy to her. "What's his story?"

"Don't even try," she said.

"Try what?"

"I heard you two talking. Everything he told you is legit."

"You looked like you were down for the count."

"I was for part of the time. Impossible to sleep straight through in the back of a car. Unless you are a child, I suppose."

"Is that where you met him?"

She lifted an eyebrow. "In the backseat of a car?"

Jack chuckled. "Guess it's possible."

She turned her attention to the menu.

He slid the menu toward him. She looked up. He held her gaze.

"Security Service."

Johanna glanced around the room. He waited for her to admit the truth.

"I was young, fresh out of college. Joined the Army as an intel officer."

The woman Jack met at the front door walked up to the table and greeted them, first in German, then in English when she saw Jack didn't understand.

"Coffee?"

"Yes," Johanna said. "Black, please."

"Make that two," Jack said.

"Ready to order?" the waitress asked.

"Waiting on a friend," Jack said.

She shrugged, tilted her head, frowned, and walked away.

"As you were saying?" Jack said.

Johanna nodded and continued.

"I suppose I showed potential, because before my six years were up, a man came and visited me and presented an offer."

"To join the agency."

"Precisely." She tapped the pads of her index fingers together while looking past Jack. "Coffee's coming."

"So's your friend."

Outside, the driver pocketed his cell phone and leaned into the car once again. He emerged with a messenger bag Jack hadn't noticed before. Presumably it had been stored under the man's seat.

"What's his name?" Jack asked.

"He'll tell you if he feels like it," she said.

"Fair enough."

The waitress reappeared with two mugs. Jack leaned back in his seat as she placed the first one in front of him. Steam wafted and disappeared. He took his first sip, and the anticipation of caffeine melted into relief as the liquid burned the back of his throat.

The driver joined them, ordering coffee and something else in German. The waitress jotted down the order as the driver took his seat. Jack changed his mind about breakfast and ordered eggs and sausage. Johanna decided on the same.

The three sat in silence for a few minutes, the driver looking between their mugs, licking his lips until the waitress returned again with his coffee. He slurped a few sips down.

"Name's Noah Lundgren." He stared at the empty host stand. "Yes, that's my real name. No, I don't care if you know."

Johanna covered her smile.

Noah shot her a look, and she apologized. After he looked away, she winked at Jack.

"You know most of my story. I just told it to you. I left some out, of course."

"Like how you recruited Johanna to join the Security Service."

She made a face. He nodded.

"Your decision?" Jack asked.

"Yes, one hundred percent," Noah said.

"How did a guy tasked with counter-everything have the time to identify intel talent in the Army?"

He stared at his palm as though he were a high schooler with test answers written on it. "It may come as a surprise due to my rough exterior, but I do have friends. Over the years, they told me about rising stars within their commands. Every so often, I'd follow up, starting with service records. I might give them a test."

"Oh, really?" Johanna interrupted.

The wrinkles in his forehead became more pronounced like a weathered barn door as a wide smile crept across his face. Jack noted Noah was missing several molars.

"Didn't know about that, did you, kid?"

"What was it? Romania? Estonia? I always had my doubts about that officer in—"

Noah waved her off. "None of it matters, and even if it did, I'm not allowed to tell you. Hell, it might destroy the fabric of whatever holds together all that confidence you walk around with."

By this point, Jack was thoroughly amused at the banter between the two. Their mentor-mentee relationship had morphed to that of a father and daughter. A special connection. What was bothering him was why they were together at this moment. And why he was with them. The urge to butt in and ask these questions threatened to take hold. Jack settled his breathing and focused on the conversation.

"That confidence came from my father," she said. "And the Army."

"And...?" He tapped the saucer plate in front of him.

"And you," she admitted with a heavy sigh.

"I always did right by you, didn't I?"

She stared at him for several seconds. Noble wondered what thoughts and memories raced through her brain. Her eyes widened, lips softened.

"Of course you did, Noah."

"Then understand what I am about to say does not come from me or anyone I represent." He clenched his scarred fists, glanced at his coffee. "I'm so sorry about this."

The calm facade evaporated. Her cheeks flushed. Her breathing became rapid. "Noah? What is it?"

Noble looked past the man. Past the woman. Saw two cars pull in simultaneously. One from the north entrance. The other from the south entrance. He kept calm and didn't say anything. Only dropped his hand to his lap so he could pull his gun when he stood.

Johanna leaned toward Noah and grabbed his arm. "What's going on, Noah?"

He looked away from her. His eyes glossed over.

"You have less than twenty-four hours to live, Johanna."

PART 2

CHAPTER 13

THE WHOOSHING OF BLOOD IN HER EARS DROWNED OUT THE woman's words. Clarissa stood there naked in the middle of a store she had broken into, holding an armful of clothing and makeup she couldn't pay for. She didn't think she could have been in a worse position than the one she found herself in the day before, drugged and tied to a chair, until this moment.

The woman's voice rose, jutting the gun toward Clarissa with each word. And all Clarissa could focus on was the woman's finger threaded through the trigger guard. One unexpected sneeze and a round would tear through Clarissa's body.

Presumably it registered with the store owner that Clarissa didn't understand a word she was saying.

"Who are you, and what are you doing in my store?"

"I..." She couldn't come up with a lie and stammered through another five or six responses.

The woman approached, taking a step at a time, stopping, gauging Clarissa's reaction. About ten feet away her eyes widened. The gun lowered. She reached out with her free hand.

"My dear, what on earth has happened to you?"

"Should've seen me before I took a bath in your sink."

The lady glanced over her shoulder toward the bathroom. Clarissa noticed the trail of blood on the floor. Why hadn't she taken a moment to clean up the mess she had made?

"Are you hurt?" The lady let go of all pretenses that Clarissa was a threat to her and now stood about a foot away. She reached out and caressed the cuts and bruises on Clarissa's face. Her eyes narrowed. Her head tilted. Her bottom lip disappeared as she bit it. "Did a man do this to you?"

Clarissa nodded and let out a meek, "Yes."

"And is he still after you?" She placed her hand on Clarissa's shoulder.

"He is."

The lady guided her toward the back of the store, had her wait while she dragged the benches out of two of the dressing rooms. They were solid wood. Clarissa had been impressed by them when she noticed them earlier. The older woman had no problem moving them. She set them a couple feet apart, patted on one and gestured for Clarissa to sit, then lowered herself onto the other.

"Mind if I put these clothes on first?" Clarissa said.

The woman raised her hand and laughed and slapped her own knee. "You must think I'm a crazy person trying to get you to sit naked in front of me."

"It's not you." She waved her off as she headed toward the changing room. "You know us Americans are just a bunch of prudes."

The fake smile she'd plastered crashed and cracked on the floor the moment she closed the curtain. She ran her hands along the back wall, feeling for any seams out of place. Not a chance here, though. This wasn't drywall. She glanced up. Drop tile. Maybe it would work? She tried to recall every image she'd ever seen of an office building with those tiles removed. There had to be some kind of support up there, right?

She faced two problems.

First, a gap of a foot-and-a-half between the top of the changing room frame and the ceiling.

Second, she'd picked a changing room without a stool. Getting up there would result in noise and would attract the store owner's attention. What if she drew the pistol again and shot?

"Everything OK in there?"

"Yes, just squeezing into these yoga pants." She grabbed them and worked them over her hips, then put on the long-sleeve merino shirt. Good enough for now. If she had to run, she'd take the rest with her.

Emerging from the dressing room, she felt somewhat normal. The woman gestured her over. Clarissa sat across from her.

"Why did he beat you?"

"Are you insinuating it's my fault?"

The woman smiled sadly, looked down, shook her head. "I'm sorry if it sounded that way. When he used to do it to me, there was always a reason. He'd sit me down later. Discuss it with me. Tell me what I did wrong and how to correct the behavior."

Clarissa now saw why the woman was so direct. She felt that she and Clarissa were sisters in this. "And did you?"

"Correct my behavior?"

Clarissa nodded as the woman chuckled.

"I doubled down on it."

"Sorry?"

The woman placed her hand on Clarissa's knee. "I made sure to piss him off the same way five or six or seven more nights in a row."

"Why would you do that?"

"Because eventually, he'd give up. He thought I was the weak woman." She mocked spitting on the ground. "He was the weak one. He always gave up, and I grew stronger, more defiant."

"You could have left, couldn't you?"

"Couldn't you?"

Clarissa averted her gaze.

"Things, they are different here. Woman can't just leave her husband because he slaps her around." She worked her right cheek in her teeth for a moment. "I did it like this to keep him away from my girls." She gestured toward the pictures on the wall. "He couldn't touch them. Ever."

"Did you eventually leave him?"

The woman reached into her dress pocket and produced the pistol. She stared at it, traced the barrel with her index finger. "I've shot this pistol thousands of times in the countryside. I'm better than any marksman soldier our army ever put out."

Clarissa waited for the woman to continue, but she seemed lost in another time entirely. Her lips twitched up into a smile, lasting mere seconds before they began trembling. Tears slipped down her cheeks, getting lost in the lines etched on her face; others falling freely off her chin, dying in her bosom.

Clarissa reached across the gulley between them and placed her hand on the other woman's knee. "Did something else happen with that gun?"

The woman placed the pistol near the edge of the bench then gripped the wood so hard her knuckles turned white. She looked up at the ceiling. Her head shook, almost convulsed, side to side. A few shaky breaths later, she lowered her chin and met Clarissa's gaze.

"It was a camping trip. Just the two of us to celebrate our anniversary. I insisted we remain home, have a nice dinner with the children. But he insisted we go, so we went. Early Spring, so you know it was quite cold. He wanted me to bring extra blankets, even an extra sleeping bag. Double up and stuff it up."

She smiled at Clarissa as though they shared an inside joke. Clarissa awkwardly smiled back, unsure if she should say something. She didn't need to.

"And a little voice in my head, probably that of my late mother, told me to go get that gun she gave me before she passed. Go get that pistol and stuff it in there and make sure, make absolute goddamn sure that I remember which bundle it is in because if he were to find it"—she held out her hand with her index finger outstretched and her thumb cocked and aimed it at her head—"well, I don't think it takes too much imagination to know what would have happened."

"So, are you saying—"

The lady held up her finger and Clarissa's voice trailed off. Silence filled the gulley between them, and Clarissa wanted nothing more than to wave it away as though it were fog and then escape this situation.

Moving out now would have more impact than hearing this woman's murder confession. But she couldn't, because she still hadn't attempted to negotiate a future settlement for her purchase.

The store owner continued. "See, I don't need imagination to know what would happen, my dear. I lived it."

Clarissa felt a wave of ice crash through. She nearly fell off her seat, feeling as though she were floating amid the frigid churn. When she regained her equilibrium, questions raced to the forefront of her mind. They slipped out before she could stop herself.

"What happened? How did he react? I mean, you're still here, so you must've escaped somehow?"

The lady's eyes narrowed to slits. "It was quite a lovely evening, that night. He caught fish. I cooked them in the cast iron skillet over the fire he built. We had red wine from Spain." Her chin dropped, and she stared at Clarissa over imaginary glasses. "From Spain. That's good, expensive."

A car honked, drawing Clarissa's attention away for a moment. She took in the scene on the street through the front windows. A few people out. A couple of cars rolled by. Nothing too bad yet. She had time until the workforce hit the pavement. That was when she'd take her leave. When she could hide herself among the crowd and get another mile or two away.

"It was a great night. I recall I kept thinking, this is what we need."

"Wine every night?"

The lady's demeanor changed for a moment, and she smiled at Clarissa as though they were mother and daughter. And it felt that way for a few seconds.

"Well, that helps. I can admit that." She continued to smile. "But I was referring to the rustic life. You know, chopping down trees. Building things. Fishing and hunting and foraging for food. A small garden to subsidize it, right? I started seeing a future where things would go better."

"But they didn't, did they?"

The smile faded, shadows returned to the etchings on her face. Her head tilted down and her eyes turned dark as coal.

"No, they didn't. You remember the warning earlier, about the right bundle?" She rolled her eyes in the way only a daughter can do when her mother was right. "Well, I, how they say where you are from, screwed the pooch." She leaned in close enough Clarissa could smell the garlic on her lips from last night's meal. "My mother's pistol, the one she gave me before she passed, was in his bundle. He came strolling out of the tent with it in his hand. He had it cocked. He had it aimed at me while wearing the most beautiful smile I'd ever seen on his face."

"Pardon?"

The woman nodded knowingly. "Doesn't make sense, right? Think of it this way. He was in love with the idea of me dying."

"And there you were, in the middle of nowhere. He had a pistol. You had a bullet with your name on it."

"Yes, see, you understand. You know what this man is like."

Clarissa nodded, hoping the woman would continue.

She did.

The smile faded. "He had a dirty job to do before he could fully experience that love. So he taunted me. Told me all the ways he could kill me, from a single tap to the back of the head, to using every bullet he had available and watching me slowly bleed out."

"Charming."

"Absolutely." They shared a quick laugh. "I had prepared myself to die years before this. I was ready for the shot. But when it happened, well, nothing happened to me. But he was on the ground with a gash on the side of his head where blood was pouring out."

"What?"

"The rocks were loose, and he misjudged. It slipped out from under his foot. He fell back, twisting, and he hit the big rock, cracked open his skull. Somehow, somewhere during that fall, he fired off a round."

"Jesus."

"Yes, He was there." She smiled. "Well, I ran over and freed the pistol from his hand and then watched as he faded away. I witnessed that light in his eyes disappear. I swear at that moment a black mist slithered from his gaping mouth and darted away to find the gates of Hell. His soul was the same coward he was in life."

"The cops?"

"Yes. Accidental death."

"Your mother's gun?"

"Now we get to the point of all this." She reached next to her and retrieved the pistol and offered it across the space between them. "You need this now. It may not work as you intended, but it will get the job done."

"I don't think I can—"

Clarissa inhaled sharply as glass shattering and a gunshot coalesced into one haggard sound. The woman in front of her lost half her head as the bullet tore through, rendering her no more.

CHAPTER 14

IT WASN'T THE FACT THAT A GUY NAMED BRETT TAYLOR WAS standing in his doorway.

Nor was it the fact that Brett appeared to be moments away from ending Brandon's life.

Amid all the investigating Brandon had been doing, he found contracts on Noble, Clarissa, hell, so many related contracts popped up the bodies could fill the L.A. morgue.

What pissed him off was that he didn't know someone had ordered a hit on *him*.

"Brett, what the hell are you doing here? Who...who did I piss off?"

"It's not always about pissing someone off." Brett lowered the pistol and sidestepped Brandon on his way inside. He looked around the house and then back at Brandon, no emotion on his face. Men like Brett never showed any.

Brandon wondered if they even had them.

"Does this have to do with the trial?"

Brett faced the sliding glass door and didn't answer.

"Is there something wrong with—"

Brett raised his hand, signaling to give him a moment. What was he doing? Listening? Did he see something outside? Brandon spun his chair around and shut the front door along the way. The bang of it hitting the frame caused Brett to turn.

"What trial?" Brett said. "Someone suing you for hacking them?"

The comment was so out of left field Brandon couldn't help but laugh at it. "Nah, nothing legal, man. The medical trial."

Brett glanced around until his gaze settled on the pill bottles on the counter. Six in total. He walked over and investigated them, picked each one up and read the labels out loud as best he could. Most people would stumble through the names, and Brett was no exception.

"The hell is this stuff?"

"It's to turn me into Superman."

Brett pointed at the crutches resting against the wall. "You're using those now?"

"A little less every day. I can get down the hall from my office. Progress is quick. They say I could be on my way to walking unassisted within three months."

"No kidding?" Brett looked impressed.

"No kidding."

Brett opened one of the bottles and emptied the contents on the counter. They clinked against the quartz like tiny marbles. He shaped them into a pile, then did the same with another bottle.

"What are you doing?" Brandon wheeled into the kitchen and rammed into the man. "I need those!"

Brett tossed an unopened container on the counter and pushed Brandon away. "If you don't listen to me and do what I say, it won't matter if you ever take another pill."

"Yes, it will. I might die if I'm not weaned off properly. They emphasized that."

"Who the hell is they?"

"Dr. Michaels."

Brett reached back and grabbed one of the pill bottles. "Dr. Michaels? As in Michaels Biotech?"

Brandon searched his internal file system to recall information he had learned about the doctor while researching him and the medicine. It had been limited, but yes, the biotech company matched what he had found.

"Yeah, that's correct."

Brett started laughing and brought his hand to his face and rubbed his eyes. "You gotta be kidding me."

"About what?"

Brandon wished he could reach the 9mm hidden in a compartment on his wheelchair without drawing attention. He'd never outdraw Brett, though. The guy made his living disposing of other people's supposed trash.

"What I'm about to show you doesn't leave this room. Got it?"

Brandon nodded.

"I'm serious, man. Because if it does, you won't."

"You gonna babysit me to make sure?"

Brett shook his head. "Don't mess with me, man. I'm only here in this capacity because of what Noble did for me."

"Yeah, well if you remember, my house burned down. My equipment was fried. I lost years of work because I helped him help you."

"Again, part of the reason I'm here, Brandon."

"Then get to the point." The rage was building, boiling over. If he wasn't careful, he might end up dead.

Brett pulled out his phone and swiped and tapped on the screen. He stared at Brandon for a moment, then turned the device to face him.

Brandon read it four times. Then a fifth time to make sure it sunk in. It took a sixth pass for the date at the bottom to kick in.

"That's tomorrow?"

"Less than twenty-four hours."

"To live?"

"If they get their way."

"But that's the doctor who's helping me walk again. Why...why would he want me dead?"

"How'd you meet this doctor?" Brett leaned back against the counter. He'd holstered his pistol and now crossed his arms over his chest and his left ankle over his right.

"They just showed up, I guess."

"You guess?"

"They just showed up."

"Who's 'they'?"

"The doc and a couple of guys who, I don't know, look like you and Noble."

Brett took a few moments to process the information. Brandon wondered if Brett had met the doctor in person. Did he know the men who accompanied the doctor on his visits? And why hadn't the doc just sent one of them to kill him? Why enlist outside help?

Brandon shook his head at the last thought. Distance. That was the answer. Michaels couldn't use men who worked for him to carry out the hit. The next question was more important, though. Why did he want Brandon dead?

Brett had walked down that same trail and apparently hadn't found the answer either.

"Why's this guy want you dead, Brandon? What'd you do? Start snooping around, found out some not-so-nice things about him?" He shook one of the full pill bottles so it rattled like an Afuche-Cabasa. "And, like, does this stuff even do anything for you?"

"I told you, I'm able to stand up and walk now."

"Prove it."

Brandon had exhausted himself earlier. His quads were still trembling. He wouldn't be able to stand. "Don't have to show you anything, man. And I have no idea why he'd want me dead. The guy's been helping me all this time."

"Maybe the trial is a crock. Maybe he's been doing something real shady with it and they have to pull the plug. How many others are involved in this? Who else is taking these pills?"

Brandon shrugged. "Apart from taking six tablets a day, I'm not involved." But he knew he could find out. He wanted to find out. He was scared of losing access to the pills if he did what it took to find out. "I can see if I can get into their system."

Brett agreed, and they went to Brandon's office.

"You think the other people involved are getting this same treatment?" Brandon asked.

"Let's get some names and find out." Brett looked around the room at the monitors hanging on the walls. "Can you pipe in security footage on these?"

With a few keystrokes, each monitor lit up with a feed from around the property. Then, Brandon opened a terminal on his desktop and started working. Within twenty minutes, he had access to everything in the doctor's practice and his company, Michaels Biotech. A pit formed in Brandon's stomach, doubling in size with every passing second as he scrolled through the data.

"The hell is this?" he muttered.

Brett put his hand on Brandon's shoulder and leaned forward. He remained quiet for twenty seconds or so. Brandon felt the man's breath on his cheek and held his breath as long as he could. Unfortunately, his lungs weren't that well-conditioned.

"Ok, you win," Brett said. "What are we looking at?"

"A whole lot of fake data."

CHAPTER 15

"WHAT DID YOU DO, NOAH?"

Noble heard Johanna's words but didn't process them fully. He didn't need to. The four men exiting the two cars each carrying a pistol told him all he needed to know. Noah had sold her out. Perhaps him, too.

The older man clenched his eyelids shut, but it couldn't stop the tears from falling. The table shook as his knees bounced under it. He choked back a sob. After a deep breath, he settled. Looking at Johanna, he spoke in a language Jack didn't understand, but the impact of his words was clear.

"Noah," she said. "What did you do?"

Noah glanced at the parking lot. He saw the same, armed men Jack did. Three waiting. One heading for the back.

"You have to hurry," he said. "Get out, now."

The two in front of the restaurant started toward the front door. The closer they got, the more Jack thought one of them bore a resemblance to Rupert, the guy who'd been on the street with Johanna and disappeared in the club. He couldn't be certain. It had been dark both outside and inside.

Noah pulled his pistol and handed it to Jack. Jack felt the weight of it in his palm.

"Just in case," Noah said.

"Sure you don't need it?" Jack said.

"I'll be fine." Noah clenched his eyes and bit down hard. "Go, Johanna. Let me face this. I'll tell them you got up to go to the bathroom and never came back. Maybe you were spooked."

Jack looked at Johanna. She had wiped the tears from her eyes, leaving a dark eyeliner stain across her cheeks.

"If we're gonna have to fight," Jack said. "Best do it in the kitchen."

Rising, she followed him to the back of the dining room. Before pushing through the swinging door, Jack looked back, saw the guys about to enter.

"Everyone should take cover," he said. "It's about to get messy in here."

There were gasps. A bell rang as the door opened. One of the men shouted in English. His accent was Anywhere, USA.

Noah shouted back at him. "She left. She must have received word from Rupert."

The other guy spoke with a thick accent and said, "I didn't say anything. Where is she, old man?"

Noah shouted, "You'll take her over my dead body."

Jack pushed Johanna through the door, looked back, saw Noah reach into an empty jacket pocket. The two guys at the door didn't wait. They each fired two rounds. All four hit Noah in the chest. The man stood there for a few seconds, glancing over toward Noble before collapsing forward onto the table.

Jack lifted his arm, sighted the guy on the left, the one that looked like Rupert. He pulled the trigger. The bullet hit the guy in the gut. Jack fired again and finished the job. The other man dumped his magazine in a fit of rage, but Noble by now was in the kitchen.

Johanna had already instructed the kitchen staff to take cover. Some were on the floor, but the rest were cramming into the walk-in refrigerator. Made of metal, they'd be safe in there.

"Are you OK?" he asked her.

"I...Noah. Rupert? What? I..."

Jack reached for her arm and squeezed it.

She shook him off. "I'll deal with it later."

She had compartmentalized. All she could control was this moment. So she did what she had to do to control it. She could deal with the fallout tonight. Or tomorrow. Or a year from now. Whenever it made the most sense to relive the trauma of the event and everything that had led up to it. First, she had to survive this ordeal.

Johanna slammed the walk-in door after the last of the staff had entered. The kitchen quieted to the whisper of food sizzling on the stove. There were no places to hide, only spots to conceal themselves for a few moments until their assailants adjusted to the angles of the stainless-steel counters and racks and the expo window.

"What do you think they'll do?" she asked.

"Try to kill us, I suppose."

She huffed. "Tactics, Jack. This isn't the time to screw around."

"If I'm gonna die, I'd rather do it with a smile on my face."

A finger of light slid across the floor as the rear door cracked open. Jack fired a round in that direction and the door eased shut again but didn't latch.

"I thought they might be organized enough to bull rush in from both ends. Maybe they'd lose one, but their chances of getting both of us increased." He stepped toward the expo window where five plates waited for a server to pick them up. "Now it seems they're gonna wait us out."

"Think there's more on the way?"

"I'd imagine they believed they could take you by surprise. Didn't go that way, so they'll take their time snuffing us out of here. That or they're satisfied with taking Noah out." He regretted the words as soon as he said them. "Sorry, that was insensitive."

She shook her head. "I've got to come to grips not only with his death, but that he took us here, was working with Rupert, and let them know our location."

"They must've been a couple miles behind us the entire time."

Johanna stared off and said nothing.

"There had to be a reason. People don't turn like that on a whim."

"Sometimes they do, Jack."

"We can debate it later. We need a plan." He eased along the wall until he came to the door leading into the dining room. A grease-coated window occupied the center just below head-height. He could see the far right side of the restaurant through it. Only one person remained in their seat, hands flat on the table. The rest were on the floor. The attackers were still there, minus one dead guy. Where were they now? And what were they doing?

"What's out there?" Johanna took a few steps closer.

Jack said nothing. He ducked and walked to the other side of the door where he had a view of the counter, the entrance, and a few more empty tables. One of the men stood by the front door. He remained armed, but kept his pistol aimed at the ground. The other guy was missing, and Jack presumed he was standing somewhere in the center of the restaurant aiming at the window in the swinging door.

There was one way to find out.

"Come over here," he said. "Stay low."

Johanna threw a glance at the rear door as she crossed the middle of the kitchen. She crouched low and made her way to his side.

"What's the plan?"

"I'm gonna bait him into a shot. He's gonna shoot right through this glass."

"OK. Then what?"

"Best guess, someone is coming through that back door hoping to catch us by surprise. So what I want you to do is keep your gun aimed at that back door. See how easily my round went through?" A beam of light penetrated the hole left by the bullet. Dust particles lit up as they floated through the light. "The moment you see that door open, take three shots, chest level, covering the width of the door. Got it?"

"Yeah, makes sense." She double checked she had a round in the chamber.

"Measure twice, cut once, right?"

"What?"

"Something my old man used to say. I was too hardheaded as a kid to follow his advice, but eventually it sunk in."

"Are you sure you're not going to be shot?" she asked.

"No, I'm not."

"Well, if you don't get shot, what are you going to do?"

"I'll figure that out when the time comes." He smiled, but apparently, she did not find humor in his words. "Just do what I said. I think I know how this is gonna go down."

"Yeah, I think I know too. And it isn't good."

He pointed at the back door. "Aim there. Moment you see it move, shoot."

She nodded, dropped to a knee and steadied her shooting hand by bracing the opposite arm over her knee.

Noble took a deep breath, held it, exhaled, waited. Four counts each step. Time slowed down. His thoughts stopped. They didn't crawl along, just ceased to exist. All his senses were tuned to the situation and surroundings.

The men in the dining room spoke in hushed tones.

Bacon and sausage burned on the flattop, spewing smoke into the range hood.

A thin layer of sweat insulated his palm from the polymer pistol grip.

His dry mouth tasted metallic.

And he homed in on the door's window.

It all started there.

CHAPTER 16

JACK PASSED IN FRONT OF THE WINDOW. HE DID IT SLOWLY enough he could make out the man ten feet in front of him. Doing it in a way that if the man reacted quickly and smartly enough, he could squeeze off a round and hit Jack somewhere in his chest or abdomen. He counted on the guy taking the headshot. There was something about how brazen they were when they entered the parking lot, as though they were above anyone stopping them. Something about how casual they were stepping out of their vehicles, as though they were beyond reproach.

They didn't fear Noah.

They didn't fear Johanna.

They probably didn't know about Noble.

Or maybe Noah had tipped them off, but undersold Jack.

Jack gritted his teeth hard enough one might crack. He had exhaled before moving and held his breath until he cleared the door. Every muscle was tense and rigid, anticipating the searing pain of lead slamming into his body, tearing through skin and muscle and organs and bone.

The guy in the dining room didn't take the bait. The shot never came. The excruciating silence hurt more in that moment than any bullet wound would have.

Jack continued a few feet past where he had planned on stopping in case the guy decided to try to shoot through the wall. Sticking out his hand, he used it to brace himself so he wouldn't collide with the steel prep table. Three chef's knives rested on a large cutting board covered in onion skins.

Voices rose from the other side of the door. The men barked at each other. They spoke fast, their voices high and excited. At that moment, it became clear to Noble that the team had a plan of their own, and now they were going to put it into action. He prepared for an all-out assault. They'd rain hellfire in the form of bullets, emptying every magazine they had. If anyone was left standing, they'd likely face an execution.

He wouldn't let that happen.

Better to go down in a hail of bullets than to take one behind the ear.

If that were going to happen, it would be now. Every second the other team wasted gave Noble and Johanna time to regroup and think up an offensive game plan.

"What's going on?" Johanna looked up at him. "Why didn't they shoot?"

"Never said the idea was foolproof." He meant it, and now wondered why he didn't come up with a backup plan before putting them in this position.

"So what now?" she asked.

Jack watched the light peeking in from under the rear door. It remained complete and undisturbed. Where was the guy who'd headed toward the back? Had he retreated to the parking lot? That wouldn't make sense. Perhaps he had repositioned at one of the corners. From that vantage point, he could cover the back, one side, and a part of the front the two men in the dining room couldn't see.

"Jack? This is your specialty, not mine. How should we proceed?" Her words came out in jerky bursts between rapid breaths.

"My specialty? OK, I'm coming around to your side. I need you to reposition to face the dining room."

"Got it."

He squatted, kept his eye on the back door. No change to the light coming in from under. He stopped behind Johanna.

"Move to the left so you're in front of the door."

"You sure? What are you going to do?"

"Trust me, Johanna. Do what I say when I say it. In front of the door is where I need you."

"OK. What are you going to do?"

"Something crazy. You focus on your job. Hit the first target you see."

Her eyes widened. "What if I hit a civilian?"

"You won't. They're all on the floor and out of the way."

"OK."

"Listen, I gather you don't have a lot of field experience. These guys look exactly like you'd expect." He accessed the part of his mind that had taken in the scene as he passed the window and combined it with his first viewing of the men. "He was about ten feet from this door. Tables next to him were empty. Black pants. Black t-shirt. Tattoos covered his right arm. He had a handgun in one hand and I think a radio in the other. Short hair, black. The other guy was dressed the same."

He thought back to watching the two cars pull in. He pictured them exiting their cars. Regret stabbed at his psyche. Why hadn't he said anything? He knew the men were out of place. His inaction led to Noah's death. He knew enough about the man to feel remorse. He'd have to deal with that later. For now, he reminded himself Noah led the guys to the diner.

"The other guys, the one who went around back, was dressed the same. You see anyone like that, shoot."

"Are you sure there were only four?"

Her words caused him to second-guess what he saw. There could have been another man in each car. Did he ever get a good look *inside* the vehicles? He couldn't say that he had.

"No, but that's what I saw. I gotta go with that right now."

"OK." She steadied herself. "You want me to push the door—"

He exploded around her and kicked the door open. It whipped toward the wall, colliding hard, coming off the bottom hinges. Three shots rang out. The guy had fired one that went high and wide, smashing into the door. The other two rounds belonged to Johanna.

Both landed. The man in black with the forearm tattoos and the gun and the radio staggered back. Two dark stains spread across his black shirt. He bumped into a table and fell back on it. His gun and radio dropped to the floor.

Jack sidestepped left. This offered him a view of the far side of the dining room, opposite to the entrance. No one was there. No diners. No killers.

"Back door!" he shouted.

Johanna spun on her heel, taking cover behind the wall and covering the rear entrance.

Several shots rang out from the dining room. Six or seven, he wasn't sure, the burst came so fast. Noble took cover to the left. Johanna to the right. Holes punched through the wall above her, six inches from her head. She lowered even further.

Jack waited for a pause. When one came, he stepped into the opening and surveyed the full dining room in one sweeping glance. The man who'd just shot at them had made it past the front door and was outside. Spray and pray. The man had emptied his magazine to buy a little time, presumably hoping one round would hit its mark.

Jack fired three rounds that shattered the large windows as the guy raced past them. All missed the man, and he made it into the car. Jack fired another round, aiming at the vehicle. The windshield shattered. It wasn't enough to stop the guy. Tires screeched as he rolled over the curb and into oncoming traffic. A couple cars came to sudden stops, but not the utility truck that slammed into the driver's side at full speed.

"Where the hell is the other guy?" he said. "Something's not right."

Johanna darted toward the rear door. "I'll check the back."

"Johanna, no, do—"

His words came too late, but they wouldn't have made a difference even if she had reacted to them. Jack felt frozen in time as the high pitch whine of air rushing past filled his ears. Then everything went white, and the explosion knocked the back door inward and Jack backward into the dining room.

CHAPTER 17

THE SHOCK OF WHAT SHE HAD WITNESSED DIDN'T HIT Clarissa immediately. The scene unfolded in a matter of seconds. The time lapse felt like hours. The world closed in with the sound of an orchestra, tight and terse, as if the camera panned in on a woman losing her mind. Literally, in this case.

Years of training, on the street—from her father and Noble, Sinclair, her time in the Treasury Department working with Beck—took over automatically.

Don't think. Just react. Trust your instincts. Follow your gut. You have a will to survive. Use it.

She'd heard these phrases and dozens of others repeatedly since she was five years old. There had been times when they had saved her life. They'd be more important in the next five minutes than at any previous time.

Clarissa twisted and dove off the bench. Flattened on the floor, she used her knees and elbows to sniper crawl toward the bathroom. Every heartbeat felt as though it would be her last. The anticipation of another shot sent shards of ice through her nerves, stabbing her spine, arms, and legs.

Slithering through the opening, she took stock of herself. Aside from the panicked response, she was OK. No new wounds.

"All right, think." She looked around the darkened bathroom. For what? Answers? This wasn't a time for answers. She needed to get away. How? First step, assess the scene.

She looked at where the woman had taken her last breath. The other lady had collapsed sideways and rolled off the back of the bench, her body hidden by the thick wooden frame. The woman had handed her the pistol at the moment the bullet hit her. Clarissa replayed the sequence and recalled that she'd dropped it. It had to be between where they had been sitting.

From her current location, she could see the side of the store facing the alley. All the window shades were drawn, offering no view of the outside or anyone who might be there. Easing her head past the door frame until her right eye could see the front of the store, she saw the bullet had passed through one of the large windows. The glass spidered outward from the hole left behind. Estimating the hole to be about chest height, the shooter either took his shot from the sidewalk or the second story of the building across the street.

Clarissa had no logical reason to believe that the older lady had been targeted. The shot couldn't have come from the sidewalk. The shooter would have noticed the contrast between the two women. They would have taken Clarissa out, not the store owner.

The shot had to have come from across the street.

She studied the room in front of her and the likely trajectory of the shot. The only explanation available was that Clarissa had been out of view. When they saw a woman, they took a shot.

How had they known she was here? Had they tracked her with a device? She thought of the burner phone and the message from Brandon.

Not him. He wouldn't have turned me in.

Clarissa couldn't accept that he would do this to her. But there were no other logical explanations. She was hot. So much so that even he had no choice but to let whoever was behind this know. Who could have that kind of influence on Brandon?

The only answer she could surmise made her sick to her stomach.

Old doubts about Beck surfaced. Fears that he was blaming her for the missing assets recovered from the theft were more than fears. He had taken it to the top. This order had to have come from within the US intelligence community.

Stomach knotted, she turned toward the toilet in fear she was going to lose its contents, not that there was much there. For a moment, her breathing was out of control. Her abdominals convulsed. Hands and feet felt like ice, then went numb.

"Easy, easy, easy," she choked out. Simply repeating the phrase lessened her panic. She worked through a breathing exercise that took less than fifteen seconds. She decided if it came down to it, gun to her head, she'd freak out then. For now, she had to escape.

Dropping to the floor again, she decided her path would be to the benches where she would collect the pistol, then to the side door where she had entered. Her movements were slow and deliberate. She kept herself within the cover she estimated to be blocked by racks of clothes. There would be a moment or two where she might be seen, but logically, she knew the shooter had moved on. Remaining wherever they took the shot from would spell disaster for them. Between eyewitnesses and CCTV, they'd be made. Yes, they'd be on film leaving. Someone might see them fleeing. But it wouldn't be a slam-dunk like standing in the street with a gun.

She stopped and quickly collected the remaining clothes. They'd be needed once she stepped outside. In these temps, she could last a while dressed as she was, but sooner rather than later, the cold would seep in and wreck her.

As she separated the clothing, she found a small round device. After a moment, she recognized it as a Bluetooth tracker. How? Where? Her mind raced and came up with no logical explanation other than they had planted it on her at the house, and through the act of changing, she had loosened it, and it had become tangled up in the bundle of clothes. By the device's nature, they would have to be within a certain range to detect the signal. She made it through the night outside only by chance that they hadn't come close enough until she had entered the store.

The explanation was one she needed, though she didn't rule out the Brandon connection.

Grabbing the pistol, she checked that it was loaded. She chambered a round, hopeful that if she needed to use it, the .380 would pack enough power. She stopped at the corpse, still warm, still seeping blood. "I'm sorry," she whispered as she went through the woman's dress pockets, pulling out a set of keys, one of which had a Volkswagen logo on it.

A way out.

Clarissa wasted no time crawling to the side door. She paused, waited, listened. Voices rose and fell. Male. Accents similar to the ones in the house, though everyone here sounded that way.

Clarissa worked her way up and peeled the corner of the window curtain high enough to see outside. There was no doubt they were the men she had encountered in the car. One had to have taken the shot that ended the store owner's life. She began to doubt the shot had been taken from across the street. Rather, the reflection of the morning sun off that building lit up the front windows of the store to the point they could only make out the shape of a woman. Assuming it was Clarissa, they'd fired.

The door handle jiggled. They were coming in.

Clarissa darted to the closest changing room, which still had a bench. Dumping the clothing there, she stood on the bench, and slid the ceiling tile over. A metal I-beam offered her something to grab hold of and pull herself up. She tucked the pistol in her waistband and jumped. She gripped the bottom lip of the beam with her fingertips, adjusted her grip, and pulled herself into the space above the tiles.

A few feet in height and with no direct support under, all she could do was work her legs around the beam and position herself on top. She slid the tile back over and waited.

Light from below shone through the cracks, but she couldn't see anything in the store from her position. The door broke free from the frame. Their heavy boots fell on the floor heel-to-toe in a deliberate manner. She imagined them with their guns out, sweeping the store before investigating the body on the floor.

A bead of sweat cut a river down the middle of Clarissa's nose, cold against her flushed skin. Slipping free, it disappeared in the dark. Her arm wrapped around the beam; her fingers holding the bottom lip. In her right hand, the pistol offered comfort. She aimed it at an angle, roughly where the store owner rested eternally. She tried following the footsteps but ruled out any attempt at shooting them from her concealed position.

The men spoke to each other. She couldn't make out the words at first. Then it seemed as though one had placed a phone call because he spoke in English.

"It's done." He paused a few beats. "Yes, confirmed. Dead on the ground." He said something quietly in his native language, then followed it up with, "Through the head. It's a mess. Yeah, yeah, OK. We'll get out of the city and lie low."

Clarissa expelled the air in her lungs over several seconds as relief washed over her. They believed they had a confirmed hit. Her skin pricked as the sweat covering it chilled from the air rushing in through the open door as they exited.

After several minutes, she pulled the tile up and set it aside, then lowered herself through the opening after poking her head out to check that the sidewalk in front of the store was clear. Once on the ground, she hurried to collect the clothing, putting it all on before making her exit.

Sirens approached from somewhere down the street. It wasn't possible for her to determine which direction. Using the front door was not an option. She headed out through the side and turned right and headed down the alley, away from the main road. The store owner's keys jingled in her left hand, creating their own rhythm that sometimes matched her pace. She had her right hand tucked in the vest pocket, gripping the pistol.

"Where is this stupid car?" she muttered to herself.

It was a newer model and came with a key fob that had an alarm. She held down the button with the red label and waited. Within two seconds, the horn blared repeatedly. She hurried to the end of the alley and saw a silver VW Jetta with flashing taillights.

She stopped for a moment and closed her eyes. For the first time, she took a real deep breath. The yelling from a man across the street cut the experience short. She looked over. Saw the guy dressed in black head to toe. Saw the guy he was waving frantically at who was on the same side of the street, maybe fifty feet behind her.

Repeatedly she pressed the unlock button on the fob. Every instinct screamed for her to get in the car. The driver's door was facing the street, so she slid across the hood of the car next to her and sprinted until she reached the Jetta. Her fingers slipped on the handle, and it took a few tries to get it open. Adrenaline raced through her body. The key shook as she attempted to insert it into the ignition, never taking her eyes off the man in front of her. She couldn't get it to slide in. When she finally looked, she realized the key was for the doors and trunk. The vehicle had a pushbutton start that she jammed with a single finger.

One of the men banged on the rear fender as he reached the car.

Clarissa mashed the lock button on the armrest a dozen times, hearing at first a loud click then a bunch of muted ones. She depressed the clutch, lowered the emergency brake, and shifted into first. The engine ramped up over four thousand RPM. The tires squealed on the asphalt. The vehicle lurched; the front passenger side fender hit the back of the car in front of her. She hit the accelerator harder, pushing the other vehicle forward at an angle.

The second guy reached the vehicle. He punched the driver's side window. Cracks spread out from the indentation his fist left. The other guy broke the rear passenger window. He tried to dive in as she broke free from the other vehicle, making it part of the way. She dragged him a block before pulling the pistol out. Aiming the pistol at his head, she pulled the trigger.

CHAPTER 18

THE SCENERY PASSED AS A GREEN BLUR WITH THE
occasional tractor-trailer breaking up the monotony. Not that Brandon
paid attention. It was all in his peripheral. For the past three hours, his
focus had remained on the screen in front of him while Brett drove them
toward the supposed address of Michaels Biotech. What they'd find
when they arrived was anyone's guess.

Brett had been adamant it would be an empty lot or a gas station or
someone's house. They'd go up, and the people would tell them they
received mail occasionally for the company but had no idea what it was
and that they'd lived there for a decade or more.

Brandon wasn't so sure. For one, he'd looked it up on Google Maps
and saw what appeared to be a warehouse building with a strip of black
asphalt surrounding it, and on three sides, woods beyond the paved
road. Brett shrugged it off. Said someone at Google could've been paid
off. If anything, the map had been hacked. Brandon gave up arguing with
the guy and decided to cede the point until they arrived.

Aside from Brett flipping an XM station every time a song Brandon
enjoyed came on, the ride had been smooth. Brandon had spent it
digging into any and all information he could find on the company and
its principals. There wasn't a whole lot, but he found a few interesting
tidbits of information.

The doctor had used a fake name associated with a recycled social security number. His credentials appeared legit. While this was within the scope of what Brandon could pull off for someone, it would only last a short time before the record was corrected. His first thought was that he had been targeted by some group who went through the lengthy process of administering the treatment. Why go through all of that? Why not just kill him?

Perhaps they did not want death. Their plans could have been nefarious in other ways. What if they had been planning on getting Brandon to a point of no return, a place and time where the treatment had taken such great effect that he'd do anything to clear the final hurdle? Then they'd drop the hammer. Do this for us, or your newfound abilities will unwind until you are confined to that chair again.

And if that didn't work, then the threat of death.

It all seemed plausible. Even Brett agreed. Neither of them could figure out what went wrong. Why Brett had been sent.

There was one problem with the argument. The doctor had been licensed for well over two decades. Brandon focused on finding the root of this.

"Telling you, man," he said. "This does not make sense."

"Maybe he's legit?" Brett checked his side mirror and eased them into the left lane. He hadn't pushed the speedometer more than seven over the speed limit the entire time they'd been on the highway. "Maybe he really is a doctor and someone got to him."

"You mean like made him an offer he couldn't refuse?"

"You tryin' to sound like a mobster?" Brett looked at him and laughed. "If so, you screwed it up big time. It's more like this." He repeated the phrase with a heavy Bronx accent.

Brandon tried again. And again. He couldn't quite get it, and Brett seemed to rather enjoy that.

"All right, tough guy," Brandon said. "I'm sure there's stuff you can't do."

"Not likely. I'm pretty much perfect at everything."

"Yeah, then unravel this mess."

Brett nodded a couple of times, held his thoughts in for a few beats, then took a stab at it. "So the doctor was probably some leading researcher, breaking new ground. Stuff like that. Someone takes notice. Someone with a *real* biotech company. They offer him some lucrative package—"

"The deal he couldn't refuse."

"Not exactly." Brett looked over his shoulder as they cleared another semi and moved back into the right lane. "Sometimes money gets them in. A little greed goes a long way. And once you've roped them, then you start setting in all kinds of hooks. They get this brilliant doctor in the door by paying him an ungodly amount. Something he'd never make elsewhere. He's not old yet. Young family, probably. Wife. Lots of student debt, too. This is the fast lane to getting everything they want before they're too old to enjoy it."

"Right, I see." Brandon started tapping away on his keyboard. Instead of trying to uncover a mystery, he decided he'd roll with the data that had been in front of him the entire time. Within seconds, he had confirmation. The doctor was legit. He was who he said he was. "I think you're onto something, Brett."

"I know I am."

"OK, here's what I'm having trouble with."

"The fake company."

"Right. How do we get from brilliant researcher with tons of promise, to a fake company and a contract on my life?"

"The offer he couldn't refuse, remember?"

Brandon nodded. Sometimes he missed the obvious. A side effect of his intelligence he'd always presumed. "Someone gets this guy in with money, then what do they do?"

"What do you think they do?" Brett looked over at him. "What would someone do to you?"

"What haven't they done?" But he thought about the question for a bit and realized he had been groomed the same way at one time. He had been the brilliant doctor, just in a different form. "Oh, I see."

"You got it, don't you."

Brandon talked it out. "After a couple years, he's handed a new assignment. Something no one ever figured out. Doesn't take him long to start cracking it, right, and he's feeling really good. But what he doesn't know is how this is being used. He doesn't know the laws he's broken. Doesn't realize the trail leads to him. Not until he gets a visit."

"Damn, Brandon, it's like you've been working with spooks your whole adult life."

Brandon laughed loudly. "I miss some things, man. I just miss them."

"So the company takes care of him, but now he owes them. Doesn't take long until this straddling of right and wrong doesn't matter anymore. He's able to justify what he's doing, and that's all that matters."

"OK, I get all this, but I'm still left wondering, why me? What did I do to this guy that they wanted to put me through all this?"

"It's not what you did. That's what you need to understand. It's what they could use you for. The better question is, what happened to make that point moot? What changed?"

Brandon took his eyes off his computer and thought about this. The events that led up to the doctor showing up. He'd been off the grid for a while. Hadn't taken many jobs. Wasn't answering messages except from select VIPs. There had to be something else.

"What's the connection with the other hits?" Brandon asked.

Brett whistled and shook his head. "You know, that's a bit of a loaded question, and it's been dancing around my monkey brain all day."

"Is that a fancy way of saying you don't know?"

"If I was gonna be fancy, I'd use an English accent."

Brandon turned to face the guy and rolled his eyes. "Seriously, man. We don't have time for jokes."

"There's always time for jokes, and situations like this call for them. But, back on track, there's gotta be a link. Perhaps that's why you were originally pulled in? They figured Noble would reach out to you at some point."

"And now they got a bead on him, so I'm not needed."

"Bingo." Brett drummed on the top of the steering wheel.

"What?" Brandon asked.

"I think we've figured your part out."

"But?"

"Why me? Why was I assigned to this? Years ago, Noble took a job to kill me. He heard me out, spared my life. A decade goes by, and it's my turn to terminate him. I heard him out, spared his life. In both instances, we worked together instead of completing the job, regardless of the outcome. Hell, I just did it with you today."

Brandon looked out the window and worked up the strength to ask his next question.

"Did you plan on killing me today?"

"Moment I saw your name, Brandon, I knew things were gonna go sideways." He pointed at the map on the dashboard screen. "Hey, look at that. A mile to go. You're gonna owe me a thousand bucks when this turns out to be something other than a warehouse."

"I never bet you."

Brett laughed and waved him down. "Kidding, man. You really gotta loosen up if you're gonna partner with me." He exited the highway and slowed to a stop at the bottom of the ramp. He paused there even though there was no traffic coming. "I don't know what we're going to find when we get to this place. You may need to wait in the car for a bit. Are you comfortable with a handgun?"

"Plenty of training."

"Ever shot someone?"

"Yes."

"Really?"

"Really."

"Open the glove box."

Brandon found a Glock 19 with a spare magazine. He retrieved it, checked it, and chambered a round. "OK, I'm good." And he meant it. He'd faced his own mortality plenty of times. Maybe never quite as close as it had been today, but enough to accept it could be over at any moment. That's the reason he agreed to the medical trial to begin with. That's what *she* couldn't understand.

He shook the thought of Kimberlee free and focused on the task at hand.

Brett took a right onto a narrow road made of worn, cracked asphalt. Gravel kicked up and pelted the undercarriage. Sounded like hail plinking off the vehicle. When they cleared the wood line and the warehouse appeared, Brandon swelled with pride.

"Told ya," he said. "Give me my grand."

"Yeah, yeah," Brett said. "Let's drive past real quick."

The lot was empty, as far as they could tell. A thick chain and padlock secured the only door in sight. A couple of windows looked boarded over. They continued on, and a quarter mile down the road, Brett K-turned and pulled onto a stretch of grass that led into some trees.

"I need to go scout this out. Wait here."

The next ten minutes were nothing short of torture for Brandon. They were steps from the address of the company who'd pretended to help him. They might have spotted Brett. They might have someone coming to the car. They might just kill them both. With his head on a swivel, he scanned front and back, left and right, non-stop, Glock at the ready.

Brett emerged from the woods and gave him a thumbs up. He opened the door and got in and started the car and backed out onto the road.

"Empty as can be. We're gonna park around back."

"You're sure?"

"Nothing but wires dangling where the security cameras used to be. Windows are boarded up. Front door padlocked. But the rear is accessible. Big roller door, which doesn't really make sense. No one is backing up a big truck in that narrow space. I got it open."

A few minutes later, Brandon stared inside the empty space. Open boxes littered the floor. Shelves towered along the walls. He spotted one area of interest: an office.

"Heading in there," he said.

"Go ahead. I'll stand watch and see what I can find out here."

Brandon rolled across the floor, wondering what the hell they used this place for, if anything. When he got to the office, he pulled the door open and his stomach sank.

It was empty.

CHAPTER 19

A BLACK CLOUD HOVERED ABOVE JACK, SEEPING OUT OF THE kitchen, crawling along the dining room ceiling. A thousand speakers blared in his ears, high-pitched and intense and stabbing at his brain. Disoriented and confused, he focused on the doorway as he rolled onto his stomach and brought one knee under him, then the other.

On all fours, he stayed under the smoke and started toward the kitchen. His right arm gave. He crashed cheek-first onto the floor. Searing pain traveled from his scapula to his elbow. Without checking, he knew his shoulder had been dislocated when the blast knocked him back.

He searched his mind for the missing moments. Johanna hurried to the back door. He called out for her to stop. Then it happened. The bright flash. The shockwave punching him in the chest, knocking him off his feet. Everything went dark until he came to and saw the smoke enveloping the restaurant.

Jack sucked in as much air as he could. He lifted his chest up a foot. Three times he practiced what was to come next. He exhaled, refilled his lungs. Then he drove his right shoulder into the floor. Bone and socket grated. Stretched or torn ligaments sent a fiery sensation that traveled across his back, chest, and down his abdomen. The sensation went from making him want to vomit, to release and relief in a matter of seconds.

He remained on his knees, but his upper body folded into a puddle on the floor.

He pushed himself up and moved forward. The smoke had thinned out to the consistency of light fog. Through it, he spotted a body on the floor, unmoving. *Johanna.* Jack rose and staggered forward. His left leg ached. Had it caught on the door frame on the way out? Hit a table on the way down? He hiked his knee up to chest level, kicked out. The pain was sharp, like someone had jabbed a thick needle into his quad just above the knee, but it didn't prevent him from moving. Nothing to worry about now.

Sunlight streamed in through the gaping hole where a door once stood upright at the far end of the kitchen. Now it dangled from the bottom hinge. Rays knifed through the smoke and it looked like Jesus might make an appearance in the middle of it all.

"Johanna?"

He was five feet from her. Couldn't tell if she was breathing. Everything looked to be intact. There was no blood on the floor. Both positives considering how close she'd been to the blast. But it meant nothing if she'd suffered internal injuries.

Whatever they had used for the blast, it hadn't been strong enough to send the door flying. Perhaps the guy had rushed. Hadn't set the explosives in the optimal position. Maybe they fell when he ran off before detonation. There could be plenty of reasons and Noble didn't care which one explained it away. He knew this could've been much worse for him. But how bad was it for Johanna?

He knelt at her side and worked his hand around her neck. He adjusted his fingers. He couldn't find a pulse anywhere. If she wasn't dead, there could be cervical injuries that might be exacerbated by repositioning her. Noble ran his hand along her arm tucked under her body and found the bony point on her wrist. He placed his index finger there and pressed in.

"There it is."

With each beat of her rapid, thready pulse, tension drained from his muscles.

"Can you hear me?"

She moaned.

"Come on, girl. We gotta get you outta here. Are you hurt?"

She groaned.

He slid his finger into her palm.

"Squeeze."

She did.

"Say something."

"Something."

His lips twitched at the corner. Too soon, he thought.

"Listen, Johanna. I need you to tell me if anything hurts. What are you feeling?"

"Numb."

He scratched at her upper arm, neck, and back.

"Feel that?"

"Yes."

He moved to her left, calf, foot.

"And that?"

"Yes."

"OK, I think you're just numb from shock. I'm gonna roll you over. OK?"

"OK."

Jack positioned himself near her head. He braced himself for what he might find as he steadied her neck and used his leg to tilt her right side up and over.

"Just need to do a once over on you."

He checked for wounds and fractures and displacements. Found none. He checked the quadrants of her abdomen. Found a concern. The bottom left quadrant was firmer than the other three.

"Johanna, there might be internal bleeding. How's your stomach feel? Any pain?"

She propped herself up on her elbow and ran her other hand across her midsection. Jack watched for any signs of distress. She didn't show any. Neither would he, regardless of what it felt like.

"Doesn't really hurt," she said. "Maybe a twinge or two. Can I stand up now?"

He pulled himself up using the walk-in refrigerator door handle, remembering there were people in there. He pulled the handle and opened the door and everyone inside shuffled out, arms wrapped around their bodies, cold from the extended time in the fridge. Two stopped and helped Johanna to her feet.

"We need to get you somewhere to be checked out," Jack said.

"The keys," she said. "Noah's keys."

Jack investigated the dining room and spotted the man. The blast had spared him and he remained in the same spot. "OK, let's go."

One of the kitchen staff helped Johanna through the restaurant to the front door and out to the car. Jack took it from there, situating her, leaning the seat back so she could rest. He was concerned by her coloring, but given everything they'd been through, couldn't determine if it was related to the blast itself, shock, or the possible internal bleeding.

As he rounded the car, he noted how still the air felt. No breeze. No sound. Almost a vacuum in the middle of a highway stop-off. It was a rural area. The blast had been several minutes ago. Where were the authorities? It wasn't a bad thing they hadn't shown up. He didn't know who was after them. He wasn't sure of their capabilities, so he assumed they had connections all over. If law enforcement and medical services were in their pocket, even as lookouts, they'd be picked off in no time. So he didn't want to risk taking Johanna to a hospital.

He opened the driver's door and slid inside. Started the engine and peeled out of the parking spot. Within twenty seconds, they had merged onto the highway and were heading east again.

"How're you feeling?" he asked her.

"Not so hot."

Jack looked over. A layer of sweat had formed on her forehead. Her shirt looked damp. Her rapid breathing indicated she was under distress. She needed treatment immediately and options were limited. The hospital might be her only chance. Pull up, say he found her on the side of the road, call her Jane Doe. Make sure anything that could be used to identify her remained with him.

But the hospital would attempt to figure out her identity. They might bring in the media. Tweet her picture out or put it on some other social media. The trees would topple, and once the larger ones fell, the ones that had weathered all the storms, the smaller ones behind them would collapse. She'd be made. She'd be killed.

Noble cursed under his breath as he pulled out his phone and dialed a number he'd never dialed before but had committed to memory well over a decade ago. The line connected and rang five times. Six. Seven. "Come on, man." Eight. Nine. He refused to hang up even though he knew every second he remained on the line his position became clearer to anyone looking for him.

The line clicked. Jack thought the connection had been terminated. Then he heard a voice he couldn't ever forget.

"Who's calling me from this number?"

"Brandon, it's Jack. I don't have much time. I'm east of Hamburg, Germany. Got a medical emergency and can't go to a hospital. Tell me you got a friend out here."

"Hang tight. I'm gonna reverse engineer and call you on an encrypted line."

The line went dead. Jack clutched the phone in his left hand, wove around traffic with his right. He glanced over at Johanna. Her condition was deteriorating rapidly. She couldn't wait for treatment much longer. Every minute that passed brought organ failure closer to reality.

The phone buzzed. He answered at once.

"OK, Jack, listen. I'm in a world of hell right now, too. We all are."

"What's happening there?"

"Gonna get to that. Let's just say, I'm hanging with one of your old friends."

"Bear?"

"God, I wish." Brandon chuckled. "I'll get to that. Let's get you where you need to go first, then we'll talk."

"OK."

"Sending you an address now. About twenty-five minutes away."

"Who is it?"

"Friendly doctor with a small practice."

"Friendly to who?"

"The Agency, among others."

"She's former Swedish intelligence."

"This guy should be perfect then. I'm notifying him now, Jack. Gonna follow along. Five minutes after you get there, I'm calling you back. Got it?"

"Yeah." Jack navigated to his messages and found one from an unknown number containing an address. He read it back.

"Good to go. Talk soon."

Jack pressed the voice command button on the steering wheel and pronounced the address as best he could. It took several attempts before the computer finally recognized it. The route required him to exit in half a mile and take back roads from there. Twenty minutes in total.

Johanna gasped and clutched her stomach.

"It's getting worse."

Jack reached over and held her hand.

"We're gonna get help now. Hang in there."

CHAPTER 20

THE ROAD WENT FROM ASPHALT TO GRAVEL AND ENDED where a dirt driveway began. The path led to an opening between white split-rail fencing. Paddocks bordered the land. Horses meandered, stopping to eat grass. A large house loomed in the distance.

"The hell is this place?" Jack said.

Johanna opened her eyes and looked around. "It's beautiful. Reminds me of my grandparents' farm where I spent summers as a kid."

He smiled at her for a moment before the gravity of the situation leveled him again. Pasty and pale, sweat coated her body and soaked through her clothing. Was hours from death, at best. He'd seen this before. Witnessed death due to untreated internal wounds. What seemed little could become a lot in a matter of minutes.

As he pulled up to the house, a man and woman were waiting out front. They started toward the car before Jack had put it in park. The woman opened the door, began assessing Johanna. Jack hopped out and met the doctor in front of the car.

"Situation?" the doctor asked.

"Bomb went off."

"A *bomb*? Where?"

"Some restaurant we were at. We were double-crossed."

The doctor did his best to hide his concern. It didn't take much to put the pieces of this puzzle together and realize he was looking at two people marked for death.

"No one followed you here, correct?"

"To my knowledge, no."

"To your knowledge?" The doctor wrapped his hands behind his head.

"Our mutual friend was tracking me. If anyone was following, he'd be the one to tell us."

The doctor looked over Jack's shoulder and studied the land beyond his fence.

"You can stand watch, correct?"

"I will. You got any firepower in there?"

The doctor smiled. "That I have. Let me check her out first. I'll have my secretary take you to the storeroom once we have her inside."

The doctor and his nurse helped Johanna out of the car and sat her in a wheelchair. Racing her in through a side door with Jack close behind. The doctor told his assistant to take Jack to the back and let him have anything he wanted, then they took Johanna into another room. The door clicked shut, and the assistant waved for him to follow her.

Once inside the storeroom, Noble found plenty he wanted. He grabbed a Winchester .308 hunting rifle with a scope. He took two Glock 9mm pistols. He found an AR-10, also chambered in .308 with a twenty-round magazine.

He took his haul to the front porch and set up there. While watching the horizon, the phone buzzed, and he answered immediately.

"We're here," Jack said.

"I know," Brandon said. "Is she gonna be OK?"

"I hope so, man."

"Who is she?"

"Name's Johanna. For the past six months, I've been working under the name Van de Berg. I assumed it when I killed him. Took on his role as a hitman trying to get close to whoever's had this contract on my life. First job was Clarissa, but it dropped right away. I've picked up eight since. Eight people who got a second chance at life. They've all offered a clue or two, but I haven't managed to put it all together.

Thought this lady might be the missing piece. Turns out, I was right, and wrong."

"What happened today?" Brandon asked.

"She had someone she trusted, was in the agency with him. Older guy, Noah, seemed loyal enough. But he turned. Don't know why or when or how, but he did. Led four goons to our location. I got one after they got Noah. Got another a bit later. Two others escaped after detonating explosives. That's what got Johanna. Internal injuries. Seems pretty bad, but I'm not a doc, so what do I know."

"This adds up, man."

"How so?"

"Brett Taylor. Remember him?"

"Of course."

"He showed up at my door."

"That's not good."

"You can say that again. Fortunately, he didn't pop me. But, man, I uncovered some stuff. There's a new job on Clarissa. There's one on you, too. They know Van de Berg is dead. They pegged you as the one who did it. They knew you were in Denmark. This Noah guy had to have been tied into it, too."

Jack spotted something moving. He brought the rifle up and looked through the scope. Just a dog in the distance.

"Figured out who's behind it all?" he asked.

"Getting there, but, and this is weird, it all traces back to this doctor."

"Doctor? The one here?"

"No, the one who showed up at my door with an experimental treatment to make my legs work again."

"Do they?"

"Almost, bro. Thanks for asking."

"Anytime. Get to the point about this doctor."

"He owned a biotech company."

"Biotech?" Jack's skin pricked.

"All a sham, though. We're trying to find evidence on site now. It's not looking good, but we know enough about the guy to proceed."

"You think what's going on with you is tied to what's happening here?"

"I do, Jack. Something crazy is going on. You need to find Clarissa."

"Any idea where she is?"

"Warsaw." Brandon said.

Jack pictured the map in his mind. There was distance to cover, but he could do it. "I can get there in about eight hours."

"I'll be communicating with her soon. Once I get an update on her situation, we can arrange a way for you two to meet."

Jack glanced through the window to the small waiting room. The assistant was sweeping the floor. Behind her was the closed door to the room where Johanna was. "You think the doc will keep Johanna here?"

"Already arranged. Once you know she's good, get out of there."

"I want to ask her a few questions first. See if she knows anything about your doctor or a biotech company." He didn't say the rest. That one of his previous targets had ties to a U.S.-based biotech company. He'd reveal that soon enough. First, he wanted to find out what Johanna had to say about it.

"Hey, Brett is waving me over. I think he found something. Gonna bounce. Call me on this line if you need me. It can only connect to your number. No one can see the traffic in or out. It's safe."

"You got it, my man. Talk soon."

Noble set the phone on the railing and placed his hands on either side of it. The cool breeze offered relief from the hurricane brewing inside. For years, he'd been the target of one government or madman or another. Every time he'd gone on the offensive. Faced down his adversaries every time. And he faced the same aftermath every time.

"This has to end," he said out loud. "Now."

"Pardon?"

Jack looked back and saw the doctor standing there. He nodded, said, "Didn't hear you come out here."

"One of the many skills I possess." The doctor smiled.

"Good one at that." Noble turned and leaned back against the railing. It bowed an inch under his weight but held firm. "How is she?"

"She'll live, that's what is important."

Jack glanced at his watch. "Didn't take long."

"There was a hemorrhage, affecting her left kidney. I gave her treat-ment to expedite clotting, drained excess blood, loaded her with elec-trolytes as well. The body will take care of the rest. She won't need surgery."

"Thanks, Doc."

"Tobias Benker's the name."

"Doctor Benker, appreciate it."

"Please, Tobias. We share a mutual friend. That makes you and her my friends now, too."

"Likewise. If there's anything I can do for you, anything at all, you say the word."

The doctor stood next to Jack, leaned over the railing and stared out at his vast property. "I consider myself blessed with this life, especially compared to my former life." He paused, perhaps to allow Jack to ques-tion him, which he didn't. After a few beats, the doctor continued. "You and I are not so different. Your battles were on the field, in the shadows. I was called in to handle things behind the scenes, and sometimes in a way that perhaps violated a code."

"I'm sure you did what was necessary."

The doctor shrugged and pursed his lips. "Sometimes what was necessary wasn't what I would deem so, but when powerful men have your number, you can't always say no."

"I can agree with that statement."

"I'm sure you can. What's your background, by the way? Agency guy? SOG?"

"Something like that."

"Come on, humor an old goat. What did"—he looked Noble up and down—"*do* you get up to?"

"Enlisted at eighteen. Marines. Guess someone saw something in me and another guy during Recruit Training. We were moved to a CIA-spon-sored training program hidden in the Appalachian Mountains. Overseas after that. Fun stuff for a few years, then Bin Laden took his shot, the world went to hell, and I ended up in the Middle East working as a door guy for the Agency's guys. Ended up in another agency after that. Then contract work. You know the deal."

The doctor grunted in agreement.

Jack continued. "When you do what I've done as long as I did, you never really escape. The fallout continues no matter what plans you've made or who you've promised you'd be there for." He turned to face the field again. The wind had picked up, slapped him in the face. He inhaled the countryside, wishing he could stay here for a month. "No matter where I go, someone is looking for me. I figure I'll be living like this for the rest of my life. Unless…"

Tobias stared at him, waiting for him to continue. "Go on."

"I've said too much already." He spun and started toward the door. "Can I see her?"

"Yeah, come on."

Tobias led him inside, down a hallway and through a reinforced door that led into the waiting room. The assistant looked up and smiled. A sad smile, as though she were hiding something from Jack. Tobias opened a door wide enough for him to poke his head through. He said something in German then stepped aside. The nurse stepped out and hurried past Jack.

"You're going to keep her here for a while?" Jack asked.

"It would be best if she remained for a few days," Tobias said.

"Good. Is it OK to go in?"

Tobias pushed the door open and moved out of the way.

Once he crossed the threshold, it felt like any other hospital in the world to Jack. The sounds of beeping equipment, pumps operating, and monitors with numbers and lines and a host of other things he didn't really understand but pretended to whenever a medical professional spoke about them.

Johanna rested with her head propped up on two pillows. Her eyes were closed. Her chest rose and fell with a peace Jack wished for most days. He took a seat on the bed next to her and waited for her to wake. It only took a few minutes.

"Hey, kiddo," he said.

"Kiddo?" Her face twisted.

"Wasn't sure what else to say." He tried to smile, but the weight of the day and the newly acquired information made that impossible. "How're you feeling now?"

She blinked a few times. Her glassy eyes and relaxed smile told him what he needed to know. She said it anyway. "I feel high. Like, really good and really high. I think I could listen to reggae all day and all night and it would just feel right."

A real smile formed, and he looked down at her and felt a moment of peace. She was going to be all right. He told her so. "Tobias says you'll pull through just fine."

"Who?" Her eyes searched the ceiling for an answer that didn't exist there.

"Doctor Benker."

"Oh, the spaceman!"

"Yeah, the spaceman." Jack chuckled and made a note to ask the doctor for some of what he'd given Johanna. "He says that the rocket will land again in a couple days and you'll be free to go."

"That sounds yummy." Her head leaned away from Jack. "What are you going to do? You're not leaving me, right?"

He didn't have the heart to tell her he was getting out of here sooner rather than later. He needed to find Clarissa. Needed to figure out who was behind all of this.

"I might have to step out for a bit, but—"

"No, no." She grabbed his hand. "Listen to me, Jack. You need to stay with me. You can't get out of my sight."

He felt a slight tug in his gut. Never a good thing. "Why's that?"

"Because."

And then she fell asleep.

CHAPTER 21

BRETT TAYLOR LOOKED LIKE A GUY WHO HAD FOUND THE Christmas gift that eluded him as a child. He waved an envelope around like it was a winning lottery ticket. Brandon crossed the room and met him.

"What is it?" Brandon asked.

"Don't know if it's much, but it's something." Brett extended the envelope so Brandon could read it.

"Meadowcroft Biotech?"

"That mean anything to you? At any time during this treatment, did that company come up?"

"I don't think so, but, that name..." He wheeled around in a few circles, a habit he developed as a child to help his brain disassociate and recall old information. "That name sounds so familiar."

"Meadowcroft?"

"Yeah." Brandon scratched his head and continued searching for the answer. "I'll get it."

"Well, while you work on that, why don't we get out of this dump? There's nothing here. This is gonna have to suffice as our best lead."

"Our only lead." Brandon scoured the room in hopes he'd find something else, anything else, that could lead them to the next step, but nothing stood out. "Since this place was a sham, perhaps that's the key to it all? Maybe the doc was brought in by that group to do this."

Brett shrugged. "Can't say one way or another, but I wanna get back to the car and get moving. Find out where this place is headquartered and we'll start heading there."

"Still feel like we're missing something here," Brandon said.

"What?"

"Can't put my finger on it."

"You're welcome to stay, buddy."

"No, I'm sticking with you. Let's get out of here."

Ten minutes later, they were back on the highway. Didn't take long to find an address for Meadowcroft Biotech. Problem was, there were several addresses, and none were in the same state. The closest was outside of Frederick, Maryland, only a few hours away.

During the drive, Brandon developed an intense headache while working on his laptop. He'd experienced this a few times recently and attributed it to allergies or something in his home, where he spent the vast majority of his time. All of his time, if he was being honest. That had been another recurring argument with Kimberlee. She wanted him to get out, experience life. Not spend all his time on a computer. He knew nothing else. She didn't accept it. Thinking about her wasn't helping. The headache intensified with every keystroke.

"You doing all right, Brandon?" Brett asked.

"Uh, yeah," he said, glancing over. "Why?"

"Your breathing, man. It's all jacked up."

"Jacked up?"

"Yeah. Can't you tell you're almost hyperventilating?"

Brandon closed the lid to his laptop and felt his pulse. His heart was beating well over a hundred beats per minute. He noticed how shallow his breaths were. His hand started trembling, then felt cold, and soon after, his fingers were numb.

"You need me to pull over?" Brett asked.

"Keep driving," he managed to spit out between breaths. "I'll be OK. It's just anxiety."

"You sure?"

Brandon reached over and adjusted the music volume, turning it loud enough he couldn't hear his ragged breaths, couldn't feel his heart beating against his chest. He closed his eyes and wished the symptoms away, but they wouldn't comply. And his head. His damn head felt as though it were splitting apart.

The car decelerated rapidly. He was pushed against the door. Opening his eyes, he saw they had exited the highway and Brett was taking a cloverleaf too fast.

"I said keep going."

"You need some water or something. Maybe some fresh air."

"I can roll the window down."

"There's no harm in taking ten. I gotta piss anyway."

A couple minutes later, they pulled into an empty Shell station lot and Brett left the windows down and trotted into the store. The guy slipped out of view as the door closed.

Brandon let the air into his lungs. He forced himself to hold it, let it seep through his lungs and into his bloodstream. Then he exhaled, waited a few seconds, and repeated the process. By the time Brett emerged from the store with a handful of Slim Jims and a plastic bag, Brandon had overcome the attack and eased back in his seat.

Brett went to his window, handed him a large bottle of water. "Here you go. Have a healthy meat stick while you're at it, too."

Brandon accepted the items with a nod and let his eyes fall shut again. His body felt better, only still a bit tense. And his head still ached. That had gone away at the same time previously. For some reason, it lingered. He kept working on his breathing, kept calming the fearful thoughts.

Back in the car, Brett reached over and squeezed Brandon's shoulder. "Everything OK?"

"Yeah, I'm good. I think I'm just anxious about what's ahead. Let's just get where we're going and get this done with."

"Aye, aye, captain." Brett hit him with a mock salute.

For the following two hours, Brandon stayed off the computer. Putting on his sunglasses, he leaned the seat back and did his best to rest. But, It wasn't easy. Waves of panic hit him. Moderate at first, then reducing in length and intensity. Thirty minutes out, he dozed off. Five minutes from their destination, he woke up when Brett exited the highway. He sat up to investigate the new surroundings.

"Morning, sunshine," Brett said.

Brandon groaned.

"Want another meat stick?"

"I think the last one is still with me." He burped and waved the air in front of his face.

"Coffee?"

"You got a Keurig in the backseat?"

"Nah, but the sign says there's a gas station close to here."

"I think I'm good." He checked the street in both directions when they reached the stop sign. "So, this is it?"

"This is it." Brett looked over at him. "You ready for anything?"

"No, but I don't have much of a choice, do I? We don't figure this out, I'm a dead man."

"As am I," Brett said. "Unless I take you out. Then I did my job." He remained stone-faced as long as he could, which was a few seconds. His laughter did little to ease Brandon's mind.

"It's talk like that that'll get you killed in the middle of the night."

Brett waved him off. "You wouldn't stand a chance."

"You don't think I can kill a man?"

"I don't think you can kill me. Big difference between your everyday guy and me, my friend."

"Likewise, *my friend*."

Brett laughed him off, but Brandon felt he got the point across. Could he beat the man into submission? No. Hell no. But could he wreck the guy's life with a couple keystrokes? Damn right.

"Switching gears," Brett said. "Remind me what we're walking into here."

"Office building," Brandon said. "Multiple businesses here, too, so we won't look all that suspicious."

Brett looked at Brandon, then in the rearview at himself. "Yeah, nothing about us together looks suspicious."

Brandon shook his head and continued. "I'm assuming this is an office staffed by a couple people. I'd bet clerical in nature. Not expecting to find anything really going on here."

"That a good or bad thing?"

"I just need one computer connected to their internal network. Then it's game on."

"Let's hope so."

It was late in the afternoon. The setting sun hid behind the six-story building. Trees dotted the parking lot, which was a quarter full. A man and woman dressed in business attire stood by the front door talking, backpacks slung across their shoulders.

"The easy life," Brandon said.

"The boring life," Brett said.

"You wanna talk about boring, man?"

"Gonna call me insensitive now?"

"Yeah, I am."

"I feel like this is a friendship that won't last, Brandon."

He laughed at the comment. "For once, we agree."

Brett circled the building and spotted a set of glass doors at the rear. Parking close to it, he helped Brandon out and into his wheelchair. Inside, the lobby was basic. No receptionist. No security guard. Just a plaque on the wall listing the businesses present in the building. Meadowcroft Biotech was located on the third floor, number three-zero-two.

They rode up in the elevator and found the office. On the right side of the door was an access card reader. On the left was a floor-to-ceiling window, clear, no curtain. Brett looked through.

"Not much of a place they got here. One desk, some boxes, shelves with stuff on them. That's about it. Single room, too."

"Occupied?"

"Nope."

"Try the door."

Brett grabbed the handle and turned, but it didn't move. "Can you do something about this?"

Brandon had his laptop open and was pecking away at the keys. "Already on it." Ten seconds later, the door beeped and Brett pushed it open.

"Good job. I might have to keep you around after all this is over. Maybe split profits with you eighty-twenty."

"Brains get the eighty."

"Maybe I won't keep you around."

"Go to hell."

Entering the office, Brandon immediately went to the computer while Brett searched through the boxes on the floor and items on the shelves.

It took Brandon less than a minute to access the system. It was easy. Too easy. Any amateur could've done this. Not necessarily the company's fault. This fell on the employee who just didn't give a crap and left stickies all over the monitor. Brandon tried the ones with single words and hit on the fourth note. He figured the others were passwords as well. One would allow him to access the company's intranet, if the computer wasn't logged in already. He quickly determined it was.

"Our lucky day," he said.

"You ain't kidding," Brett said.

"What'd you find over there?"

"Just some boring corporate literature, but it ties your doctor, his fake company, and this real company together. What'd you find?"

"I'm in their system."

He zoned out as his fingers did the work, accessing files that led to a database that led to his name. His name sitting in one cell, and in the cell next to it, the word canceled was written in red. Capitalized and in bold. **CANCELED.** He continued to scan the row, taking note of the IDs in each field. Most were numeric, which he figured were records in other database tables. He'd search them one by one, but first he stopped to write down a phrase that caught his eye: **PROJECT STEEL BANYAN.**

Brandon typed out a SQL command and inputted the various record IDs he had found. Each linked to other databases that contained more information about him. Basic information like height, weight, date of birth, social security number, previous addresses, his criminal record. That's where things started to get weird. He accessed a table solely about him. They knew things no one should. Secret government projects he had worked on. Private jobs he had completed off the record for some higher-ups in the government and intelligence communities. They had lists of his allies and enemies. He was chuffed to learn he had more enemies than he realized. He wondered if Brett had ever heard of them.

Brett walked over and looked over his shoulder. "I recognize some of those names."

"You kill any of them?"

"Might have." He pointed at the notepad. "What's that? Project Steel Banyan?"

"I think it's the name of this medical trial."

"Looked it up yet?"

"No, not yet. Been trying to get through all these databases. These guys know a lot about me. Too much about me. They shouldn't have access to some of these jobs I've done and projects I've worked on."

"You sure this company name doesn't ring a bell?"

"I've been hoping it'd pop up, but it hasn't." Brandon looked up at the guy. "Let me get back at it."

Brett slid a chair over near the door and took a seat.

Brandon finished up with his initial list of commands and entered one more. The database returned a link, and that was it. He clicked it. A password box popped up. He tried the remaining single words written on the stickies, but none worked. However, the handwriting on one of them was different. The letters didn't match. He turned his head sideways and saw why. It was written upside down. When he flipped it over, a sequence of numbers and letters that made no sense appeared. When typed into the box, the system allowed him in.

And what he saw horrified him.

Project Steel Banyan was not about trying to fix his condition. It was a program designed to engineer a super soldier. And it was in its infancy. Every test subject they had tried previously had passed away around the timeframe a bit further along than where Brandon was at now. He scanned through the other participants' information. All had been disabled like him. All had made progress like him. All had experienced the headaches like him. All had died from stroke.

He opened the file with his name and read through the reports. They started off promising, but as time went on, they became more ominous.

The same symptoms were popping up. The outlook was death. They knew it.

The door beeped. The handle turned. Brett pulled his pistol and Brandon began sending the contents of the hard drive to his private server.

CHAPTER 22

THE HOURS MELTED INTO ONE ANOTHER. THE SUN TRAVELED across east to west as she drove south, stopping for gas and food once, wearing a hat and sunglasses and zipping her vest all the way up. No one paid her any attention. No one cared. She craved for that to be the everyday experience of her life. If everyone would just leave her the hell alone, she could find her peace.

She'd found it a few times. Sort of, at least. Most recently, in Italy. The serenity it had provided made her believe she deserved that peace. Fool. It shattered and crumbled under the false foundation it had been built upon.

When would this end? When would she be free again? Soon. One way or another, her life would change, and she'd leave all of this behind.

First, she had to find Beck and straighten things out between them.

Clarissa exited the highway and pulled into an empty lot. She backed into a spot in the middle that offered her a view of the on-ramps and off-ramps and all traffic heading in both directions. Grabbing the bag off the seat, she pulled out the phone and SIM she'd purchased at the gas station.

A moment later, the line was ringing in her ear. "Come on, pick up, pick up."

The call went to a generic voicemail she'd heard several times in the past. Beck wouldn't check the message. She'd have to try again, and again, until he finally answered.

The sun had started its descent. The western sky was bright with deep orange and red. The east had turned pinkish. Stepping out of the vehicle, she took it in for a few minutes. The cool air made her lungs feel tight. Working in breath after breath, loosening her chest, relaxing.

"Where did it all go wrong?" she said. "One minute, things were perfect; the next you got dragged into this world, and now it feels like there's no escape." Looking around, she almost hoped someone was there. Whether to hear her out or take her out. All she wanted was to unload her thoughts and feelings and be done with them. Death would be much quicker than a shrink.

Knowing she had to get moving, she returned to the vehicle and took her seat. She decided to stick to local roads for a while and had her map application reroute her before pulling out of the lot. She hadn't made it two miles when her new phone rang. The number was blocked, but there was little doubt who was calling.

"Beck," she said.

"Clarissa," he said.

"Thanks for leaving me to fend for myself."

"Didn't have much of a choice, did I? Not after what you did six months ago."

"Someone had to help him."

"Yeah, and now he needs help again."

Clarissa felt a tinge of panic at the thought of Noble being in trouble. Or was it guilt? She'd dragged him into this mess. But the mess had turned into a huge problem. At this point, she was certain Beck had a hand in all of it.

"Look, I don't want to get off on the wrong foot," Beck said. "I know you need help. I'm here to help you."

Clarissa shook her head as though he could see her. She wished he could. She wanted him to see the look on her face in this moment. "Do you have any idea what I've been through? Six months, Beck. Six months without a soul to help me. I've been on the move, trying to figure out where you went and why. Hoping I'd make some connection between all these events that would let you off the hook in my mind. But I can't get there, Beck. The road's closed. Blocked. All signs point to you, but I'm not sure how to get across the map."

"What are you saying?"

She considered how to respond to the question. Outright accusing him for her current situation might cause him to drop the call and block her. Again.

"I'm not saying anything," Clarissa said. "I'm just frustrated."

"I told you we had to separate for a while. This is a lot of money. We need to let things cool off before we can turn this all in."

She knew he never would. The story always changed. "The money means nothing to me. This job means nothing. I just want to be free. Can you set me free, Beck? Can you make them forget I ever existed?"

There was a long pause, and she thought he had disconnected. He cleared his throat and said, "Why don't you come in, Clarissa? We can meet in Ticino, Switzerland. You remember the house we used there?"

She thought back to their early days working together, when their personal and business lives intermingled and she thought that, perhaps, he could be the guy she needed. Things had changed so much.

"What do you think?" he asked.

It was a terrible idea. She didn't trust him, but she had to make him think she did. "It'll take me a while, but I can get there."

"Great. I'll get a flight booked at once and meet you there."

"Hey," she said.

"Yeah?" he said.

"What's going on with Jack?"

Beck sighed and took his time answering. "He's in trouble. Again, I might add. Seems that six months ago, when you broke protocol and offered him aid, he took out this assassin Van de Berg. Can't blame him for that. It was Jack or the other guy. But instead of moving on, he assumed the guy's identity."

"Why?"

Beck laughed. "Why does Noble do anything? Look, I have no clue what makes the guy tick. You're better at this guessing game than I ever could be." Pausing a beat, he coughed, then continued. "So, he starts racking up jobs as Van de Berg, but intel is saying he never actually killed any of them. We're trying to get info on the marks, but it's slow-going. We don't know if they were—"

"Who's 'we'?" she asked.

"I'll explain that in person," he said. "As I was saying, we don't know who these people were and why they had contracts out on their lives, but chances are, they were not good people and probably deserved to die."

"'Chances are'? 'Probably'? Who are you?" She let her anger simmer before continuing. "If Jack let them live, he had a reason."

"Oh, yeah? What?"

She had no response. He'd debate anything she could say. If Jack had assumed this identity, there was a reason. And by not killing his intended victims. That made it even clearer he was trying to piece together who was behind all of this.

"Right, that's what I thought," Beck said.

She didn't take the bait. "Well, do you know who might be after him? And is it related to me?"

Beck's breathing grew louder, which indicated he was thinking through his words. He had a habit of rehearsing them, including moving the vocal muscles to produce the words before actually saying them. It was odd at first, but she had adjusted to it.

"I really shouldn't say this over the phone, Clarissa. It's the kind of thing that could cause *problems*."

"I'm out here alone, Beck. On my own. I need to know."

"You're right. I know you're right. OK, six months ago, Van de Berg picked up a contract on you. We now believe that Noble had already assumed his identity. The theory has been floated that he assumed the identity because you were marked for termination. Did that mean he wanted to help you or kill you? We don't know."

She burned at the insinuation.

Beck continued. "For some reason, the job was pulled and canceled within forty-eight hours. From that point on, he worked those eight jobs and picked up a ninth on a lady named Johanna Karlsson. Ever heard of her?"

Clarissa searched her memory but came up short. "Can't say I have."

"Swedish intelligence. Analyst for most of her time but did some field work. She left and has been working on her own. Mostly. There's a few associates as well."

"Why was she targeted for termination?"

"We don't know. Don't know why any of them were. That's why we hope to find Jack, so he can tell us. There has to be some connection between one of those eight people and her." He paused a beat. "And possibly you."

"So, are her people after Jack over this? Do they assume he's Van de Berg?"

"No, he's been outed. A body was found in the woods in a shallow grave some forty miles south of Amsterdam. They identified the corpse as Van de Berg. Apparently, whoever is running that organization had already suspected Noble, and this confirmed the truth."

"How long had they suspected this?"

"Unsure, but it's telling that the contract on you was pulled so quickly. Also, it wasn't reinstated until the determination that Jack had assumed Van de Berg's identity."

"This doesn't sound good."

"It's not, Clarissa. It's open season on the guy, and now you. There's zero chance he survives this. You're in the same boat if you stay out there. You need to come in. Now. Your history with him is lengthy. Even after he's dead, they'll keep coming after you. You've got nowhere to hide."

"Except with you."

"That's right."

She closed her eyes tight and thought of how to best respond. Would she go? Could she go? Or should she say she was on her way to buy a few more hours?

"I'll alter my course and see you in Ticino."

She hung up the phone and pulled off the main road, coming to a stop in front of a row of small homes. Windows were lit up with artificial light. Families sat around together or ate dinner together or played games together.

Feeling claustrophobic with the weight of all the revelations weighing down on her, she exited the vehicle and took a walk down the road. The temperature had dropped significantly since sunset. She hugged her arms over her vest and squeezed. Once past the strip of houses, the road disappeared into the blackness of night, and her mind wandered.

She had a few options, none of which were ideal. Only one was definite. The others required luck or patience. She considered waiting for Brandon to reach out again. Maybe he'd gained some ground. Maybe he'd tracked Jack down. Maybe she should just reach out to him. She pulled out her phone and stopped.

Clarissa had essentially gone off-grid. Chances of some hit squad showing up in this small town were slim unless they'd managed to track her again. She'd been careful to check her clothes and the vehicle and found nothing. Would making that call expose her?

She also needed to locate Jack. By the sound of it, he'd been working in Europe. If Brandon knew Noble's location, she could go to him. Together, they'd make a formidable team. They could watch each other's back. Maybe they wouldn't survive. If the worst happened, they'd go out together. The way she always thought it would end.

Lastly, she could make the trek to Switzerland and meet Beck. Was it the obvious choice he made it out to be? Or were her instincts correct and showing up there would be her last bad decision in a long line of them? The guy could've helped her at any point during the last six months. He hadn't. The same excuse of waiting for things to blow over had been used time and again. Things never blew over. Not for her. She'd faced all the trials and difficulties of surviving, while he had the government's protection. Probably had returned to the States and had been yucking it up in his office.

"This is all too much," she said to herself. "There's another option. Disappear."

An hour passed. Her hands were numb. Her face burned. Her lips were chapped. She returned to her car and began driving without a destination. Close to the border of Slovakia, she pulled into a mostly deserted motel parking lot, a flashing vacancy sign welcoming her.

CHAPTER 23

THE POUNDING ON HIS DOOR JOLTED JACK AWAKE. HE THREW the covers off, barely registering the chill of the night on his sweat-covered body. He grabbed the Glock off the nightstand and aimed at the door.

"You need to hurry," Tobias shouted.

Jack rushed around the bed and opened the door. The doctor stood there in a pair of shorts and white t-shirt.

"What's going on?" Jack asked.

"I just got a call. Some men are on the way. They want you and the woman."

"We can stand our ground."

"No, we can't. These are mercs, highly trained ones. I don't need them shooting my place up, which they'll do if you're here."

"And if I'm not here? What'll they do to you?"

"Nothing," Tobias said. "I'll explain I didn't know who you were. You visited and left. They'll leave me alone."

"They won't do that."

"Let me handle them. You and Johanna need to leave now. You have to clear that road before they get on it."

Jack turned around and threw on his clothes and gathered his things, including the two pistols and the AR-10. Tobias didn't argue. He only kept telling Noble to hurry.

"Let's go get her," he said.

"She's already being helped to the car," the doctor said.

"What about her injury? The sutures? Medicine?"

"Meds are in the car with her. The stitches will dissolve. She's fine. Trust me. And if things get worse, bite the bullet and go to the hospital."

"This is stupid, Tobias. I can handle these guys."

"I can't risk it, Jack. I just can't."

The doctor ushered him down the stairs and out the side door where the car was waiting. Someone had started it and moved it and left his door wide open. Jack stopped there and looked around. A cow mooed from somewhere in the distance. A couple of dogs barked. The activity had awoken the farm animals a few hours early.

Noble closed his eyes and inhaled the smell of the pasture, cold and clean and sweet. It settled his nerves and helped him focus on the task at hand. Taking his seat, he reached for Johanna, who lingered somewhere between sleep and awake. They had sedated her after she drifted off, so she'd sleep through the night. Presumably, that would make the next couple of hours easier. She wouldn't have to worry or try to convince him to take a different action.

Jack turned the car around, got his bearings, and cut off the headlights. When the white fence came into view, he adjusted his course to drive through the opening. At this spot, he had a better view than when he came in. He was on top of a small rolling hill. He could see clear down to the road. He would see any headlights approaching before they spotted him. So he cut his on and eased down the road so as not to disturb Johanna in her slumber.

When he reached the main road, he didn't continue much farther. He pulled over a hundred yards down and retrieved the AR-10. He hustled back to where the road ended and the gravel began, crossed over and found a perch. There, he waited until a vehicle came rolling down. A small car with two men inside. The driver cut off the headlights and turned on the interior lights. Two sitting ducks who thought they were invincible.

Noble sighted the driver in his scope and pulled the trigger. The shot could be heard for quite some distance, he presumed. All the way back at the house. He imagined Tobias panicking at the sound of it. The same way the passenger panicked, just as Jack had thought he would. The guy opened the door and stepped out with his pistol aimed at nothing. The light flooded his legs and Jack lined up a shot and took it and blew the guy's left leg off at the knee. The man fell and screamed and shouted and cried.

Jack ran over with the Glock in one hand, the AR-10 in the other. He kicked the guy's pistol out of the way and aimed his at the guy's head.

"Who are you?"

The guy couldn't put the words together.

"Who do you work for?"

The guy closed his eyes and bit down hard.

"I swear on your mother I'll end you right here if you don't tell me."

"What does it matter?" the guy yelled. "You're a dead man walking."

"That's all you got to say?"

The guy said nothing, continued grunting in agony.

"Enjoy Hell."

Jack put him out of his misery. He stepped over the guy and leaned inside the vehicle. The driver slumped over the steering wheel. A backpack rested on the rear seat. Two unopened cans of soda were in the center console cup holders. Was that going to be their celebratory drink? Soda? He opened the glove box and pulled out the contents.

"Interesting."

There were two envelopes. One was full of cash. The other contained two passports and airline tickets to Dulles airport outside of D.C.

"Who were you guys going to meet?" he said to the dead driver.

Approaching headlights caught his attention. Tobias. Jack reached over the passenger seat and grabbed the backpack. He stuffed the envelopes inside and hustled back to his car and tossed them in the trunk. Then he ran back to meet Tobias at the scene of the carnage.

Tobias was already there, hands on his head, staring up at the sky.

"What did you do, Jack?"

"Told you I could take care of these guys."

"Don't you realize what you've done?"

"Started a war?"

"Damn right you started a war. One you're not gonna hang around for."

"Get your people and get out then." Jack held the guy's eye for a moment. "Who are these guys? Why did they have tickets to Dulles?"

"I...I don't know what you're talking about." Tobias glanced back at the house, then down the road.

"You seem pretty scared for a guy who doesn't know what I'm talking about. Who'd you tell we were here?"

"What do you mean? Why would I—"

"Don't screw with me, man. Someone I trust contacted you. You did what you had to do, upheld that oath and fixed my friend. But then you talked to someone. You mentioned we were here. Maybe you said a name. Maybe it was my name. And the person on the other end of the line recognized it, and you knew they would. Next thing, I wake up to you pounding on my door 'cause these guys were sent. You needed me out of the house so they wouldn't kill you. Got news for you, Tobias. They would have. I almost kept going. Almost bailed and left you to deal with these guys. Why? Because I ought to kill you for mentioning my name."

Tobias looked like a deer in headlights, standing in the wash of the car's lights. His mouth opened, closed, opened again. He squeaked out something but couldn't say anything.

"Don't even try to make something up." Jack looked back at the dead guy slumped over the wheel. He gestured to where the other dead man was on the ground. "Who are they, Tobias? Who sent them?"

"I don't...I don't know."

"You don't know who you called? You don't know who warned you these guys were coming?" Jack took a step toward the doctor, causing Tobias to flinch when Jack brought his hand up. "Maybe that's it. No one called you back. You knew they'd come tonight."

The other man tried to keep his gaze fixed on Jack but failed. He looked past Jack again. Back at the house.

"That's it, isn't it? Whoever you called told you they'd come tonight, around three a.m. You bastard. Why didn't you just refuse us? Why set us up?"

"I didn't know who you were. I'd give you the name of the guy, but he's nowhere near here. He just…"

"He just what?"

"He wants me to let him know when things happen."

"Who?"

"I can't say."

"Why?"

"He'll kill my daughter." Tears filled his eyes. There was sincerity behind his words.

Jack backed off a bit at that. He stepped to the side and looked toward the farm. "These guys were headed back to the States. To Dulles. Not far from the Pentagon. Not as close as Reagan, but not that far. Never got to talk to them, well, at least not while the dude wasn't in agonizing pain. Hard to maintain your accent when you're speaking through a groan after having your leg shot off."

Tobias turned his head to look at Jack. "You think they were American?"

"Was your contact?"

Tobias nodded, then hung his head in shame. His eyes, misted over, were clenched tight.

"Just give me a name."

Tobias sobbed twice, choked down the third one. "David."

"David? That a first name or last?"

"I only know him as David."

"How did you meet this David?"

"At a medical conference in Las Vegas. Four years ago. He was looking for funding. Looking for doctors who were willing to participate."

"Participate in what?"

"Some medical trial. Helping paraplegics and whatnot."

The information slapped Jack across the face. Was this the same trial Brandon was taking part in? He had been about to call bullshit on the guy until this. He took another look at the man in front of him. Fear devoured Tobias. He'd turned against two formidable people, one of whom was standing in front of him, and the other had the kind of resources where he could send a couple of guys from Northern Virginia to Germany to take care of a washed-up spy.

"Are you serious about your daughter?"

Tobias sobbed again. That was answer enough.

"Get your things and get out of here, Tobias. Got a feeling you're next on the list. Call our mutual friend. He can help you out."

He turned his back on Tobias and returned to the vehicle thinking he might need to place a call to Brandon as well.

CHAPTER 24

A MAN WHO LOOKED LIKE HE WAS PROBABLY WORKING IN THE office for his college internship stared down the barrel of Brett Taylor's 9mm. His eyes were wider than his glasses. His khaki pants turned several shades darker around his crotch.

"For Christ's sake, man," Brett said. He grimaced at the smell and took a step back. "Who the hell are you?"

"N-n-nobody."

"Well, Nobody, if you turn your ass around, I won't blast you into oblivion with this gun. Sound good?"

The guy didn't move. Tears streamed down his face, and he convulsed.

"Dammit, Brett, I gotta roll through that spot."

Brett scratched the back of his head and stepped to the side. He grabbed the young guy and guided him to the corner of the room. "Just face the wall, OK? Stand there like you're the dunce in class and don't move until the teacher tells you to. Got it?"

The guy couldn't say a word. Probably went into shock and wouldn't remember a thing about them. Brandon wheeled back and stopped. What if the guy knew who he was? He'd glanced over at Brandon at one point. Hadn't he? A sharp pain started above his right eye and traveled toward his scalp. He kept trying to remember if the guy had looked at him. Had he stared long enough to make an ID? Did it even matter? Everything he just saw told him he was already a dead man walking. Why was he concerned about this guy identifying him? A bullet to the brain was better than what he imagined death from whatever they were pumping into him would be like.

"You all right over there?" Brett asked.

"Huh?" Brandon said.

"Your breathing, it's all jacked up again."

The guy looked over his shoulder. Met Brandon's gaze. He gasped.

"You're him."

"What?" The pain spread. His lungs burned. His heart pounded. "I'm who?"

"The guy from the current trial. But..." The man turned around. He glanced down at his pants and shook his head.

"But what?" Brandon forced the words out. His chest tightened.

"You died."

"When?"

"Like, yesterday. I just updated your entry."

"Canceled." Brandon's attack subsided. The pain dissipated. In death, Brandon had the ultimate freedom. "They think I'm dead?"

"Clerical error," Brett said. "You're a dead man walking, though. They won't stop until you're gone."

"Comforting."

"What do you mean?" the guy asked.

"Any idea who you're working for?" Brett said.

The guy shrugged. "I mean, the name's on the door. This is just an internship. I go to Georgetown."

"Yeah, well, good for you, rich kid."

The guy sulked into the corner and tried to cover the piss stain on his pants.

"What are we gonna do with him?" Brandon said.

"Hey, kid," Brett said. "If I told you you're working for a guy who puts out hits on people, and once he finds out you let us in this office, he'll likely dispose of you as well, what would you say?"

"Uh..."

"About what I thought." He pointed at the door. "Get out of those vile clothes and let's go."

"I can't go out there naked!"

"You can stop and wash your underwear then, but you're not wearing those pants in my car."

The guy stripped, tossed his pants in the trash, and covered himself with his soiled underwear. They exited the office after Brandon confirmed the files had been transferred securely. He killed the connection and erased all evidence he'd accessed the system. Was it foolproof? No. Someone could have seen everything remotely. Would they have been concerned? He couldn't answer that, so he presumed someone had seen, and they were pissed.

"Let's get this kid to a bathroom and get the hell out of here."

Thirty minutes later, they were twenty-five miles east of Frederick, Maryland on I-70 halfway between Mt. Airy and the city of Baltimore. Brett took an exit off the highway and continued driving north.

Brandon contemplated his future. What was left of it, at least. Nothing was set in stone. He was a smart guy. He could research and figure out a way to counteract the effects of the trial once he dug in and understood it better. Waves of optimism were met with resistance. He told himself it was over. He should go out guns drawn, blaze of glory style. He compartmentalized the thoughts with a promise to himself to deal with it after he figured out who was at the heart of this.

At Westminster, Maryland, Brett drove northeast for a spell, before finally turning north at a sign that said *Gettysburg 10 Miles*.

"Feeling like you need to brush up on your history?" Brandon said.

Brett cracked a smile. He seemed to be warming up to Brandon. "Got a place we can crash just past Gettysburg, near Michaux."

"What's a Michaux?"

"State forest." Brett rolled down his window and spat his gum out. The imbalance in pressure caused a pain in Brandon's ear until Brett rolled the window up again. "My property backs up to it. No one can build back there. Pretty nice."

"Who all knows about this place?"

"Not a soul."

Brandon gestured to the backseat where the guy sat in his wet underwear.

"Sure it's safe to bring him?"

"That momma's boy?" Brett laughed and shook his head. "Kid just wants to live. My cabin is the best place for him until we get this squared away."

"So now you're gonna babysit him?"

"No," Brett said, looking Brandon in the eye. "You are."

"What do you mean I am?" Brandon turned in his seat and looked back at the kid. "You planning on leaving me with him?"

Brett pulled over on the shoulder and slammed on the brakes. The car skidded on loose asphalt and gravel. Brandon thought it might veer off the road, but all it did was fishtail a little. When it came to a stop, Brett rested his left arm on the steering wheel as he shifted in his seat to face Brandon.

"Look, man. You and I each have talents the other doesn't. Let's face facts, OK? Your brain is a marvel. But the brawn ain't quite there. I'm also guessing you're not too keen on walking into someone's living room and executing them and whoever else is there to bear witness."

"If I could walk—"

"You wouldn't do a damn thing. And that's OK. The world needs a few guys like me, a lot more like you, and none of the pissants like that one in the backseat." He repositioned himself and eased down on the accelerator. Gravel crunched underneath the tires. "Skills, man. Skills. You use yours. Let me use mine. We'll get this figured out."

Twenty minutes later, they were in thick woods on a narrow road that a single car could barely traverse. Brett navigated it like he'd been doing it for over twenty years. Because he had, Brandon had learned. The guy had picked up the place in '99 and had renovated and added on over the years. He had fifteen acres surrounding it. He had an advanced security system monitoring the entire fifteen acres. If someone managed to get to the house, they'd be greeted with sounds loud enough to incapacitate them and lights strong enough and flashing so rapidly they'd induce a seizure in the strongest of people.

Not only that, but he had a shelter underground, a hundred yards from the house. It could be accessed from a hidden entrance in the woods. It could also be accessed from three locations within the house that Brett wouldn't divulge. Chances of needing the shelter were slim, anyway.

Brandon knew all this because Brett wouldn't shut up about it once he had told Brandon that's where they were going.

They turned onto a gravel drive. The car crept along as Brett swept his head from side to side, investigating his property. He slowed a couple times, took a closer look. Satisfied nothing was wrong, he moved forward until something else looked amiss.

"Really, how many people come out here, man?" Brandon said.

"I think it's pretty," the guy in the back said. "I'd come out—"

"Nobody asked you," Brett shouted.

"Gonna make him piss himself again." Brandon laughed, and it started a fit between the two of them. Brett had to stop the car because they couldn't stop giggling like a couple of school kids.

"You know I'm sitting right here." The guy in the back crossed his arms and his legs and looked quite uncomfortable.

Brett looked up into the rearview. "Kid, will you—"

"My name is Thomas, OK? Can you call me that?"

Brett made a face where his eyes widened and his mouth formed a tight O. "Well, he wants us to call him Thomas, my good man."

"Whatever you want, Tommy." Brandon pinched the tip of his nose to keep from laughing again.

"All right, all right," Brett said. "Thomas, we're gonna take good care of you."

"Doubt that," Thomas said.

"I can back up, drive twenty miles down the road, and drop you off if you'd like? Just say something, anything, and we'll go that route."

The kid kept any snarky comments he had to himself as Brett continued down the driveway. A decent-sized house rose in a clearing. Brett pulled out his phone and tapped a shortcut. Lights cut on, illuminating a circular driveway and the porch.

"I think you're gonna like the setup in my place. You load up all that data you stole and do what you gotta do with it. I'm gonna take a seven-hour nap. In the morning, we're gonna reconvene and figure this out."

CHAPTER 25

JACK DROVE STRAIGHT THROUGH UNTIL THE SUN threatened to rise. The sky lightened and dark blue turned to pale orange. Wisps of pink clouds offered the promise of a beautiful day. For some, at least. He glanced over at Johanna, who hadn't stirred in a couple of hours. She looked younger in the morning light. Dawn had a way of doing that. He recalled the ghettos, war zones, places that had been bombed to hell and left to rot. And somehow, some way, those moments before the sun peeked over the horizon made everything look new and safe and welcoming.

The Polish border drew close. He had considered driving south to Switzerland. Still had accounts there, including two that hadn't ever been accessed. Some stashed deposit boxes with passports, property deeds and keys, and lists of contacts around the world. People who could make his problems disappear by letting him take a position on their yacht so he could get safe passage to the Caribbean, or anywhere else, for that matter.

Perhaps when this was over, he'd go wherever Mia was.

After clearing the border, they drove another twenty miles, then stopped for gas and coffee. He bought two of the largest size, figuring if Johanna didn't drink it, he would. He grabbed some snacks and paid for it all at the automated register. The only employee in the store was a young guy who stared at his phone the entire time Jack was there.

The sun sat low above the horizon when he stepped back outside. It was large and wide and shaped a little differently than normal. An illusion he appreciated.

Jack set the coffees and snacks on the roof of the car and pulled out his phone. He redialed the number for Brandon and waited. The line kept ringing. He kept waiting. The call disconnected. Shaking off the doubts creeping into his mind, he got behind the wheel and tried to offer Johanna some coffee. She didn't respond. He gathered his thoughts, pulled out of the parking lot, headed toward Warsaw with two people occupying the free space in his mind.

He needed to hear from one to find out about the other. Brandon would call back soon or answer the next attempt at reaching him. He'd tell Jack where Clarissa was and that he had it all under control. Brandon would tell him where to go and who to kill to put this whole thing to bed. The guy had come through a million times before. He'd do it again.

The call came one hour and thirty minutes after Jack pulled out of the gas station. The call came one hour after Jack passed a car full of guys who were shouting at him and sped up to keep shouting at him. The call came thirty minutes after Johanna opened her eyes and said good morning.

Jack answered and wasted no time on formalities. "Tell me you got this whole thing figured out, Brandon."

The guy on the other end of the line remained silent.

"Brandon? You there?"

Several seconds passed before Brandon said, "Yeah."

"What's going on? What've you got for me?" He thought about pulling over in case bad news was incoming.

"How do you deal with it, Jack?" Brandon's voice was soft and lacking its usual playfulness. The guy always had a way of making the worst news sound fun and exciting. This was different.

"Deal with what, old friend?"

"Knowing that every time you wake up, it could be the last time."

"I got news for you. Every time anybody wakes up, it could be the last time they do so."

Brandon sighed as though he was disappointed by Jack's answer. "I get that on an intellectual level. We're always one heartbeat, one breath, one second closer to death. Blah, blah. I'm not talking about that, man."

"If not that, then what?"

"You shoulda checked out years ago, Jack. I can think of a dozen incidents over the past ten years where I can't believe you didn't die. I mean, three times, I thought for sure you were a goner. I had proof of it. Yet, here you are. Outlived your nine lives, so some benevolent or malevolent sky-being granted you nine more."

Jack didn't have a response. He tried not to dwell on such thoughts.

"How do you do it?" Brandon sounded agitated. "How do you face the very real possibility that you might die today, Jack?"

He gripped the steering wheel tight with his left hand and eased off the accelerator after moving into the right lane where he wouldn't have to worry about some car coming up on him at a hundred miles or more an hour.

"So, you have no answer?" Brandon said.

"Brandon, tell me what's going on. This isn't like you. Even during the worst times, I can't recall—"

"Just answer me, man."

Noble took a deep breath and considered his response. "OK. Yeah, I mean, I think about it. Did I when I was in my twenties? Not a chance. I was invincible, man. My thirties? A little bit. You know, the bumps and bruises, they lingered a little longer. In my forties? Yeah, it pops into my head more frequently than I'd like to admit. But I can't let it linger. It can't worm its way into my brain like an earwig, because that's how it manifests. Once it manifests, it spreads, and not only to you, my friend. To all those around you as well. You start obsessing about death, and it'll find you."

"You've lost a lot of people, Jack."

"I have. But I can't blame myself for most of them."

"Interesting," Brandon said. "Makes sense, in a way."

"Almost everyone I know who died thought about it too much. All we can do is get up and do our job. We put one foot in front of the other and move ahead. The only way is forward. Whatever it is, you've got this."

Brandon chuckled softly and paused before replying. "When's the self-help book coming out?"

Jack laughed.

Brandon said, "Appreciate the encouraging words, but I'm not sure they apply to me."

"Is this about the job? Brett showing up at your door?"

"I wish that's all it was, Jack. I really do."

Noble tried to figure out what was driving the conversation. What had happened to his friend that he was talking like this? Through all the years, even during the worst times, Brandon never lost that sense of being young, cracking jokes, having fun. He was the kind of guy that didn't look at his disability as a hindrance. He found ways around it. Hell, he made up his own ways to get around it. All Jack could surmise was this had to be something serious.

"If it's not Brett, what is it?" Jack asked. "Level with me and just say it. What's weighing so heavily on your mind?"

"You're right. Guess I should just say it instead of torturing you with this. The medical trial is what has me upset. This doctor, he's a sham. His company doesn't exist. We tracked the office down. It was an empty warehouse. We've done extensive research on these people and come up with so little. A bunch of shell corps behind it. So far, I can't figure out who they belong to. I've got some more info to dig through when I go inside, but, I'm not sure it matters."

Jack listened and said nothing.

"Wanna know the worst part, Jack?"

"Yeah."

"It's some goddamn super soldier program. And before you say it, no, I am not going to turn into an elite operative. They wanted to see what would happen to people like me when they provided this treatment. I guess if the results were nothing short of amazing, like they were, and there were no permanent side effects, which there might be, then, they could sell it to the government. And if they don't take it, probably offer it to the highest bidder."

Jack thought about the revelation. "What potential permanent side effects are you afraid you're dealing with?"

"Been getting headaches followed by intense anxiety. Like, thirty-minute panic attacks while my head feels like it's going to explode. My pulse skyrockets. I can't breathe."

"Take anything for that?"

"I can't take anything but what they've been supplying me with."

"I know it might not matter now, but did you tell anyone about these symptoms?"

"They just started."

"Sorry to hear this, man. You think going off the meds will help?"

"Tomorrow is day one. Guess we'll find out." Brandon took a few seconds before continuing. "I accessed a database on the trial. Started matching records to tables. They know so much about me. And also…"

"Also what?"

"All the previous participants have died."

"You're kidding."

"Right."

A long lull persisted between the men. Jack stared ahead, only registering the car in front of him. He had the auto-cruise pacing the vehicle so he could focus on the conversation.

"One more thing," Brandon said. "Maybe this'll liven up the chat."

"What is it?"

"I think we got a lead at the warehouse. An envelope with the name of another biotech company on it. After some research, I found multiple offices, one only a few hours away. So we went there. All the info I found on the program and myself, it came from a computer in that office."

"What was the company name?"

"Meadowcroft Biotech."

Jack felt an icy razorblade slice down his spine.

CHAPTER 26

THE ALARM CLOCK BLARED AT SIX-THIRTY IN THE MORNING. Clarissa reached over and smashed the top of it with her palm until it ceased to annoy her. She should've yanked the cord from the wall and tossed it across the room, because it started up again seven minutes later. This time, she sat up and switched it off.

Sunlight peeked in through the slit in the curtains. Why was it that blackout shades always drifted apart a fraction of an inch overnight?

Rising, she walked over to the coffee machine, another thing she'd yet to conquer in Europe. Every hotel and apartment she'd stayed in had the oddest single serve coffee makers. She struggled to find pods for them in the stores, too. After several minutes of fiddling with the small appliance, she figured it out and felt soothed by the bubbling of the water as it heated and filtered through the pod.

After brushing her teeth, she took care of her other needs. By the time she finished, a small cup of coffee waited for her. Another issue she had with Europe. Why were the coffees so damn small? Tiny as it was, the caffeine hit her quickly. She downed the first mug and made a second.

The seconds passed. A cool stream of air piped down from the ceiling, smelling a bit musty, like so many other places. She peeked through the peephole in the door to confirm no one waited outside for her. Then she peeled back the curtains, one layer at a time, until she had a view of the empty parking lot. The other cars were gone. The vacancy sign no longer blinked. An older woman with tangles of long gray hair swept the parking lot, pushing cigarette butts and other trash toward the street.

Clarissa retrieved her second cup of coffee and returned to the window. There was something about the old woman that caused Clarissa to watch her intently. Perhaps it was the way her back hunched, likely from years of hard work like sweeping parking lots and cleaning motel rooms. There was something else, though. A few sips further, and she realized the old lady reminded her of the store owner. Their dresses were almost identical. The old lady reached her hand into a side pocket and retrieved a phone from her dress.

The time felt meditative in a way. Clarissa's head emptied, her thoughts faded, and she focused on the woman a hundred feet in front of her until a van pulled into the lot. The window rolled down, and an arm stuck out. Clarissa gasped, fearing the worst. But the old woman looked up, smiled, waved. The van pulled into a spot a few spaces from the silver Jetta and a bunch of kids hopped out and ran toward the motel office. A woman stepped down from the driver's side and went up to the old lady and hugged her.

This, Clarissa thought, was a safe space. A place she could take her time and recuperate. Figure a few things out before deciding how to proceed.

Finishing her coffee, she added water to the machine, but didn't start another cup. She wanted some fresh air first, so she put on the clothes she'd worn the day before and left her room. Crisp air greeted her at the threshold. The air had a tainted smell, as though a factory were nearby, upwind of the motel. The taste in her mouth soured, but she adjusted.

Bounding down the stairs, she saw the old lady and who she presumed was the woman's daughter enter the motel office. Clarissa hurried in after them. The older woman greeted her with a smile and began speaking to her in Polish. The lady hadn't been in there the night before to witness the comedic scene of Clarissa attempting and eventually succeeding at renting a room without being able to communicate with words.

"I'm sorry," Clarissa said. "English?"

The woman looked at her daughter and raised her eyebrows into her already wrinkled forehead. Clarissa worried they might be swallowed whole.

"How may I help you this morning?" the younger woman asked.

"I was wondering where I might go for breakfast?"

"You can eat with us here if you'd like?"

Clarissa glanced through the open doorway and saw all the kids huddled around a table. "I don't want to impose, plus, I need to get a little work done. Any diner nearby that you can recommend?"

The woman told her of two places, and Clarissa set out for the nearest. It was only a few blocks away, so she decided to walk. Along the way, the peaceful facade she had erected began to crumble. Her thoughts turned to Jack and Brandon and Beck. Having not heard from the last two in a while, she couldn't stop worrying about the former.

Seating herself in the diner, she ordered more coffee and eggs with bacon. The meal was spent considering all her options again. Going to Beck was a non-starter. The last six months had made it painfully clear he had no interest in helping her. She had convinced herself the only use he had for her was to set her up to take the fall. He sure as hell wouldn't own up to stealing the stolen funds and locking them away. Even if he *recovered* them, the losses sustained from funneling the money into crypto, then further mixing it through networks of shady exchanges, would not go unnoticed. He'd be a hero, and he'd need someone to blame. Who would that be? Who could he say made off with ten million dollars? In the grand scheme of things, it would be nothing compared to the two-hundred-plus million he *found*. He'd be the hero. She'd be hunted.

Pushing Beck off had bought her a little time. It had an expiration date, though. Mid-afternoon, maybe early evening, if she sent him an update. She contemplated this strategy. It was not without risk. There was little doubt he was tracking her. A message would alert him to her new location, which was well short of where she'd be had she traveled straight through the night.

What if he was tracking her now, though? He had people who had the capability of triangulating her cell signal. It wouldn't be in real time, she believed. More like snapshots through the day. There were few people she was aware of that could do more than that. Beck was not one. And anyone he knew with the ability likely worked in a walled garden and would need more than his word to pull off the request.

She glanced down at the phone. It was her only connection to Brandon. Did it have to be, though? She remembered the number. She had initiated the outreach. All she had to do was send another message from a new line. She picked up the device and fired off a message through the encrypted tunnel they'd been using. She updated him with her location and plan. To a point, at least. She didn't want to leave too much information on the device, so she told him she thought she was hot and was going to pick up a new phone. She'd send a message from it so he could reestablish this connection with her.

Five minutes later, she received a thumbs up emoji from him.

Two out of three. Now, she had to figure out how to reach Jack. Brandon would help, that was a given. She had to hope that the tech wizard already had a bead on Noble. If he didn't, she'd be walking into a buzzsaw with no protection. She paused for a moment to consider why she was doing this. Things could have been different just six months ago. If she'd trusted her instincts instead of whatever pull she had to the sense of duty she felt, none of this would be happening. Or, if it were, they'd be dealing with it together.

"Don't beat yourself up, girl," she muttered.

The lady sitting at the table across from her looked up, a quizzical look in her eyes. Clarissa nodded and grabbed her fork and shoved a helping of eggs into her mouth.

The sentiment held truth, though. Half a year ago, she believed she was doing the right thing. That she and Beck were on the path of retrieving what had been stolen from the Vatican. But now? She questioned it all. Even the story of the theft. Their investigation had remained on the periphery. Information came secondhand from agents she'd never met. Beck told her they were an elite group within the Treasury Department, much like the top one percent of the CIA's Special Activities Center. These men had no past. They were true ghosts. They could take the investigation no further, so they handed it to Beck.

And she fell for it. She was certain now that the truth would be simpler and reveal a conspiracy she didn't want to unravel but now felt compelled to be the one to do so.

She devoured the rest of her meal. Before leaving the diner, she shot a message to Beck that she had fallen asleep at the wheel and decided to get a room for the night. She said she'd be on her way soon. She said the phone was running low on battery and she'd rather keep moving than worry about it right now. All of it seemed plausible enough.

Back in her room at the motel, she grabbed the few things she had with her and tossed them on the passenger seat. She went to the office to check out and left enough information with the women that if someone showed up looking for her, they'd have a simple answer.

"Leaving already?" the younger woman asked.

"Have to get to Ticino by tomorrow. Driving the whole way."

The woman placed her hand on her forehead. "My dear, that is going to be a long drive. The train would be a little faster."

"I need my car, though."

"You Americans." She shook her head. "I don't know how you live the way you do."

Clarissa shrugged as if to say, what else can I do? None of it mattered because she wasn't going to Ticino. Not even close to it.

She smiled at the old woman who was smoking an unfiltered cigarette while sitting on a bench outside the office. The lady said something to her in Polish. Clarissa looked back and saw a wide grin on her face. She returned it, then jogged to the Jetta.

She drove west for an hour or so until she reached the Czechian border. She pulled over at a service station and powered down her phone. After gassing up, she went inside, paid for the gas, and bought a new phone, then went to the restroom. She pulled the SIM card out of the old phone and flushed it down the toilet, then dropped the device in the trash. If Beck sent someone to find her, they might look here for her, at this gas station. They'd work their way back to the motel where the younger woman would smile at them with the older woman by her side, and she'd say that Clarissa left an hour before this moment on her way to Ticino. Maybe they'd believe it. They'd waste time searching for information about her. Was there an accident? Was she in the hospital? Had she been captured by someone else?

Meanwhile, she would put hundreds of miles between them. She would become a ghost.

And if for some reason she needed to find Beck, she knew exactly where he'd be.

PART 3

CHAPTER 27

BRANDON MANAGED TO SLEEP THREE HOURS uninterrupted. Then he received a message from Clarissa and his brain wouldn't shut up long enough to string together another hour's worth. He laid there as long as he could, but the silence was maddening. Why'd the place have to be so damn quiet? It felt like he was in a vacuum where sound was being pulled out.

He got up, showered, and went to the kitchen where he found Brett seated at the table with his laptop open and a mug of coffee in his hand.

Brett tilted the mug toward Brandon. "Morning. Want some?"

Brandon nodded and rolled up to the opposite side of the table. "What are you looking at?"

"Anything I can find on Meadowcroft."

Brandon resisted the urge to grab the laptop and see where Brett's searches had led. "Any luck?"

Brett returned to the table, set the coffee in front of Brandon. He stood in front of the laptop, nodding. "I think you'll find it interesting." He spun the computer around and slid it across the table.

Brandon read through the short article explaining that Meadowcroft Biotech had lost their government funding four years ago. It had been their main source of funding. In its place, they had taken on private investors. Not only that, they had begun rescinding patents they had given the government permission to use. They had also canceled programs in place with various agencies. It took several months to unwind it all, but it appeared that since that time, Meadowcroft had operated on its own with practically no oversight.

"What happened four years ago?"

Brett shrugged. "That's what we've got to figure out, eh?"

"Suppose so."

"Hungry?"

"I could eat."

"I'm gonna go check on our friend." Brett padded up the stairs.

"Four years ago," Brandon muttered.

He tried to put together a timeline of events in his own life. What had he been doing then? Why would the company pinpoint him for this super soldier program—Project Steel Banyan—some three-plus years later? How did they even know about him?

Nothing stood out from that time or even from a few previous years. The only link to the current situation was Jack Noble and his connection with Brett. Beyond that, it all made little sense. He needed to dig deeper, and for that, he needed his laptop.

Brett returned. "The kid doesn't feel like eating yet."

"You mind grabbing my computer out of the car?"

Brett held up a finger. "Ah, yeah." He disappeared for a moment and returned with the laptop.

Brandon woke the machine up and saw that he had a new message from Clarissa. She'd coded it the same way she had earlier. Sent it to the same number. Firing up a terminal, he established an encrypted channel and sent her a message confirming receipt.

A few minutes later, he received another message from her.

"Situation went sideways. Had to leave but am going back to Warsaw now. Beck wanted me to come to Ticino. Don't trust his motives. He's been avoiding me for six months, and I think he's trying to set me up to take the fall for this heist. Can you find out if he's behind the attempt on my life? Do you have any other contacts in or near Warsaw who can assist?"

"A lot to unpack here," he muttered.

He started by looking up Ticino and any active players there. It took less than three minutes to determine the place was a ghost town. Probably why Beck wanted her to go there. He had a hunch Beck had nothing to do with the contract on her life. No, that had to be related to Noble somehow. Beck might be shady, and he might have done something illegal, but Clarissa was worth more to him alive than dead, especially if she was correct that he wanted her to take the fall.

Brandon set that aside for the moment and started looking for friendlies in and around Warsaw. He felt as though he'd let her down earlier when he hadn't come up with someone to help her when she had first reached out. There wasn't much choice in the matter. Once Brett showed up, the day took a serious turn for the worse.

It didn't take Brandon long to locate an old warhorse of an ex-CIA operative named Clyde Kemp. He scanned Kemp's file. The guy was a relic from a time before computers and internet and modern intelligence. The job was a lot tougher for those operatives. At seventy-five, he had spent every year since fifty in Poland. He owned a bar that expats frequented. Some of them from the same community as him. If Clarissa wasn't safe there, she wasn't safe anywhere.

Brandon found a common contact and reached out to Kemp through the intermediary and waited for a reply.

"Bacon?"

Brandon looked up, confused by the word until he saw Brett turned at the waist, tongs in hand. "Oh, yeah, sure. Eggs, too."

"You got it."

"Hey, man, how secure is your setup?"

"Iron clad."

"You're sure about that?"

"Paid an expert to set it all up. No one can detect traffic coming in or out of this location."

Brandon ran a program to confirm. The network passed. He'd feel better tunneling into his own system but had concerns that it had been compromised. Brett's system would have to do.

He accessed the server where he'd dumped the Meadowcroft Biotech files and began wading through the trash. The Banyan project was his primary concern, but he wanted more than that. He needed names, dates, locations. He wanted communications in the form of internal and external messages, but couldn't find any of that. If the files he stole contained this information, someone had gone to great lengths to hide it.

Brett came around the table with a blue Fiestaware plate loaded with a dozen strips of bacon and probably four scrambled eggs. "Eat up. You're a growing boy."

Brandon rolled his eyes at the guy as though he were a teenager aggravated with another comment from his dad. "Piss off."

"We'll leave that up to Tommie."

They both shared a quick laugh. Then both fell silent just as quickly. This wasn't a day to joke around. There was too much at stake.

Brandon didn't realize how hungry he was until he took the first bite of bacon. "Damn, this is good. Where's it from?"

"Trader Joe's." Brett held up the package. "Black Forest bacon. It's meat candy, man."

Thomas finally plodded down the stairs. He looked different this morning. The scared kid had left. The guy showed more concern now than yesterday. He took a seat at the end of the table and scratched at the shadow of stubble on his face.

"Changed my mind," Thomas said.

"About what?" Brett said.

"Breakfast. Smells good."

"I'll get you a plate."

Brandon slid his plate over. "Take a few slices of bacon. No way I can eat all this. But, man, is it *good*."

Thomas grabbed three pieces and thanked Brandon. His face melted when he took a bite. "Damn, this *is* good. Where's it from?"

Brett and Brandon both replied. "Trader Joe's."

All three shared a smile. Brandon realized it was moments like this he missed most, with Kimberlee gone. Sitting around, laughing at random comments and situations. If he survived this part of his ordeal, he'd find her by whatever means possible and straighten things out. He wanted and needed her by his side for whatever was left of his life.

Brett set a plate in front of Thomas, and the man placed the remaining bacon on his fresh pile. "Guys, look. I need—"

Brandon held up a finger. "Hold on a sec."

A message through the intermediary had come in and he needed to check it. He accessed the program and read the response. It was a go. Kemp would take Clarissa in. He had a secure setup attached to the bar where she could wait things out. He thanked his contact, then shot a message to Clarissa with the address of the bar and the name of the ex-CIA operative.

"All right." He filled his mouth with eggs and talked through them. "What did you wanna say?"

Thomas set down his fork and swallowed his food. He looked at Brett, then Brandon, then at his plate. "I'm afraid I misled you guys yesterday."

Brett walked over and angled his chair. He took a seat facing the younger man. "How so?"

"I thought that if you believed I was an intern, you might leave me alone. You know, figure I was worthless, and maybe if you scared me enough, I'd agree not to say anything. I even forced myself to piss my pants." He looked down at his plate as he turned a light shade of red. "In retrospect, that was a bad idea."

"Yeah, and not as funny now that we know you did it on purpose," Brett said. "Kinda sick, if you ask me."

Thomas nodded without looking up. "I just want you to know I was trying to save myself, is all. I didn't *want* to deceive you. The gun freaked me out a little."

"If you're not an intern, what do you do?" Brandon asked.

"Things I don't want to do anymore," Thomas said.

"Can you expand upon that?" Brett asked.

"I know who you are, Brandon. I know all about you, including when you were earmarked for the trial."

Brandon processed the information. Was this guy for real? He looked closer at Thomas, noticed things he hadn't the day before. His boyishness was a facade. There was a line etched in his forehead. Crow's feet extended from his eyes. His lips sagged a little. He wasn't some twenty-two-year-old intern after all.

"How long have you worked there?" Brandon asked.

"Long enough to know David Meadowcroft is a bad man with bad intentions."

"The doctor who was administering my treatment, Dr. Michaels, what do you know about him?"

"Seems like he was probably a decent enough guy at one time. From what I could gather about him, and most of the doctors and scientists, they were behind a wall on the true intentions of this project. If they got wind, or voiced their concerns, David would offer them more money while also pointing out he knew their deepest, darkest secrets. It was never a bluff. The guy could get dirt on people like you wouldn't believe. Dr. Michaels knew he was screwed, so he sold his soul to Meadowcroft for money and a promise to not reveal his secret." Thomas leaned back in his chair and shook his head. "Guess you could say the same about me."

"He blackmailed you?" Brett asked.

"No, I just haven't left even though I realize the company isn't exactly on the up and up."

"Why does this name sound so familiar to me?" Brandon said.

"David Meadowcroft?" Brett asked.

Brandon nodded while working through unconnected events, looking for a link.

"We learned that the company lost most government funding a few years back," Brett said. "Any idea why?"

Thomas shifted in his seat. His lips thinned as he pressed them together tightly. "That was before I really had any access to the higher-ups, so I've only heard rumors. I've never actually heard David talk about this."

"What were the rumors?"

"There were a few."

"Tell us."

"That he'd slept with someone's wife. Multiple someones at that, and they were wives of powerful people. Also, I heard that he'd played hardball with someone very, very high up in the Pentagon and they called his bluff. Oh, and that the guy leading the charge on the Banyan project from inside some government agency had died, and with him out of the picture, no one else stood up for the project, so the funding was moved to another project by some subcommittee."

This information appeared to do nothing for Brett, but it punched Brandon square in the gut.

CHAPTER 28

TWO WORDS ON THEIR OWN MEANT NOTHING. LIKE A LETTER torn in half, only a piece of the story could exist, fragmented. You could glean some context, sure. But the blanks had to be filled in. And when that happens, the mind runs wild.

That's how Jack had felt in general for the past thirty-six hours. He'd been working with two halves of a story and couldn't figure out how to match them up.

The hit on Johanna.

Oskar the club owner's place in all this.

Noah's deception.

The compromised doctor.

The hit team sent to kill him at the farm.

None of it made sense until he heard the name Meadowcroft. It took precisely a half-second for the memory of Tobias saying the name David to scream in Jack's mind. On their own? Coincidences. Together?

David Meadowcroft.

A man he'd met when Feng, the Old Man, had offered him a job to take out a guy named Marcus Hamilton Thanos. A woman, an FBI agent —who turned out to be a double agent—named Lexi, had been involved. She perished. When Jack went back for David Meadowcroft, his office had been abandoned and he'd lost track of the man. It all happened over a decade ago and had been filed away in that place in Jack's brain where he buried the memories he no longer wanted to interfere with his life.

And now it had resurfaced, and he was starting to tie together the two halves of the story he couldn't figure out.

Driving for hours, he recounted that period of time in his life, trying to figure out why Meadowcroft would want Jack dead after all these years? Could he be the one who had put the hit out on Clarissa? On Johanna? All the other jobs Jack had taken after assuming Van de Berg's identity? Van de Berg had been hunting Noble. Had Meadowcroft ordered that hit? If so, this went back quite a few years, at least.

Meadowcroft seemingly had unlimited resources a decade ago. Jack could only imagine how his wealth and power had expanded in the time since. With that came reach that might equal some of the largest nations. How else could he explain what happened in the early morning hours? It appeared Meadowcroft had his hands deep into someone's pockets if the two men sent to kill him and Johanna were out of Langley.

Were they, though?

Two halves of a letter he thought he had pieced together, but he considered he might be wrong on this point. The possibility existed that Meadowcroft had his own team of elite operators. Operatives who could move in and out and do the dirty work that his network of for-hire hitmen weren't equipped for. The two men could have been part of a rapid-action team that didn't need days or weeks to prepare. Operating solely on brute force, they got in, got out, and even if they were detected, got away because Meadowcroft had the money to buy off anyone.

Thoughts jumbled together into a mass of congestion, rivaling the traffic around D.C. or Atlanta. It was time to shift his thoughts to something else: finding Clarissa.

But before that, he needed gas, coffee, and a bite to eat.

Reaching over, he tapped Johanna's knee. "You up?"

She stirred, blinking away sleep. She stretched her arms out, rolled her head in a circle. "I'm getting there. Woke up a few times already and drifted away again."

"How's your stomach?"

She touched her abdomen as though it were a porcelain doll with a fracture line running down the middle. Surprise worked through her face, and she poked a little harder. "Doesn't hurt at all." Hiking up her shirt, she investigated the few sutures there. The skin was red, and a little swollen, but other than that, it looked fine.

"Great. You'll need to take it easy for a bit, though. No Superwoman stuff, got it?"

"Yes, dad." She chuckled, then grimaced and placed her hand over the incision. "OK, maybe not feeling entirely perfect."

"Hungry?"

"No, but I could go for coffee."

"Great."

Jack pulled off the motorway at the next exit and found a gas station that had a little diner attached. It wasn't much. Six bistro tables lined up along a long window. Three inside. Three outside. He helped Johanna to a table outside, went in, and ordered coffees and a couple of small things to eat. He kept watch over her the entire time.

When he returned to the table, Johanna had her eyes closed, facing the sun. The morning light brightened her pale face, accentuating her attractiveness. He set the coffee and a croissant in front of her, then took his seat. Minutes passed without a word spoken. Jack wasn't sure what to say. There were plenty of topics to choose from. Two stood out most.

The contents of the briefcase. And his recent revelation.

"Where are we headed?" she asked.

"Warsaw," he said. "I think."

Her eyes narrowed, indicating follow-up questions. Jack could only imagine where the conversation would go, but she kept them to herself. At least for now.

"Is there more to the story with Noah?"

"No." Doing her best to hold his gaze, to not appear as though she were deceiving him, she failed.

"I understand this is upsetting. Hasn't even been twenty-four hours. I've hardly processed it, so I can't imagine what you're feeling right now." Sipping his coffee to allow her a chance to respond. She didn't. "I also know that you're lying. We haven't known each other long, but you've gotta trust me. This might be larger than you or I thought a day ago. What's going on here? Who was the guy in the street? Rupert, I think his name was? The one who led us into the club? I thought I saw him in the diner." He noticed her nodding slightly, a reflex, perhaps, confirming what he saw. "Any idea why Noah turned on you? And the briefcase, what's in there? Things went so sideways after we left."

Staring at the crumbs on the table, she wiped them away with her hand. "There's things I can't say."

"Why?"

"You wouldn't understand." She glanced up at him and reconsidered. "Maybe you would. I don't know. This whole thing is a mess. A huge mess. I'm sorry you were dragged into it. Sorry that I lured you into this. When I first saw you in the street, got a real good look at you, I knew you weren't him."

"Who?"

"Van de Berg."

Jack eased back in his chair. He studied her for a moment, turned his head, scanned the parking lot and the pumps and the traffic racing back and forth on the motorway.

"What do you know about that?" he asked.

"Only that you're not him," she said.

"So, you were expecting him?"

"We put out a lot of misinformation to attract attention. When we received confirmation it had worked as intended, I went to the apartment in Denmark."

"It's yours?"

"No, it belongs to my agency."

Snippets of their past conversations flashed in his mind's eye. "You said you were done with that line of work."

"Officially."

"Unofficially?"

"I'm in deep."

"The guy you were with, Rupert? Who was he?"

"My handler. And, obviously, Rupert was not his real name."

She showed no signs of deceit, though recent revelations told Jack she could play both sides well. He might never know how much truth every sentence contained.

"What's your real name?"

"Johanna Karlsson."

"Oskar?" he asked.

"A glorified criminal," she said. "He gets information. We trade for it. Sets my moral hackles on fire, but it is what it is. Right?"

"For the greater good and all that. I get it." He took another sip of coffee. "What's in the briefcase?"

"A lot of intel that I'm not sure matters anymore."

"Why?"

"When did you kill Van de Berg?"

The conversation was flowing. He didn't hesitate to tell the truth. "Six months ago."

"That's why. Everything since was you, not Van de Berg. Do you know who you were working for? Do you know why those people you killed were targeted?"

"No, on both accounts. And I didn't kill any of them."

"Why did you kill *him*?"

This time, he hesitated. "It's not a long bridge to walk across. You can probably figure it out with the info in that briefcase." He waited for the follow-up question she didn't ask, so he took control of the interrogation again. "Who was Noah?"

"Who wasn't he?" She laughed, a harrowing sound which was followed by a grimace and her hand going to her stomach again. "My trainer … confidant … adopted father, basically. My original handler. The story about him is true, mostly. The only thing he loved more than me was his own daughter, though I helped fill the hole in his heart after she shunned him a decade ago. She wanted nothing to do with him, and that killed him. Even years later, he still loved her with his whole heart."

"Enough to double-cross you if it meant saving her life."

"I can't blame him." Her body language suggested otherwise. "He paid the price for it."

"They'll still kill his daughter."

"That might have been a bluff on Noah's part. He knows how to get to me." She swallowed the rest of her coffee. "I'm sure there was more than just that. Noah had a habit of getting into debt to dangerous people. He'd often pay it off by offering his services. There's a chance he got in over his head, and this group used that to their advantage."

"When you say 'this group,' who are you referring to?"

"Do you know who was on the other end, Jack?"

"Of what?"

"The line? The computer? The text? However you accepted your contracts, do you know who it was?"

"Not a clue. I did all of this to find out. I gathered what I could from my targets and then gave them a second chance. A new lease on life, you could say."

"Why did you want to know?"

"Because the bastards have been trying to kill me for years. I want to end it. It has to end. I have a daughter who needs me." He dropped his chin to his chest. "More like, I need her. I need the redemption."

They remained silent for several minutes as they processed the words hanging in the air between them. Did they understand each other better now, or were things worse? He understood why she didn't say something sooner. She had her own stuff to deal with between Rupert's and Noah's deception, and her injury.

The question now was how much more to reveal to her. Was she considering the same? If he took it to the next step, said a name, waited for her reaction, would that change the dynamic? Would it change the course they were on?

Two things happened in the next thirty seconds that did.

Jack felt his phone buzz against his leg. He retrieved it and accessed the message from Brandon.

"Clarissa's at a safe house in Warsaw. Sending you the deets. Also..."

The message lingered for several seconds. Another came in. An address for a bar. Helpful, but not what was keeping him on the edge of his seat.

"Jack?" Johanna said.

Looking up over the phone, he nodded.

She said, "I need to ask you if you've ever heard of a name before."

He said, "OK."

She said, "If not, you just need to forget it. Nothing good can come from knowing this."

He said, "Understood."

She took a deep breath, placed her hands flat on the table, closed her eyes. This was a big leap of faith for her.

The phone buzzed again. Jack glanced down.

Brandon messaged, "Frank Skinner."

Jack looked up at Johanna.

She said, "David Meadowcroft."

CHAPTER 29

THE FOG DISSIPATED INTO A LIGHT MIST AND BURNED OFF when the sun had risen four fingers into the sky. The view from the porch of the hostel she'd spent the night in was less than spectacular. Some would appreciate the countryside, the cows, the green that stretched for miles. Clarissa would if she were here under different circumstances.

Today, it meant she had to return to the city where she'd been taken. To the place where she had escaped. To the heart of the neighborhood where she'd witnessed a woman murdered by a bullet that was meant to assassinate Clarissa.

She'd blocked the memory. Being on the run and doing her damnedest to survive aided in the effort. This morning, while watching the fog lift and the sun burn through, the memory of the store owner lingered. Her story had been harrowing. Her death even more so.

She considered that most basic of tenets, *an eye for an eye*.

The older lady had confessed to a murder, even if it was only murder in her mind. As far as Clarissa was concerned, her husband had driven her to it. Even if the story she told had been whitewashed, toned down, a slight spin on the truth. She could have walked up behind him while he was reading his paper and put the barrel to the back of his head and pulled the trigger, and Clarissa would have said it was justifiable homicide.

She spat at the word. *Homicide.* The woman did the world a favor. That man didn't deserve to breathe the same air as others.

Needing respite from the images dancing with fire in her mind, Clarissa picked up her phone and read the message from Brandon for the fifth time. It filled her with hope. It filled her with anxiety. Beck couldn't be trusted, a man she'd spent the majority of her time with over the past five years. How could she trust a man she'd never met named Clyde Kemp?

Moments like this enhanced the drought in her life since her father passed. At times, she had Noble to fill the void. But no one could replace her father. More than just the little things, if he were alive, she could contact him and maybe get out of this mess. At worst, he might have information on Kemp. If Brandon had found the guy, he had ties to the U.S. Whether through military, intelligence, or some other position, she had to trust the guy would be friendly toward her.

And if he wasn't?

It wouldn't be the first time she found herself in such a situation.

She procrastinated a short while longer before gathering her things and driving the last leg of the journey. Anxiety clawed at her chest with every car that passed. She saw the face of the man who had clung to the Jetta's rear door. Imagined his lifeless body, nothing more than a speed bump on the road after she shot him.

Were these men and whoever they worked for looking for her in Warsaw? Or had they also gone to Ticino, Switzerland? Was she right thinking that no one would imagine she would return to the city?

Exiting the highway early, she found a parking lot to ditch the car. It could be the one thing that led to her downfall. Not wanting to take public transportation, she ordered a ride through Uber. Time passed slowly. The last five minutes felt excruciating. The city center wasn't far off. She could see the Warsaw Spire. The fields had turned into concrete. The trees into row homes.

The driver showed up and nodded at her as she slid into the back-seat. He confirmed her destination and didn't say another word. The lack of conversation was nice compared to some rides she'd had in an Uber or taxi. Still, she kept her vest unzipped with the pistol grip in reach should something happen.

Fifteen minutes passed and nothing happened. The driver pulled to the curb, said thank you and drove off the moment the door clicked shut.

Clarissa looked up at the sign that read THE RED, WHITE & BREW! An image formed of her contact. Rolling her eyes, she thought of her father's friends when she was a young teenager, about the time everyone started treating her like an adult. Their terrible jokes. The innuendo that perversely made its way into all of those jokes. It had not been directed at her. Rather at each other. This guy would probably fit right in with them. Hell, he might have been one of them.

She opened the door and saw five older men lined up at the bar all facing a guy with a buzz cut and faded tattoos running up and down each of his arms. He stopped mid-sentence and stared at her. The other men turned, out of synch with each other. Presumably, alcohol made the difference.

"Look at this sweet thing," the guy on the right end said.

"Eve warned you, Teddy. Not in my bar." The guy behind the bar leveled the other man with a look that said try me and find out. He looked up again and smiled at Clarissa. "This is an American bar, my friend. You gotta be able to speak *American* to be in here."

"I'm American," Clarissa said. "I believe we have a mutual friend."

His smile dropped. His eyes went vacant. "Bar's closed guys. Come back in an hour."

"Clyde, what the—" was all one of the guys could spit out before Clyde told them to leave.

"You all can come back in an hour or never again. Your choice." He stepped around the bar, gestured for Clarissa to head in.

The five guys downed what was left in their mugs. Sliding off their barstools, they filed out through the door, muttering curses under their breath.

Clyde waited for the door to shut behind them before turning toward Clarissa. He smiled. The corners of his eyes bunched up and dozens of lines spread toward his temples. Figuring him to be in his seventies, he had the physique of a man half his age. His features were hardened, no doubt from his years of service, but his eyes had a softness to them.

"Don't mind those guys and their foul language."

"I'm a military brat," she said. "Heard a lot worse."

"Suppose you have." He sized her up. She held her ground. "They'll be all right, though. In an hour they'll return, try to drink me out of business like they do every night."

"Did you know them before?"

"Before what?"

"Before you retired and came out here?"

"Ah, yeah, I see what you mean." He returned to his post behind the bar and grabbed a hand towel and began wiping down the bar top. "Other than Teddy, I've known them all for a long, long time."

"What's Teddy's story?"

"Teddy, yeah, well, let's see here." He grabbed each mug and dunked them in a sudsy sink. "He was a teacher back west."

"Back west?"

"The States."

"Oh, gotcha."

"Lost his wife and son and daughter in a car crash."

"Oh no." Clarissa thought about the comment he made to her and let it go. "Was he involved?"

Clyde nodded. "He was driving. Fell asleep at the wheel. It ate him up."

"I can imagine." She sat on the middle stool. "How'd he end up here?"

"Via San Francisco then Thailand, onward to Goa, India. Ah, Naples, Italy. And eventually here, teaching English."

"He taught English in all those places?"

"No, 'fraid not. Something much more violent."

Clarissa did not press for more information. Instead, she looked around the bar. The myriad of items on the wall hung without care or organization. The pieces didn't fit, and due to that, the decoration had its own charm.

"And you? When did you move here?"

"I never left, really." He pulled down a bottle of vodka with a Russian label and two rocks glasses, dropping three ice cubes in each before pouring a layer of vodka. "Eastern Europe was my theatre, if you know what I mean."

She nodded and said nothing.

"Yeah, I figured you would." He hoisted his glass and met hers halfway across the bar. "Cheers."

"Cheers."

"I did go back to the States, but I found a homeland that didn't want me anymore. Things had advanced so much. Computers and internet and cell phones. Granted, we have all that here now. But twenty years ago, this area was pretty far behind. You could get by as God intended, punching actual buttons on a phone and having a conversation. None of this texting or emailing, or... What is it they do now? Facing? Snapping? Ticker-talking?"

Clarissa giggled and his face flushed.

"Sorry," she said.

"It's the Irish in me." He smiled at her. "Don't let the fellas know that I even know those terms."

"I won't. Promise."

He refilled their glasses with a healthy pour. He leaned against the bar top, resting his forearms on the edge of the aged wood. "What kind of trouble are you in?"

"The bad kind," she said.

"Someone after you?"

She nodded.

"Who?"

"Not sure. Could be someone I know, or someone I knew, or maybe someone I've never met. Hard to tell, you know?"

"Sounds like you keep interesting company."

"Funny you say that, because I've been thinking the exact same thing lately. Like, what good are these friends if they're no better than enemies?"

"After years of straddling the line between love and hate, life and death, good and evil, I know one thing for certain. The main difference between friends and enemies is that enemies have seen our darkness and have mirrored it, while friends illuminate our path out of it."

She lowered the glass from her lips. "That's beautiful."

"I think I read it on a bathroom stall in a strip club."

"Well, it's still beautiful. Guess someone was inspired by what they saw on stage that night."

They shared a laugh and finished their drinks.

"All right," he said. "Let me show you to your room before those clowns come back for more of my beer."

Clarissa looked over her shoulder toward the front window before following Clyde through a door just down the hallway behind the bar. She couldn't help but notice two men leaning against the glass. Probably the guys who'd been here when she entered.

She hoped.

CHAPTER 30

"So explain this to me," Brett said. "I want to make sure I know what I'm looking for."

Brandon sat at the table with Brett across from him and Thomas to his left. They were eating again, sandwiches Brett had picked up from a little store nearby. Brandon wasn't fond of the dill pickles on it, but he managed.

During the time Brett had been gone, Brandon put together several pieces of the puzzle, but it had all fallen into place after Thomas revealed that a subcommittee pulled Meadowcroft's funding after an Agency guy died. He figured it was a stretch when he began digging. But the data lined up, and now he was certain.

Brandon started from the beginning. "Frank Skinner was the head of a small intelligence agency—more of a unit, really—that operated without license. It was called the SIS. He recruited Noble in the early 2000s. Jack stayed on board with him for a few years before going out on his own, though he kept picking up work from Frank."

"They had a good relationship then?"

"Then, yes. As time went on, it became tenuous at best." Brandon thought back on several missions. "It was Frank who assigned Jack the job to kill you."

"Right."

The events surrounding that ordeal clouded Brandon's memories for a minute. Jack and Bear had suffered greatly. So had Brandon.

"Sometime after that," Brandon said, "Jack took an assignment from a crime boss to handle a guy named Thanos. This ultimately led to him meeting Meadowcroft, who even back then was pretty damn rich. His influence and power was starting to grow back then."

"Interesting," Brett said. "Wonder if Meadowcroft remembers Jack from that incident?"

Thomas piped up. "He doesn't forget a name or a face. Remarkable, really."

They both nodded at the guy.

Brandon continued. "Jack and Frank's relationship fell apart a bit after the job to take you out, Brett. Some seven years or so later, Jack was corralled into working with the guy again. They maintained some semblance of a working friendship for a short time, but it went south again. Then *you* showed up to kill Jack—"

"Such a tangled web, isn't it?" Brett chuckled.

Brandon didn't. "Things came to a head four years ago."

"Jack killed Frank."

"Correct." Brandon reviewed the diagram he had made piecing this all together. "And at that time, Skinner was high up in the Agency. He had some pull. No, not some. He had a lot of pull. He also had quite a few enemies in the Agency, as well as the House and Senate. Frank didn't care, so long as he maintained his connection with his powerful allies. One of those allies was none other than David Meadowcroft."

"Frank secured the funding for this project?"

"You are on fire, Brett!" Brandon returned the guy's smile. "Skinner wanted that project to come to fruition. Apparently, it had become an obsession of his. He got Meadowcroft anything he wanted. Frank figured he could pilot the program, advance his career further, and get rich as hell. Didn't end that way for him, of course. Whether that's fortunate or unfortunate is up to how well you knew him, I suppose, and not many people really knew Frank Skinner. He'd spent so many years in the shadows. Even in his position in the Agency, few interfaced with him. And I'm guessing he liked it that way."

"All right," Brett said. "Skinner climbs the ranks. Noble takes him down. Anyone clued into our world figures the reason Noble was being hunted was because he killed Skinner, and people assume it's us hunting him."

"Us?"

"You know what I mean. The Agency, whoever."

"Yeah." Brandon looked at Thomas. "This make sense to you?"

The guy nodded. "Like I said, I never dug into the details, but David had, well, actually, *has* contacts like this Skinner guy in intelligence communities around the world. He tried to get support from some of them following the U.S. government pulling out, but there wasn't much success. He took another route, self-funding and untraceable funds."

"Terrorists," Brett said.

Thomas shrugged. "Beyond my paygrade. But, like I said, the guy is an awful human being. Could've done so much for humanity and instead seems hellbent on destroying it."

"Well, we can't let him do that," Brett said.

"No, we can't," Brandon said. "That's why I need you to go to Chicago."

"What's in Chicago?"

"The main office," Thomas said. "If you are going to find David, that's the place. He probably won't be there, but there are people there who know where to find him. It'll be tough getting to them, though."

"I don't need him to get to them," Brandon said. "I need access to Meadowcroft's personal information. His calendar, contacts, and email accounts. Is Chicago where we can get that, Thomas?"

The man nodded and looked at Brett. "If you can get to the tenth floor, you can get Brandon this access."

"Why not you?" Brandon said.

"They'd suspect something if I showed up there," Thomas said.

"Guess I know what I gotta do," Brett said.

Twenty minutes later, Brett was at the front door, packed, flight booked, ready to leave for Chicago. Thomas briefed him on the security challenges he might face while there. He drew a map of the main floor and showed Brett an exterior door that was unmonitored. Knowing a disguise would go a long way, Thomas told Brett how to get from that entrance to the janitors' room.

After Brett departed, they turned their attention to the Banyan project. Brandon had to know how deep this went. Who was involved? Who had been killed due to their involvement in the project? Who had been killed because they wanted to stop the project?

"There's gotta be something here," Brandon said. "A record of someone who disappeared one day. Never showed up for work again. Was never heard from again."

"I don't doubt that's happened," Thomas said. "But you won't find evidence of it in the system."

Brandon knew the guy was right; spending time searching was an exercise in futility. Meadowcroft would be sure to have the coverup in place long before taking action.

"Employment records exist, right?" Brandon said.

Thomas nodded. He squinted as he looked over Brandon's head.

"Dates of employment would exist in those records." Brandon tapped at the keyboard. "We just need to find everyone who left and then run a script to Google all of them with a few keywords like missing, obituary, deceased, and so on."

"That might work." Thomas moved a chair close to Brandon and sat down. He reached for the keyboard. "May I?"

"Have at it."

A few minutes later, Thomas had an employee database opened and filtered down to every employee who had stopped working for the company. He copied all the names into an Excel file, then added home addresses and phone numbers. There were hundreds.

Brandon took over again. He wrote a script to cycle through the names, adding bits of information and additional keywords. The searches took place in the background while they were talking through the next steps.

"I've got some ways to check on any possible leads," Brandon said.

"How so?" Thomas said.

"Less you know, the better. Let's just say I've got access to some systems very few other people do."

"OK, so you'll be able to find out what the police know?"

"Something like that."

"Will you notify them of possible wrongdoing?"

"Not sure we have time for all that. But with those reports, we can get the family information. With that, we can find out who knows what. Like, did the missing or deceased confide in them prior to losing their jobs?"

"Ah, I see." Thomas leaned over the table toward the computer. "We can act like we're new detectives assigned to the case, following up."

"There you go, man! Getting the hang of Geekspionage."

Thomas laughed. "Geekspionage. I like it."

"Just coined the phrase. With all these advancements going on with AI and such, one of us is going to be the next James Bond."

Thomas pointed at the screen. "It's done searching."

Brandon's smile faded and his hopes sank when he looked at the results. "That can't be right." He ran through his script one more time. He wanted to throw the laptop in the trash. "Not a single one turned up as missing or dead?"

Thomas squeezed Brandon's shoulder. "If it happened, it never filtered down to my level."

"There's gotta be..." Brandon stopped as he watched Thomas stiffen up, face turned toward the ceiling. "You all right, dude?"

"Casey Whitworth." The two words ran together.

"Who's that?" Brandon asked.

"She was before my time, but there were rumors that she'd been... taken care of, if you know what I mean."

"Yeah, I think I do." Brandon's fingers returned to the keys. He searched the name in the database filtered for past employees. His heart thumped against his chest while waiting for the results. He sighed. "Let down again." He shook his head, turned and looked at Thomas. "You sure this lady actually worked there?"

"I know it." Thomas pulled out his phone. He started to type out a message.

"Whoa. What're you doing? You can't text someone now. Get us all shot up."

Thomas sat the phone down. "Sorry, you're right. I was thinking—"

Brandon held up a finger. He backed out of his current query and began typing a new one. Twenty seconds later, he hit return. The system processed for several seconds before returning a single row that started with the name Casey Whitworth.

CHAPTER 31

AN HOUR INTO THE DRIVE TO THE ADDRESS IN WARSAW, JACK hadn't spoken a word despite multiple attempts by Johanna to get information out of him. Focusing on the road in front of him, he cursed at anyone who got in his way. This wasn't the time to slow down. He laid on the horn frequently. This drew a healthy dose of criticism from his passenger, which he ignored.

Rolling the window down a few inches, He let the cool air saturate his face and hair and hands. The smell of the highway infiltrated his nostrils. The sound of tires on asphalt overwhelmed the cabin, and he couldn't hear the radio. Not that he'd paid much attention to it. Couldn't recall if rock or jazz or classical had been playing.

After the windows were rolled back up, he looked at Johanna, who met his gaze with an icy stare of her own. Hiking her eyebrows, she widened her eyes as if to say, "What's your problem?"

He couldn't blame her. When she had mentioned a name and Brandon had texted a name, Jack went into a shell. He had helped her up from her chair and took her by the arm and led her back to the car. Hadn't said a word since. Kept the pedal down until someone got in his way. Kept rolling the window down to shake the cobwebs free. Kept thinking of the last time he saw David Meadowcroft and Frank Skinner.

The connection had been made. Now he had to figure out why. Perhaps he needed to talk through it.

"I met David Meadowcroft well over a decade ago. I'd been working with an FBI agent on a messed-up case and he was her contact. He helped us out a bit, but something was off. I returned to see him at the end of the ordeal, and he'd packed up his facility and was gone. Things didn't work out for me to find him again. Tell you the truth, I'd forgotten all about him."

Johanna took a few moments to respond, likely letting go of her aggravation to get the words out clearly. "Why'd you lock up with me over this if he didn't mean much to you?"

"Because I got a text."

"Yeah, I noticed."

"And it had a name as well."

He saw her in his peripheral, staring, waiting.

"Are you really going to make me ask?" she said.

"Frank Skinner."

"Oh my God." Reaching out, she touched his forearm. "It was you. You killed Skinner in France. What was that? Four years ago?"

Jack nodded his response.

"You never paid a price for it?"

He laughed. "Yeah, I received my freedom a year or so later. I've been the hunted ever since."

"I can imagine. Taking down a CIA—"

"The CIA wants nothing to do with me. I did them a favor. Did the country a favor. Hell, Johanna, I did you and the rest of the world a favor getting rid of that pathetic, double-crossing son of a bitch."

"What's the link then? Between Skinner and Meadowcroft?"

He'd hoped she could answer that question. Perhaps her resources had a way of making the connection. She'd been the one to bring up Meadowcroft.

"I was hoping you knew," he said.

She shook her head.

"What do you know of Meadowcroft?" he asked.

She blew a puff of air through pursed lips. "We know he's funneling in money to work on some super-soldier project. from anybody willing to donate. He lost his government funding a long time ago. Once we were turned onto him, we started noticing lots of cryptic communications coming from all over Europe and Africa and the Middle East. Some of it from terrorists. But other communications revealed something else sinister."

"Contracts."

"Yep. He was putting out hits on people who'd interfered. All through an intermediary, of course. We believe that's who you've interfaced with all this time. The hope was Van de Berg could lead us to that person once we hit him with the evidence of all his kills. But then he turned out to be you and we quickly surmised something else was brewing."

"I left all of them alive," he said. "None of them gave up information about Meadowcroft."

"None had direct ties to him. They wouldn't have ever figured he'd want them dead. They played some integral role in a company, or as a witness to someone who the company needed. It took digging on each of those victims, I mean targets, to make these connections. We went deep to find the links to Meadowcroft. They were all there."

"Every single one?" he asked.

She nodded. "We can hunt them down if need be."

"Never find them. Not in time, at least. Their new identities are solid."

Jack pulled off the highway at the next exit. A mile down the road, they stopped at a roadside table. Johanna didn't feel up to climbing out, so he rolled down the windows and they sat there for a few minutes, both lost in thought.

A gentle breeze rolled through the car. A family was seated at a picnic table. Children laughed and yelled as they played nearby. Noble closed his eyes and absorbed the peaceful situation. A moment or two was all he needed.

He broke the silence in the car.

"Why does Meadowcroft need funding from terrorists and other unsavory characters? Guy was loaded and had tons of connections."

"He lost his funding." She angled her phone so Jack could see what she had looked up. "One month to the day after you killed Skinner."

It took a few moments for him to process the information. "Skinner was his connection? Frank Skinner? He got him the funding?"

"Makes sense, right? Look at what he did in the CIA. He would want that program to succeed. I know if I was the link to something like this, I'd sure as hell get promoted when the program came to fruition."

"I knew Frank well," Jack said. "At least some of the time. He was a go-getter. Always wanted to advance. But, he was also shady, so I'm not sure his involvement with Meadowcroft had good intentions behind it."

Leaning against her door, the wind whipped strands of her hair about her face. Jack was admiring her looks at that moment when he noticed her wince.

"All OK?" he asked.

"Sharp pain," she said.

"Stomach?"

She grabbed her abdomen.

"This been happening all along?"

Shaking her head, she closed her eyes.

"Do we need to find another doctor?"

"It's abating. I think I'm good, but I'd like to lie down in the back."

Jack hopped out and ran around to the other side of the car. Two kids stopped playing with sticks and stared at him. He offered a salute. They returned it with smiles and laughs and went back to trying to poke each other's eyes out much to their mother's dismay as she called after them in a language Jack didn't understand.

A few minutes later, Jack and Johanna were back on the highway. Johanna had dozed off, leaving Noble to the meditative passing of the road. His thoughts weren't still. Racing to make connections between people he'd encountered and places he'd been over the past decade, particularly the past four years.

He thought about Clive and Sadie and the rest of the team. A team he could have joined. Probably should've joined. Then he would've had a leg up on this situation before it came to a head. Did Clive know what was going on? He thought about establishing a channel to connect with the man, but decided against it. No point bringing Clive in to risk his and his teams' lives. The guy would jump right in without a second thought. That was if Clive *didn't* know what was happening. Noble had to consider the opposite, that Clive was somehow involved. The guy worked for the highest bidder, after all. And in that case, giving Clive a beacon, even for a second, would spell doom for Jack.

The road stretched open as far as Noble could see. A few cars dotted the lanes ahead. There was plenty of distance between them. Jack settled into the lull. For the first time since leaving the gas station, his thoughts melded into his breath, and he cleared his mind. There were a few remaining connections that needed to be made, and he couldn't make them yet, not without input from Brandon and Clarissa. The former he'd call when he reached Warsaw and made face-to-face contact with the latter.

It'd been a while since they'd spent any real time together. The last time had been in the months following Skinner's death. He'd hid out in Italy, using her place. She would show up and spend weekends with him when she could. Sometimes she'd even be there during the week. It was nice while it lasted.

When it came to Jack and Clarissa, it never lasted.

Would this experience be any different?

Doubt crept into his mind. Not just doubt, more like a resounding "no" from a choir of baritone angels. No one should hitch themselves to Noble, least of all her.

Johanna moaned and shifted in the backseat. Jack turned his head to observe her, noting she'd started sweating and looked a little pale. Neither were good signs.

"Hang in there," he said. "Two hours to go."

CHAPTER 32

BRETT STARED AT THE GROUND BELOW. ROADS AND HOUSES and cars all looked like the miniature decorations around the train table his dad had set up in the basement. The guy next to him was too big for his seat and kept elbowing Brett. He hated window seats in coach. He hated coach, especially row thirty-two on a 737.

The drive to his contact's house would take longer than the flight from Philly to Chicago. Once there, his contact could outfit him with anything he needed. Guns. Ammo. Comms devices. Listening devices. How much of the mission would be recon versus attack? That depended on what he encountered at Meadowcroft's headquarters. Try as he may, and as skilled as the man was, Brandon couldn't locate David Meadowcroft. Couldn't even find a last known location that wasn't three months old, and that came from a photo snapped as he walked out of a swanky L.A. restaurant and posted on an obscure activist blog calling Meadowcroft the devil.

The odd photo struck Brett. Why would someone so high-profile within the government and so well-known to the people that hated him allow himself to be photographed? He tossed around the idea that Meadowcroft employed a body double. Perhaps several body doubles. If that were the case, why weren't they being deployed around the world to sow confusion as to the man's whereabouts?

The train of thoughts looped around like an infinity symbol. He pulled out his phone and opened a Sudoku app, tapped on the third to hardest level and spent the rest of the flight knocking out two puzzles. Before Brett knew it, they were on the ground, shuffling off the plane. He made his way through O'Hare, his least favorite airport in the country, and rented a car under one of his assumed names. From there, he hopped on 94, crossed the border into Wisconsin, and drove to Kenosha.

His contact had a place on 1st Street with a view of the lake. It was a chilly afternoon, and the wind whipping off the water made it feel like the middle of winter. He hopped from foot to foot while waiting at the door for his guy to answer.

A man with a long beard that stretched from an inch under his eyes to the middle of his chest and even longer hair on his head, answered. The two exchanged the kind of nod and smile that only two people who'd been through some serious shit together could. The man welcomed Brett in.

"Good to see you, Chris," Brett said.

"Likewise, old friend. How's life been treating you?"

"Hard to complain. Keeping busy."

"I can see. Glad you were able to stop by amid all the madness." Chris patted him on the shoulder and smiled. "Wanna get down to business?"

"Let's do it."

Chris led Brett upstairs. They stopped at a door that required an access code. After punching it in, Chris put his shoulder to the door and pushed it open.

"Reinforced everything up here. Steel door. Steel framing with no more than three inches gap between each stud. And this is just to get into the airlock."

"Airlock?"

"Well, that's what I call it. Feel like I'm a spaceman or something when I say it."

Looking at the guy's bloodshot eyes, clothing, hair and beard, Brett figured Chris was a spaceman morning to night, smoking pot all day.

The next door required another access code. Chris said the same thing about the door, the framing. The door popped open, and Brett saw a room about twenty feet long and ten feet wide. The right wall was essentially a large gun rack. Three quarters of it was long guns, pistols, and MP7s. He had body armor and knives and other weapons.

The opposite wall was tech central. Phones, GPS, comms equipment, a few parabolic listening devices, and a few smaller devices.

"You know what you need?" Chris asked.

"Pretty simple, I think. This is a walk-in, walk-out situation, so two of those HK VP9s, and that Sig P938 with an ankle holster. I'll take a shoulder holster and an IWB for the HKs."

"All right." Chris started digging through a drawer along the far wall. He pulled out the holsters. "Saw you eyeing the MP7s. Want one?"

Brett did indeed want one. "You don't mind?"

"Not at all. Just gotta promise to put it to good use."

"If I find the bastard I'm looking for, he's likely to be surrounded by a team of guys like us. I think the MP7 will be a nice equalizer."

"Love the way you think, Brett. Always have."

Brett chuckled. "You too, bro." He glanced over at the comms equipment. "Any chance you wanna ride along? Be my eyes in the field? You were the best at that back in the day."

"You care if I smoke pot in the car?"

"Just roll down the window so I don't get a contact buzz."

"Pull your car around back. I'll get the gear downstairs and meet you at the rear door."

Brett exited the room and headed outside. The chilled wind hit him in the face, made his eyes water. He stared out at the lake. He felt small for a moment and took stock of his place in the world. His job wasn't glorious. It wasn't always easy. Sometimes good people had to die because they did something stupid, made a bad decision, crossed the wrong person. Those were the worst.

But this? Destroying Meadowcroft? While not a sanctioned job, he'd accept it a hundred times out of a hundred and take pleasure in completing it. Meadowcroft had destroyed many lives for nothing more than gaining more power.

He hopped in the car and drove around back where Chris waited with the comms equipment. Brett went back inside and fit the holsters to his body and placed the weapons inside them. They concealed the MP7 in the trunk. Chris sat in the passenger seat with a MacBook on his lap and another device Brett had never seen perched on the dash. Brett didn't ask what it was for. It was like asking Brandon a question. He wouldn't understand.

Brett looked over at Chris. "Ready?"

"Let's roll."

CHAPTER 33

CASEY WHITWORTH WAS BORN IN NEW HAMPSHIRE AND moved around until the age of ten when her father was stationed at Norfolk Naval Air Station. She spent the rest of her youth in Virginia Beach. Attended public school. Played soccer and ran track. She was a straight A student who only missed one day of high school. She went to Duke on a full scholarship and graduated in the top one percent of her class. Graduate school followed, then her PhD.

She began her internship with Meadowcroft during her junior year of college and never left the company. She never married and rarely dated. She never had kids. She rarely spoke to her parents who, by all accounts, loved and supported her. They figured she was a shut-in who had become all-absorbed with work and solving a single problem.

The problem? According to her father, she wanted to engineer the soldier of the future. It consumed her. It was all Casey would talk about on the rare occasions they spoke. He and his wife had concerns, of course. She stopped visiting when she was twenty-eight. Emails were rare, as were texts when they became the more common form of communication among people. Phone calls were almost non-existent. They'd hear from her two or three times a year.

Until 2014.

She sent a text on December 31, 2013.

The content was different than her other messages.

"Happy New Year. Miss you, Dad. I'm coming home soon."

She never made it there.

CHAPTER 34

BRANDON STARED AT THE NOTES FROM HIS CONVERSATION with Mr. Whitworth. The man broke down and sobbed a couple of times. He pleaded for this new detective to take action against Meadowcroft, the company and the man. Brandon muddled through his responses. It was easier to act like someone he wasn't through other forms of dialog. Over the phone with a still-grieving father? Forget it. He found himself choking up during the conversation.

Ending it with a promise that they'd find his daughter. No actual detective would say that. But they didn't have the skills Brandon had.

Thomas reviewed the information and went back to his room to think about every story he'd heard regarding Casey. It had been a while, he said, since anyone last spoke of her. He mentioned that he considered her to be a myth of sorts. A real person whose legend had blown up after she disappeared.

And was it all that strange?

People escape their lives every single day. In this day and age, it had somehow become easier to ghost most everyone in your world. But *most* was the key. With technology, the lure to reach out to that one friend could be strong.

If Casey was alive—and that was a big if considering who she worked for—would she have done so?

Her father had provided him with a list of all of her friends on social media. There weren't many. Some acquaintances from high school and college, a few people from work, and other professional contacts. When Brandon asked if any of them were especially close with his daughter, he scoffed, saying she had never maintained a close friendship for more than a few months, even when she was a little girl, and it got worse in high school and college.

Brandon considered this as he painted an image of the woman's personality and psychological make up. She wasn't introverted, according to her father. Rather, she disliked most people, and there was no obvious reason. Her drive was as intense as anyone he'd ever seen. Casey refused to fail, no matter what pain she endured. Once, she had completed a four-hundred-meter race on an ankle that broke a hundred meters in.

She had fortitude *and* an intense dislike for most people.

Sports had always been a major part of her life. Even after college, she routinely played in pickup games and adult leagues up until her disappearance. All this while she refused to hang out with old friends, co-workers, and her family.

Brandon sat back and looked over the list again. Her father had been building it since the year Casey disappeared. He'd added as much information on each person as he could find. When they knew his daughter. Where they lived at the time and now. How they were associated.

Relaxing his gaze, he scanned up and down the columns looking for anything that stood out, whether a pattern or an anomaly.

"A teammate," he muttered.

Brandon sat up straight and homed in on the only cell in the spreadsheet that said college teammate.

He called up the stairs. "Hey, Thomas, come down here."

Thomas plodded down the steps and jogged over to the table. "What's up, boss?"

Brandon felt a bit of pride at hearing that. It also made him feel old.

"I was looking through this list her father provided," he said.

"Yeah?"

"Tell me if anything stands out to you."

Thomas reached for the laptop. "May I?"

"Sure." Brandon leaned over his phone. Waiting messages attempted to draw him in. Flipping the phone over, he reminded himself to take it one thing at a time. Clarissa was settled. Jack was on his way to her location. If things had blown up, anything he could do from the middle of Pennsylvania could wait a few more minutes.

He gave Thomas a few minutes to stare at the data, not expecting the guy to understand. Brandon had spent several minutes thinking it through before the revelation smacked him in the mouth.

"She only remained friends with one teammate?" Thomas leaned so close his nose nearly touched the screen. "And there's, like, hardly any co-workers on there. At least that I recognize. Could she just not make friends?"

"I don't think she wanted to."

"Why?"

"Sometimes life is better lived alone."

"Do you really believe that?"

Brandon nodded, though he was thinking about Kimberlee while he did so. Would this all have gone down this way if she hadn't left? There was a chance it could have turned out worse.

"Not me," Thomas said. "Something had to drive her to be like that."

"Not everyone is like you, and that's probably a good thing." He squeezed out a chuckle that came across as half-hearted and condescending.

"Whatever."

"Yeah, whatever." Brandon paused for a beat to collect his thoughts. She had driven people away. Parents, classmates, teammates, and co-workers. "Let's follow up on the woman she played soccer with at Duke."

"Chastity Braun. OK, on it." Thomas walked around the table to where his laptop was set up. He asked for the spelling of her last name, then got to work.

Brandon took a moment to pass along the information to Brett. He opened up a terminal window and ran a program to establish a channel for secure contact. Once connected, he transferred the call to his cell phone.

"That you, Brandon?"

"Yessir."

"On my way to HQ now. What's up?"

"Perfect, perfect. I got a couple names for you to look into while you're poking around."

"Go ahead."

"Casey Whitworth." He paused a beat while Brett repeated the name. "Chastity Braun."

"Context?"

"Whitworth worked for Meadowcroft until she disappeared in 2014."

"Disappeared?"

"Yeah, and get this. She's still listed as an employee."

"Interesting. What about the other lady?"

"Braun," Brandon said. "We're not sure. She's not an employee, but she's got a connection with Whitworth. Kinda stands out among all her other contacts and people connected through social media."

"How so?" Brett asked.

"Whitworth was an All-American soccer player at Duke. Athlete her whole life. Braun is the only teammate that showed up in her contacts."

"That's odd. Really odd, right?"

"Well, I was never much of an athlete," Brandon said with a laugh. "But some of the guys from chess club are still my best friends."

Thomas looked up with a smile and mouthed, "Nerd."

It didn't make Brandon feel any better. "Look, be careful and make sure you call me when you get there. I think we can hijack the security feed, but I'm gonna need you to be my eyes once you're inside."

"Got it." Brett disconnected the call.

Thomas stood up and stretched and went to the fridge and grabbed a Michelob Ultra. He held it up in the air. "Want one?"

"Why the hell not," Brandon said.

He wheeled back from the table and met Thomas next to the fridge. The bottle was wet and cold and so was the brew. Brandon grimaced at the bitter taste. He knew it would abate with each further sip. He wasn't accustomed to day drinking, or drinking at all, really. It never suited him. But he figured he could use a little mental lubrication today. It'd keep him a little more relaxed, a little less anxious.

"We need to find something that directly ties David Meadowcroft to the contracts on Jack Noble and Clarissa Abbot. I know it won't be in any of these files on any of these servers. We might need Brett to rip the confession out of him."

Thomas nodded and smiled. "I wouldn't mind witnessing that. You know, I feel like a total jerk for getting wrapped up in this. I try to tell myself I was in too deep before I realized I'd waded into the water, but that's a lie. The signs were there. I ignored them."

"Why?" Brandon asked. He knew the answer.

"Money, for one," Thomas said.

"Of course. It's always about the money."

"Is it?" Thomas leaned back against the counter and crossed his right ankle over his left. "What about power? Influence? Maybe even fame?"

Brandon understood where the guy was coming from. He had wanted all of those things before, too. Every time he acquired more money or influence, he felt a little worse about himself. Up to a point. Eventually, the soul is corrupted past the hope of salvation.

Was he unredeemable?

Thoughts of what was going to happen to him soon resurfaced. There had been plenty of distractions to keep his mind occupied enough that it didn't dwell on the deaths of the other trial participants. He hadn't dug too far into their history yet, but he knew they had all been on the pills longer than he had. How long had they suffered from symptoms like his? Only thing he knew for sure was that they were all dead. He might be soon, as well.

And if that were the case, he wanted to see everyone involved with the Banyan project destroyed before he died.

Thomas notwithstanding.

The other man had returned to his laptop and continued his search. It wasn't long before he stood up again, this time white as a starched bedsheet. He rubbed his forehead, slid his fingers down the sides of his nose, and pinched his nostrils shut.

"You got a nosebleed or something?" Brandon asked.

Thomas clenched his eyes shut. He bit down hard. His jaw muscles bulged. His lips curled back.

"Dude, are you OK?" Brandon hurried toward the man. "You need to sit down again?"

Thomas's face went slack, his eyes drooped, his shoulders slumped. He eased back into his chair and looked at Brandon. "The headaches from the medication." He blinked rapidly. "They're a bitch, aren't they?"

CHAPTER 35

JACK STOOD ON THE STREET BESIDE THE CAR AND LOOKED UP at the sign. "The RED, WHITE, AND BREW!" Shaking his head, he slammed the car door shut.

Gasoline vapors hung in the still air. The storm-cloud-darkened sky did little to make the working-class neighborhood attractive. Not that it was unattractive. It just existed, as did the people here. The kind of folks who got up and went to their jobs and came home in the evening. They'd have a bite to eat. Maybe watch some TV and have a beer or glass of wine. If they were social, they'd probably head out to their favorite bar, which was unlikely to be the RED, WHITE, AND BREW!

Presumably, the locals hated the place. Or rather, what it stood for. Americans coming in and taking up space in their town. Americans who had no idea what it was like to grow up in Warsaw. Americans who didn't live with the threat of annihilation from the enemy across the border. Americans who probably worked hard and busted their ass and saved up enough and had enough retirement to come live here, in *their* neighborhood.

The looks Jack received from a couple of old men hustling along with canes in their right hands and beanies on their heads did nothing but confirm Jack's suspicions.

He didn't care. Nowhere for long, he wouldn't be in Warsaw for long.

Opening the rear passenger door, he knelt down. Johanna looked as bad as she had before Tobias the doctor had fixed her. A temporary solution, it seemed. He reached and brushed her hair out of her face, tucking it behind her ear.

"How are you holding up?" he asked.

She blinked him into focus and wiped drool from the corner of her mouth. "Not so hot." Looking over his shoulder, she made a face at the sign behind him. "Where the hell are we?"

"Warsaw."

"I thought so." When she smiled, he couldn't help but return it. "Jack, I really need to get to a hospital. I...I'll deal with whatever consequences come of that. OK? You know I won't mention you, right?"

Jack hesitated before answering. He wanted to believe her. He needed to believe her. After all, he could've bolted and left her behind at the restaurant and after a couple hours on the road, he'd be in the wind again. Pull over at a random rest stop. Head off into the woods. Hike along the highway until civilization returned. Usually wasn't that far off.

"I know you won't, Johanna." He took her hand in his and she pulled his hand to her face. It was soft, warm. "The guy who owns this place is a friend. I think he'll be able to help get you to a hospital, and it won't require me to be there. Are you comfortable with that?"

Her eyes shut, and her head eased down. He ran his hand through her hair, startling her awake. "Yeah, sure. Just get me there."

"Do you think you can get out of the car?"

She squeaked out, "No."

He rose and checked the street. Empty for the most part. The old guys had reached the other end of the block. A few women hung around outside a laundromat. Not much else going on.

"I'm gonna run inside. Doors'll be locked, but if anyone touches the car, scream as loud as you can."

She mocked him with a weak, "Ahhh," which made both of them smile. Then said, "Go, we're wasting time."

After he shut the car door, he confirmed it was locked. He took a deep breath as he turned around and walked up to the door. The sign on it said OPEN. Leaning his shoulder into it, he entered. Five guys occupied five stools along a wooden bar top. All of them looked over their shoulders at him. One looked at him more intently than the others. That was the guy to watch out for.

"Looking for Clyde," Jack said.

No one said anything back. Staring at him like he had entered the wrong place at the wrong time.

"He's hosting a friend of mine," Jack said.

The guy on the end, the one who stared hardest, hopped off his stool and walked over. He carried himself with confidence, but the guy was no match for Noble, even if he was armed.

"Not looking for any trouble here," Jack said. "We have a common contact who helped my friend get here and I need to help her. There's also a woman outside in need of medical attention. Now, if you'll just point—"

"Jack."

He turned his attention toward the voice he could never forget. Clarissa smiled as tears welled up in her eyes, covering her mouth to keep a sob at bay. She ran over and slammed into him with a hug so tight he thought she was going to dislocate a vertebra.

"I have so much to tell you," she said.

"Same here," he said. "But first, I really need some help out here. My friend has internal injuries. She's not the kind of person who should go to the hospital, but I think if your host or these guys are willing to help, we can make up a story that they found her on the side of the road. It would make sense. She has an incision. She can say she has no recollection of the events of the past few days."

"Yes, let's do that." A new guy appeared from a doorway in the hall. This was the type of guy Jack was used to dealing with. The kind of man who took shit off no one. Give you the shirt off his back and take it back if you acted out of line while wearing it. An old warhorse, reporting for duty. "Name's Clyde."

"Noble."

Pointing at the guys on the second and third stool, he said, "You two, go out and get his friend. I'll pull my vehicle around. You others, remain here with Clarissa and Noble. Lock the place up after I leave." He turned toward the back, then tossed a look over his shoulder. "We'll be back shortly."

Jack followed the guys out front to unlock the car. Hung around a few minutes longer as they pulled Johanna out and placed her in Clyde's vehicle. She was barely coherent, hardly able to open her eyes. Jack stopped them before they shut the door. Kneeling on the curb, he leaned over her and brushed the hair out of her face.

"Don't know if you can hear me, Johanna," he said. "I'm gonna put an end to this. I'm gonna find the bastard who's responsible for hurting you, and I'm gonna put an end to him." He took her hand in his and felt a little comfort when she squeezed. "You're going to be all right."

Her eyes fluttered open. Johanna looked younger, almost childlike in that moment. The words strained against her parched mouth and lips. "Promise?"

"Promise."

"We better get her to the hospital," Clyde said.

Jack rose and stepped back. All three men hopped in and drove off. Jack waited until they turned out of sight and went back inside.

Clarissa met him with a sad smile. He reached out and cupped the side of her face. He wiped away the tear streaking down her cheek.

"Come on now," he said. "Hasn't been that long, has it?"

"Six months since we last talked?" Her gaze danced from eye to eye.

"Something like that. To tell you the truth, I wasn't sure what to expect when I got here."

"Did it match your expectations?"

Trying to laugh, the gravity of the situation outside made it impossible. "Can't say yes, and can't say no. But this is the kind of place I think you'd find anywhere in the world."

"Except back home."

"*Especially* back home."

Both shared a smile, and she stepped in closer. Her arms threaded through his. She leaned in and pulled him close. Her head rested on his chest. He inhaled her scent. It always felt natural. Moments like this. In the beginning, at least. Over time, the longing faded, and all they were left with was twenty-plus years between them.

"Why don't you two go get a room?" one of the guys said, and the others cackled and Jack wanted to join in, if only to feel a moment of relief.

He pulled back and looked Clarissa in the eye. "Is there somewhere we can talk?"

Nodding as she let him go, the tips of her left fingers traced down his arm, found his palm, intertwined with his fingers. "Come on." She pulled him past the bar. He tried to stop to pour a drink. "Not now. This is serious."

"So's my thirst." He couldn't help it. Something about her brought it out in him. The situation didn't feel as dangerous. Though, he knew it was.

"Come on." Then she looked back at the guys on the stools. "Make sure you lock up like Clyde said."

He followed her down the hall and through a door that fed into another hall. At the end of it, they entered a room set up like a studio apartment, with a small stove and fridge, a small table, a two-seater couch, old TV, and a bed in the far corner.

"It's homey," he said.

"It's just for a few nights," she said.

"Until you get back on your feet," he said.

When she smiled, he grinned and for a moment, he wanted to lean in and kiss her, and he could tell she wanted him to. But for every happy second that passed, there was one not so pleasant. Johanna danced through his thoughts, vibrant like the night he met her, then dying, like the way he left her.

Clarissa noticed the swing in his mood and reached for his hand. "Your friend?"

He nodded.

"Is she going to be OK?"

"First doc patched her up, seemed confident. Didn't take but fourteen hours before she started going downhill again. Gradual at first. Seemed to ramp up the closer we got to Warsaw."

"What happened?"

He popped open the fridge and was disappointed when there wasn't a beer there to greet him. Looking around, he caught her shaking her head at him.

"What?"

"Do you need a drink that badly?"

"Any idea the week I've had?"

Clarissa rolled her eyes as she turned away. He watched her lift onto the tips of her toes and open a square cabinet door. She came down with a glass bottle full of clear liquid with Russian words on the label.

"Is that all you got?" he said.

"Are you in a position to complain about it?" she said.

"Well, there kinda is a bar right down the hall."

She produced two cups from the drying rack and set them upright. The air between them smelled like a hospital when she opened the lid. The vodka sloshed in the cup and crested one side then the other before settling down. Clarissa picked up both cups, shoved one toward Jack.

"Drink," she said.

"It's warm," he said.

"It'll put hair on your chest."

"Maybe I'll catch up to you."

"Are you kidding me?" After she stopped shaking her head, she lifted the glass to her lips and downed half the contents.

Jack had no choice but to follow suit, only he downed the entire glass. Fire followed the vodka down his throat. He grimaced against it. He stifled a cough. He looked away when Clarissa laughed at him and then poured him another double.

"So, tell me about your week?" She forced a smile, which Jack appreciated.

"First you. I heard it's been rough."

"It has. I knew something was wrong. It was obvious. When they took me, I honestly thought that was it. I was done. Managed to escape, and now here I am. Maybe I'll tell you the longer version after a few more of these." She held up the glass. "Now your turn."

"Right, back to what happened." He sipped from his glass and set it on the small table. "How far back do you want me to go?"

"Six months."

"After you helped me?"

Nodding, she twirled her finger, prompting him to continue.

"I was done. Sick of being hunted. After I took out Van de Berg, I decided to assume his identity. Figured it might lead me to someone who could tell me why I was being targeted and who was behind it." He hesitated a beat, not wanting to bring the next point up. "You were my first target."

"Me?" She stepped back until she hit the counter. "Six months ago?"

"Yeah, but the job got pulled within a couple days. There were more assigned. Technically, I completed them. But I gave the people a choice, and believe it or not, all chose to live."

"Funny how that happens." Her eyes were distant as though she were listening, but the words took a few extra seconds to pass through a filter.

"Wound up in Denmark, took a new assignment. Ended up getting into a scrap in the street saving her. Or her saving me. Not really sure which yet. Fast forward, her former handler double crossed her with me sitting there. An explosion. Dead people. She's injured. Turns out she's active Swedish intelligence, too. "

"Go figure."

"Right. Brandon hooks us up with a friendly doctor out on a farm. Nice enough guy. Fixed her up. Called in that a couple of strangers were at his place and apparently the description he gave of me matched the description of a person someone else wanted dead. A hit squad arrived middle of the night. Pros. Possibly from Langley. Rest of the time was finding my way to you."

"Well, you found me," she said.

"That I did," he said.

Whether the alcohol or the time away or just their simple magnetism, they slowly started toward each other, ready to begin a dance that would end on the bed.

Until they heard gunshots from the bar.

CHAPTER 36

BRETT STOPPED ONCE ON THE DRIVE TO CHICAGO. HE PULLED off the highway and into the parking lot of a Target. It was Chris's idea.

Brett stopped off at the Starbucks inside the store and got an Americano with an extra shot of espresso. The cup burned his hand as he walked to the men's section. He found an abandoned cart. There were clothes and a couple of food items in it. He tossed them on the floor and strode off with the cart, his Americano resting insecurely in the child seat.

"Is this really necessary?" he said to Chris.

"I think it's better we look like we're coming on shift," Chris said.

"What's that even mean?"

"We're supposed to be janitors, right? Well, you think a janitor is coming to work looking like you?"

"What's wrong with the way I look?"

"Nothing, unless you're a janitor."

"You're pissing me off, Chris."

"I don't care." He started toward a rack of jeans. "Come on, let's get this over with."

They were out of the store ten minutes later, each with a new pair of jeans and t-shirts. Brett chose Nirvana, the one with the smiley face. Chris opted for Green Day, because of course he would.

Brett and Chris reviewed their plan as they neared the destination. Brandon had told them where to go and what to do. He would be available to hop on comms and guide them. With five minutes to go, Brett pinged him and got a reply that Brandon was ready.

Brett drove around the building and parked at the back right corner. The entrance they were to use was twenty feet away. Cigarette butts littered the loading dock. No wonder the door remained unlocked. That's where they took their breaks.

With the trunk popped, Brett hopped out and retrieved both his and Chris's backpacks. They didn't look overly full. But each came in at well over twenty pounds. They were loaded with equipment, half of which Brett hoped they wouldn't need. He was concerned the bags would weigh them down. Maybe even get them in trouble.

He received a message from Brandon with instructions to connect to a voice chat server where Brandon could communicate through their gear. Within a few minutes, he was in their ears.

"All right guys," Brandon said. "This should be pretty easy so long as you can get to that janitors' room."

"How far is it?" Brett asked.

"Once you're inside, it should be pretty simple. Let's get moving."

The two men walked over to the loading dock and melted into the shadows under the overhang. It felt ten degrees cooler, with a slight breeze wafting past. They hung out there for five minutes before Chris checked the door.

"Open," he said.

"Keep going," Brandon said.

Chris pulled the door back, and Brett went through first with his hand resting on the butt of a VP9. The door shut with a whisper, and Chris took a couple of long steps to catch up with Brett.

Over half the lights in the corridor were out, leaving the space feeling more like an underground tunnel at a facility that didn't exist, instead of a modern office building. Making it worse, a permanent layer of Lysol hung in the air like dense mist in the woods.

"OK, when you reach the bathrooms, go just past. There's one more door along that wall before you dump out into the lobby. That's your special place."

"Nothing special about this place," Chris said. "Feeling some weird juju here, man."

"That's from all the pot you smoke," Brett said.

"Keep it down for a minute, guys," Brandon said.

The bathrooms came and went, and they now stood in front of the door.

"Doubt we'll get as lucky this time." Brett reached for the door and cursed when he found it locked.

"Don't worry," Chris said. "Your stoner friend has done locked himself out of enough hotel rooms and cars and even his own house once or twice that he's picked up a special set of skills."

Brett watched as Chris produced a lock-picking kit and went to work on the door. A few moments later, they were standing in the room. Chris tossed his bag on the couch, unzipped it, and pulled out some gear. He took over communicating with Brandon, and they tossed around a bunch of nerd terms that Brett knew little about.

"That should do it," Chris said. "You got visuals?"

"Stand by a sec," Brandon said.

Brett watched and listened with anticipation.

"I own them now," Brandon said. "Hop into those overalls and get your asses up to the tenth floor." His voice became muffled. "OK, listen up. Thomas just said that once you get up there, there's likely to be a security guard. Most of these guys don't care, but don't let your guard down. The ones that work up there are a different breed."

"Got it," Brett said. "I'm built to handle guys like that."

"I'm built to smoke a little weed and—"

"Yeah, we got it, Chris. You like to get high."

"I mean, I'm high right now."

"Probably couldn't function any other way," Brett said.

"Get moving, guys," Brandon said. "I got a lot of other stuff I'm dealing with here."

Brett felt a surge of lightning shoot through his arms and legs. He shot Chris a look and the other man hiked an eyebrow and shrugged.

What was Brandon facing? Was he OK? Brett had to assume Brandon wouldn't be on the phone right now if he was in danger.

Both men finished changing and arranged their guns for easy access. If it came down to it, they'd use them. It wouldn't be ideal by any stretch, but hell if they'd go out any other way.

They exited the room and entered the lobby, finding it deserted. The only sound was a slight humming. The unmanned wooden front desk stood dark against the light gray walls. A board hung behind it with various company names. Brett mentioned it to Brandon.

"You want a picture of the other companies in the building?"

"That might be a good idea. I can cross check it with what's listed online and run a query against all of them through government and Meadowcroft databases."

Brett snapped a pic with his phone and followed Brandon's instructions for uploading it when they entered the elevator.

The ride up took about twenty seconds. Neither man spoke. Brett stared straight ahead, enjoying a moment where no one could spot him. His enemies were numerous. That came with his job. He accepted it long ago. Every night, he laid his head down and was prepared to never wake up. In fact, he hoped it would happen that way. No chance of seeing it coming.

The elevator slowed down and rocked to a stop. The doors opened. Cooler air penetrated the small space, and Brett inhaled it deeply.

"Go time," he whispered.

Chris took point and exited first, which surprised Brett. The guy had been out of the business for a while, and even back then, he wasn't exactly a point man. Maybe he needed to feel the rush, the surge of adrenaline. His life couldn't be all that exciting in Kenosha, Wisconsin. Then again, it'd been over a decade since they'd worked together. Brett knew little about the guy anymore.

"OK, guys, head left. You'll pass two doors. Stop at the third. There's a keypad there. The access code is... 9483771." He repeated the code. "Let me know when you're in there."

Brett punched it in. A soft beep followed. The lock audibly disengaged. He grabbed the handle and turned.

"Opening."

Chris took position, extended the MP7, aiming it at where the door met the frame. Brett watched his eyes for any sign of surprise. He inhaled and held it until Chris nodded slightly.

"Go time," he whispered. Then added, "We're in."

The room was about thirty feet wide and about twenty feet deep, door to window. The lights were off. The sun was on the other side of the building. Fading afternoon light filtered in. There were a few desks with monitors and keyboards and pens and notebooks, but no personal effects. Along the back and side walls were file cabinets and tables littered with papers, which didn't stop there. They were all over the floor, too.

"This place someone's trash can?" Chris said.

"What's that mean?" Brandon said.

"Just a lot of junk everywhere," Chris said.

"Are there offices in there? Desks? Anything like that?"

"Yeah, a couple." Brett walked over to the nearest and sat down. "Keep me covered, Chris." He moved the mouse, and a screen came to life. "Looking at a login screen of some sort, Brandon."

"OK, I want you to enter these credentials." His voice softened. "Go ahead, Thomas."

Thomas gave Brett a login and password. The dialog box disappeared, the screen flashed, and a moment later, Brett was staring at a command prompt.

"OK, now what?"

Brandon walked him through a series of commands that made no sense to him. Windows popped up on the screen, loaded with gibberish. He kept inputting what Brandon told him exactly as he told him. He never figured himself to be a transcriptionist, but he felt he was doing a fairly decent job.

"OK, man," Brandon said. "I've got access. Sit back and watch me work."

"No offense, but I'd rather watch two dogs humping."

"Suit yourself, perv."

Brett rose and walked around the room while Chris went through the papers. He appeared to be sorting them into piles. The rest of the office looked tidy, which made the disturbed area all that more concerning. Didn't take a big leap to figure someone was clearing out of the office in a hurry.

He began walking across the room toward Chris when he noticed two shadows spaced a couple feet apart under the door.

"I think we've got company," Brett said.

Chris stopped what he was doing and aimed the MP7 at the door. Brett hurried across the room to Chris's side, positioning himself at the far corner where the window met the wall. He had his VP9 drawn and ready to fire.

The keypad beeped its approval.

The lock disengaged.

The door handle turned.

And light from the hallway flooded in.

The woman that entered was tall and lean with dark brown hair and eyes that probably weren't that wide when not staring down the barrel of a pistol. She turned and reached for the door.

"Don't do that," Chris said.

She froze in place, her hand mere inches from the handle.

Brett moved in her direction. "Who are you?"

"Nobody," she said.

"Kinda hard to believe that," Brett said.

"What's going on?" Brandon asked.

"We've got a visitor," Brett said. "Probably harmless, but she's had a good thirty seconds now to stare at our faces."

"I won't say anything," she said.

"Again, kinda hard to believe," Brett said. "Step back from the door with your hands up."

She complied, taking five steps toward the middle of the room. "This fine?"

"Who are you?" Brett asked again.

"Really, I'm nobody." She held her gaze steady on him.

Brett took three more steps, stopped, refocused his aim for effect. "Listen, lady, I'm not asking again. The next words out of your mouth better be your name. And before you say nobody, understand this. I pull this trigger for a living. You're literally nobody to me. You die, it doesn't affect me or my partner the least bit."

Her eyes glossed over, and she bit her lip.

"What's it gonna be?"

"My name is Brittany Schau."

CHAPTER 37

TEN SHOTS RANG OUT. POP-POP-POP. ONE AFTER THE OTHER. They echoed through the bar and down the hallway and into Clarissa's room. Had to be two shooters at least. The screams of men rose above the silence on a wave of anguish. Confusion spread across Clarissa's face, turned to fear.

Jack sprang into action. One of those moments where he stopped thinking and his training took over. It was second nature now, no matter how badly he wanted to forget how to do it all. He retrieved his gun and turned toward the door. Clarissa grabbed his arm, pulled him back. He shook her off and crossed the room and peeled the hunk of metal back. It hadn't been latched. If it had, would they have heard the shooting?

"Shut it, Jack," Clarissa yelled. "They can't get in."

He ignored her request. He wasn't sure if they could get out or if they'd be sitting ducks with a team of assassins waiting them out. And running wouldn't solve anything, it'd only lead to more of the same.

He left the room. Closed the door behind him. The stifling hallway was filled with the echoes of a man shouting.

"Where is she?"

No accent. The guy was as American as Noble.

The only replies were sounds of pain and choked sobs.

Another gunshot.

Another scream.

Another round of shouting.

"Tell me where she is!"

"Not here," the wounded man answered. The words sounded guttural, as though he had to force them out through clenched teeth.

Another shot.

No scream this time.

"Your turn." The shooter's voice was lower. A long pause ensued. "Where are you pointing? The ceiling?"

Jack took a few steps toward the end of the hallway.

The wounded expat grunted something Jack couldn't decipher. Noble took a few more steps, braced his left shoulder against the wall and cupped his right hand with his left, steadying the pistol.

Just show your face. That's all I need.

"If I go back there, and she's not there, you know I'm coming back for your life. And if you don't believe me..."

Another shot rang out. Silence followed. He'd killed the second man, Jack was sure of it.

"You're my last hope, friend," the shooter said. "Don't let me down."

The expat mumbled something between his cries. It didn't matter what he said. The shooter had no intention of letting him live.

Ten initial shots. Three men at the bar. All three were left living, but in obvious pain. Now one guy remained.

Was there a silent partner lying in wait? Jack tried to imagine how a single shooter could've done it. With the way the guys sat at the bar, facing away from the street, he would have had time to set up. First three shots swept left to right. Next three in the opposite direction. Two bullets each in the backs of three men. Four more rounds placed anywhere as long as the guys lived for a little while.

Plausible.

Noble refused to rule out another shooter until he saw the carnage and who was behind it. And even if it turned out to be just one guy, there'd be spotters outside. Had to be. Someone had to warn the shooter when the police closed in.

The shooter had on heavy boots or some other footwear with thick soles. His plodding steps slapped the floor louder with every step. Noble waited for the man to appear. Seconds dragged on and felt like minutes. The footsteps stopped. The agonized groans continued mixed in with crying. The sound of a man with minutes left to live. Death was imminent, naturally or otherwise.

Jack's heart pounded as though he'd sprinted a quarter mile. He felt his pulse hard in his throat and at his temples. This wasn't the first time he'd experienced the sensation. He doubted it'd be the last. He breathed steadily, in for four through his nose, hold for four, out for four through his mouth, hold for four. The process kept him focused, prevented the anxiety from penetrating his mind. He could handle the physical reaction. Cold hands going numb, muscles tightening, abdominals clenching. But if he let the thoughts in, his world would turn real bad real fast.

The footsteps resumed, slowly and deliberately, heel-toe, heel-toe. The shooter whistled. It was off key and disturbing, like he was trying to play with his victims. Might've been. But he didn't count on running into Noble, and Jack had a surprise for him.

A gun barrel appeared, followed by four hairy knuckles. Jack sighted in midway between the wall and the center of the opening and eight inches above the level of the gun. He pulled in one long breath and held it.

The shooter whipped around the corner. He shot blind, sending three rounds down the hallway like he hadn't already expended a dozen minutes before. The light behind the guy obscured his face. Jack could tell it was wide and covered with a beard. The whites of the guy's eyes stood out as his frame blocked the doorway.

Jack squeezed the trigger before the guy had a chance to zero in on him.

A single shot hit true, center mass.

The guy tried to lift his gun.

Jack sent another round down the hall, hit him in the chest a second time.

A third caught the shooter in the face.

He collapsed where he stood.

"Anyone else out there?" Jack called out. There was no need to worry about his position being compromised.

"No. Help."

"Clarissa," Jack yelled. "I think we're clear."

Jack moved forward and stepped over the lifeless body of the shooter. He didn't bother to look down at the guy. Wasn't worth it. He turned the corner toward the bar.

The scene in the room was straight out of an action flick. Blood soaked the old hardwoods. The barstools were toppled over. Mugs laying sideways on the bar top, puddles of beer surrounding them.

On the floor, the lone survivor held his stomach. Blood oozed between his fingers. He saw Jack and reached out with his other hand. His breathing was rapid and shallow. He didn't look like he had much time left.

The other two expats had already expired, their wide eyes stared up at a reaper Jack couldn't see and didn't want to see. Not like this.

"Help," the lone survivor pleaded.

Noble carefully approached the front door and looked through the narrow windows. The immediate sidewalk was clear. Maybe the spotters had a time limit they were operating on. Perhaps they had already attempted to reach the shooter, and his non-response was their cue to bail. Or they could be just out of sight, ready to take action if anyone other than their man exited the bar.

"Jack?"

He turned toward the sound of Clarissa's voice.

"I'm in the bar. Don't come in here."

She leaned through the doorway, her gaze fixed on the dead guy. It wasn't the first she'd seen, he knew that. But the look on her face made it seem that way.

"I know him," she said.

"What?" Jack started back toward her.

The guy on the floor said, "Help me, man."

Jack stopped and knelt next to the guy. "There's nothing I can do."

The guy clenched his eyes and leaned his head back on the floor. "Then put me out of my misery."

Jack looked over his shoulder at Clarissa. "Step back in the hall for a second."

"Why?"

"You don't want to watch me do this."

She dipped back, and he placed the pistol against the side of the guy's head and pulled the trigger. Jack didn't watch. He didn't look back to see if the guy died instantly or was convulsing on the floor as the final traces of energy worked through his body.

Clarissa was down on a knee, searching through the shooter's pockets. She pulled out a money clip and took his gun.

"Who was he?" Jack asked.

"One of the bastards that tried to kill me." She stood up and pulled the wad of cash and cards from the money clip. Jack noticed the determination on her face as she rifled through it. She found an ID and slapped it against her palm. "I thought they were all Polish."

"This guy's definitely from the States."

"I know." She held up the driver's license issued in Illinois. The address was just outside Chicago. The name could've been fake, but they'd leave that up to a guy who had the tools and skills to figure out that kind of thing.

"The men that captured you," he said. "You're sure they were Polish?"

She ran her left hand through her hair, grabbed a fistful of it as she shook her head. "Can't be sure of anything anymore, I guess. They had Polish accents and spoke in Polish."

"Could've been part of the game. Screwing with you either because they were worried you would escape or—"

"Or they intended to let me go."

"Did it seem that way?" Jack asked.

"Not at all. Why would they kidnap me just to turn around and let me go?"

"Because you were the bait."

"For who?"

"Me." He pulled out his phone and snapped a picture of the dead guy. A few more taps, and the photo was on its way to Brandon.

"Who would want to do that?"

"I've been trying to figure that out, but the names that have popped up don't make sense. They have no connection to you. They'd just as soon kill you to get to me as have to deal with holding you captive."

"OK, who's that leave then?"

"Someone who didn't want to see you killed but would gladly watch me die."

Her eyes widened. "Beck?"

CHAPTER 38

BRANDON TYPED OUT THE NAME, SPELLING AS HE WENT.

"No, not S-h-a," Brett said. "It's a S-c-h-a-u."

"Really?"

"We saw her company badge."

He typed it in: Brittany Schau.

At once, a record returned in Meadowcroft's database. Thomas leaned over his shoulder to get a better view. He shook his head so fast his hair whipped against Brandon's cheek.

"Are you seeing this?" Brandon said.

"Seeing what?" Brett said.

"Sorry, not you. But don't let that woman out of your sight." He leaned out of the way so Thomas could have some space. "In fact, get her out of there. I've got all I need from that system you linked me up with. Guarantee this woman is more valuable than anything else you'll find."

He muted his mic and pushed Thomas back a few inches.

"You ever seen that name before?" Brandon asked.

"I have *never* seen *that* name before," Thomas said.

"You know, it seemed familiar to me, but the fact it isn't to you has me concerned, especially when she's the head of the Banyan project."

Thomas scraped the floor, dragging a chair closer to Brandon's laptop. "It doesn't make any sense." He tapped on the edge of the keyboard. "Scroll over. Check her employment date."

Brandon navigated to the cell where the employment date should've been.

"Missing?" Thomas leaned back and put his hands on top of his head. "The hell is going on here?"

Brandon held up a finger and unmuted his mic after Brett told him they were heading into the elevator. The line went silent for thirty seconds.

"Back in the lobby now." Someone was whistling, sounded a bit distant. Chris, most likely. "In the hallway. Need to stop off and get the comms gear out of the janitors' closet."

"Do you?" Brandon asked.

"Already had this convo with Chris. Some of this can be traced directly back to him."

"Some spy."

"Tell me about it. OK, we're in. He's clearing out. I got the woman. Standby."

Brandon turned his attention back to his computer, continuing his search for records on the woman. There were no others in the company system that he could find. He opened a program he'd written to search all government databases at once. After entering the name in the search box, he clicked a button and watched as results started pouring in. Some databases might take up to three hours. Others came back immediately. So far, every result returned as not found.

"And we're out. Quick walk to the back door. Chris is going first, then me and our new friend." He paused a beat. The door banged free from the jamb. "Just waiting for his signal."

Brandon sat frozen for the next ten seconds until Brett came back online.

"Good to go, man. When do you want us to check in with you?"

"Wait a sec." Brandon opened up a private browser and pulled up a map. He zeroed in on Chicago, then moved the cursor northwest. He tapped on the screen when he found what he was looking for. "OK, look, there's a private airfield your side of Madison, Wisconsin. I'm gonna send you the name and address. Get there. I'll arrange for a private jet to meet you there. You might have to wait nearby for a bit, but my guy is guaranteed to show up."

"Sounds good," Brett said. "Call if you need anything."

"You do the same." Brandon pulled out his earpiece and stretched his neck, rolling it in a circle to the right, then left.

Thomas paced the kitchen. He looked worried. Scared. Sweat covered his brow and soaked through his shirt. When he'd spotted the name, he seemed genuinely shocked to see it in the database. He'd said he'd never seen it before. Had it been a ruse? Was *seen* his way of making the lie believable? It made no sense he didn't know of the head of the program.

"You know, we never talked about your headaches," Brandon said.

Thomas slowed his pace to something a little faster than a crawl and turned his head toward Brandon. His gaze was off elsewhere.

"How long have you been taking the pills?" Brandon asked.

"About as long as you," Thomas said.

"What's it done to you? For you?"

"Processing, mostly. My ability to take in data and process and spin it is insane now. Physically, I'm faster and stronger than I've ever been. But it's really the increases in brain power that are unbelievable."

Brandon mulled it over for a moment. He felt the same as far as intelligence and capacity went. "Do you think the physical changes are as drastic as me being able to walk?"

"The goal was never one trait over another. You already have superior intellect. It made sense for your physical attributes to improve. They specifically engineered your formula to stimulate nerve and muscle growth. For me, well, I really didn't know what I was getting into. He just...well, they told me it was something to help my distracted brain. Better than the Adderall I was on, they said. And they were right. I found focus and flow, and it went so well at first."

"Yeah, at first mine was great, too. The gains were fast. There weren't any side effects. At least none that I recognized." He backed up from the table and decided to rise out of his chair. Once standing tall, he said, "I mean, look at this. I couldn't do this when I was five years old."

"It's remarkable."

"Were you hired to take part in the program?"

Thomas nodded slowly as he presumably measured his response. "I didn't realize that was the case. It was a mailroom job. I was offered it by a friend of a friend. Didn't think much of it when they said I needed to focus better or I'd be fired. Then they told me they had a solution, so I took it. Three months later, I'm behind a desk. Three months after that, I'm at the office you eventually found me in."

"Who did you think was running the program if not this Brittany Schau?"

"You know, now that I think about it, I never knew. Once they revealed what was going on, how I was a test case not specifically geared toward the military, I just kind of went with it. Like, I'm ten times smarter than the smartest person I ever knew, and he went to Harvard. Why give up that and a six-figure salary? I was the kind of guy destined to work in Big Lots the rest of my life. Not doing this."

Brandon sat down and scooted back toward the table. "Bet you never thought it would lead you here." He looked down at his legs. "I didn't either. I thought this was some kind of thank you from the people I'd helped. Now I realize it was a slow way to assassinate me."

Thomas opened the fridge, grabbed two more Michelob Ultras, and returned to the table. He twisted the cap off a bottle and set it in front of Brandon.

"It's not an easy way to go," he said.

Brandon had presumed as much. If he stopped taking it now, could the effects be reversed? "Maybe this Schau lady will have an answer for us."

"How is Brett gonna get back here?" Thomas asked. "He left his car in Philly, right?"

"He's resourceful. He was trained to be. He's had to be to survive in his business as long as he has without getting caught or killed. He'll figure it out."

They sat in silence for several minutes. They didn't look at laptop screens. Didn't incessantly check their phones. Just two guys having a beer together.

The silence in Brandon's mind didn't last long. How could it? On a normal day, his brain was in hyperdrive. With everything he was dealing with, it had been a feat of world-class mental strength to just sit there, beer in hand, breathing in and out.

Thomas's concern over the new woman in the picture played over and over in his mind. He also had issues with the lack of information he'd been able to find on Casey Whitworth after 2013. There was still an angle he hadn't chased down. The lone college teammate she'd remained in touch with. He set the beer down on the condensation ring it had left behind and pulled his laptop close.

"Couldn't stay away, huh?" Thomas said. He wore a goofy grin. Had the beer affected him already?

"So much about this bothers me," Brandon said. "Thought of something. Give me a second."

He opened Chrome in an incognito window and typed out her name and hit enter. The results came back. A row of images of an attractive woman, fairly tall, dressed in her Duke basketball uniform. Headshots. Action shots. A few more of her a couple of years later, dressed in business clothing.

He scrolled down and saw old sports news mentioning her name. Casey's, too. The two of them were a force to be reckoned with on the pitch.

Then he stopped on a result toward the bottom of the page, past the old YouTube videos. It was dated four years ago.

Urgent Search Underway: Former Duke Soccer Standout Chastity Braun Disappears Without a Trace

"Holy hell." Brandon looked up and saw Thomas staring back wide-eyed.

"What is it?"

Brandon zoomed in on the google result and turned the laptop toward him. "Have a look."

He looked over the top of the laptop. "May I?"

"Go for it."

Thomas began reading the article, "Chastity Braun, a standout soccer player for Duke University and now a prominent defense attorney in the research triangle, has gone missing, according to her husband Brad Locke." He stopped reading, but his eyes scanned through the remainder of the article. He looked up. "When was this?"

"It said four years ago. Is there a date on the article?"

Thomas swiped on the trackpad. "December 14, 2018."

"Why does that sound familiar?" Brandon said.

"Yeah," Thomas said. "It does to me, too." He spun the laptop around and pushed it back to Brandon. He jumped out of his chair and ran around the table. "Go back."

"Go back where? The search results?"

"No, go back to Meadowcroft."

Brandon switched over to Meadowcroft's database and looked over at Thomas. "What am I looking for now? That date?"

Thomas nodded, tight and terse. His eyes bugged out, his fingers trembled. "Yeah, put it in. I swear I saw it in here somewhere."

"Wait, you think Meadowcroft had something to do with Chastity's disappearance?"

"Is it so far-fetched? One of Casey's only friends goes missing four years after her?"

Brandon created a SQL query to search for the date and waited. The search took thirty seconds and returned nothing. He shrugged. "Worth a try, I guess."

"What date did Casey go missing?" Thomas asked.

"Already crossed my mind. Her dad last heard from her on December…" He saw a flash of light in front of his eyes and felt an intense pain through the middle of his skull. For a moment, thought and reason left him, and he couldn't feel himself breathing.

Thomas grabbed his shoulder. "You OK, man?" He shook him a little. "Brandon?"

As quickly as it started, it dissipated. His vision cleared, the pain subsided. And he had a thought.

"Dude, you all right?" Thomas asked.

"Not sure what the hell just happened, but I think I know what happened in December of 2018." He cleared his query and selected one he had previously run that day. One record returned. He scrolled all the way to the right. "What do you see there?"

Thomas leaned forward. "Hire date December 21, 2018."

Brandon scrolled left to the beginning of the row.

Thomas almost fell back in a chair. "That can't be right?"

Brandon read the name. "Brittany Schau."

CHAPTER 39

THE ACTIVITY ON THE STREET INTENSIFIED. SIRENS. SHOUTS. Banging on the front door, which threatened to cave in due to the force applied on its decades-old lock. The windows on it rattled long after the last thud. Someone blocked the light. Likely a cop. If anyone else had accompanied the shooter, they'd be long gone by now.

Jack stepped back and turned toward the barroom.

Clarissa reached out and grabbed his arm, turned him toward her.

"What are you doing?" she said. "They won't help us, Jack. They might turn us over to *them*. Let's go through the back."

He took another look at the carnage leading to the front door. Bodies littered the floor and blood stained it. Three lives cut short all because of him. Had he been played from the moment he took over as Van de Berg? Had he been walking right toward a trap all along?

His thoughts turned to Johanna, and he shoved them to the side. He had to assume she was getting the treatment she needed. He had to get out because if he didn't, whoever came through the front door would cuff him and carry him away and in jail he'd be helpless prey.

Clarissa yanked him free from his thoughts as she pulled him down the hallway toward the back of the building. Had to be a door there. Reaching it, she pulled it open, and they entered another hallway. It was dark and dank and smelled like urine. The journey was short, thankfully, but the next door wasn't as easy to open. It was stuck against the frame from years of warping.

Jack drove his shoulder into the door and broke it free from whatever had held it in place. Sunlight knifed through slits in the darkening clouds and the brightness blinded him for a second or three. A man stood in front of him, thick and tall. He heard Clyde's voice.

"What the hell happened in there? There's cops all over the street."

Jack reached back and grabbed Clarissa's hand and said, "You need to get us out of here now."

"Tell me what happened!"

"Someone showed up and murdered your friends. He's dead now. Nothing you can do to him or for them." He paused for a moment to make sure Clyde was looking him in the eye and could see the seriousness on Jack's face. "We gotta get moving. Either hand me the keys or hop in and drive. I don't care which."

Clyde spun on his heel and ran toward his car, telling the guy in the back to scoot over. Clarissa climbed in, and Jack followed her. Clyde jammed the accelerator before the back door was shut and the clutch was off the floor. The tires squealed against the pavement and the sedan lurched forward, jostling them all as he took the speed bump at the end of the alley without slowing down.

He turned away from the bar. Made a right at the next intersection. A left at the one after that. He continued on for an uninterrupted half-mile and turned again. Then he pulled over.

"Get out," Clyde said.

"Us?" Jack said.

"No, these two."

"What for?" the guy up front said.

"Because you need to get home and lock your doors and don't come outside until you hear from me again."

The men complied. Jack crawled out of the back and moved to the front passenger seat. Clyde stared at him for several seconds without saying a word. Jack waited a few beats longer.

"We need you to get us out of town."

"What happened in there?"

"We were back in Clarissa's room. Heard ten shots and a lot of chaos. I went into the hall. The shooting stopped. The guy showed his face, and I put a bullet through it."

"Any idea who he was?" Clyde said.

"We got his ID," Clarissa said.

"Doubt it's legit," Jack said.

"But it's from Illinois," Clarissa said. "And..."

"And what?" Clyde said.

"I recognized him."

"From your ordeal?" Clyde asked.

"Yeah."

"I thought they were Polish?"

"So did I."

"We figure they were faking for the coverup," Jack said.

"What coverup?" Clyde asked.

"It's better you don't dive that deep into these waters, man. I'm not sure where this leads, and I don't know if there'll be a chance to ever come up for air again."

As the clusters of buildings dissolved into empty space, an ominous sky beckoned them to turn around. Clyde pulled off the road near a train station. A good enough place to stop when you didn't know what your next destination was. Hop on and figure it out along the way.

"You two take my car," he said.

"Can't do that," Jack said.

"Yes, you can, and you need to. I don't know the extent of the trouble you're facing. And you were right, I don't need to know. But I've been there before. I've needed the kind of help I can give you right now, which is a mode of transportation."

"Are you sure, Clyde?" Clarissa asked.

"As sure as those black clouds advancing toward us are going to unleash their deluge upon our little slice of the earth." Shifting into neutral, he applied the emergency brake. "Jack, in that glove box are some items that might help you two out."

Jack reached for the latch. Clyde stopped him.

"Wait until I'm gone. You'll know what to do with them."

"Appreciate it."

Noble exited the car and opened Clarissa's door. She squeezed his hand as she brushed past him. It felt soft, warm. He met Clyde at the front of the vehicle and exchanged a nod and read a decade's worth of information in the look he gave Jack.

"You two find yourselves back in Warsaw, give me a shout. The RED, WHITE, AND BREW! will rise again." A shimmer of light reflected off his moistened eyes.

"I'm sorry about your friends. It should have been us."

Clyde shook his head. "No, the world needs people like you, not a bunch of old drunks who whine about every little thing." With that, he trotted toward the platform without looking back.

Seated behind the wheel, Jack shifted into gear and drove toward the advancing storm. Streaks of lightning snaked their way down from the sky. With every mile, the thunder intensified. Rain hit the windshield lightly at first, then the heavens opened up and the road before them disappeared behind a thick veil. He white-knuckled the steering wheel until the storm let up some twenty miles later.

"Hell of a day," Clarissa said.

Jack laughed and considered whether this one made his top ten list.

"I know where he is," she said.

"Who?"

"Beck."

"Where?"

"Ticino."

"Ticino?"

"Switzerland."

"Ah, that's right. The Italian area." He pulled up a mental atlas and generally knew where it was. "What's he doing there?"

"He wanted me to meet him. Probably figured out by now I ditched him." She turned toward her side window.

"And now you're gonna call him."

"What?"

"Tell him you thought you were being followed, so you detoured and hid out for a couple days. You're on your way now."

"So you want to tell Beck—a man who at the moment has far more resources than us, that wants you dead and maybe me as well—that we are coming to see him?"

"Not 'we,' you."

"Just gonna drop me off on a street corner and let me saunter up to him and smooth this over?"

Jack chuckled at the thought. "You do saunter well."

"Damn right I do." She smiled, but it was short lived. "Hey, what do you think's in the glove box?"

"One way to find out."

Pulling the latch with one hand, she caught the door as it fell with the other. The contents were neatly arranged. A phone. A GPS and tracker. Two wireless earpieces. A thick wad of Euros and a couple of credit cards. Rail passes. And a small Sig, either a .380 or 9mm.

"Well," she said. "At least we know he's on our side."

"After what happened in his bar," Jack said. "I don't know how he could be."

"Wasn't our fault."

"Not directly." He reached into his pocket and pulled out his phone. "I'm gonna see if I can connect with Brandon." He dialed the number and put the phone on speaker while it rang. After thirty seconds, the line disconnected.

"I'll shoot him a message," she said. "Catch him up on what happened."

He diverted his attention back to Johanna while Clarissa tapped on her phone. She had fascinated him from the moment he first saw her. Their time together had been a whirlwind. He realized he barely knew her but felt as though they'd spent years together. When she started going downhill, he felt the hole forming in his gut. The one that said this won't end well. Bury all the feelings in here. So he hadn't asked Clyde how it went and Clyde hadn't offered. Presumably, this meant bad news. He'd find out sooner or later, and if the report wasn't good, he preferred to hear it later. Grieving over the woman he hardly knew but spent an intense two days with would be a hindrance in their current circumstances.

"He got back to me." Clarissa's voice broke the spell.

"Who? Beck?"

"No, Brandon. I haven't reached out to Beck yet, and I don't want to do it from this phone. We'll find a place to call in the next town."

"Gotcha." He looked over at her while she read the message to herself. "What's it say?"

"Brett's en route back to him with someone from Meadowcroft. Also, untangling a mess here. Things don't make sense. Starting to follow the money trail now."

"Sounds like he's got things under control."

Clarissa laughed. "Sounds like he's in as much of a mess as we are."

"Because of me."

She reached for his hand resting on the shifter. Her fingers wove between his. "I got him involved. And it's good because he's pieced a lot of this together along the way." Pulling her hand back, she returned it to the phone. "I'm going to bring up Beck and see if he can pinpoint his location."

"You thinking about showing up unannounced?"

She nodded. "Bad idea?"

"Great idea," Jack said. "He won't expect it. He thinks you're in the wind now. We can catch him off guard this way. I'll handle whatever security detail he's got while you distract him with your story. Then we'll turn the screws on him and find out what's going on."

"Easy peasy," she said.

"Easy peasy," Jack said, and he felt dirty for doing so.

PART 4

CHAPTER 40

THE HOURS MELTED TOGETHER WHILE WAITING FOR BRETT, Chris and their detainee. Brandon kept in constant communication with Brett. The situation was under control. The woman didn't struggle and went on the plane willingly. While Brett sensed she wanted to talk, he didn't trust her. Getting her off the plane and to the house was a different story. There weren't many options for getting a ride where they were flying into. Brett had to call in a favor. Now, they were on the way to the house.

Brandon had stopped searching for more information a while ago. It all ran together now, like a massive pile of spaghetti. He couldn't find where one thread ended, and another started. Every answer brought more questions. What had happened to Casey? Who was this Brittany woman and why was she hired a week after Chastity had disappeared? It all had to be related, right?

"I'm driving myself crazy," Brandon said. "And apparently I don't have many more days left, so I'd rather chill out."

Thomas went back to the kitchen and retrieved two more bottles of beer. He opened them and handed Brandon one. "This'll help."

"I suppose." Brandon clinked his bottle against Thomas's and pulled hard. He wiped the bubbly wetness from his lips. "This sucks."

"That it does," Thomas said. "But it's all we got."

"Probably shouldn't have anymore. Things might get serious in a bit."

"How close are they?"

Brandon pulled out his phone and looked at the tracking app he'd linked to Brett's cell. "Not far, maybe ten minutes now."

"Guess we oughta finish these up."

Brandon shrugged. "We're adults. He's not gonna bust us."

"Just wanna look professional, you know?"

"What? For the woman who you didn't even know was the one behind the program slowly killing you?"

Thomas drained the last of his bottle and carried it to the trashcan. "I don't know, Brandon. Whatever." Laughing as he dropped the bottle, it shattered against one of the other empties. "How are your friends in Europe?"

"On their way to Switzerland. We'll need to provide some support in the early morning. Before that, I need to do some digging on Clarissa's partner, Beck."

"Don't trust him?"

"I don't trust anyone."

"Yet, you trusted that doctor."

Brandon had no response to that other than to say, "We all wish for what we can't have. When someone comes along offering a miracle, it's not easy to turn it down."

"I feel that." Thomas then let out a loud belch that echoed up the stairwell.

Brandon laughed and shook his head. "Anyway, something doesn't add up, and I'm starting to wonder, is Beck involved with the things going on over here? He left Clarissa in the wind for over six months. Then she's grabbed and taken off the street by a group of pros. They drugged her and everything."

"That's insane. And she escaped?"

"Tough woman, man. She's smart, *and* she has street smarts. The things she's been through, man, you wouldn't believe me if I showed you video. She saw Beck as a way out, but he only dragged her in deeper.

If she gets through this, I swear I'm gonna do right by her and give her a new life."

"Maybe I might be able to help with that."

"You?" Brandon side-eyed the guy.

"I've got a few contacts, too." He crossed his arms and leaned back. "This Beck guy, what's he do? Agency?"

"Treasury Department. Secret Service, but really deep. Kinda like a special operations group. He's been in and out of Europe for, I don't know, seven years now." Brandon's face tightened. "I don't like how things went down with Clarissa this week. Don't like that people showed up exactly where she was, took her, but they didn't kill her. It's a gut feeling, but it's telling me he's involved, and he used her to get to Jack."

"Are you sure that's not the beer lingering in your stomach?" Thomas smiled, but it faded quickly. "Why Jack?"

"Why not?" Brandon huffed out a laugh. "Well, one reason why not is his damn record was expunged. Literally wiped clean. Shouldn't be anyone after him since the Skinner mess."

"Frank Skinner, right?"

"Well, you do listen." Brandon reached over and slapped Thomas's shoulder. "Yeah, that guy." He thought back to when all this went down. "The crazy thing is when the government forgot about Noble, they *forgot* about Noble. I know someone in the CIA or NSA has to hear all this chatter surrounding him. Not a damn person has stepped in to help him, despite all he's done."

"Maybe *they* actually want him dead."

Brandon looked over at Thomas. "I think you're right, at least partially. I don't know about *they*, but I'm sure *someone* in that community wants him dead."

"Beck."

"It all goes back to him."

Thomas flipped the lid of his laptop open and started typing. "Let's see what I can find."

"Tell you what, Tommie. You really slow played us. I'm impressed. I mean, you can get things by me. I want to believe in people. But Brett, man, that dude's seen everything and then some."

"It's a talent, I guess. You know, I still remember what it was like to be an idiot. I still play it up a lot around friends and family. Don't think they could handle me with this brain I have now."

"If it's true that we don't have much time left, you might want to let them in."

Thomas looked over the top of his laptop. "You got anyone like that in your life?"

Brandon nodded as his thoughts turned to Kimberlee. "Yeah, a bit different, though."

"How so?"

"Because she is the love of my life. The only love I ever had in my life, actually. I pushed her away because of my changes. Ignored the negatives of this new body because I was so focused on the end goal. I really screwed it up."

Thomas pointed at Brandon's phone. "There's still time."

Brandon sat quietly for a few minutes. He wanted to think it over, find reasons not to reach out, continue to be stubborn about the whole thing. But all he could picture was her face. Her smile. The way she looked while sleeping. The sadness in her eyes and tears staining her cheeks when she left. Scooping up his phone, he rolled toward the front door and began typing out a message.

Headlights swept across the front windows. Tires crunched gravel. An engine revved, then settled to silence. Doors opened at intervals. Closed the same way.

Brandon tensed, concerned who it might be. The rational part of his mind knew it was Brett returning. He couldn't trust that blindly. A message arrived a few seconds later. He backed out of the one he was typing and opened the incoming text. Brett messaged they were ten minutes out. Brandon started to back away from the door, spun around, but it opened before he could get to the kitchen. He looked back, relieved to see Brett standing there.

"Your message said you were ten minutes out," he said.

"I sent that ten minutes ago," Brett said.

A tall woman who looked vaguely familiar in the way all tall, slender, brown-haired, attractive women looked similar stood behind him. Brett escorted her to the table and sat her along the back wall. Chris slid a chair over and took a seat next to her. He leaned back, crossed one leg over the other, and rested his hands in his lap. His eyes closed and his breathing slowed.

Brandon figured the guy wasn't too worried about the woman and Brett must not have been either, because he disappeared into the back of the house. She looked around the room, clearly unimpressed, and asked for a drink. Thomas obliged her and brought her a Michelob Ultra. He brought one for everyone. Guy must've been hooked.

After taking a sip and closing her eyes and leaning her head back, she locked eyes with Brandon. Pretty as she was, she had the coal black eyes of the devil. He'd seen eyes like that. Heartless and full of hate. But he wouldn't let her win. He stared her down until she turned her attention to Thomas. He backed down after a few seconds. So she cut a look at Chris, who was still meditating or whatever the hell he was doing.

She looked bored and disinterested, as though she were often in this predicament. Hell, maybe she was. Brandon hadn't heard of her before, but what did that mean? His world was small and tight, and she hadn't wormed her way into it.

Except she had. She headed Banyan, and Banyan was killing him. Rage rose like bile, and he looked away from the unsent text on his phone and into her dark eyes.

"Hello," she said.

"Brittany Schau, I presume," he said.

"Brandon Cunningham, I presume," she said.

"Glad to see you can put names to your victims' faces."

She smiled as she reached for her beer, held the bottle an inch from her lips for a second or two, then took a small pull.

"No one forced you to enter the trial," she said.

That was true, and Brandon had no response to it.

"And Thomas," she said while still staring at Brandon. "Our company wunderkind, dumb as a rock, screwing up in the mailroom until you started taking those pills."

He looked up and squinted at her. "December 14, 2018."

"What about it?" she said.

"December 21, 2018," he said.

"Is this supposed to mean something to me?"

Thomas's face took on a dark look at that moment. Maybe the light and the way he held his head. Maybe the pure disdain he felt for the woman. "I don't know? Does it?"

Rolling her eyes, she looked toward the hallway leading upstairs.

"How about the name Chastity Braun?" Thomas said.

Something struck Brandon at that moment. The name, the familiarity of it. Chastity Braun. Brittany Schau. He put his fingers on the keyboard and typed the letters out, one space between them. His eyes danced back and forth as he mentally crossed the letters out. Every single one was accounted for in both names.

"It's an anagram," he said.

"What?" Chris said, eyes still closed.

Brandon stared at the woman. "You're Chastity Braun."

She didn't say anything.

Thomas said, "What the hell? The dates, the one-week gap. But..."

Brandon flipped through the tabs on his laptop and came to the article about Chastity's disappearance. He turned the screen toward her. "There's some resemblance, but you don't look exactly like her."

She shrugged but offered no retort.

"Why? How?" Brandon said.

Breaking off her stare, she looked toward Brett as he emerged from the hallway. He stood at the end of the table opposite her, remaining silent for several seconds, then took a seat. He worked something out from between his teeth using his fingernail. He flicked it to the floor, placed his arm on the table, leaned over it. Everyone looked at him and then her as they were locked in a stare-down. Brett cleared his throat, then spoke.

"You wanna tell them the truth, or should I do it, Ms. Whitworth?"

CHAPTER 41

THEY DROVE THROUGH THE NIGHT, ALTERNATING DRIVERS every few hours. Neither Jack nor Clarissa could sleep for more than thirty minutes at a time. Stops were infrequent, and when they happened, it was a sprint to use the restroom, refill the coffee, top off the gas tank, and get back on the road. Jack didn't want to linger anywhere for too long. Not even the highway. So they got off the highway for a few miles here and there and took long, winding, boring roads until they found an on-ramp again. They decided against the most direct route and instead headed west of Warsaw. Skirting Czechia in favor of Germany, they headed south for the final leg of the journey.

They emerged from the thirty-five-mile-long Gotthard Base Tunnel early in the morning. A soft pink sky welcomed them. The sun threatened to clear the white-capped mountains. Jack rolled down the window to clear out the lingering heat and exhaust fumes the tunnel had bestowed upon them and breathed in the crisp air.

The rushing wind woke Clarissa. Stirring, she smiled at him.

"Morning," he said.

"Back at ya." She sat up and looked around. "Are we close?"

"About thirty minutes away."

"Got a plan yet?"

"Was hoping you thought of one while sleeping."

As she stretched her arms over her head, she arched her back. "I thought of nothing, Jack, and it was marvelous." A grin stretched across her face. He always thought she was most beautiful in the moments after she woke up, her hair a mess and no makeup.

Jack veered off the highway at the next exit and backed into a parking spot on the far side of a service station. After engaging the emergency brake, he notched his seat back a few inches and closed his eyes. What would today bring? After the past few days, he supposed anything was possible, but ruled out puppies and rainbows. Maybe tomorrow.

What they needed was a plan, and thus far, one had avoided him. It was damn near impossible to come up with anything beyond the basics. Beck might be ready for him. Beck would be ready for anything. What kind of team did he have with him? Chances of him rolling solo were slim, though not impossible. And that was *if* the guy had hung around waiting for Clarissa to show.

They'd worked out her part. At least the portion where she walked up to the door and said hello and sorry and gave him a story about thinking she was being chased. Jack figured he'd wing the rest. Sometimes that was his best plan. Sometimes that was his only plan.

"I'm going inside. Do you need anything?" She gave him a second, then in her mock-Jack voice, said, "Coffee."

Jack got a laugh out of it and said, "Coming in with you." He opened the door and had one foot on the ground when the phone in the glove box began ringing. He looked over at Clarissa. "Expecting a call?"

She pulled the latch and retrieved the phone and offered it to him. He waved her off, so she answered, put it on speaker and said, "Hello?"

"It's Clyde."

"I figured."

"Forgot to mention this when we were saying our goodbyes. Check the trunk. You'll need to pry up the floorboard, but I think you'll appreciate what's under there. Call me when you guys are headed back with my car."

The call disconnected. She shrugged at Jack and pocketed the phone. He popped the trunk. They met at the back of the sedan. The cargo space was vacant save for a few empty bags. Jack stuck his fingers down

into the nearest corner and lifted. It took a few yanks before giving way
with the sound of Velcro ripping apart. He worked his other hand under
and pulled harder until he had it lifted.

"Now isn't that a thing of beauty," he said.

"Guess we know how you're gonna watch me now," she said.

Sitting in the well of the trunk was a sniper rifle, broken down in a
foam insert case. He reached in and pulled out the high-powered scope
and aimed it toward a V-shaped valley in the mountains.

"Can see plenty far with this thing." He put it back and performed a
quick check to make sure no one was watching them. "I'll have to do a
little recon once we figure out the best spot for you to meet Beck." After
closing the trunk lid, they walked around the corner to the store
entrance.

Clarissa stopped by the front door. "Do you think he'll go for it?"

"Meeting you somewhere? Probably not, but it's worth a try."

"Won't it make him more suspicious?"

"That's what we want."

"Are you sure?"

Jack pulled the door open and ushered her through. "He's not
expecting me to show up if you can sell it to him. Convince him you
were scared because of everything that happened. He might suspect
something, but he'll have his guard down with you, Clarissa."

"How can you be sure of that?"

He paused while pouring his coffee. "Because I let my guard down
with you, Clarissa."

Twenty minutes later, they were fifteen minutes closer to Ticino,
about halfway there. Every so often, one of them would say, "Maybe that
spot," then the other would nod or not. They kept driving either way.
Five minutes from town when cell phone reception improved, he
stopped, and Clarissa stepped out of the car and made the call.

The wind whipped her hair around her back and shoulders. Turning
away from the gust, she covered the phone with her free hand. As the
wind died down, she walked away from the car.

Jack kept his gaze loose as he covered all angles in a sequence of
front, rearview, left then right. A single car passed. The driver didn't

even look over. In rural areas or places where cell signal was spotty, it wasn't that uncommon for someone to stop and make a phone call when reception became available.

The call took no more than five minutes. Clarissa jogged back to the car and climbed in. She stared straight forward, phone clutched in her hand.

"What's the verdict?" Jack asked.

Clarissa turned in her seat to face him. "The house."

"Dammit." Jack studied her for signs of betrayal and saw none. Still, he didn't like the idea of walking up to the house where Beck had time to prepare.

"I know but look at it this way." She pulled her hair back into a ponytail, strands still revolting due to the gusts. "I bailed on him and went back to Warsaw. If he's legit, that looks bad on me. Right?"

Jack nodded.

"And if it is a setup, he knows I went back there. Knows I went to that bar and I would assume he is aware it's a safehouse. So, the guy that showed up that you killed was his man. He either believes I did it or Clyde did it—"

"Or I did it."

"Someone." She opened the glove box and removed the concealed Glock and the comms equipment. "I can handle him."

"What if it's not just him?"

"Then you'll have to figure that out."

"So we both go out in a blaze of glory?"

Clarissa shrugged. "I'm done, Jack. I can't do this anymore. Either kill me or set me free."

"Run then."

"What?"

"Let me take you to the border of Italy. You have people there, right? The old people in that town loved you. They gotta have family throughout the country in small towns and on farms. Someone'll take you in. You can live a simple, peaceful life."

She scoffed. "And spend the rest of it looking over my shoulder. Waiting for some hired gun to show up and put a bullet in my brain. Or worse, haul me in so I can rot in a cell for whatever Beck's pinned on me. Does that sound like a great way to live out my years?"

Jack knew it wasn't and said as much. "I just don't see today ending well for either of us if you walk up to that door."

"I'll have you watching. I won't go in until he assures me he had nothing to do with what happened in Warsaw. Both times."

"And you'll believe him?"

"I know him, Jack."

"Then tell me why he abandoned you for all those months and only had interest *after* you escaped from his … those men."

"Either he sent them or he didn't." She reached for his hand. "There's no gray area here."

Jack sat back in his seat and rested his head and thought it over. They'd come this far, there was no choice but to see it out. If they pushed meeting elsewhere, Beck would get spooked and he might run. If he ran, he'd go to a place where they would have no chance of getting to him. At least out here, they could dictate some of the terms of the fight.

When his thoughts turned to the meeting possibly going sideways, he had to shut it down. If he thought that way, it'd happen that way. Instead, he had to control what he could control.

"Hand me that GPS," he said.

Reaching into the glove box, she grabbed the Garmin and handed it over.

"Give me the address." He waited while she recited it from memory and punched it in. Then he studied the terrain surrounding the house and determined he could set up on the hillside across from the property.

She leaned over and took a look as well.

"Pull this up on your phone. I want to see a satellite image as well as what's on either side of that point."

A few seconds later, she had Maps up and switched over to the image view. The area was surrounded by thick woods. The kind of place Jack could disappear just inside, and Beck wouldn't see him. Conversely, Noble would be blind to any lookouts or cameras Beck had placed there.

"This house," Jack said. "Does he own it?"

"We've been there before," Clarissa said. "Some years back. He said it belonged to a friend."

"You believe that?"

She nodded. "There were personal effects all over the place. Pictures of family, young and old. You could see the progression of the kids from babies to adults. Once they grew, the couple didn't need so much space, and they wanted to be someplace warmer, so they moved to Barcelona and use this as a getaway when the summer heat in Spain is unbearable."

"Do you recall any surveillance equipment?"

Clarissa laughed. "There's no crime out here, Jack."

"How did Beck know these people? Did they work for any government?"

"Friends of his parents. And before you ask, his dad was a carpenter and his mother a first-grade teacher." Zooming in on the image, she showed him the old swing set in the backyard. "These are family people. They don't know what Beck does. Probably figure he hangs out at the White House all day keeping toddlers from getting through the gates."

"Switch that map back to the regular view."

She zoomed out again and changed the setting so they saw the roads.

"OK," Jack said after looking the area over. "We're gonna drive up here." He pointed to a road a quarter mile east of the house. "I'll get out and trek down the hill until I have a clear view."

"OK."

"You're gonna have that burner in the glove box switched on. You wait for my call and then you drive to the house. Park on the street before the driveway."

"Won't that look weird?"

Jack thought it over. "Park on the driveway as far to the left side as you can. If I gotta move, I don't want anything obstructing my shot."

"OK."

They sat there for several minutes. The wind gusts picked up again, shaking the sedan. A rock formed in Jack's stomach and he couldn't ignore it. He'd been in several precarious positions in his life, but this felt off. It felt final. No matter what happened today, life would change forever for one of the three of them. Maybe all of them.

He wanted to turn to Clarissa, tell her he'd go to Italy with her. Spend his life on a farm in the middle of the country with her. They'd always have each other's backs. No one could sneak up on them if they were together. And if trouble found them, they'd move again. Resources weren't an issue. And there were plenty of places in the world they could take up residence.

Jack looked over at her. Her eyes were closed. Her hands were folded in her lap. She breathed in and out steadily. He almost reached for her. Then he thought of everyone in his life no longer with him, whether by death or choice, they'd all gone.

If they survived the afternoon, it would be better to let her go than hold her close and destroy her life.

CHAPTER 42

BRANDON STARED AT THE WOMAN AND SEARCHED HIS mental cabinet for images of Casey Whitworth while recalling the heartache her father still felt when he spoke of her.

Licking his lips, which still tasted of cheap beer, he tried to speak but only croaked out half a word. She stared at him with eyes devoid of emotion. Her expressionless face told him nothing, matching the images he'd seen of her. But she also looked somewhat like Chastity Braun. The more he stared and imagined the pictures he'd seen of both, he thought she could be either of them. A little work performed by a skilled plastic surgeon, and it could go either way. Or maybe she really was Brittany Schau, who since birth was the perfect blend.

Whatever the case, it broke Brandon's brain. Everything he'd heard and learned and seen over the past couple of days meant nothing to him anymore.

"I can see this is troubling for you," she said.

Brandon nodded his head for several seconds. "I just don't understand what's going on here."

"That's to be expected." Interlacing her fingers on the table, she leaned forward. "I'm impressed you cracked the names. And I have no clue how you reached that employee file and found Brittany."

"You speak of her like she's someone else."

"That's because she is."

"What?"

"Brittany's in Irvine, California, leading a team that believes they are working on a legitimate bioengineering project. They get fake data back so they don't realize how destructive their work truly is. They follow a madman who should've been killed many, many years ago."

"Well, we can agree there," Brandon said. "Is Schau really Chastity Braun?"

"Chastity was a lawyer, not a scientist. She had no idea any of this was ever going on."

"The names though?"

"Coincidence. I'm impressed you made that association. I really am. Maybe if you were working at Meadowcroft, Banyan wouldn't have been such a disaster."

Brandon pushed back from the table and looked at Brett. "Do you wanna fill me in here?"

Brett shrugged and said, "I still don't know what the hell is going on. Halfway here she started talking up a storm and said if we'd help her with immunity, she'd spill everything she knew."

"OK," Brandon said. "What does she know, 'cause she ain't saying anything I can use."

Brett looked down at the woman and gestured for her to continue.

"I always struggled with others. From the time I was a little girl, I had very few friends. The other smart kids hated me because I could physically dominate them. The other athletes couldn't stand me because I could run circles around them when it came to math and science. My parents tolerated me—"

"I spoke with your father," Brandon said. "Well, if you really are Casey."

"How is he?" she asked.

"He misses you. Wonders what happened to you."

Her eyes glossed over. "When this is all over, I'll reach out to him. Like I was saying, they tolerated me, but later, after college, I formed a bond with my father. I needed his guidance. My mentor was a terrible man. I just didn't see it at first."

"Meadowcroft."

She nodded.

"Why'd you stay around as long as you did?"

"Do you know much about David Meadowcroft?"

"I see your point," Brandon said.

"Good," she said.

"How long did it take for you to realize this?"

"Once I was in so deep I couldn't get out."

"He could've destroyed your life is what you're saying."

"No ... he did destroy my life is what I am saying."

Brandon paused before speaking again, needing to absorb everything that had been said and think about his next words. "Over eight years ago, you disappeared. If you're not Brittany, and Brittany isn't Chastity, what happened to Chastity, and where have you been all this time?"

The confidence left her as she dropped her chin to her chest and closed her eyes. Brandon had struck gold and asked the question she didn't want to answer.

Brett placed his hands on the table and leaned over her. "If you want any shot at immunity, you better tell the story."

When she lifted her face, tears streamed down her cheeks. They caught the curve of her jaw and fell from her chin. Not bothering to wipe her eyes, she spoke through light sobs, which dissipated after a few sentences.

"I was young when I started at Meadowcroft. A junior in college. I caught David's eye when I was barely twenty-one. To me, at the time, he was a god. He had the brains. Was good looking. Older. He took me under his wing and, well, I'd lived a pretty sheltered life and spent all my time with my face in a book or on the track or the pitch. I didn't have much experience with men. None, really. A few short flings just to experience it all, but never any connection."

"I can relate," Brandon said.

She smiled at him. Had he pierced the veil?

"Anyway, I was young, and he took advantage of that. Took me about eight years to realize it, and obviously, by that time, I was in very deep. I saw the things that were covered up. Knew all the secrets. When I tried to break away from him, he told me he'd retaliate. He'd make sure I went to jail and spent the rest of my life behind bars so thick even the guards wouldn't be able to get me out. I'd never see my few friends or my father ever again."

"So, you complied." Brandon shrugged. "I can see that. But you did manage to get away."

"Sort of."

"How do you mean, sort of?"

"I told him I just needed to go home for a little bit. You know, see my parents, spend some time away from the lab and the stress that went along with Banyan and dealing with David. Of course, I never said the latter to him. That would have been a disaster." A smile lingered for a few seconds. "I flew to Dulles and rented a car, but didn't go straight to my parents' house."

"Where'd you go?"

"South on 95, picked up 85 in Emporia. Final destination: Durham, North Carolina."

Brandon saw it now. "To see Chastity, your lone friend from your school days."

She glanced toward the corner of the room for a moment, perhaps collecting her thoughts. "I wouldn't say lone, but most definitely my best friend. As I mentioned before, I got sidetracked. Had a hard time with all the other kids. But Chastity was like me. Well, that's not accurate. Everyone loved her. But we connected because we were both good athletes—"

"Don't sell yourself short," Thomas said. "All American? That's pretty damn exceptional."

"Thank you," she said. "But that was a long time ago. Anyway, we were both highly intelligent, too."

"Right, she's a lawyer." Brandon paused a beat. "Was a lawyer."

Casey's face twisted with pain. "We went out for drinks on New Year's. Didn't think I had too much, but I still don't know exactly what happened. I lost control of the car and went off the road."

"New Year's 2013."

Tears streamed down her face. "It was a rural area. Even on a holiday, no one was driving that road."

"What happened, Casey?" Brandon asked.

"Chastity was ejected. It wasn't a horrible crash, but the car was a convertible, it was unseasonably warm that night, and she wasn't wearing a seatbelt. Dead on impact." Her hands trembled. Had she ever spoken of this before? "I was banged up as well, but could move, walk. After I managed to get her into the trunk, I drove the car down this long dirt road, found a clearing and there was a pond. I put her in the driver's seat and pushed the car into the pond and watched it sink."

The room was silent as everyone absorbed the confession.

"I went back a few days later to see if the car or a body had surfaced and neither had. The water was practically black. I did a little digging around and found that it was an old farm named Belle Grove and had been abandoned a hundred years earlier. The heirs had just left it to overgrow. If anyone ever took it over and found the car, well, they'd figure it was me in there after they traced the plates and VIN back to the rental company."

"You became Chastity."

"I called her firm and said I was her and had been in an accident and needed to take some time away. They granted it to me. I got a little work done to look more like her, which wasn't hard. Everyone always thought we were sisters."

Brandon started looking for holes. "How did no one know?"

"My parents had no clue I had flown in as early as I had. David didn't know my itinerary." She paused. "Once he said I could go, he forgot about me for a bit. Probably hadn't noticed I had left. He was so absorbed in Banyan, and with good reason. Progress was being made."

"Fast forward four years. Skinner dies, and some months later, Chastity disappears and Brittany Schau arrives." Brandon held out his hands. "This is related. How?"

"Frank came along sometime in 2013, maybe sooner. Wasn't like David told me much about that side of the business. But he mentioned he finally had someone on the inside who would push for government funding. Unlimited government funding, as he put it." Her expression soured. "This is when things started to get really bad. With all that money being thrown around, expectations were high. From the straights who didn't know what we were really doing, to the people like Skinner who pushed for bigger and faster advancements."

"It can be like that sometimes."

"Tell me about it. When I heard Skinner had been killed, I knew things would take a nasty turn, but I had no idea David would go to the lengths he did to secure funding."

Brandon waited to hear what she would say, knowing that the new sources were not people on the up and up.

"I hacked into his system ... well, hack is a strong word. He used the same three passwords the entire time I knew him and was still using them years later. I saw the people he communicated with. He'd managed to launder a couple hundred million dollars from terrorists through some crazy scheme to run it through a covert financial entity linked to the Vatican. He was working with a Treasury Department agent named Bent, I think."

Brandon felt ice slide down his back. "Beck?"

"Yeah, that's it. David had given him instructions on further funneling the money through Bitcoin and, I don't know, a whole bunch of stuff I didn't understand at the time. Beck would get a cut of everything, and a stake in the company. Beck had also agreed to finish tying up the *loose ends*."

Brandon kept his poker face in the midst of her confirming his suspicions. "Anything else?"

Sighing deeply, she shook her head. "I was careless."

"What happened?" Brandon asked.

"I accidentally hit reply while looking at an email in his inbox and left an empty draft. Guess he saw it. I received an anonymous communication that I would be found soon if I didn't stop."

Brandon had another answer, but more questions. "So, you made Chastity disappear?"

She nodded and leaned back in her chair and drained the rest of her beer. "Can I get another?"

Brett headed to the fridge. "I think we all need another."

Brandon said, "Back to Beck. Were there any other names you can recall from those communications?"

She laughed. "I hardly remembered his name. So much has happened since then, and it was only a few communications."

"Can you still access Meadowcroft's personal email and files?" Brandon asked.

She shook her head. "I tried a few times when I was in different locations, but he changed the passwords."

Brandon began typing out a message to Jack and Clarissa, warning them that he had confirmation Beck was involved with Meadowcroft.

Brett set a beer in front of everyone and stopped next to the woman. "Casey, we have reason to believe that David Meadowcroft put out contracts on several people, including two friends of ours who are actively being hunted. Did you ever hear of him doing something like this?"

"I wouldn't put it past him, and come to think of it, I'm sure he did it in the past, but..."

"But what?" Brett asked.

She looked at each of them in turn. "You don't know?"

"Know what?"

She closed her eyes. "David killed himself last year."

CHAPTER 43

JACK STOOD ON THE SHOULDER WITH THE RIFLE IN HIS right hand aimed at the ground and watched the sedan fade out of sight. He had twenty minutes to make it down the hill. Any more than that, and Clarissa would be late to meet Beck. The distance wasn't an issue. The steep decline proved worse than the GPS indicated. He stood at the top, stared down, worked out his initial line. Treat it like a switchback, he thought. He'd have to measure every step to stay on the path so he wouldn't have to double back when he reached the bottom.

Starting off wasn't too bad. The decline intensified ten yards in. The trees were spaced far enough apart that he couldn't always find a hand-hold, so he traveled horizontally until he reached a point he could slide down and latch onto a young tree or low branches.

The journey proved arduous. He slipped often, skidded five, ten feet at a time. Almost lost the rifle when the strap caught on a rock.

After ten minutes fighting with the mountainside, the grade less-ened, and he hiked the final hundred yards. The early-morning sun penetrated the outer layer of the woods. The leaves looked neon green as they shimmered in the breeze. Debris kicked up as a gust whipped through, carrying with it the smell of dying embers from an overnight fire. At any other time, it'd be a peaceful scene.

His thoughts turned to Johanna. He had no idea what hospital she was in, if she was even still in one, or what name they checked her in under. Did she have the capacity to use an alias? Did the owner of the bar, Clyde, make one up? Or call her a Jane Doe. These were questions he should have asked on the drive out of Warsaw, but the adrenaline and lingering shock and exhaustion from the previous two days rendered his mind incapable of processing his thoughts.

Once he was done with this mess, he'd find her. Make sure she was all right. Talk to whoever she needed him to talk to and back her story up. He'd let her know she didn't suffer for no reason. And that Noah, no matter how misguided his intentions had been, didn't die in vain.

The tree line lay fifty feet ahead. A two-story stone house with an even number of windows on either side of the front door and one more upstairs sat on a spacious lot with minimal but pleasant landscaping. All the window curtains were white and pulled back, creating a reverse V-shape from the top of the window down. A wide barren driveway led to a detached garage made of brick, indicating it had been built in recent years.

Jack slowed as he neared the edge of the woods, keeping about twenty feet of distance in a spot where the shade concealed him. He rested the rifle against a tree, buttstock on the forest floor. Holding the scope to his eye, he worked it methodically left to right, down to up, back to the left. The only movement came from the birds and the breeze.

He pulled out his phone and sent a text to the burner Clarissa had pulled out of the glove box. The message said, "We're a go." He didn't want to send it. He didn't believe it was safe to proceed because he didn't have faith that Beck had any honorable intentions. The plan was an aberration as far as tactical planning went. They'd be better off storming the house and detaining the guy than having Clarissa walk up to the front door. He estimated a fifty percent chance one of the three died today.

But there was that voice in his head. *Listen to the woman.* Was it from *Lethal Weapon*? Or *White Men Can't Jump*? One of those lines from a movie he loved and watched too many times as a kid. There were hundreds that popped up in the most random moments, like now. He admitted there was something to it, though.

He might not trust Beck. Clarissa might not trust him either. But she could read the guy, the same as she could read him. They had worked out a signal before he left the car and she drove off. Right hand behind her back, inverted peace sign. If he saw that, he was to take the shot.

Jack grabbed the rifle and gave it a final once-over. He started to reattach the scope when the sound of a door opening cracked the wind's whisper through the woods. Stepping to the right, where the rifle had been, he took cover behind a thick tree. He'd chosen this specific tree for this specific reason.

A White Swiss Shepherd darted through the opening and ran halfway across the yard. He stopped. Ears perked. He lifted his nose in the air. He sniffed.

Turn around, buddy.

The dog walked to the edge of the property and stared into the woods to the left of Noble's position. The dog's mouth closed and opened and closed again. He took a few more steps to Jack's left, walking along where the grass met the road until he was at the corner of the driveway. An electric fence, perhaps, kept him penned in.

The dog turned and strutted in the opposite direction, stopping a couple of times to sniff the air. Then he locked in Noble's position. Jack searched his mind for any facts he had on the breed. He couldn't recall if Shepherds were more sight or smell. Either way, the dog knew Jack was there and didn't make a sound.

A man appeared in the shadows and whistled, then called for the dog. Jack identified the voice as Beck's. He hoped the dog wouldn't be a problem. Not now, and not when Clarissa arrived. Another whistle caught the dog's attention, and he turned and trotted back inside.

Beck had been in Noble's sights for a good fifteen seconds, which was more than enough time had he been better prepared to take a shot. He had considered taking it anyway. It wasn't that far. He'd have to hit Beck, for sure. He could put an end to this chapter and call Clarissa and tell her not to come because someone else was out there, too. Someone who had gunned down Beck before Clarissa could look in his eyes as he answered her questions. Before she could determine the truth.

But it hadn't gone down that way because the dog went inside and Beck slipped in after him and shut the door.

The tension in Jack's shoulders eased, and he stepped back from the tree. He realized his current vantage point wasn't ideal, so he moved ten feet to the left where he'd have a better angle of the doorway. Clarissa would need to be set up perfectly for it to work. He sent her a text telling her to stand to the right of the door. It would force Beck to step at least into the doorway to see her. He'd probably think nothing of it, though he might wonder why she was standing so far over. Jack used the scope again and zeroed in to the right of the door and saw the bell. No reason to worry.

There was nothing left to do but wait for the sedan to pull up. For Clarissa to park in the driveway all the way to the left. For Beck to check through one of the front windows and see her get out of the car. He'd head to the door and wait there. Wouldn't open it until after she arrived.

But if he did open it, if he came out onto the porch and welcomed her with a hug, he wouldn't let her step to the right. Beck would keep her right in front of him. Because it worked in his favor, but not Jack's. No, he was in the worst possible position should that happen. So he grabbed the rifle and went back to his first spot and checked the angle again. Head on. Wouldn't work. So he moved to the right about ten feet further and felt like that could work, but he'd need to tell Clarissa to position herself to the left of the door.

He fired off another text and pocketed the phone. He picked up the rifle and attached the scope. He sighted in on the center of the door about middle of chest height and breathed in, held it, breathed out. Breathed in again, held it, waited for his heart to slow down, breathed out. Once more, he breathed in, held it, and this time knowing when the pause in his heart's rhythm would occur, he imagined squeezing the trigger and putting a bullet through Beck's heart.

The sound of an approaching car broke the silence.

Noble didn't move.

The vehicle appeared, turned into the driveway, parked to the left.

Noble didn't move.

The door opened and slammed shut. Clarissa came into view in his peripheral.

Noble didn't move.

The front door opened. Beck stepped out. He stopped dead center of the scope.

Breathe in, hold.

Clarissa hurried past the five windows to the left of the front door.

Breathe out, hold.

Beck opened his arms wide. The expression on his face was not a welcoming one. It was fraught with worry or anxiety.

Breathe in, hold.

Clarissa stopped short of his reach. She stuck her right arm out, held up a finger.

Breathe out, hold.

His arms dropped. He spoke quickly. The sound of his voice carried up the embankment. The words were indecipherable.

Breath in, hold.

Clarissa shook her head. She wrapped her right arm around her back.

He continued to hold. His heart continued to slow. Thump-thump. Thump-thump.

She made a fist.

He exhaled and waited for the signal.

Beck's chin dropped to his chest, he clenched his eyes tight.

Clarissa reached out with her right hand and placed it on his shoulder.

Beck looked up. He spoke and Jack read his lips. "I could never do that to you. This all got out of control. These same people are after me, too."

Jack looked up from the scope as Clarissa and Beck walked toward the front door together. The second part of the plan had started. He was to wait five minutes, then exit the woods and head to the front door. Clarissa would meet him there. If she didn't, he was to break in and do what was necessary.

The walk to the last of the trees was easy. He got there and took a position behind the thickest he could find. His phone buzzed, and he reached for it. The number on the screen didn't match the one he had been messaging. Several messages popped in one after the other. He scrolled up and felt his heart drop. All the messages were from Brandon.

Meadowcroft died a year ago. He wanted you dead over Skinner.

Beck had been working with him, laundering money for the Banyan project.

Beck's in deep. Was going to get a cut and share of the company.

Beck agreed to tie up "loose ends" Jack. That's you! It's all about Skinner!

The implications struck him like lightning.

Beck was behind all of this now.

Jack had suspected it before.

He knew it now.

"Clarissa."

Jack dropped the rifle and the phone and sprinted toward the house.

CHAPTER 44

JACK DIDN'T SLOW DOWN WHEN HE HIT THE PORCH. PISTOL in his left hand, he grabbed the knob with his right and half twisted as his shoulder hit the door. It broke free before the latch cleared and crashed open. He felt the same pain in his upper arm that he'd felt after the explosion, but it didn't stop him.

The Swiss Shepherd met him at the door, his lips peeled back, teeth bared. He growled and barked but held his ground and didn't attack. Jack kept the dog in front of him. It was all he could do in the foyer. He didn't have far to go, though. Down the hall stood Clarissa and Beck. She spun, shock on her face at the sight of Jack standing there, pistol aimed at her. Beck stood behind her. He reached behind his back.

"Don't do it, man!" Jack yelled.

"Jack, what are you doing?" Clarissa screamed back.

He ignored her. "I will end you if you bring that gun around. Don't test me, Beck."

Beck brought his hand back around slowly. It was empty. He lifted both arms in the air. "OK, Jack, you got it. Look, it's just us here. Let's talk—"

"Call off the dog."

"Jack," Clarissa said, her voice dialed down. "What is going on here? What are you doing?"

He ignored her again. "Call the dog off, Beck."

"Mischa," Beck said. "Come."

The dog stopped growling. Her ears relaxed, she lowered her head. Beck repeated the command, more assertive this time, added a short whistle. Mischa turned and walked over to him. Spinning in a half-circle, she sat next to Clarissa and stared at Jack.

Clarissa held her hands out to placate Jack. Her wide eyes betrayed her calm demeanor. Presumably she thought Jack had flipped. And he couldn't blame her because he had.

She said, "Why don't you lower that gun?"

Jack said, "Why don't you step aside?"

Beck still had his hands up. He stepped around Clarissa, moved in front of her. "Look, Jack, if you feel you gotta take that shot, do it. But you're making a mistake if you kill me right now."

"Am I? The way I see it, I'll be doing the world a favor." He glared at Beck, shook his head. "Funneling money from terrorists? Jesus Christ, man, you took an oath."

Clarissa's face twisted, and she took a few steps back. "Beck, what's he talking about?"

Beck ignored her. "Jack, if you want out of this mess, you need to hear me out."

The only thing separating Noble's index finger from the trigger was a thin layer of sweat. He wanted to squeeze it; hoped he'd sneeze so it would happen without him thinking. He almost pulled it, but he couldn't do it with Clarissa directly behind Beck, and Beck knew that.

"Clarissa, move," Jack said.

"Jack, whatever you think is going on here," she said, "let's talk about it first."

Beck made no movement. Stood there like a guy who knew he was as good as dead and had at least one card left to play to extend his life and possibly save it if he could be useful enough.

"Come on, Jack," Clarissa said. "One conversation."

The muscles around his eyes and mouth relaxed. The pain in his shoulder throbbed. He could move it, so he knew it wasn't dislocated, but it hurt like hell. He hadn't really noticed until now because the edge from the adrenaline had worn off slightly around the same time Clarissa's words had gotten through his thick skull.

"Are you armed?" Jack asked.

Beck nodded. "In my waistband, middle of my back."

"Clarissa," Jack said.

"Yeah?" she said.

"Get his gun, eject the magazine, clear the chamber, and slide it toward me."

Beck lifted his arms and interlaced his fingers behind his head and allowed Clarissa to retrieve the pistol. She ejected and tossed the magazine toward Jack. She set the pistol down and slid it across the hardwood. Beck didn't move. Jack stopped the sliding gun with his foot and then kicked it behind him and heard it bang against the sill plate.

"We good now?" Beck separated his hands but kept them above his shoulders.

"You and I will never be good."

Clarissa stepped forward and stood next to Beck. The shot was there if Jack wanted it.

"Can we talk this out?" she said.

"What did he say to you?" Jack said.

Beck said, "I told her—"

"Not you, asshole."

Clarissa said, "He told me he messed up. He got me in trouble a while back and subsequently put you back on the map of some people who really don't like you—"

"Tell them to take a number."

"—and he's been trying to fix it, Jack."

Noble took his eyes off Beck for a moment and saw the sincerity on Clarissa's face. Whether the story was a crock or partly factual, Beck had convinced her it was the truth.

"One question, one answer. OK, Beck?"

Beck nodded.

"If you lie to me, that'll be it for you. Got me? Taking your life will mean absolutely nothing to me. I'll probably enjoy it. Understand?"

Beck nodded again.

"Did you launder terrorist money for Meadowcroft?"

Beck closed his eyes. His hands dropped to his side and he nodded a third time.

"Why?"

"Money. Power. Meadowcroft was persuasive. Plus, he had something on me that would've ruined me. It made more sense to lie in bed with that devil than face the consequences."

Jack's jaw was clenched so tight he expected a molar to crack in half. In that moment, the anger and rage he felt for what the man had done, how he had endangered Clarissa, himself, and countless others had no parallel in Noble's recent memory. The only person he'd ever wanted to kill more had been Frank Skinner.

But Beck had been honest. He deserved another chance.

"Who else is here with you?" Jack said.

"Just me." He licked his lips and wiped the sweat from his brow. "Look, if anyone shows up here, we're all dead. OK? Me, you, Clarissa. They'll have a bullet for each of us." He lowered his hands a bit more. "I screwed up, Jack. I'm trying to make it right. At least let me do that, then you can do whatever you feel you gotta do to me." He shook his head and forced a laugh. "I'd almost prefer you do that, because there's a six-by-nine cell in a federal prison waiting for me, and I don't think I can live out the rest of my life like that."

Every fiber of his being said not to trust the guy. That this was a setup. That the moment Clarissa arrived, he had made a call and dispatched a team that would show up any moment now. They would finish the job the guys at the farm and the guys in Warsaw failed to do.

The rawness in Beck's voice gave him pause. Beck had admitted to what Brandon had said he had done. The specifics were in a text on the phone he'd dropped in the woods.

"Jack," Clarissa said. "Will you hear him out?"

Noble took a moment to clear his thoughts. A few minutes of dialog couldn't hurt. It might provide the answers Jack had been seeking for so long. Then Beck would pay the price for his betrayals.

"OK, but we can't do it here."

"I'll go wherever you want."

"Leave your phone, wallet, keys here. Put nothing else on. We're going into the woods to get my phone and the rifle. All three of us. Then, Clarissa, you'll drive us away from here. We'll find someplace secluded. And if I don't like what I hear, you're a dead man, Beck."

Five minutes later, they were on the road. Twenty minutes later, they stopped in the same secluded location where Clarissa had placed the call to Beck. They got out of the car and walked with Beck in front and Clarissa and Jack behind him until they were far away from the road, obscured from view. Someplace no one could see them.

Jack pulled out his phone and opened the voice recording app and pressed record. "State your name and tell me everything from the beginning."

Beck cleared his throat, said his name, then began his confession.

"It was probably ten years ago when I was first turned on to David Meadowcroft. We thought there were some inconsistencies in the funding he was receiving and investigated him. Couldn't prove anything. We could've run him up on some trumped-up charges, but they wouldn't have stuck, and with the way the guy's wealth, power, and influence were growing, it wouldn't have done any good.

"I kept tabs on him for a bit, but then your buddy Frank Skinner made a deal with him. Frank was sure he could secure the funding if Meadowcroft would see to it that Skinner led the project once it was ready for widespread use in the military. Meadowcroft agreed. Frank went to work, pressuring the members of the subcommittee that approved funding for these types of projects. Soon enough, Meadowcroft had unlimited funds. Now, whether he intended to make good on the promise he made to Skinner has always been up for debate. Obviously, they never got that far because—"

"I killed Skinner." Jack looked down at the phone and shrugged. It was public knowledge, and the Agency had swept it under the rug. No one would come after him now.

"Right, and you know what? A lot of people were happy you did."

"Probably those same politicians Skinner blackmailed into writing Meadowcroft a blank check."

Beck smiled and nodded. "I'm sure of it. Well, the subcommittee bailed on the Meadowcroft project, and the funding dried up. He started burning through his own funds, but with the amount of cash being used, his liquid assets soon dried up. He tried to secure funding, but no banks would work with him."

"So he got creative, and that's where you came in."

"I'm not proud of this, Jack. It wasn't like the guy called me up and said, 'Hey, why don't you launder money for me?'"

"How'd he get you to do it, then?"

"I had a daughter."

"What?" Clarissa said. "A daughter?"

Beck glanced at her and nodded, then stared off away from them. "She was sick. The treatment she needed would've cost more than my salary at the time. This is back when I was a rookie."

"You had government benefits," Jack said. "They would've taken care of everything."

Beck clenched his eyes tight. "She was illegitimate. Her mother was married to another man, and not just any man, but my best friend at the time. I couldn't... I just didn't think I could do that to him. So I agreed to help someone in exchange for her treatment."

"Meadowcroft."

"Yeah."

"What'd you do?"

"I was an accomplice in the murder of a high-profile state senator in California."

"An assassination."

Beck nodded.

"Did you pull the trigger?"

Beck nodded again.

"Say it."

"I pulled the trigger."

"We're not so different, Beck."

He looked up at Jack and met his gaze. "He had me."

"So, you did his bidding, used your connections and skills to move a quarter of a billion dollars all the while lying about where it came from and making up a fake investigation. Is that right?"

"Yeah, that's pretty much it."

"Pretty much." Jack shook his head. "Here's what I don't get. Why keep pushing it? And if you're not the one behind the attempts on me and Clarissa, who is?"

Beck looked confused. "Meadowcroft. That's the whole point here."

"I was just told he killed himself a year ago. Brandon messaged me. They got some woman, Casey Whitworth, who has a couple aliases all intertwined with Meadowcroft. She told them all about it."

Beck shook his head. "I'm not sure what you're being told, but Whitworth died on December 31, 2013, and I spoke to David Meadowcroft two days ago."

CHAPTER 45

SUNLIGHT STREAMED IN THROUGH THE WINDOW. BRANDON had forgotten to close the drapes before collapsing into bed. The brightness amplified the lingering headache from the beers he'd consumed the day before. He hadn't been drunk when he went to bed. He also wasn't used to a bunch of crap in his system. Shielding his eyes, he grabbed his water. Before going to bed, he shot three squirts of lemon-lime Mio into it. He downed half the glass, took a breath, and finished it off. It tasted like watered down Gatorade. Not the best, not the worst.

He tapped his phone and checked the time. Only six a.m. Far too early, considering he had been up past one a.m.

Maneuvering off the bed and into his wheelchair, he rolled over to the window. Tall trees rose into a clear sky. The sun was hovering just above them. It might be a good day after all. His stomach growled, so he spun around and went to the en suite bathroom to freshen up and splash some water on his face. Before leaving the room, he grabbed his phone, and when he reached the door, he looked down at it.

"Ten messages?"

The app icon connected to the secure channel he had in place with Noble. He was certain there were updates on the Beck situation. Hopefully, it was all resolved without harm to him or Clarissa.

But what he saw when he scrolled through the communications

turned his stomach more than any amount of beer could have. He backed away from the door, read through the messages again, absorbing the information. Whitworth was dead. Meadowcroft was alive. The hell was going on? Had the woman he'd been led to believe was Casey Whitworth conned them all? They had no solid proof of anything, and while her story had required some disassociation with reality to absorb, it was believable.

Tapping on the reply button, he started to type out a message. His hands started shaking, then convulsing. The phone fell into his lap. His head throbbed down the middle from the base of his skull to his chin. Pain tore through him. His eyelids fluttered. He couldn't see or hear anything. But he felt the pain and the terror gripping every nerve ending in his body. He wanted to scream out, but his mouth wouldn't open. He wanted to get out of his chair and run, but his legs felt as though they were wrapped with cement.

His thoughts trailed off. The panic faded. The room seemed to brighten even though his eyes were closed. The spasms slowed, then ceased as he faded into oblivion.

THE SHOUTING WOKE HIM. IT TOOK SEVERAL SECONDS TO recall where he was and what he had been doing the previous forty-eight hours. Once the fog lifted, it all came rushing back, everything from Brett showing up at his door to the attack he had suffered moments or minutes or hours ago. He wasn't even sure what time it was. He checked his phone and saw it wasn't even six-thirty. It hadn't been that long.

Brett yelled again, this time for help. Brandon rushed past the kitchen. Brett stood in front of the couch, facing Brandon, his hand over his eyes. The man heaved through a couple of sobs. About that time, Thomas hurried down the stairs, only wearing his boxers, his hair a disheveled mess. He stopped next to Brandon and put his glasses on.

"Brett? What is it?"

Brandon already knew. Chris's head hovered just over the top of the couch. His hair was matted with blood.

Thomas took a few steps and had the same revelation. "Oh, Christ!" Spinning around, he grabbed his stomach and ran for the bathroom. The sound of him throwing up filled the room.

Brandon wheeled past the couch and took a deep breath before spinning around, but nothing could have prepared him for the mutilation he saw.

"What the hell did she do?"

Brett shook his head. "I'm gonna kill her." He went to the door and pulled it open. "Dammit! She took the car."

Brandon followed him over, noticed a trail of blood leading away from the front porch. "She might not have gotten away unscathed."

Brett looked down at him. His eyes were dark. His lips quivered. He looked back at his dead friend. "We should cover him up."

A few minutes later, Brett and Thomas carried Chris's corpse down to the basement. Brett had a freezer down there big enough to store the body. They reconvened in the kitchen. They each glanced at the couch and the bloody stains on the front door. Finally, Brett positioned himself to block the view.

"I woke up to these messages." He handed his phone to Brett. Thomas crowded in to read along. "My initial thinking was we have to consider the source, since all of this intel came from Beck. But the guy admitted to Noble that it was true he had laundered money for Meadowcroft. He was willing to say so while Jack recorded the conversation."

"Do you have that conversation?"

"Hang on." Brandon sent a message requesting it. Fifteen seconds later, he had a link. "Here goes."

The three of them listened to Beck spill his guts on how he had funneled the funds for Meadowcroft and the reasons why. The revelation at the end that Casey Whitworth was dead and Meadowcroft was still living wasn't as shocking as it would have been if the woman were still detained in the house.

The recording finished, and Brandon sent a new message to Jack that said, "Next steps?" Then he went back to his room and grabbed his laptop and set up at the table again. He wasn't sure what he was looking for when he pulled up the window connected to Meadowcroft's system. He queried email accounts, locations, phone numbers. He printed twenty pages of information.

Thomas and Brett came over to join him.

Brett said, "Hear back from Noble yet?"

Brandon checked his phone and shook his head.

Thomas said, "Do you think she's going back to Chicago?"

Brett said, "Doubtful."

"Where do you think she's going, then?"

"If I knew who she was, I could probably tell you, but I haven't got a clue, man. Best guess is she ditched the car a quarter mile away from a Sheetz and hiked back to the service station. There, she used the restroom to wash up and get the blood off her skin. Maybe bought a change of clothes and a hat. Found a trucker going anywhere but here and hitched a ride."

"That story she gave us," Thomas said. "There has to be some truth to it, doesn't there? It was too real."

Brett shrugged. "Whole thing could've been true. We could go find that pond on the deserted farm and pull out a car with a body trapped behind the wheel. Doesn't tell us who it is or was or who this woman is and was. She managed to kill a guy that did two tours as a Green Beret in the Stan. Sliced him up and gutted him like he was a damn fish. Maybe he screwed up and fell asleep. Maybe she got to him with more of her story, offered to get him a beer, grabbed a chef's knife as well, and then did it."

Brett walked to the front door and traced his finger across the dried blood. Then he turned back around. "We can't do anything about her. And that's fine. For now. I'll hunt her down. What we need to focus on now is finding Meadowcroft and exacting revenge on that spawn of satan."

Brandon started searching for information on David Meadowcroft. "She wouldn't have said that bit about him killing himself if there wasn't something behind it. She had to have figured we would check on it eventually, right?"

Thomas said, "She might have just been trying to buy some time. Remember, she said that Schau and Beck had covered it up. Any media clips that went out were artificially created."

"True." Brandon scrolled through the results, finding nothing that could confirm the story. Nor anything that could disprove it. "David Meadowcroft, where would you go to hide out?"

"Guy's got almost unlimited resources," Brett said. "He could go anywhere."

"Does he, though? He needed someone on the inside to help him launder and funnel money. Really dirty money. The kind that won't go unnoticed forever. That takes time, especially if they went the crypto route. Remember, she mentioned Bitcoin and other things she supposedly didn't understand. To do that effectively, you're routing through multiple wallets, then you're using a blender."

"A what?" Brett looked as though he were hearing someone talk about particle physics.

Thomas said, "It's some really advanced stuff that makes it almost impossible to ever trace the source wallet once the process is complete. There's maybe five people in the world with the capability of tracking these transactions down, start to finish."

"And with this much money," Brandon said, "a quarter of a billion dollars, no one could get through it all. But still, you have to let it rest for a while. Cash all that out at once and someone's showing up at your door."

"So what's all this mean?" Brett said.

"It means that Mr. Meadowcroft and whoever is still on his side may not have as much cashflow as you might suppose. Think about that when you're trying to figure out where he's hiding out."

Brett nodded. "He's as close to home as possible."

"Gotta be."

"California," Brett said.

A message lit up Brandon's phone. They all held their breath while he opened it.

Brandon looked up at Brett and smiled.

"Burbank, to be exact."

CHAPTER 46

BECK ARRANGED FOR A FLIGHT OUT OF SWITZERLAND. JACK had concerns, but Clarissa eased them. It took every favor he had left to make it happen. He found someone in the private sector with too much money who was in need of an even bigger favor. Beck contacted a prominent politician who he'd helped not too long ago. It took some negotiation and required Beck to accept a job from the politician that was deeply disturbing, involving a mistress and her kids. He joked that he'd probably be in jail anyway, so there was little chance he'd have to complete the job.

The person in the private sector lent Beck their personal Gulfstream G650. The flight showed up at a regional airport at one p.m. They boarded fifteen minutes later. An attractive flight attendant offered them a drink. Clarissa had champagne. Beck had scotch. Noble had bourbon. Two, in fact. They lifted off just after two.

To say the interior of the jet was opulent was an understatement. Two plush chairs that folded into beds were up front. In the middle, there were two couches that faced each other. Four captain's chairs at the back of the cabin were in a two-by-two configuration, also facing each other. A table rose out of the floor in the middle of them. Jack and Clarissa and Beck had their drinks and a small meal consisting of chicken, green beans, and salad, and talked a little strategy.

The short of it was they had none, really. The best they came up with was Meadowcroft's childhood home. A place he hadn't visited in decades according to an interview in Newsweek from eight years ago. An obscure reference, for sure. But still one that had been made. And a guy like Meadowcroft didn't make references for no reason. Was it a stretch to say he had placed a clue that day? Probably. But not entirely. So they decided that was where they'd start. A little house on a little street in a little town a little bit away from Burbank, California.

After finishing his meal and his second drink, Jack took one of the couches and settled in for the flight. Clarissa took the other. Facing each other, they said nothing. Beck remained in the back. He lowered the table and reclined his seat and was out before Jack or Clarissa had even closed their eyes.

Jack last checked his watch at five 'til three, which left him about ten hours to catch some sleep. Flying backward through time, it would be around four-thirty p.m. in California when they landed. Plenty of time to get a car and get past Burbank to the little house on the little street in the little town. Plenty of time to start an investigation that might go anywhere, but even if that were the case, they'd be able to check one item off the list. They'd find another place to check. They'd find a lead. Jack had committed to going to the ends of the earth to hunt Meadowcroft down.

THEY STEPPED OFF THE PLANE INTO PARADISE. THE AIR WAS warm, the sun was heading toward the ocean, and L.A. was enveloped in an orange haze of smog. Jack breathed in the air. He knelt down and scraped his fingers across the asphalt. It felt good to be on American turf again.

The private airfield was north of the city, close to Burbank. Brandon and Brett were set to arrive soon with another man named Thomas, who had details of the inner workings of Meadowcroft.

Beck pointed at a blue Suburban parked nearby. "That's our ride. I'll go take care of payment and all that."

Clarissa walked with Jack to the small terminal. Not even five minutes on the ground and both were ready to get out of the heat.

"Sleep well on the flight?" he asked her.

"Well enough," she said. "It was nice to relax, knowing no one was gonna kill me for a little while."

Jack laughed. "Fair enough, and I get that."

"Think we're safe here, Jack?"

He chewed on it for a moment. Could they trust Beck to be true to his word? The guy could've sold them out while in the air. Their next stop could be their final one.

"I can't trust the guy," Jack said. "But we've got no choice. This needs to end, and I don't care how, really. I mean, I do for you. You've got the potential for a great life, Clarissa. When we're through this, I want nothing more than for you to disappear."

She tilted her head and rested it against the wall she leaned against. Her gaze cut right through him. "What if you disappeared with me?"

"We've been down this road too many times before. I thought..."

"What?"

"In Italy, you know, I really thought we had a chance."

"So did I." She bit her bottom lip.

"Once this is done, someone else is coming. And then someone else. I'll never be done with this. I can't drag you into it."

"Shouldn't I be able to make that decision for myself?"

"No, you shouldn't. There's something else at play with you and me, and I don't know that it's healthy for you to be around me."

Lowering her chin, she glanced down at the ground. "Yes, you're right. I knew it in Italy, too. It was nice, and maybe even a glimpse into what life could've been like if we were normal people."

Jack chuckled. "Normal. What the hell is that?"

Shrugging, she continued. "But I knew it could never be permanent. I guess ..." She exhaled hard through her nose. "I guess there's always that part of me that was a fifteen-year-old girl with a huge crush on my father's protégé."

"Protégé?"

"One of his projects, I guess." She laughed. "And as I grew into a woman and we really got to know each other, well, I mean, Jack, you were my first love. I knew then it was a fantasy that I could tie you down. No one ever could. And, frankly, I don't know that I want to be tied down."

"You shouldn't be." Gently, he reached out and brushed her hair out of her face. "Go live. See the world. We'll talk to Brandon to get you set up with whatever you need, IDs, passports, all of it."

"I know you're right. I just can't shake the feeling that—"

The door whipped open, and Beck walked in. "Their flight just landed. Let's get them, get loaded up, and get moving."

Clarissa sighed. "To be continued, I suppose."

"I suppose," echoed Jack.

They walked outside together and found Beck near the Suburban. He had the tailgate open and waved them over.

"Let's go see what he wants," Jack said.

Beck grinned when they got closer. He looked like a little kid on Christmas. Jack soon saw why. There were eight handguns and two HK MP7s.

"Take your pick, friends," Beck said.

Jack grabbed two Sig 9mm handguns. The MP7s could wait. Clarissa grabbed a 9mm as well.

"Just one?" Jack said.

"We'll see where the night goes," she said.

"Any chance you have a way to reach Clyde?"

She shook her head. "Not without that burner. I'm hoping Brandon does. I want to check in on him."

"I need to check in on Johanna."

The woman had been on his mind intermittently since leaving Warsaw. During the early part of the drive, he worried about her frequently. The nearer they got to Switzerland, the less he thought of her. He had to focus on the task ahead. Worrying about something he couldn't control in those situations had always spelled disaster.

"I hope she's OK," Clarissa said.

"I hope he's OK," Jack said.

Beck tapped Jack's shoulder. "That's their plane."

He turned and watched the smaller jet taxi next to the Gulfstream. The ground crew went to work. A few minutes later, the door opened, and Brett climbed down, followed by a man Jack had never seen before.

His relationship with Brett had been tumultuous to say the least. They had always worked things out, though, and he figured today would be no different. The fact that neither was there to kill the other was a good start.

They met halfway across the tarmac and shook hands.

"This is Thomas," Brett said. "Meadowcroft employee of sorts."

"Of sorts?" Jack extended his hand and Thomas took it.

"Limited to one area, really," Thomas said. "And worked solo in a satellite office, so never had much interaction with the rest of the group."

"You know David Meadowcroft?" Jack asked.

Thomas nodded. "Haven't seen him in a couple years. When that woman, whoever she really is, said he was dead, I found it plausible. There were rumors that David hadn't been seen for some time."

Jack turned his attention back to Brett and asked, "They wheeling up a ramp for Brandon?"

"Nah, stay here and watch this."

Brett ran back to the jet and climbed up the steps. Brandon appeared in the doorway, standing straight. With Brett walking backward in front of him, Brandon descended each step on his own until he reached the bottom of the stairs. He looked wiped out when he got there, but he made it.

Jack hurried over before Brandon was seated in his wheelchair.

"Had to look you in the eye, man," Jack said.

Brandon smiled and held out his arms. Jack embraced him.

"Been too long, old friend," Jack said.

"Sure has."

Jack felt the man's tears on his neck. "You crying, you big baby?"

Brandon laughed as he pulled back. He didn't bother to wipe his eyes. "A real man isn't afraid to shed tears, Jack. It takes strength to face one's emotions and vulnerability to express them."

"You read that in one of those fortune cookies you love so much?"

"I don't eat them anymore, man."

Jack took a step back and eyed him up and down. "Yeah, you look great. Kimberlee did a good job getting you abs, huh?"

The smile faded from Brandon's face. "We'll see about that."

"Let's get you over to the car and get the hell out of here."

"Sounds good. I'll tell you what I figured out about Meadowcroft during the flight over here."

CHAPTER 47

BRETT TOOK THE WHEEL WITH BECK SEATED NEXT TO HIM.
Clarissa and Thomas took the back row. Jack sat in the middle behind
Brett to keep an eye on Beck. Brandon was next to him.

The Suburban was big and comfy and surprisingly nimble. It registered two thousand miles on the odometer. Still smelled new. There
were crayons in the cupholder and little bits of goldfish crackers on the
floor.

They cleared the exit, and Jack turned toward Brandon. "What's this
about info you got on the flight?"

Brandon looked ahead and then shrugged at Jack with his palms up.

"Don't worry about Beck," Jack said. "He's on our side for now. Well,
as much as he can be."

"For good," Beck said.

"I'll settle with for now," Jack said.

"Suit yourself, but I'll surprise you."

Clarissa squeezed Jack's shoulder. Maybe her way of asking him to
cut the guy a break for a few minutes.

"All right then," Brandon said. "I have access to most of their system,
but one thing I kept encountering was records that corresponded to
another table that just didn't exist. No matter how I tried, I couldn't
find it."

"What kind of records are we talking about here?" Jack asked.

"Boring stuff, mostly. But enough that it caught my eye, and I wanted to see where they led, especially things that were related to Banyan." He paused and grabbed his stomach for a moment. Jack noticed the pained look on Brandon's face. "Whew, that was something."

"You OK?" Jack asked.

Brandon nodded. "I'll be all right. So anyway, I get to thinking, maybe this thing is hidden or requires some extra code to access. I started trying all these combinations related to Banyan. Came up with nothing at all. I was ready to throw my laptop out when Thomas started talking about the woman."

It felt as though the air left the cabin. No one had mentioned what happened to Chris. Brett had compartmentalized and pushed through the loss of his friend, but the scene would affect him sooner than later.

"I had an idea. That random record I found with Brittany Schau had an email address. I accessed the corporate web mail and started playing with the login."

"Was it related to Banyan?" Jack asked.

"No. Well, yes, but not yet," Brandon said. "The name, though, and this is the key."

Brett looked at Jack in the rearview and smiled. "This is cool."

"Casey Whitworth, Chastity Braun, and Brittany Schau. Three women somehow all linked together in this mess. Through Beck, we learned Whitworth did in fact die years ago. She wasn't the one in the house with us, though she claimed to be her. She managed to get really emotional when I brought up her father and when discussing the accident, and I think that caused us all to suspend disbelief for a short period of time."

Jack shrugged. "She could've rehearsed the story mentally on the way over. Gotten herself to believe it. She might have been saying this for years, right?"

Brett shook his head. "She really didn't shut up on the plane once she started talking."

Brandon said, "She made it a point to talk about this farm where she sunk the car with her friend, Chastity, inside of it, dead. The emotions were real and raw, man. She said the name of the farm, and for some reason it stuck out to me."

"What was it?" Jack asked.

"Belle Grove."

"OK. Does that mean anything?"

"On the surface? No. But how often do I linger around the surface?"

"Rarely. I mean, you can't swim, can you?"

Brandon laughed. "Right, so I dug and found something on, get this, Ancestry.com of all places. Had to pay for a damn account to view it. I mean, this is a legitimate problem in our world now, Jack. Everything is behind a damn paywall, and to make it worse, it's all subscriptions. I don't even know what I'm—"

"Brandon," Jack said. "I might die of old age by the time you finish this story if you go on this rant."

The remark earned a couple of laughs from the others, including Brandon.

"Yeah, right. Guess who owned the farm at the turn of the century?"

"2000?" Jack asked.

"1900." Brandon said.

"I couldn't tell you if my life depended on it, but if their last name is Logan—"

"Nothing to do with Bear. I'll save you the struggle. A woman named Brittany Schau, descended from Swedish immigrants, people who bought the land and built the farm and died when Brittany was seventeen years old. She dedicated the rest of her short life to that place, and when she passed, the only heirs were cousins who didn't care and left the place to nature, passing it down to their kids, who passed it down to their kids."

Jack paused a beat to absorb the information. "So, Casey Whitworth really is Brittany Schau now?"

"Casey Whitworth is dead," Beck said.

"How do you know?" Brett asked.

"Because I recovered the body from that damn car." Beck turned in his seat and looked at Jack. "It was one of the things Meadowcroft had me do. I flew into Raleigh. Rented a car. Bought a tarp and shovel and some heavy-duty waders and I went into the pond and got the body out. I buried her close by."

"She must have been all distorted by then," Jack said. "How could you have determined whether it was her or her friend?

"Yeah, she was. I still remember the sight of her. But she had a tattoo on her ass that Meadowcroft told me would identify her."

"What was it?" Brandon asked.

"Coordinates. 42.438480, -76.496891."

"How in the world did you remember that?" Brandon asked.

"I was forced to remember it," Beck said, "and there was something about the way that woman looked when I pulled her out of the water, all bloated, and I had to check for the tattoo and the skin was distorted and so were the numbers. It just stuck after that."

"Where's it lead to?" Jack asked.

"Never checked," Beck said. "Didn't want that in my memory."

Brandon had his laptop open. "Say those coordinates again slowly."

Beck repeated them. Brandon typed them in.

"Taughannock Falls State Park in New York." Brandon looked up. "That mean anything to anybody?"

No one spoke up.

"Wait," he said. "What if?" He typed furiously. "Beck, what email did you use to reach him? Was it corporate?"

"Yeah, but one he didn't give out. DaM678@meadowcroftc.com."

Brandon punched it in and moved to the password section. He tried a few different combos before finally getting it. "That's it! Taughannock with a zero in place of the o."

"These rich people baffle me," Brett said. "Smart enough to earn billions, yet dumb enough to get hacked."

"If you want to see real hacking," Brandon said. "Talk to me after this is over."

"Anything good in there?" Jack asked.

"Oh, man, this is good." He leaned forward. "Brett, turn around, we need to head to Irvine."

Brett looked over his shoulder. "You sure? 'Cause that's a good hour from here."

"Trust me," Brandon said.

CHAPTER 48

THE SMALL WAREHOUSE OFF PORTOLA PARKWAY WAS NESTLED in the foothills of Limestone Canyon. The sun hovered far to the west, bathing the building in a wash of pink and red. The barren parking lot made them think the intel might not be correct. But they knew looks were often deceiving.

Brett drove past and continued on for a quarter mile where the road turned away from the corridor. ,Continuing until they were out of sight, he pulled off on a patch of dirt.

Beck had further filled them in that it was Chastity who had gone to David after the accident. She'd feared for her life. Meadowcroft then sent Beck out with her to reclaim the body. From that point, the woman lived under Meadowcroft's thumb, doing anything he needed until he apparently needed her to be a part of the company. They staged her disappearance, and she assumed the identity of Brittany Schau. That part was fuzzy, and to Jack, it didn't matter.

Brandon had found recent communications in Meadowcroft's secret email account between David and Brittany. They surmised that something happened between the two recently that led her to declare she was going public with details that would bury Meadowcroft and his company. He wanted to negotiate. She didn't. He convinced her she could have half of his recent payout. Beck confirmed that he had recently received messages from Meadowcroft asking for the keys to the wallets that held his money.

"OK, I think I have this set," Beck said, handing his phone back to Brandon.

Beck had spent the better part of the drive moving a hundred million dollars' worth of Bitcoin and Ethereum between crypto wallets. He'd called in to the Treasury Building to speak with a contact in their little-known crypto assets division, a group of guys a lot like Brandon who got off on tracing transactions around the globe until they finally reached a place where identifying information could be gathered. People in the crypto community thought they had total anonymity. Never the case. The guys were able to flag each wallet address and even provided four of their own. These were rigged in such a way that no matter what Meadowcroft or Brittany tried to do with the funds, it would be tracked from the source IP to the final destination.

"Give me the rundown," Brandon said.

"He's getting twenty sets of keys to twenty different wallets. Four of them are controlled by the Treasury Department. The rest are earmarked, and these guys will be watching every move made with them. They know this is terrorist money, and they desperately want to get their hands on it."

"Gotcha." Brandon connected the phone to his computer via a USB cable. "I'm injecting some hidden code into the headers that'll let us know the moment the email is opened and from where."

"What kind of accuracy?" Jack asked.

"The exact moment it's opened, we'll get an alert. As for the location, there's ways around that, so we'll see. If it says Turkey, then we know he's on a VPN. I'm sure his computer is set up with one, but most people don't think about it on their phones. If it's anywhere near here, then we know he's in the warehouse."

Brett turned a little farther in his seat and looked at Jack. "Let's talk about tactics."

"I'm sure there's a way in over these hills, but I don't think it's necessary. It'll be dark soon enough, and we can walk along the road, then climb up and use the hill for cover. Might not be a bad idea for you or me to scout it out now. Maybe not, though. If Meadowcroft pulls up at the right moment, we'll be made."

Brett nodded. "Was thinking the same thing, but you're right, it might be too risky."

"Break up into three teams. Brandon and Thomas are going to take the car and move to a safer place. Just keep heading this direction until you're a few miles away. Each of you is gonna have a 9mm in your hand."

"Got it," Thomas said.

"The rest of us are gonna head out on foot together. We'll get close before deciding where to split. Once we do, Clarissa's with me. Brett, you keep an eye on Beck."

"I'm on your side," Beck said. "You saw what I just did."

"Yeah, well, people say all kinds of things," Jack said.

"It'll be all right," Brett said.

"Remember, this guy has pros in his corner. I watched them execute the man that turned over Johanna, and her current handler, guy named Rupert, was in bed with Meadowcroft also. They nearly killed us with an explosion. Later, I caught two of his guys by surprise at the doctor's farm, because the doctor had called it in then had second thoughts, but it was too late. I don't think I'd be here today if I hadn't been given that notice. They also got to Clarissa. So, let's make sure he's alone before we rush in. I don't know how many more lives I've got left against these guys."

Jack kicked open his door and let the warm breeze wash over him. He wished his visit to the L.A. area could be for different reasons. Perhaps after this was over, though, he could find a spot to relax.

The sound of distant traffic from the corridor served as white noise. No one spoke. Each person had their way of handling the real possibility this could be their last day among the living.

Brandon was the first to break the silence. "We've got an alert." He tabbed over to the program window and confirmed the message had been opened. Then he grabbed the IP address and ran a trace on it. "Just like I thought, no one ever thinks about their personal phones. I bet his business cell couldn't be traced."

"Where's he at?" Brett asked.

"Quarter mile from here," Brandon said.

"Can your Treasury guys confirm any transactions?" Jack asked.

Beck held up a finger and fired off a message. A few seconds later, his phone dinged. He read back the answer. "Yes, we see money moving."

"All right, guys," Jack said. "It's go time."

CHAPTER 49

THE WIND WHIPPED UP THE SIDE OF THE HILL, KICKING UP dirt and debris. Jack tasted it in his mouth. It stung his eyes. Made its way into his nose and clogged his throat. He and Clarissa were perched diagonally behind the warehouse. The parking lot was empty. A single light illuminated a small portion of the loading dock.

Brett and Beck were on the other side of the building, taking cover amid the chaparral. From their vantage point, Brett said he could see lights on inside. They hadn't spotted any movement.

The front of the building was outfitted with a large roller door. There was a good chance Meadowcroft had driven his vehicle inside.

Brandon had done some research on the warehouse. It was owned not by Meadowcroft, but by a company called TLG Holdings. A little digging revealed it to be a shell corporation. A little more digging tied it to Brittany Schau.

Headlights broke free from the stream of cars on the corridor as someone turned off Portola. They aimed straight at the warehouse. The vehicle pulled up to the front, and out of Jack and Clarissa's view. The engine cut off. The lights followed, dimming the area beyond the building. A single car door opened and closed.

"You got eyes on this?" Jack asked.

"Got it," Brett said. "It's her. We're moving forward."

"Coming down," Jack said. He looked at Clarissa. "You ready for this?"

"Sure am."

The MP7 bounced against his chest as they descended the hillside. A minute later, they were on the ground.

"Hold your positions," Brett said.

Jack was about to ask why, but then the sound of another vehicle approaching tipped him off. "Must be Meadowcroft." He got on the radio. "You got eyes on this one?"

"Big SUV. Looks like multiple people, but hard to tell."

"Brandon," Jack said. "Any movement on Meadowcroft?"

"Activated a trace the moment he opened that email on his phone. Haven't seen it move at all. Best guess is he's inside the warehouse."

"They've got visitors then." He muted his mic. "Let's move toward the front."

Clarissa took the lead.

Brett came back on the comms. "This doesn't look good."

At the same time, Jack heard multiple doors open.

Jack and Clarissa picked up their pace and continued forward, moving away from the building to where the vegetation would offer some cover. They passed the front of the warehouse. Two cars were parked one behind the other. A smaller sedan and a larger SUV, maybe a Tahoe or Suburban. The SUV was in front of the entrance door.

A light attached to the exterior wall illuminated a small swath of the ground.

Two men stood stacked up, close to the warehouse, in front of the door. A third walked up, grabbed the knob. A fourth stood behind him, holding a gun similar to the MP7 Jack had. He had it aimed straight ahead. The guy at the door held up his free hand and appeared to countdown.

"Holy hell," Jack said.

"This is a kill team," Brett said.

"Doing us a favor?" Jack said.

"Wouldn't count on it," Brett said.

The door opened. The fourth man covered it. The guys against the wall went in one after the other, the door opener following.

A woman's faint voice said, "What's going—"

She never finished. Several shots rang out.

"Oh no," Clarissa said.

"We gotta move in now," Jack said. "We'll ambush them as they come out. Last guy lives for a few minutes. Aim for his knees."

In the midst of shadows, the two teams moved out from their cover and crossed the parking lot. Brett took the wall fifteen feet from the door, armed with an MP7.

Jack crouched at the front of the SUV, also armed with an MP7.

Clarissa was his backup.

Beck took the rear of the SUV. Both he and Clarissa were armed with 9mm handguns.

This was a huge risk. The highway wasn't that far off. Traffic was nowhere near rush hour level, but there were plenty of vehicles. The only thing that worked in their favor was that the warehouse was situated in a gulley that hid the front entrance from the corridor. Across the highway were apartments. None faced their direction, but the sounds of the gunfire would raise suspicions. They had to operate quickly.

"Brandon?" Jack said.

"Go for Brandon."

"Need you guys to make your way back here. Stop about a hundred yards away and be ready to roll. OK?"

"You got it, hoss," Brandon said.

"You remember what Bear told you about saying that long ago?" Jack said.

Brandon laughed. "The big goof said it didn't fit my demographic. Overgrown ogre. I'll show him a demographic."

The radio went silent, and Jack and the others dialed in for the encounter ahead.

The door banged open, and the first guy stepped out.

Everyone held position.

The next guy came out, followed by the third. The first guy stopped and lit a cigarette, and as he looked back up from the flame, his head turned toward Brett. He dropped the lighter and the smoke and reached for his gun.

Brett fired and caught the guy in the chest. He pulled the trigger again and hit him there a second time. The guy staggered back into one of his partners, who didn't know whether to catch him or shove him to the side so he could return fire. In the end, it didn't matter because Jack stepped out from his position and squeezed the trigger of his MP7, which was set to three-round burst mode. All three hit the second guy in a line going up from his mid to upper back. He collapsed, and his partner fell on top of him.

The third guy squeezed off a couple of rounds in Brett's direction. Brett grunted and then returned fire, missing wide.

Beck picked up his slack as he rounded the back of the SUV. He fired four individual rounds from his MP7, hitting the third guy in the chest, neck, and face.

"Jack!" Clarissa called out.

Noble dropped instinctively as the crack of gunfire sounded. A bullet whizzed past his head and slammed into the dirt somewhere behind him.

Clarissa dropped to the ground as well and fired five rounds from the ground. The bullets traveled underneath the SUV and two found their mark on the guy's lower shin. He went down hard, and Beck was ready with a few rounds of his own, placing one in each leg.

The guy lost his weapon somewhere along the way and was rolling around in agony.

"Check on Brett," Jack said.

Clarissa rolled over and got off the ground and ran over to Brett. He was holding his stomach. His hands were red with blood.

Jack called out over the comms. "We need you now." Then he said, "Beck, go see if you can find anything on the woman inside, anything at all in there. We don't have a lot of time."

Beck moved inside the warehouse, and Jack waited by Brett's side with Clarissa for Thomas and Brandon to show up. It only took a few seconds for the Suburban to arrive. Thomas hopped out and helped Clarissa and Jack get Brett inside the vehicle.

"I gotta stay," Jack said.

"Wait," Brett said.

"What? You need to get to a hospital. Now."

Brett's hands were shaking and his lips were trembling. He didn't look good, and Jack feared he wouldn't make it.

"My wallet," he said.

"You don't have time for this."

"I don't have time at all." He tried to smile. He tried to reach for his wallet. He couldn't do either. "Get it."

Jack reached into his pants pocket and pulled out the wallet.

"There's a pic-pic-picture of Reese. Take it."

Of all the thoughts to have at that time, Brett's sister Reese McSweeney was not one Jack imagined would pop up. He rifled through the wallet until he found a photo of a woman he had loved and lost twice and didn't want to be reminded of.

"Have Brandon help you with the code on the back," Brett managed to say.

"OK. Now you stay still. They're gonna get you to the hospital. It's just a few minutes away." He turned to Clarissa. "Go with him."

She hopped in, and Jack shut the door and then turned away before the Suburban drove off.

Beck had dragged the wounded member of the hit team just inside the warehouse and left him there while he searched Brittany's clothing. The guy writhed on the floor, getting blood everywhere.

Jack walked past the guy and took in the warehouse. It was empty for the most part. A few shelves with papers on them.

"Anything there, Beck?"

Beck stood and waved a cell phone, wallet, and an envelope.

"Guess that'll do." Jack turned toward the guy on the ground. "Let's get him in the SUV. Cops are bound to show up soon."

Beck kicked the guy in the knee. "Who the hell are you?"

The man had no response.

Beck grabbed him by his hair and dragged him outside, creating new blood streaks on the floor. He continued yelling at the guy and was getting nowhere with it.

Jack took one last look around. Spotted something on a desk butted up to the front wall. A phone. Probably the one Meadowcroft had emailed from. Maybe he wasn't so dumb about his phone after all. Jack pocketed it and stepped outside.

They lifted the guy into the SUV, and Beck climbed in after him. Jack took the wheel and pulled out of the parking lot, down the long access road, and onto the corridor.

In the backseat, Beck worked on the wounded man some more.

"I know who sent you. I need you to tell me where he is."

"For Christ's sake, man. Get me to a hospital."

Beck punched the guy's leg, causing him to cry out.

"You want another bullet hole?" He had his pistol in his hand. Maybe not the smartest move on the bumpy roads. One pothole, and their prisoner's brains would be all over the interior. "Tell me where he is. Where were you supposed to meet him later?"

"I don't know."

"How the hell can you not know?" Beck threatened to smash the gun over the man's leg.

He held out his hands to stop him. Through his sobs, he said, "You killed the guy who knew. I'm the FNG in the unit."

"What unit?"

"Meadowcroft's security detail. All I know is he left a phone behind for us to find. He'd have details on it."

"What's the password?" Beck said.

"Wrong guy, man."

Beck leaned forward and said, "This guy is worthless to us."

"I'll find a quiet spot."

The man started crying again but offered no additional information. He must not have had anymore. That was his problem, not Jack and Beck's.

"He said Meadowcroft left a phone," Jack said.

"Yeah."

"I found a phone."

Jack checked his mirrors and yanked the steering wheel to the right and veered across two lanes to make the exit. He wasn't sure where they were, but both sides of the corridor were full of hills and no houses. He took a dark road to the end, K-turned, and stopped.

Beck looked at the wounded man. He was pasty. Eyes closed. Pained breathing. Beck slapped him.

"All right, last chance. What do you know?"

"I told you. I don't know a damn thing."

Beck got out, walked around the back, and opened the side door. He grabbed the guy by the hair and dragged him out of the car. One gunshot later, and it was done. He climbed into the passenger seat and buckled in and then adjusted the radio volume as if nothing had happened.

They moved to another dark street where they got ahold of Brandon. They had made it to the hospital. There was no news on Brett yet. Brandon was able to help them crack the phone's password. It was another version of Meadowcroft's email password.

Jack found the notes app already opened. It contained two lines.

An address in Burbank.

CHAPTER 50

THE FRONT WINDOWS OF THE UNASSUMING HOUSE AT THE end of the dark street full of unassuming houses were lit up. The porch light was on. There was no garage. A Mercedes S-class was parked in the driveway. The house sat in the middle of at least two acres, giving it plenty of space from neighbors.

David Meadowcroft's childhood home. Apparently, he'd held onto it after both his parents passed away.

Jack pulled to the side of the road and cut the engine and the lights. They watched the house from a distance for a while. Within the first few minutes, a curtain shifted, and they saw a hand and part of a face. This occurred a few more times.

"Looks like he's expecting us," Beck said.

"Shouldn't keep him waiting too long," Jack said. "Four years is enough, I'd say."

Beck nodded. "Look, Jack, before we go in there, I just want to say—"

"Don't."

"What?"

"Just don't. You and I, we're two of a kind of a different breed, man. Not many like us, and I figure that's a good thing. I believe there's just enough of us to balance out the world. Any more, it'd be an asshole revolution. Too few, a different kind of asshole, would take over."

Beck smiled and nodded. "OK. We'll leave it at that, then." He continued staring at the house. "One thing, though."

"What?" Jack didn't want to hear it.

"If I don't make it out of there, tell Clarissa I'm sorry for everything."

This was the part where Jack was supposed to tell him something like, "You tell her yourself." But he didn't. He didn't say it because he didn't mean it. Jack had no vested interest in the man. If he lived, he lived. If not, so be it.

Jack unlocked the phone from the warehouse and opened the messages app. The note had instructed the team to report in when they were seven minutes away. Why seven minutes and not six? No clue. Meadowcroft had a reason, and Jack and Beck were going to exploit that reason.

"It's time," Jack said.

They exited the SUV and blended into the shadows. According to Brandon's research, there was no alarm service. Dogs weren't a concern, since no one lived there most of the time. Meadowcroft could be armed, but he'd never be as quick or as sure of a shot as Jack and Beck.

Jack's phone buzzed. Too much had happened in the past forty-eight hours for him to ignore it. He signaled Beck, then veered off the path and found a spot to check the message.

It wasn't good news.

"Brett's gone."

His heart burned for a moment. They'd never been close, but they were the type of men who understood each other. They could be comfortable around each other. Anytime they weren't adversaries, friendship blossomed. They had an appreciation for each other despite the fact they'd each been sent to kill the other.

Jack silenced and pocketed the phone without sending a response. What could he say? OK? Sure, why not? No, he'd deal with it later, along with everything else he'd shoved to the side.

He met up with Beck at the corner of the house.

"I wish we had the others here," Beck said.

"Two of us should be enough." Jack didn't feel like telling him about Brett.

"Yeah, but they could pull up in the SUV. He's expecting that. Then we'd get him at the door when he let his guard down."

Jack looked at Beck, back at the vehicle, then at Beck again. "There's two of us. One of us can drive the thing in while the other waits."

Beck shook his head. "This is why I'm Treasury Department." His smile faded as he took another look across from the front of the house. "I'll do it if that's OK with you."

"I'd prefer it that way."

Noble watched as Beck made his way back to the SUV, wondering if he'd make a call to Meadowcroft and tell him Noble was outside. It didn't go down that way. The engine roared to life and settled into a purr. Headlights cleared a path a few hundred feet long, sweeping the street. The SUV rolled forward at maybe ten miles per hour and turned into the driveway. Beck stopped close to where the concrete met the street. A good move. It'd take longer for Meadowcroft to identify who was getting out.

A deadbolt slid free. The front door stuck a bit to the frame before opening wide. The porch lit up even more as light bled out from the house. A face poked out and retreated. A few seconds more passed before Meadowcroft emerged from the house. He took three steps to the edge of the porch. He had his hands in his pockets. He stared at the SUV, presumably anticipating good news from his hit team.

The SUV door opened and hung there for a while before a foot appeared below it, barely perceptible in the dark. Beck slid off the driver's seat in a way that concealed his face. From Jack's angle, he couldn't tell who it was, and he was certain Meadowcroft couldn't either.

Meadowcroft leaned forward from the waist, probably squinted. He called out, "Come on, let's get inside."

It was time.

"Hands up! Hands up where I can see them!" Jack shouted.

Meadowcroft turned his torso toward Jack, mouth open, eyes wide. He bent his knees like he was going to run. Jack yelled some more, which had the effect of freezing the guy in place. No matter what he had done, how many hit teams he'd sent out, he wasn't the kind of man who was prepared to face an attack. Jack closed in, gun drawn and aimed right at his middle. If he moved, he was dead. Should've already been dead, but Beck needed one more thing from him first: a confession.

Jack stepped into the light. Recognition spread across Meadowcroft's face. His weight shifted, and he rose to the balls of his feet. He was going to flee.

Let him. He wouldn't get far.

CHAPTER 51

MEADOWCROFT SPUN TOWARD THE DOOR. JACK WAS ABOUT TO pull the trigger when Beck flew into the frame. He collided with Meadowcroft, and both men slammed into the unlatched door, sending it whipping into the interior wall and bouncing back into them.

Jack raced up the steps and pushed past the door. Beck and Meadowcroft were engaged in a wrestling match with Meadowcroft somehow having the upper hand. Jack put an end to that with a kick to the guy's ribs. Before the air could leave Meadowcroft's mouth, Jack delivered another strike to the same spot, then again and again until Meadowcroft fell to the side.

Jack lunged over Beck and dove onto Meadowcroft, wrapping his hands around the guy's throat. He turned red in an instant and struggled to get a hand on Noble's face in an effort to drive him away.

"Not yet, Jack."

Beck grabbed Noble's arm and pulled him back. Jack struggled against the restraint, but settled a bit when he noticed Meadowcroft wasn't going anywhere. He remained on his back, desperately sucking in air, looking like a fish while doing so. The handgun in Jack's waistband begged him to use it. Pulling it out, he took aim.

"Wait!" Beck shouted.

"Why?" Jack said. "So the rest of his security detail can show up and finally put me down?"

"Because I need some answers," Beck said. "This guy put me under his thumb and held me there while destroying my life and career."

"You could've said no," Meadowcroft said, massaging his throat.

"Don't you want to know, Jack? How he found you those times? Why he wanted *you* dead and not the politicians that shitcanned his beloved project?"

"No." Jack lifted the gun again.

Beck moved in front of him, held out his hands.

"I will shoot you, Beck. Don't test me."

"Just give me five minutes, man."

Jack couldn't believe what he was hearing. Meadowcroft didn't deserve a chance to speak and twist his actions into something meaningful. Given enough time, the guy could buy his life back. He was a master manipulator.

"Come on," Beck said. "A couple minutes is all I'm asking. I've got a lot more to lose after this is over than you."

Noble felt like a prize idiot for even considering it. Even more so for saying, "Go for it. But if anyone shows up, I'm shooting both of you, and I won't wait to watch you die."

"Fair enough." Beck turned toward Meadowcroft. "All this time—"

Meadowcroft had risen to a seated position, his long legs stretched out. "Before you start, let me say something."

"What?" Beck said.

Here we go.

Jack prepared to end this. Curiosity as to what the man was going to say also gnawed at him. Two minutes, he decided. Two minutes to let him spill it and then it would be over for good.

"Look, we know things went a bit sideways," Meadowcroft said.

"They went a lot sideways," Beck said. "I did everything you asked. Sure, I had a good reason, but I did it. Never once did I bail on you. Never once did I say anything to anyone. I risked it all so you could have it all."

"You know I was going to take care of you with this one, though, right?"

"So you say." Beck glanced back at Jack, then returned his gaze to Meadowcroft.

Why? What had he not told Jack and Clarissa in Switzerland? He had good enough reason for complying at the time. He set up the flight, the car. None of it was done in malice. Was he scared of them finding out about the potential payout he was receiving for laundering the money? That somehow that would make all his criminal actions even more ignoble?

"You were set to make enough to disappear, Beck." Meadowcroft had managed to get to his knees now. He placed a hand on the wooden coffee table and lifted himself to his feet. "I imagine this guy had you in a precarious position if you gave all that up for this moment."

"You don't know a damn thing, David," Beck said. "I've been trying to find the perfect moment to take you down for the past ten years."

"Why now, when you're in so deep? You won't escape prison."

"Wanna bet?"

Meadowcroft smiled. "I do, actually. You see, anything happens to me, there's a laundry list of factual data going to the FBI and police departments across the country. There's names going to the CIA and foreign intelligence services. Dozens of names, Beck, and you're one of them."

Beck shrugged. "We've got access to your files. How do you think we were able to find you here? Our guy figured out the password to your hidden email address and that phone you left behind."

"I presume you're talking about Brandon?"

Beck nodded.

Meadowcroft said, "He'll go to jail, too." He took a step forward.

"That's close enough," Beck said, waving his pistol like a parent wags a finger at a toddler doing something they shouldn't.

"Clarissa, too." Meadowcroft glanced at Jack and made eye contact. "Do you want to see her go to prison, Jack?"

Jack glared at him, said nothing.

"Funny thing is, out of all these people, you're not on the list, Jack.

Wanna kill me?" Meadowcroft yanked his shirt up from the hem. "Go ahead. Put a bullet right here." He slapped his other hand over his heart. "You won't pay the price for it. Will you?"

All Jack wanted to do was pull the trigger. Was it a bluff? The master manipulator at work? Jack hated that he couldn't read the man. He waited to see where this would go.

"What's your angle?" Beck asked.

"Angle?" Meadowcroft said. "I'm like anyone. I want to live out my days and revel in my successes."

"And what of Banyan?" Beck asked.

"It's dead. I'm shutting it down."

"That's the reason they found Brittany in Chicago?" Beck paused a beat. "The reason you had her killed tonight?"

Meadowcroft shrugged. "Chicago, yes, she was trying to dig up evidence that had been destroyed. Tonight? Well, there were several reasons behind that, many of which are personal and don't concern you."

"All right. So, what's your offer?"

Meadowcroft's lip twitched. Almost imperceptible, but Jack spotted it.

"All that crypto in the remaining wallets," Meadowcroft said. "It's yours, Beck. No strings attached."

"It's mine after I kill you. That plus the wallets I gave you earlier that you haven't drained yet."

"It's true, you still have a lot of the funds in your own wallets. But are they really yours, Beck? What if every single one of them is flagged?"

"No way you could do that after what we did to the coins."

"There's a handful of people in the world who can trace those transactions. I happen to employ one. If the funds go anywhere besides wallets that end up in my possession, the Feds and the donors will be on you. Just some friendly advice, turn yourself into the Feds fast. You don't want the donors to find you first."

"You're bluffing," Jack said. That smile, no matter how brief, gave it away. Meadowcroft knew Beck had taken the bait; he just had to keep talking, keep painting that picture.

"You don't know that, Jack," Beck said.

"Who gives a damn about the money, Beck," Jack said. "It's blood money. Let's end him now."

Beck looked over his shoulder at Jack and glared back. That's when Noble knew this was going sideways.

"One last time, Noble. Let me finish this with him." He returned his attention to Meadowcroft. "David, I told you from the onset of this, leave Clarissa out of it. I know we played a game back there in Italy, we had to in order to make this look legit. Once she broke away from me, she was supposed to be left alone."

"The hell are you talking about, Beck?"

"They wanted you, Jack," Beck said. "She was the bait to reel you in. It worked, but it got out of control. She wasn't supposed to still be involved at this point. I have to know that she's off the hook and out of his network."

The rage boiled over. Noble raised his arm and aimed his gun at Beck.

That's when he noticed Meadowcroft looking behind him and smiling.

CHAPTER 52

DAVID MEADOWCROFT WENT RIGID WITH HIS EYES WIDE AND a smile on his face. Looking like a madman about to see all of his hard, manipulative work come to fruition. Beck spun around, lifted his hand, and squeezed the trigger. Thunder erupted in the room.

Jack ducked and spun and fell back. Watched the baseball bat whip past his face. He dialed in on the man holding the bat. He looked familiar, but so had so many others recently. Jack fired two rounds. One caught his attacker in the forehead, and he dropped where he stood.

The momentum carried Jack backward. He tucked and rolled over his shoulder. The open doorway was a few feet away, and he bolted through it, turning as he staggered through the opening. He caught sight of Meadowcroft, who produced a pistol and fired at Beck. Jack fired two rounds, then he tripped over the threshold. Before he hit the ground, he fired again. Meadowcroft dove backward.

Had the bullet landed?

Jack's momentum carried him past the edge of the porch. Crashing hard on the concrete steps, he felt the right side of his rib cage snap. The gun fell from his grasp. He managed to roll onto his back as he slid across the sidewalk and onto the grass. He tried to get up, but his body wouldn't comply. Gritting through the pain, he rolled the opposite way, put his hand in the dirt and shoved himself up.

Through the doorway, Meadowcroft stood tall. Aiming his gun down, He pulled the trigger. Jack contorted his body and watched in agony as Beck's torso came into view before slapping the floor, his head bouncing before coming to eternal rest at Meadowcroft's feet.

Meadowcroft turned in Jack's direction and fired multiple shots, emptying the magazine. Jack dove to his left, letting his good side absorb the impact. It didn't matter. His entire chest and core screamed in pain. He rolled through it. If he'd been shot, the pain in his upper body drowned it out.

Jack ended up on his stomach, his left hand supporting his cheek. The right tucked under his chest.

The man stepped through the open doorway and stood on the porch, glaring at Noble. Meadowcroft had wanted Jack dead for years. Noble suspected even before Skinner's death. Their first encounter with each other, well over a decade ago, was tense. When Jack went back for him, he'd closed up his office and warehouse and disappeared for a while. It was only fitting they should finish it here. Too bad Noble was all but done.

"Gonna be fun putting you down," Meadowcroft said.

Jack spat a mouth full of blood to the side. "Just come within two feet of me. I'll end you."

"I don't think so." He smiled as he jogged down the stairs. Something must've caught his eye because he did a double take toward the yard in front of him and changed course. "What's this?"

Noble knew exactly what it was.

Meadowcroft bent down and retrieved the pistol Jack had lost. He straightened up and strutted over. He glared at Jack. His overly whitened teeth stood out in the dark as his smile threatened to consume his face.

Jack moved his head, letting it fall toward his right shoulder. He closed his eyes so as not to have to look at the demented man hovering above him.

Meadowcroft laughed.

"What? Are you scared? This is good, Jack. Open your damn eyes. I said, open them! I want you to watch as I finally get to exterminate you with your own—"

The muzzle flash felt like lava on Jack's face.
The gunshot like a cannon in his ear.
His head felt like it split in two.
He was grateful he had closed his eyes.

CHAPTER 53

CLARISSA RACED DOWN THE STREET AS THE GUNSHOT RANG out. Slamming on the brakes a hundred feet or so from the house, she skidded to a stop next to the lawn, almost crashing into the SUV parked at the end of the driveway.

Two men lay on the ground. She couldn't tell who they were or if they were alive or dead. Nobody was moving. Flinging open the door, she leaped from the Suburban. Her feet carried her along automatically. Jack lay to her left, and who she assumed was Meadowcroft on the right. Sliding on the wet grass, she came to a stop next to Noble.

"Jack? Jack? Come on, baby, open your eyes."

She felt along his back for wounds, pressing along his spine. When he groaned, she broke into tears.

"Oh, thank God. You're not dead."

"Not yet," he muttered. He pointed toward Meadowcroft. "Is he?"

Clarissa glanced. A set of lifeless eyes stared back. "I'd say yeah." Looking around the yard, she spotted the open door on the SUV. "Beck?"

Jack shook his head slightly. "He got Beck when Beck saved me from a second attacker."

Clarissa felt tears well in her eyes. *Not now. Not here. Do it later.*

Threading her arms under Jack, she helped him get his left side off the ground. The damage to his face was obvious and looked bad.

"What happened?" she asked.

"Had to hide the gun somewhere." He touched his cheek and grimaced. "Is it bad?"

She stroked his hair. "Depends on what look you're going for, I guess. If it's Phantom of the Opera, you got a chance at the lead."

The smile he graced her with looked like it pained him greatly.

"We gotta get you up before the cops get here."

"Let them come."

"That's not a good idea. Come on."

First pulling him to a seated position, she then moved to the front and yanked on his arms until he was on his feet. With his left arm draped over her shoulder, she wrapped hers around his waist and guided him to the Suburban. His breathing was labored and ragged and she noticed he favored his ribs. She touched him lightly on the side of his chest.

"They're broken," he said.

"I think you might have a punctured lung," she said. "Gonna have to get you to a hospital."

"Great," he said.

He reached for the door, and she helped him pull it open and supported him as he climbed into the passenger seat. He sat straight as he could, arms tight to his side, hands on his stomach.

Racing around to the driver's side, she messaged Brandon, and pulled herself up behind the wheel.

Less than a minute later, she had the Suburban turned around and cruising toward the end of the street. She turned right, away from the main road, and navigated through the neighborhood across the street. Sirens rose to a fever pitch, then faded as they turned toward Meadow-croft's house.

"Why'd you come?" Jack asked.

"Would you have preferred I hadn't?"

"Not really. I'm curious, though."

"A feeling, I guess. The guys told me to follow it, so I did."

"Brett's really gone?"

She stared at the lights ahead for a moment, trying to find the right words. "I'm sorry."

"Not the way for a guy like him to go out."

"No, it wasn't." She'd had limited interaction with Brett during the few times Jack had worked with him. She knew he respected the guy, and with Jack, respect was everything. She reached over and squeezed his forearm. "I'm sorry, Jack."

Grimacing again, he thanked her. "I'm sorry about Beck. The other guy was gonna brain me. I ducked it, but that was only buying some time. Beck's shots distracted the guy enough, and I took him down. When Beck turned around, Meadowcroft got him before opening fire on me. I'd made it through the door and tripped. Meadowcroft emptied his magazine. I lost the gun in my hand when I hit the stairs. That's what did this to me."

She winced as he patted his ribs and grunted.

Jack continued. "I managed to get a few feet away, but it was almost impossible to move. I repositioned and took out my backup piece and hid it under my chest. No way he could see it coming. I pulled the trigger when he got close and burned half my face off."

"You're alive."

He nodded. "That I am. I don't know whether Beck deserved what he got or not, but I wish it hadn't gone down like that."

"Me too." She put both hands on the wheel and stared over them at nothing.

They drove on in silence for a short while. The street lights grew brighter, and the traffic a little thicker, but it was late, and there were only so many cars on the highway.

Her phone interrupted the lull. Putting it on speaker, she answered. "Yeah?"

"OK, we got a friendly. Don't laugh, but it's at a veterinary clinic."

"Christ, are they gonna put me down like Old Yeller?"

"Good to hear your voice, Jack." Brandon's smile could be felt through the phone.

"I'm not out of the woods yet."

"Yeah, well you better make it, man. I'm taking you to a game this year. Getting seats on the fifty-yard line."

"Promise?" Jack said.

"Promise." Brandon said.

"Wait a minute, aren't you a Cowboys fan?"

"We dem boys, Jack. We dem boys."

At that moment, Jack let his head fall to the side and his eyes closed.

Clarissa took the phone off speaker. "I think you killed him with that." She chuckled at her own joke. It felt unnatural, given all that had happened.

Brandon gave her the address. She punched it into the GPS, and ten minutes later, they arrived at the Golden Paws Veterinary Clinic.

A man and woman were waiting outside with a wheelchair. They escorted Jack to the back and Clarissa waited for three hours alone with her thoughts.

CHAPTER 54

BRANDON SAT IN HIS HOME OFFICE, STARING AT THE SAME blank screen he'd been staring at for the past hour. He hadn't accessed any of his systems since returning home and had rerouted all of his incoming traffic to an associate. It was too much right now, and considering he only had a short time left on earth, it was too much for him to ever worry about again.

He'd come to grips with the facts quickly. Maybe it was the adventure he'd gone on, something he'd never experienced before. Perhaps he felt accomplished in everything he'd done in life. All the people he'd helped. The lives he'd saved, both indirectly and directly. And he'd loved, if only briefly.

The first thing he'd done after returning home had been to message Kimberlee's mother and sister. He didn't beg for her to come home. Didn't ask for her to call him. Just told them to tell her he was sorry for being a shortsighted jackass.

After hitting send, he felt at peace with the situation.

Titus hopped up on the desk and demanded his attention. Brandon scratched the cat's head.

"What are you gonna do when I'm gone?"

He'd been thinking about it a lot. There weren't many people he knew that could take on a cat, even one as independent as Titus. Maybe he'd put an ad out during his final days. *Please rescue a dying wheelchair-bound man's cat.* He laughed at the thought. Titus didn't find him amusing and jumped down and ran out of the room. Brandon figured he was just being a jerk, but then someone knocked on the door.

Exiting his office, he rolled down the hallway and entered the great room. A beaming face appeared in the window next to the door.

Brandon hurried over and unlocked it, then waved Thomas in.

"What are you doing out here?" Brandon said.

"You told me to stop by if I was ever in the neighborhood, and I was in the neighborhood." Thomas walked past Brandon and looked around. "Nice place you got here."

"Hacking pays decently."

"Might have to go into business with you."

Brandon laughed and shook his head. "I don't know that's a good idea, my man. You and I are good as dead, remember?"

Thomas walked past him toward the kitchen. "Are we?" He opened the refrigerator and pulled out two bottles of beer. "Michelob Ultra?"

Brandon laughed. "Kinda acquired a taste for it at Brett's place."

The mood turned solemn for a minute as both men looked at each other. Thomas twisted the caps off both bottles and handed one to Brandon.

"To Brett," he said.

"To Brett," Brandon said. "May his memory live on."

Thomas took a swig, set the beer down, crossed his arms over his chest. "You think there's anyone out there that'll miss him?"

"Gotta be someone somewhere. He had a sister. Jack knew her pretty well."

"Did anyone tell her?"

Brandon shook his head. "She's in witness protection. I assume someone in WITSEC will tell her at some point, but who knows? She might have dipped out of the program."

Thomas nodded, his gaze fixed toward the door. "Oh, I almost forgot amid all this talk about death." He hustled over to where he'd dropped his bag.

"What is it?"

Thomas held up a finger as he hoisted his bag off the floor and carried it over and set it on the island. Reaching inside, he pulled out a folder with a picture of a sloth on it.

Brandon eyed him. "A sloth?"

"What? I like them. Got a problem with that?"

"Guess not." Brandon stared at the folder with anticipation. "Gonna show me what's in there?"

Thomas opened it, pulled out the contents and flipped them around so Brandon could see them. There were a bunch of numbers and markers on the front page in a colorful format. The second page looked the same. The third similar, but slightly different.

"What the hell am I looking at?"

Thomas pointed to the third sheet. "The last person who died from the Banyan. This was at the six-month mark. See how distorted all the values are compared to yours and mine?" He pointed at the individual markers for comparison. "Ours are much later in the process. Your printout is from just a few weeks ago."

"Yeah, they did take blood samples recently." Brandon stared at the papers and made the correlations between his and the dead guy's. "What's this mean?"

"Not one hundred percent sure yet, but I've talked to the scientists who were working on this, and they think we'll be OK. They need to run some tests to—"

"No way in hell I'm going anywhere near Meadowcroft."

Thomas held up a hand. "Look, these guys had no idea. They were behind a wall that David Meadowcroft had built to keep them in the dark. You and I are the only two remaining subjects. They want to help us. If we're healthy, fine. If something needs to be done to fix us, they'll do it."

Brandon tipped his head back and drained a little more of the beer. Reality hit him. "We're *not* going to die?"

"Not anytime soon." Thomas smiled widely. Looked like a schoolkid. It didn't fade.

"What's with the clown face? Creeping me out, dude."

Thomas gestured with his head toward the door.

"What?"

"Get up and go look."

Brandon turned his chair around and went about halfway. He stopped when he thought about what Thomas had said. He hadn't tried to stand since getting home.

"You can do it," Thomas said. "You'll want to do it."

Brandon looked back, certain that the look on his face made him look like an idiot. He planted his hands on the arms of his chair and worked himself up. His thighs quivered a bit, but he ignored it and walked to the door slowly and surely. He looked out the window but saw nothing.

"Get over there and open it."

Brandon tossed a glance over his shoulder at the smiling man. He reached the door and pulled it open.

"Kimberlee?"

She grabbed him and pulled him in and kissed him. "I'm so proud of you."

"What? How?"

"Your goofy friend over there tracked me down and told me about everything, including the talks you guys had. I just wanted you to love yourself the way I do, Brandon. And now that you've been through what you've been through, I think maybe you will."

He nodded.

"Let's give this another chance. What do you say? Can you look past me leaving?"

"What? Me look past something? I'm the jackass here, girl."

She laughed and moved closer and hooked her arm around him. They walked together to the kitchen island, where Brandon took a seat on the nearest stool.

Thomas raised his eyebrows and said, "Guess I should get going now."

"Wait up," Brandon said. "No rush to leave. We're gonna have steaks tonight."

"Guess I could hang around for a steak."

"Yeah, and we got a business idea to plan."

CHAPTER 55

THIRTY DAYS HAD PASSED SINCE THE NIGHT MEADOWCROFT died. When Jack had come-to at the veterinary clinic, he had been greeted by Thomas, not Clarissa. The man had looked down at him with one of those forced, tight, almost-a-smile-but-not-really-a-smile looks. Placing his hand on Jack's shoulder, he'd squeezed.

Clarissa had gone. The story was she had driven back to Brandon and Thomas. She didn't say much about what had happened, just that Jack was banged up and Meadowcroft and Beck were dead. Then she had asked Brandon to help her get off the radar, for a while, at least.

Brandon could, and Brandon did. It took about an hour, but in the end, it was as if Clarissa had never existed. No record of birth. No credit file because he changed her social security number. Every police and FBI and CIA file evaporated. Even the Treasury Department had no record of her. She didn't need a new name. Clarissa Abbot had no history. He offered to set her up with a never-ending stream of funding. But she declined. While she didn't explicitly say, Brandon was under the impression Beck had transferred crypto to her at some point and it was enough to get by on.

Brandon did all this because he figured he didn't have much time left. So what if he was picked up by a couple of guys in black suits? However, during their most recent call, Brandon told Jack there'd been good news about his health, and he was going to stick around a little bit longer, but his days of hacking and working with spies were over. Thomas and he were going legitimate and starting a new business. Something about digital forensics and becoming private investigators. Brandon didn't go into the details on the phone but said he would.

One day.

Jack had received good news on Johanna, too. The doctors had fixed the internal bleeding, and she had recovered well enough to return to Sweden. She'd said her days in the field were over, and she was happy to sit at a desk for the rest of her career. He asked about Noah, and she didn't say much. It'd take time, she figured. She told Jack if he was ever in the country to look her up. He told her the same. Both knew they never would, though. After what they endured over a couple of days, it was better to leave their relationship in the past.

Jack rose from the couch and walked into the kitchen. He poured a couple of fingers of Woodford into an empty glass and took a pull. It smelled like hot honey, and it burned like habanero for a few seconds on his lips, tongue and throat on the way down.

He'd been in a small Airbnb rental located outside of Austin, Texas, for the past few weeks while nursing his injuries. His ribs felt good enough he could jog at a slow pace. It'd take a while to rebuild his endurance, but once he was able, he'd hit it full steam. His face had healed up nicely. There might even be another scar to add to the collection.

A magnet held a piece of paper to the fridge. Ever since that night, he'd read it every single day. Multiple times a day at first. Just once a day lately. Clarissa had penned it while Brandon was resetting her existence.

Dear Jack,

This might be the hardest yet most logical letter I've ever written.

We can't be together. Please don't try to find me. I'm taking your advice and getting away from you. I'm gonna build a real life with a real guy who I can settle down with and maybe have a kid or two.

LOL can you imagine me as a suburban housewife???

Maybe it'll happen. Maybe I'll drift around for a while. Who knows? Maybe someday you and I will cross paths again.

Just don't force it to happen.

I'll know.

You can't lie to me, and you know it.

Stay safe out there, Jack. Keep out of trouble. Get out of the life. That little girl needs you, you know.

OK, Brandon says we gotta get moving. Well, they do. I'm bailing.

See ya, bud.

- C

He still got a laugh from the valediction. When Clarissa was a teenager, he always called her bud, and when she tried to sneak one last hug on him, he'd stop her and turn around and look back and tell her, "See ya, bud."

Pulling the note from the refrigerator door, he carefully folded it and carried it into the bedroom. All his things were laid out on the bed, including the items from that fateful night. They hadn't been touched. Blood still caked everything. The t-shirt he had been wearing that night went into a trash bag. Then the socks and underwear and even the light coat that hadn't made it out of the SUV.

The pants remained, stained with grass and dirt in addition to blood. He pulled the left pocket inside out and found it empty. But in the right pocket, a picture fell to the bed. Reese McSweeney stared up at him. He'd forgotten Brett had given him the picture. The man's words after giving him the photo came back to Jack.

"Have Brandon help you with the code on the back."

Turning it over, he saw a sequence of letters and numbers that meant absolutely nothing to him. He pulled out his phone, snapped a photo, and sent it to Brandon.

After tossing the phone on the bed, he trashed the pants and began packing up his things. This was his last night in the house. His last night in Austin. He was going to check out Interstellar BBQ for dinner. His Airbnb host had insisted if he did one thing during his time in town, it was to eat there.

Jack thought of a bunch of things he'd rather have done, but his body hurt like hell most of the time he was there, and he didn't want to deal with crowds and noise.

But he had felt different the past few days. *Almost* like himself again. Well enough to go pick up the 2006 Jeep Wrangler TJ he'd bought sight unseen from a dealer. The longer wheelbase was nice for a little extra storage. Plus, he figured he'd head into the Rockies for a little bit, camp in the middle of nowhere while the weather was decent.

He packed everything but his clothes for the evening. He'd only be in them for a little bit, so they'd work for tomorrow. After changing, he ordered an Uber to take him to the dealership. The transaction was in cash and took less than twenty minutes to complete.

He found the BBQ joint and ordered the Jalepeño Popper Sausage and a pound of sliced brisket. It'd be the perfect finger food for his road trip. He had finished his meal and was just about finished with his second beer when his phone buzzed.

He opened the message from Brandon and read it.

Lewiston, Montana...

Was Reese there? Why else would Brett give him the photo?

Another text came in.

Someone should tell her about her brother...and by someone, I mean you.

Jack agreed, and he didn't wait for the next morning to leave. He headed back to the Airbnb, grabbed his stuff, and started the long drive to Lewiston, Montana.

***

Jack Noble returns in NEVER LOOK BACK. ORDER NOW:

https://www.amazon.com/B0C5JNN6T4

Join the L.T. Ryan reader family & receive a free copy of the Jack Noble prequel, *The First Deception* with bonus story, *The Recruit*. Click the link below to get started:

https://ltryan.com/jack-noble-newsletter-signup-1

Love Noble? Savage? Hatch? Maddie? Get your very own L.T. Ryan merchandise today! Click the link below to find coffee mugs, t-shirts, and even signed copies of your favorite L.T. Ryan thrillers! https://ltryan.ink/EvG_

ALSO BY L.T. RYAN

Find All of L.T. Ryan's Books on Amazon Today!

The Jack Noble Series

Noble Judgment

Never Cry Mercy

Deadline

End Game

Noble Ultimatum

Noble Legend

Noble Revenge

Never Look Back (Coming Soon)

Bear Logan Series

Ripple Effect

Blowback

Take Down

Deep State

Bear & Mandy Logan Series

Close to Home

Under the Surface

The Last Stop

Over the Edge

Between the Lies (Coming Soon)

Rachel Hatch Series

Drift

Downburst

Fever Burn

Smoke Signal

Firewalk

Whitewater

Aftershock

Whirlwind

Tsunami

Fastrope

Sidewinder (Coming Soon)

Mitch Tanner Series

The Depth of Darkness

Into The Darkness

Deliver Us From Darkness

Cassie Quinn Series

Path of Bones

Whisper of Bones

Symphony of Bones

Etched in Shadow

Concealed in Shadow

Betrayed in Shadow

Born from Ashes

Blake Brier Series

Unmasked

Unleashed

Uncharted

Drawpoint

Contrail

Detachment

Clear

Quarry (Coming Soon)

Dalton Savage Series

Savage Grounds

Scorched Earth

Cold Sky

The Frost Killer (Coming Soon)

Maddie Castle Series

The Handler

Tracking Justice

Hunting Grounds (Coming Soon)

Affliction Z Series

Affliction Z: Patient Zero

Affliction Z: Abandoned Hope

Affliction Z: Descended in Blood

Affliction Z : Fractured Part 1

Affliction Z: Fractured Part 2 (Fall 2021)

Love Noble? Savage? Hatch? Maddie? Get your very own L.T. Ryan merchandise today! Click the link below to find coffee mugs, t-shirts, and even signed copies of your favorite L.T. Ryan thrillers! https://ltryan.ink/EvG_

ABOUT THE AUTHOR

L.T. RYAN is a *Wall Street Journal, USA Today,* and Amazon bestselling author of several mysteries and thrillers, including the *Wall Street Journal* bestselling Jack Noble and Rachel Hatch series. With over eight million books sold, when he's not penning his next adventure, L.T. enjoys traveling, hiking, riding his Peloton, and spending time with his wife, daughter and four dogs at their home in central Virginia.

* Sign up for his newsletter to hear the latest goings on and receive some free content ➜ https://ltryan.com/jack-noble-newsletter-signup-1
* Join LT's private readers' group ➜ https://www.facebook.com/groups/1727449564174357
* Follow on Instagram ➜ @ltryanauthor
* Visit the website ➜ https://ltryan.com
* Send an email ➜ contact@ltryan.com
* Find on Goodreads ➜ http://www.goodreads.com/author/show/6151659.L_T_Ryan

Made in the USA
Monee, IL
07 March 2025

13669733R00184